# The Great Train Robbery and the South Coast Raiders.

A novel by Graham Satchwell

Published in 2024 by Seventy-Four Books.

Print copy ISBN 978-1-0686073-1-8

# Other books by the Author

**'A Sick Business - Counterfeit Medicines & Organised Crime.'** (Published by the Stockholm Network, 2004). The earliest expose of the international trade in counterfeit medicines. Extensively quoted on news media across the world, Graham Satchwell was called as the only expert witness to give evidence on this subject before the United States Senate. The book also led to several television documentaries in which the author took a major role. One of them, entitled, 'Is Your Medicine Fake', was nominated for a television industry award.

**'An Inspector Recalls.'** Published by the History Press in 2016 was described by The Guardian newspaper as, 'The best of the genre' (police memoirs). It has received numerous 5 star reviews on Amazon. To be released as a paperback late in 2024

**'Great Train Robbery Confidential'.** Published by the History Press in 2019, also wins 5-star reviews on Amazon and received widespread national press coverage. Soon after publication it was nominated for the prestigious 'Gold Dagger' (non-fiction) award.

**'Rot At The Core.'** An expose on police corruption, it was published by the History Press in 2021 and has assisted several wrongly convicted individuals to win successful appeals. Once again, the book received widespread national news coverage and is given 5 star rating on Amazon. It is now available in paperback and on Kindle.

# Acknowledgements

Many people helped my very lengthy research to establish the facts upon which this book is built, and they have been thanked elsewhere (1) but I owe by far the greatest gratitude to former Great Train Robber, Tom Wisbey. It could not have been written without him.

Thanks are also owed to Tom's daughter, Marilyn, who since her father's death, has been generous with her time in helping ensure I have not made any obvious blunders.

In addition, old colleagues, including Andy Bicknell, Wayne Clayton-Robb, Roy Clark and Peter Holden, were kind enough to devote a good deal of time reading the drafts and making recommendations. I'm sure I have missed at least one person, and if that is you then please accept my apology.

I must also thank John Tidy, a more recent friend, for his continuous encouragement over the years to complete and publish this book.

My search for a suitable image for the front cover was ended once I saw Jack Taylor's excellent night time image of a red signal. Jack is a very successful British photographer and when I asked him for permission to use it he responded generously and kindly. Thank you, Jack.

Every writer needs a proof-reader. The trick is to find one who not only has the technical skills but also the personality and confidence to be part of the writing team. Christine Deane has all of that, and she did a great job for me without breaking the bank. Thank you, Christine.

A final thank you goes to you, the reader. Without you it has all been a waste of time!

One more thing, if you enjoy this book, please take the time to share your feelings with others on social media or by Amazon rating or review (or elsewhere).

# About the Author

Far from being a typical writer, Graham is dyslexic and left school without any formal qualifications. A short spell as failed footballer, there followed a succession of labouring jobs before Graham joined the police.

He became a successful detective before the remarkably young age of 22. He went on serve in every rank of the CID up to and including Detective Chief Superintendent.

Before his retirement he had received numerous commendations from Old Bailey judges, the Director of Public Prosecutions, chief constables, ministers of State and others for outstanding police work, related to organised crime, corporate manslaughter, kidnapping and other serious crimes.

In 1980, Graham took charge of a team of specialist officers investigating serious theft of high-value mailbags across Britain. It heralded the most successful period of high-profile detections against such professional criminals, including a case against the greatest number of accused ever to stand together at the Old Bailey (charged with conspiracy to steal).

Those in the dock included some of the most notorious gangsters in London, including former members of the Kray gang and an ex Great Train Robber.

For many years, before he retired in 1999, he was Britain's most senior railway detective. During his 30 years of service he won two scholarships to university, gained a law degree, served as Director of Studies on the command courses at the national Police Staff College, became a Fellow of the Royal Society of Arts, and was the main author of the first official Code of Ethics for the Police Service of England and Wales.

After leaving the police, he conducted a number of well-known national and international criminal investigations.

He has been writing fiction and non-fiction for many years. This is his first published work of fiction.

# Introduction

The best books of historical fiction always contain a good deal of accuracy. There is evident value in telling as much of the truth as possible and only creating falsehood in order to better illustrate the essential truth of the story. That is what I have tried to do.

It is often thought the Great Train Robbery (1963) was a brilliant one off. It seems to have been largely accepted that train robberies before that time had hardly ever, or never, taken place.

Yet nothing could be further from the truth.

It was only the scale and audacity of the Great Train Robbery that marked it out as a sensational crime.

From the 1850s (until the late 20<sup>th</sup> century), the railways carried the Royal Mail across the country. And from the earliest days, the mail was attacked by robbers and thieves.

During that long history, the railway police endeavoured to prevent and detect those crimes, and used ad hoc and full-time squads to do so.

By 1961, it was obvious to all, including the national press, that a particular gang was enjoying outstanding success in stealing mailbags across the south of England. They became known as 'The South Coast Raiders'.

At that time, elsewhere across the country, other professional thieves were trying to do the same, but without sufficient technical knowledge they resorted to violence or other extreme behaviour.

So how much of this story is true? Most of it, but don't expect to read an account you are familiar with.

My book, 'Great Train Robbery Confidential'[1] describes the evidence I gathered to support the story you are about to read. Many parts of the received wisdom about that robbery turn out to be definitely or probably false. One of the many important revelations in that book is the Great Train Robbery rehearsal of February 1963.

'Great Train Robbery Confidential' challenged and destroyed many of the myths surrounding the robbery. Naively, I thought a rational and evidence-based exploration of the facts would be generally commended by Great Train Robbery 'experts'. How wrong I was. If you want to make an enemy of an expert – prove them wrong!

In this novel I have used (and added to) the very detailed description of that rehearsal provided by Train Guard Owen[2], as well as details provided directly to me by the train robber I got to know quite well, Tom Wisbey, as well as from public records (and other sources). I spent a year conducting meetings with Tom and he travelled down to Hampshire and stayed at The Grosvenor hotel in Stockbridge, near my home, where we regularly met. And I visited him several times in hospital after his stroke.

After Tom died in 2017 (aged 86), I became aware of the determination of the sole surviving Great Train Robber, Bob Welch, that this book would never be published. Then I realised why. Tom had, at first, been hesitant to reveal details of the robbery's rehearsal. You see, none of the robbers had been charged with that crime, and theoretically, they were still liable to arrest and trial. No wonder Bob Welch wanted no more said!

One of the numerous myths about the Great Train Robbery is the leadership of Bruce Reynolds. Another strange fact is the almost complete invisibility of 'The South Coast Raiders' (also called 'The Red Light Gang' in the press of the day). This novel describes, for the first time, the key part that gang played in the robbery.

In the late 1950s and early 1960s, the South Coast Raiders were the only gang in the country that could stop any train at any signal. And no one outside their circle knew how.

For years they travelled the old British Rail Southern Region (which included all trains travelling from Waterloo, Charing Cross, Victoria, London

Bridge, Cannon Street and Blackfriars to stations across Kent, Surrey, Sussex, Hampshire, Dorset, Somerset, Devon and Cornwall). Sometimes they went further afield. And the gang remained undetected right up to the time they merged with other experienced and hardened criminals to commit the crime of the century.

To get the most from this book, park your prejudices, but hold in the back of your mind just how normalised police corruption was in the period concerned. Remember also that after the robbery, gangster Billy Hill was all but named as the 'brains' behind the crimes by both the national press and later the trial judge.

As for my assertions in this novel about the infamous Kray twins, once again suspend judgement and consider their friendship with several of the train robbers, their mutual closeness to Hill, and their pervasiveness across organised crime in the capital in the early sixties.

Remember too, when weighing the story, no other 'Great Train Robbery' author has read the whole of the official and 'classified' Metropolitan Police, Great Train Robbery file, or actually led numerous successful investigations into serious mail train thefts.

Tom Wisbey was an undefeated member of a group of old time villains who simply would not inform on others. His loyalty to that clan was remarkable.

Bruce Reynolds, in his self-promoting book about his role in the Great Train Robbery, dismisses Tom Wisbey as just 'muscle.' But nothing could be further from the truth.

In fairness to Reynolds, he clearly always avoided 'helping the police' too. But Wisbey's loyalty went further, even when I pointed out Reynold's jibe, he refused to make any adverse comment about him. In fact, I never heard Tom Wisbey say a negative word about anyone. 'Muscle', he certainly was, but stupid he certainly was not. Tom's interesting life of crime is well-described in his 2015 book, 'Wrong Side of the Tracks.'[3]

If you look at 'Wiki' you will see a passing reference to a case in the 1980s involving Tom Wisbey and a small number of travellers cheques. In reality, the gang, of which he was a part, were concerned in the theft of over £2m worth of property. It led to the largest number of people ever to appear at the Old Bailey charged with conspiracy to steal (mailbags). All but one were convicted. I kept Tom in custody for nearly two years prior to that trial, despite attempted bribery. That's how I came to know him.

No doubt Tom ensured that whoever made that Wiki entry was misled into diminishing the extent of that crime. Downplaying his part in any villainy was an established part of his modus operandi.

Over 30 years later, I stumbled across Tom Wisbey via a mutual friend. I told him I was thinking of writing about the Great Train Robbery and to my great surprise he offered to help. That is how this book was born.

Was there animosity between us? No, his early life had led to his being a professional thief, and mine had led me in a very different direction. But I truly believe there is both policeman and robber in all of us, perhaps he thought so too.

Tom's only concern was that nothing he shared with me should result in a surprise knock on the door from the police for himself or anyone else. So, we created a formal agreement. It is intended to protect against any over-zealous policeman who might decide, regardless of whether the crime was an ancient crime, that if fresh evidence of illegality came to light, then the wheels of justice should turn (I have put a copy of our agreement at the end of this book).

There is no doubt in my mind that Tom enjoyed helping me write this. In fact he so enjoyed it that he suggested other book ideas for us too. Sadly, he died long before that could be.

Have no illusions, I never had any time for Wisbey the 'robber'. But as surely as none of us can be judged solely by our occupation, so Tom Wisbey cannot be entirely defined by that single word.

So, this novel contains a lot of true information about the Great Train Robbery that has never before been in print. Only one central character is entirely fictitious (identity revealed at the end of the book), but all other central characters really did, or may have, take part in the 'Crime of the 20th Century'. For the sake of fairness, where any doubt exists about the participation in crime of an individual, I have used a pseudonym.

I hope you enjoy the read.

References:
1. Satchwell, Graham. 'Great Train Robbery Confidential'. (History Press 2019).
2. Owen, Howel. 'The Forgotten Train Robbery'. (Kindle Books 2013).
3. Wisbey, Tom. 'Wrong Side of the Tracks'. (2015 Amazon).

# Chapter 1

He ducked and jabbed, running with sweat, he could taste the blood in his mouth. The man facing him, taller and sharper, threw another jab, this time Alfredo dodged it. A bell rang, they returned to their corners. Both men pushed out gum shields, grabbed a towel and came together smiling. They touched gloves and briefly embraced. The taller man looked at his opponent, "Good to see you back, Alfredo. How's the leg holding up?"

Alfredo grinned, "Good thanks. Great to be back."

Meanwhile, a couple of miles away, in a block of council flats, a heavy pounding on the front door interrupted Shirley's thoughts. She thought the noise would wake the baby and rushed from the kitchen to the door. She expected to see the distorted image of someone behind the obscured wired glass. But no one was apparent.

"Who's there?"

'Kids.' She thought.

She waited for the sounds of laughter of silly children as they ran back to the floor below, but there was silence.

Annoyed, Shirley unbolted the door and stepped out to look along the landing. In that moment, the intruder overwhelmed her. The big ginger-haired Irishman clamped her in his powerful arms and smiled down at her. "Where's the greasy Itie then sweetheart?"

Shirley attempted to pull free, attempted to retreat inside. In that moment she recognised, just along the landing, his fat, middle-aged, balding sidekick leaning against the wall. He was smiling broadly.

Ginger laughed. "So he's out, and there you are trying to pull me into your arms."

She cried out. "Let me go you bastard."

She tried to push him away, but her arms were trapped and he easily pushed her back inside as he entered.

As she passed over the threshold, struggling to escape his grip, she accidentally kicked an empty champagne bottle. It rolled beneath their feet and clattered against the skirting board. Once in the living room, Ginger moved around behind her, and with one hand, he twisted her arm hard and high behind her back. Shirley cried out as the pain shot through her arm and instinctively bent forward and tried to lessen the twist. With the other hand, Ginger grabbed the hair on the back of her head and yanked her head backwards. He put his mouth against her ear. "Got it 'ave ya?"

The front door closed behind the fat man and he entered the sitting room carrying the empty champagne bottle. "Look Ginge, champagne."

The redheaded man was still standing behind Shirley, her arm still twisted painfully.

He looked across at the champagne bottle. "So you can drink champagne but can't pay your debts?"

Shirley could hardly speak, she was in considerable pain, bent forward awkwardly. She spluttered. "It ain't like that."

The Irishman was holding her with one hand now, his other was pulling her hair. "You ain't takin' me seriously."

Shirley squealed with pain. "You'll get it. I promise."


Little Tony started to cry loudly from the bedroom. Ginger held her twisted arm but let go of her hair. His hand reached down and onto her thigh. Then he ran his hand up the back of her leg to her buttock. "Be quiet or we'll find another way to quieten the kid."

The Irishman laughed. "Pretty girl like you, sitting on a fortune you are, and if you won't pay, well you can earn for us on your back."

Ginger looked at the fat man. "Look round, see what you can find."

But the fat man, sweating and breathing heavily, moved up close to Shirley and gave Ginger a look which seemed to ask for permission. Ginger nodded, the fat man gave a contorted grin exposing his nicotine-stained teeth. Shirley was still bent forwards but could see and smell the lower half of his unwashed body. "Keep away from me, you bastards."

Alfredo had made his way home from the gym contentedly. He had been thinking about the evening before, the pleasure of his wife's company, the meal, the champagne, and the intimacy they had shared for the first time in months. And it was the first time in ages they had had any money to spend. Life was sweet again.

He was always starving after a workout and couldn't wait to get home. But first he popped in to the local grocery shop and spent freely, something he had been used to.

Some decent coffee, an early lunch of fried eggs on toast, not with butter but olive oil, accompanied by a pint of milk and fresh fruit.

Ten minutes later, In warm contemplation he looked up towards their second floor flat. Smiling, he picked up his pace. Carrying a bag in each hand, he bounded up the stairs two at a time. He was his old self again.

But as he approached his front door, he heard his baby son crying. In the next moment he saw the front door was slightly ajar. His heart skipped a beat and his mind was raced, something was wrong.

He rushed in and instantly took in the scene. A chair and the ironing board had been upturned, Shirley's torn underwear and other clothing lay on the floor, the TV was missing. Heart pounding and sweating in fear, he dropped the carrier bags and his gym bag and called, "Shirley." No answer. He rushed to his crying son's room. A quick look in, Tony looked safe and immediately stopped screaming, perhaps simply to take breath. But in the few seconds of silence, Alfredo heard Shirley's gentle sobbing.

He ran to the bathroom and pushed at the locked door. The sobbing was louder now. His voice was high, pleading. "Shirley, what's happened? Let me in."

But she didn't answer, she just continued to sob. He pressed on the door handle and against the door. He called again and again, frantic with worry. Then she spoke almost inaudibly. "Go away."

Alfredo. "Shirl, let me in, what's happened?

Silence.

"Let me in or I'll break the door open."

She mustered her strength. "Go away, go away."

Alfredo didn't know what to do for the best and walked back into the sitting room. He stared at the open front door, the disarray, listened to his son crying again. He stared at the carpet, Shirley's bra and torn knickers. His eyes fell on the shopping bags full of treats for the three of them.

Now, his training session, the shopping and feelings of elation all seemed so pathetic and trivial. He lashed out at the shopping with a heavy kick and dashed back to the bathroom door. He pressed the handle down and threw his shoulder against the door. The small bolt gave way easily.

Shirley cowered in an otherwise empty bath, trying to conceal her beaten face and near naked body. She felt ashamed, soiled, spoilt. She couldn't look at him and muttered just one word. "Tony."

Alfredo was being overwhelmed by sorrow, love, pity and boiling rage. He left the bathroom, picked up a blanket from the bedroom and collected his son. He took both to his wife. She turned towards Alfredo for just long

17

enough to take her son. Alfredo draped the blanket around them. He tried to put his loving arms around her but she pushed him away. Her tears continued and she closed her eyes.

"Was it that ginger bastard?"

She nodded, still crying.

"Was the slimy, fat bastard with him?"

Shirley cried more loudly.

He tried again to comfort her, but she didn't want him near, but neither did she want to be left alone. Alfredo wanted to take immediate revenge and knew where to find the culprits. But he also knew he had to stay and try to make her feel safe, or at least feel less vulnerable. From that moment, shared rage, stress and fear, separated them completely.

Eight hours went by and they had hardly uttered a word to one another, and neither had eaten. Shirley was in the bedroom, perhaps because that room had not been violated it had become her sanctuary. She was cuddling Tony, and had made it plain to Alfredo she didn't want to talk or even be near him.

Alfredo was in the sitting room, it had become his cave. He had done his best to tidy the sitting room and had thrown away his wife's torn and discarded clothes. He couldn't understand why she seemed so angry towards him, or why she was shutting him out.

During that afternoon, Alfredo had asked his wife several times to tell him what had happened. But she could never tell him, the hurt was too deep. And the more determined his questions became, the more painful they were to her, and the more distressed and distant she became.

Eventually, silence had settled, and it had reigned for hours. How he hated the silence.

She broke the quiet occasionally, not to converse but to make the odd declaration, or to give an instruction. "I can't live here anymore."… "Don't you tell anyone." … "They might come back."

Alfredo had tried several times to comfort her and now felt blamed and powerless to help. At about 7.00pm she left the bedroom to prepare food for Tony. After she had fed, changed and put him to bed, she returned to her sanctuary. Fully clothed, she got into bed and closed her eyes tightly once more.

Alfredo entered the bedroom and sat on the side of the bed. He didn't speak; he knew she was awake and just wanted her to know he was there. They remained silent for about an hour before Shirley opened her eyes and focused her attention on one random spot on the ceiling.

Alfredo had been turning it all over in his mind time and time again. He was in turmoil and his anger had not diminished. He sat, fists clenched, heart racing, dry-mouthed, watching his wife's glazed, staring eyes. But turning it over in his mind a thousand times had made no difference. He knew what he had to do; he had no choice. Alfredo stood up. "I'll finish it. Tomorrow morning."

Shirley understood exactly what his words meant and came out of her trance. Her husband was fiercely protective of her, and she wouldn't have wanted any other sort of man. A fistfight was one thing, but she knew the violence to win this battle, to satisfy this outrage, was on a completely different scale, and it frightened her. It would result in grievous harm to Ginger and the fat man. That didn't bother her, far from it, but if things went wrong, and they easily could, then equal or worse harm would be inflicted on the man she loved.

Even if Alfredo won the physical battle, Ginger's boss, the bookie, Green, would send other enforcers. And Old Bill might well get involved if Alfredo did serious injury to her rapists. Then Alfredo could easily end up in prison. She knew him well enough to know he would never explain the mitigation, he would never tell another soul what had happened to her. Although he would never say it, the shame was too great. She wondered how she could extricate him. There seemed to be no way out.

Shirley blew her nose. "The last thing me and Tony needs now is you gettin' nicked or smashed up."

But Alfredo didn't respond. She knew he felt revenge was his duty. She also knew he didn't know the train robbers he now worked with well enough to bring this trouble to their door.

They argued, she cried, he shouted. Then silence, both lost in their thoughts, both knew, but for their sudden show of wealth, this disaster would have been avoided.

Alfredo thought the next 18 hours would put him at the greatest risk he had ever faced. He bit his lip hard. Why had he been so stupid? How had he become involved in all this in the first place? He thought back just a few short weeks...

# Chapter 2

A few weeks earlier, August 1962, almost exactly one year before the biggest robbery of the 20th century. A warm summer evening at a suburban railway station a few miles south of London. Wafts of black smoke gently left the locomotive's chimney as the train driver waited impatiently for the passengers to leave the train and others to board.

A fat old postman and his younger colleague were busy offloading a few mailbags from the mail coach onto a bright red trolley and loading local mailbags for carriage to other towns and cities. Once finished they slammed the mail coach doors. Oblivious to all around them, the two postmen, now in conversation, pushed the postal trolley towards the ticket barrier.

Meanwhile, Alfredo, wearing a white T-shirt and jeans, entered the mail coach via the adjoining passenger coaches and set to work with his flick knife cutting open mailbags and examining the contents for valuables.

The postmen had walked no more than 50 paces when the older one halted, patted his pockets and turned to his colleague. "Shit, I've dropped me keys, in the coach I think. Come on, before it goes out." They headed back quickly.

Alfredo was still rifling the mailbags, flick knife in hand. At his feet, a dirty purple plastic duffel bag was gaping open and was already half-full.

Suddenly, the older postman threw open the mail coach doors and quickly realised what was happening. He stepped aboard to tackle Alfredo and in support, his younger colleague stepped aboard behind him. Alfredo was startled, fear filled his mind, he immediately took a step forward and lifted the knife. "Keep back, I'm warnin' ya."

The older postman moved back sharply and bumped firmly into his younger colleague, who was still moving forward. Alfredo seized his chance; he snatched up the duffel bag and launched himself towards the platform. His timing could not have been worse. At that moment the elderly train guard arrived back at the mail coach doors and instantly collided with Alfredo in flight between train and platform. Both fell to the platform.

The two postmen quickly held Alfredo where he had fallen, Alfredo struggled hard and cursed loudly. Passing passengers stopped and watched and some shouted for the police and for help. Alfredo knew time was running out, he had to escape fast; the welfare of his family depended on it. He struggled hard but the two postmen, both ex-soldiers, were equally determined to hold him down.

The train guard, who was not in any condition to take part in a fight, slowly got to his feet, recovered his cap and started brushing himself down. The older postman, still struggling, shouted at the guard. "Call the police. Hurry up for Christ's sake."

But the old guard looked away. He simply wanted to get back on his train and take it out on time, he didn't want any complications, didn't want to get involved.

"I've got to get the train out."

Alfredo sensed an opportunity and called to the guard. "I ain't done nuffin'. I was just getting off the train and they grabbed me."

Four well-dressed men in their thirties were standing together further down the platform and were engaged in earnest, whispered conversation. Within a few seconds, one of them, the oldest and most slightly built, turned and walked away. But his three colleagues approached the crime scene quickly. On arrival, one of them assumed control.

"All right, what seems to be the problem?"

He spoke with the calm, confident manner of a man who wasn't easily ruffled.

Alfredo, seeing his opportunity to escape diminishing, snapped back. "What the fuck's it got to do with you?"

"Railway Police. Detective Sergeant Watson. Keep a civil tongue or you'll be sorry."

Now the elderly guard seemed to gain a little public conscience. "Oh thank goodness, Officer... we caught him stealing."

Watson turned to his colleagues. "Take him into custody."

Alfredo sensed the hopelessness of his situation and stopped resisting as Watson's colleagues led him away. The train guard looked pointedly at his watch. "I've got to get the train away, we're already late."

Watson sighed. He had apparently heard it all before. "Okay, but I'll need your name. You'll need to make a statement later."

Watson took the postmen's names too and told them he was taking the duffel bag containing the stolen property. It was now evidence. The younger of the two postmen couldn't resist asking.

"Is he one of the South Coast Raiders then?"

Watson permitted himself a slight smile. "We'll soon find out."

Within a few minutes the prisoner, flick knife and the stolen property were being loaded into an unmarked, high-powered saloon car parked 50 yards from the station front. Watson sat up front next to the driver who had been waiting in the car. The other two plain clothes men were squeezed into the back with their prisoner between them.

They drove off. The slim, plain clothes man grinned and looked out into the darkness.

"Never liked night duty much. It plays me piles up."

Watson smiled, but the driver, a hard-faced man of about forty, showed no response.

Apparently unhappy at the lack of appreciation for his humour, the slim one spoke again. "It's sitting on me arse all night doing fuck all, that's what does it."

They drove for only three minutes before pulling up in a quiet industrial area. Watson flicked on the internal light, turned in his seat and offered a cigarette to everyone, including the prisoner. Alfredo declined. Watson turned to face forward again took one for himself, and lit it. As he unwound his window, he took a drag of his cigarette and blew the smoke out into the night. "What's your name?"

Alfredo hesitated. "Allan, John Allan."

Watson looked out into the darkness. "Listen. We'll take you down the nick, take your prints. Then we'll call at the address you are about to give us. If you're not known at that address we'll keep you in custody until we find out who you are. So don't give me any shit. What's your name?"

Alfredo sighed, he had no choice, "Alfredo Pantelli."

"Good. Now, Alfredo, how many times you pulled that stroke before then?"

Alfredo answered honestly. "Never. First time. It's just, I'm skint."

Watson's voice continued without emotion. "Workin' on your own was ya?"

"Yeah. On me own."

Watson. "Where you live then?"

"I ain't sayin'." Alfredo knew if he gave his address, the police would go straight there and search it. He couldn't put Shirley through it.

"Ain't sayin'? Got something there you don't want us to find then?"

There was silence for a few seconds before Alfredo responded.

"Yeah. My missus and kid. That's all."

Watson waited a few moments. "So when was you last nicked?"

Alfredo responded without hesitation and the resignation of knowing for the first time in his life, in the eyes of the world, he was now a common thief.

"I ain't never been nicked before."

Watson thought for a moment. "We'll find out soon as we check your fingerprints. Better save yourself some grief and tell us the truth now."

Alfredo responded evenly. "I ain't lyin'. I can't find a job... need money for me family, rent and that. We're gonna be evicted and we owe money..."

The slim detective sitting next to Alfredo sniggered. "Fuck me, I'm wellin' up."

Alfredo had publicly confessed his failure, and it had been met with ridicule.

"You bastard."

The driver twisted in his seat and without hesitating, struck Alfredo a blow across the face.

"You a tough guy then? You want another one?"

Alfredo wasn't hurt, not physically anyway. His instinct was to retaliate immediately, but he contained himself, knowing this was a battle he could not win. Watson placed a restraining hand on the driver's arm and continued where he had left off. "Who told you about the bags?"

Alfredo. "Nobody. It's all over the papers, you know, South Coast Raiders and that."

Watson sighed and paused. "Okay, we're gonna give you a chance. But listen, son, keep away from mailbags, you understand me?"

Alfredo could hardly believe his ears. "You lettin' me go?"

The slim, smiley-faced, plain-clothes man got out of the car, held the door open and leaned back in. "Come on, fuck off quick before we change our minds."

Alfredo climbed out and turned. "What about me bag and err, the stuff?"

Watson grinned. "You got some nerve. The stolen property goes back where it belongs."

Alfredo hurried off into the darkness counting his blessings.

An hour later Alfredo was approaching his council flat in South London, tired and still dirty from the soot and grime of the railway platform. By now the relief of being released had been replaced by the desperation which had haunted him earlier. He wearily climbed the poorly lit two flights of stairs and approached his front door. He knocked gently. A few seconds went by before Shirley pulled the bolts and opened it. She looked concerned as she stepped back in and whispered. "I've been worried. Where you been? You look terrible, what happened? You all right?"

Alfredo shook his head. "I'm all right. They been round for the money?"

Shirley put her arms around him. "No...What we gonna do?"

Alfredo answered wearily. "I'll get the money. If they come near you or Tony I'd kill 'em."

Shirley moved her hands to his shoulders and felt the tenseness. Then she reached for his hands and found clenched fists.

# Chapter 3

Old Compton Street in London's West End. The flashing neon lights outside The Modernaires nightclub competed with countless others. A limo, driven by a man who looked like a retired heavyweight wrestler, stopped outside. In the back sat two men. Both looked to be in their late forties. Both stood about 5ft 10ins. Both were used to getting their own way by whatever means. Both were prone to outbursts of violence. Both lived sordid lives of crime, cronyism and deceit. There the similarities ended.

One wore a merino wool topcoat over a Savile Row suit, Jermyn Street shirt, silk tie purchased from Sulka of Bond Street, Rolex watch and handmade Italian shoes. The other's suit had been bought in Burton's some years ago, and, like his shirt and tie, was crumpled and shiny.

One was Billy Hill, King of Soho. People had often told him he strongly resembled Humphrey Bogart, the actor. It had become common knowledge he liked the comparison. Billy had a thousand friends and smelt of toothpaste and expensive cologne. His nickname was 'Smiler' and he could with equal ease, charm the flowers into bud, or slash your face from eye to mouth. The other was Detective Inspector Aldridge of the British Transport Police. Aldridge had no charm and smelt of stale tobacco, stale beer, greasy chips and officialdom. Aldridge had no friends, only cronies. Hill also had his cronies, both junior and senior, at Scotland Yard and in both Houses of Parliament, as well as lawyers, crime reporters and of course, many of the most determined criminals in the country.

Aldridge, although junior in rank compared with most of Hill's corrupt contacts, had information Hill could not get anywhere else. Information gleaned from the Railway and Post Office authorities with whom Aldridge met regularly. Billy leaned forward and tapped the heavyweight driver on the shoulder, he immediately got out of the car and walked a few paces away and waited for further orders.

Billy turned to Aldridge. "You confirmed it?"

Aldridge was impassive. "Yeah. After a Bank holiday, after the punters been spending. No less than two million. Perhaps as much as ten. All in used notes."

Billy nodded, tapped his heavy gold and diamond ring against the car door window. His driver returned immediately. Billy instructed him. "Drop Mr Black wherever he wants."

Billy headed for the club. As he strolled into the foyer, the doorman moved swiftly towards him. "Good evening, Mr Hill."

Billy smiled, nodded and took a 'Players Full Strength' cigarette from his silver cigarette case, lit it with his Dunhill lighter and looked casually around. A black pianist was singing the Tommy Edwards classic, 'It's all in the Game.' The atmosphere was warm. Billy was behaving as if he owned the place – he did. He sauntered through the club. It was reasonably busy, Billy spotted the men he had arranged to meet.

Ronnie and Reggie Kray were in their late twenties. Their dress style was like Hill's. When in public they always dressed expensively and rather conservatively. The Krays had been tearaways since childhood, beating up other kids – two on one – and taking money off them. And if no one was about, they would steal whatever they could lift. As children they had also enjoyed going down to the nearby railway lines at Bethnal Green and firing an air rifle at passengers on the passing trains. Eventually, the railway police had caught them. Their first brush with the law. Their childish crimes involved bullying, taking what did not belong to them and the use of weapons. Nothing much had changed.

Keen to impress the man they most looked up to, they had arrived at Billy's club early. On arrival they were immediately recognised by the staff and taken straight to Billy's private table. A waitress hurried chilled champagne to waiting glasses. They stood up as Billy approached and he offered his hand warmly to them both. They shook hands, and exchanged smiles as they sat down.

Billy said how well they looked and asked if they were still keeping fit by boxing. The twins told him they hadn't sparred for some time. They discussed the apparently insane young American heavyweight, Cassius Clay. They drank, smoked and talked. Clay had defeated some of the best heavyweights in the world; Donnie Freeman, Alonzo Johnson, George Logan and a dozen more. Now it seemed our own 'enry Cooper was being lined up. It was at least 20 minutes before the preamble was complete.

A pretty young waitress wearing a miniskirt put down Billy's second orange juice, he rarely drank anything stronger, she smiled briefly and left.

Billy lit another cigarette, took a deep drag and blew a smoke ring. "Remember the Eastcastle Street business?"

Ronnie responded. "Yeah course, Billy."

Billy continued. "Ten years ago now... I should 'ave got the money on the train, stopped it out in the sticks, had the lot away."

Reggie sighed heavily. "Yea, if it was only that easy, eh Billy?"

Billy pressed on. "I know Goody and a few others having been having a go at the trains and I know it's been one cock-up after another... but done right, it could earn serious money."

Reggie leaned in. "Accordin' to the newspapers, one firm's makin' real money, that's for sure."

Ronnie looked keenly at Billy. "You got plans then?"

Billy paused. "Your share, if I let you in, would be an even whack, 50k between ya, perhaps more, in used notes, completely untraceable."

"Fifty, just our share?" Reggie checked.

Billy nodded almost imperceptibly. "Minimum. I'm puttin' a team together, all you gotta do is manage 'em, and keep my name right out of it."

The twins looked at one another and smiled. Ronnie was eager. "Tell us a bit more about it then, Billy."

Billy took a sip of orange juice. "We'll get the team the papers are callin' the South Coast Raiders and beef up their numbers, I'm thinkin' Reynolds, Buster Edwards... a few more."

Reggie. "You know the South Coast Raiders then?"

Billy didn't bother to answer.

Billy had long since learned the first rule of working in a criminal gang, 'Never work with mysteries' (strangers). He had known some of the Raiders for more than ten years, Tom Wisbey, Bob Welch, Ted Harris and Freddie Sansom. They were all members of a fairly small group of seasoned, professional, London robbers. He knew they would do whatever was needed to get a job done, and none would ever grass. They were 'sound.'

Billy also knew the leader of the Raiders, Danny Pembroke, but he did not know him so well. Importantly, he was aware that Danny had always been smart enough to avoid police suspicion. But there was another member of the Raiders Billy had never met; their excellent technician, Roger Cordrey, who, he had heard, was instrumental in their considerable success. And Roger Cordrey's involvement was crucial to his plan.

"How many blokes we gonna need then Bill?" Ronnie picked up the questioning.

Billy had been planning it for weeks, "About 15 on the plot, perhaps a couple more, and one or two others off the plot an all."

The two brothers exchanged glances. "That's a lot. How much they gonna make?"

Billy allowed himself a moment. "An even whack."

Ronnie began calculating. "Say twenty on the team, times fifty K... that's err...about a million. Fuck me."

Billy grinned and looked out across his club. Everyone seemed to be having a good time.

The twins were the apprentices in the presence of the master, and more than willing to listen and learn.

After a few moments, Reggie asked. "What sort of train carries that amount of money?"

Billy smiled. "TPOs. Travelling Post Offices... carry old and dirty notes back from the banks across the country to the Bank of England for washin' or destroyin'."

Ronnie shook his head and smiled.

Reggie was hooked. "TPOs? They armed or what then?"

Billy shook his head and eyed a beautiful young woman he had not seen in his club before.

He smiled. "No, but there'll be 'bout 'undred postmen on board."

The twins looked at one another, alarmed.

Reggie. "What, 'undred security people?"

Billy was at ease and continued to eye the young blonde. "Postmen. It's a travelling post office. They sort the mail as the train heads towards the smoke."

Ronnie. "Hundred postmen though? Sounds like a bloody war, Billy."

Billy smiled. "That ain't exactly what I got in mind."

Ronnie. "So where these trains run from then?"

Billy's eyes moved from the young woman to the bar. He watched the way his barman served; it was a smooth operation.

"All over the place, all the big cities."

Reggie. "No passengers?"

Billy thought the old barman, a former brawler and thief, had settled brilliantly into his new role. "Some have passengers, some don't."

# Chapter 4

'Luigi's' was owned and run by Alfredo's parents. The warmth of the atmosphere, the aroma of fresh coffee and the sound of romantic Italian music hit every visitor. The cooking was rustic Italian– simple, full of flavour, fresh and delicious. At this moment, the record player in the kitchen was playing Mario Lanza's 'Vesti La Giubba' (Be My Love). The whole place was a slice of Italian life.

Luigi's was empty but for an Italian couple in their fifties. The man, Alfredo's father, tanned, plump, short with receding black hair combed straight back, was wiping clean the plastic tablecloths. The raven-haired woman, Alfredo's mother, very plump and once pretty, was refilling an ancient Italian Gaggia coffee machine while dreaming about Italy and the latest Mario Lanza film.

Alfredo entered sheepishly. His father looked up without acknowledging him before continuing his cleaning.  His father was still angry his only son had chosen to leave the family business and make his own way in the world. Angry his son had married a non-Catholic, an Englishwoman from a bad family. Angry his son was living in poverty without job or money. Angry the son he was once so close to, now rarely visited. Angry his only grandson was a stranger. But Alfredo's mother smiled widely and rushed towards him and spoke too enthusiastically in her heavily accented English. "Alfredo, how wonderful to see you. You're walking good now."

Alfredo glanced down at his mending leg, then back at his mum and smiled sadly.  "Yeah. Leg's fine again now, Mum. I'll soon be earning again. I just came over to ask if I could borrow a black tie... for a funeral."

His mother kissed him and held him lovingly. Alfredo's father, whose grasp of English was less than his wife's, stopped cleaning and looked up, stony faced. "I get tie. What else you want?"

Alfredo's mother cut in. "Why you being so rude? We don't see him for weeks and now you speak like this."

Alfredo could see a full-scale family row was about to erupt. "Look, I just came in to borrow a tie."

But his dad was determined to make his point. "What else? What else you want? You no come 'ere just for tie."

His mother was becoming angrier and her tone hardened. "He told you, he came to get a black tie. Why don't you just fetch it?"

Alfredo's father sauntered to the counter then behind it and out of view. Alfredo's mother's anger disappeared with her husband. Her tone dropped and her voice slowed. "How is Antonio?"

Alfredo felt both guilty and pre-occupied. He knew his father had seen through him. "It's Tony, Mum. He's fine thanks."

Alfredo stood waiting like a customer. His mother was desperate to get into conversation with him. She raised her eyebrows. "You want coffee?"

"No thanks."

She returned to cleaning the coffee machine. Her son relaxed a little and his voice softened.

"He'll be one soon."

"And Shirley, how is she?"

At that moment, Alfredo's father returned carrying a tie wrapped in brown paper and handed it over. Alfredo looked at the brown paper parcel and stuffed it into his pocket. "Thanks, Dad."

Alfredo's father put his hands on his hips and took a deep breath.

"What else you want?"

Alfredo's mother slammed a cup down on the counter. "If you can't be polite then don't speak."

Alfredo cut in. "It's okay, Mum. Dad's right. I do need to ask you... if... er, there's any chance..."

Alfredo's father interrupted. "I told you, as long as you stay with that woman, no money. You want food? Eat. Your baby want food? Bring here. But nothin' for her."

Alfredo could feel himself starting to tremble with frustration and anger.

"I can't find any work, Papa, and I owe people money."

Alfredo's father shook his head. "You choose. You want help, I give, but not when you with woman not Catholic. She not even go church. Her family bad. Nothing change. You choose."

Alfredo pleaded. "She ain't got no family, not no more."

Alfredo's father wasn't listening. He turned away. "You choose."

The love between father and son was buried beneath a ton of circumstances. Alfredo looked more drained of spirit than his parents had ever seen him. He turned slowly from his father and walked towards the door and spoke over his shoulder. "I'll make sure you see Tony, Mum, don't worry."

30

Alfredo's mother ran to her son and put her arms around him. She begged him to stay for a while and began to cry. She cursed her husband and tried to hold on to her son. Alfredo was choked and desperate, and though he had nowhere else to go for help, he could not stay a moment longer.

The following day, Alfredo, Shirley and little Tony were amongst the congregation gathered at a graveside in South London. The deceased had once been a friend of Shirley's father. Both had been notorious South London villains. The church service had concluded and the congregation was now standing around the burial plot as the vicar was finishing his prayers.

Arriving almost too late, several well-dressed men hurriedly found a path between the gravestones. It seemed everyone noticed their arrival. They stood together, some of them nodded at various individuals who were already in attendance. Some of those already gathered nodded back in recognition. But Alfredo was glaring at them. He turned to Shirley and whispered. "Bastards."

Shirley responded with a questioning look. Alfredo nodded towards the new arrivals. "Look... Old Bill."

Shirley looked around and whispered back. "Where?"

Alfredo motioned towards the late arrivals, his eyes fixed on them. "Look, five of them, Sergeant Watson and his team. Just arrived."

Shirley looked mystified. "Old Bill? No they ain't."

Alfredo's fixed gaze hadn't changed, his voice was low, his tone was certain. "Yeah, they are, I recognise most of 'em. Gave me a tug, couple of weeks ago."

Shirley was equally sure. She stared at him. "I know every one of 'em and they definitely ain't coppers."

Alfredo knew when Shirley said she was certain, she was indeed certain, but this was difficult to accept. "You sure?"

Shirley didn't answer in words. She gave him a look that meant. "I said, so didn't I?"

There was a brief pause while Alfredo took it all in. Then his expression changed from anger to rage. "Who are they then?"

Shirley hadn't a clue what was unfolding. "South London 'faces'; Danny Pembroke, Bob Welch, Ted Harris, Freddie Sansom and Tom Wisbey."

Alfredo clenched his fists and jaw, his eyes still fixed on the new arrivals. Shirley could now hear her husband's breathing. "What's wrong with you?"

But Alfredo didn't answer. He moved away from Shirley and approached the Raiders. He stood behind them and whispered loudly. "You bastards, you took the food from my baby's mouth."

Danny half turned towards him and spoke quietly. "Be quiet... Dunno what you're on about."

But Alfredo was not going to be brushed off. "You stole my stuff. I want it back."

Ted Harris, who had been driving the 'police car' on the night Alfredo had been 'arrested', turned to Alfredo and snarled. "Listen, if you want a fuckin' good hidin' you're going..."

But he didn't finish his sentence. Alfredo was enraged and his voice was getting louder. He glared back. "Yes, you and me, follow me, come on."

Danny gave Ted a quick infuriated glance and turned to Alfredo. "Calm down, son, and keep your mouth shut, a funeral's goin' on."

Shirley, who had been watching all of this, had made her way over, baby in arms. She moved up close to her husband and spoke as if to an old friend. "Hello, Danny. What's wrong?"

Danny smiled in recognition. "Hello, Shirley. Is he with you?"

Shirley gave a half-smile and nodded. "Yeah, me husband. What's goin' on?"

Danny lowered his voice and looked at Shirley and Alfredo. "Listen, this ain't the time and place is it...? Just hang on."

Within a few minutes, the service concluded, and the congregation had largely moved away. Now only the vicar remained, consoling close relatives at the graveside. The Raiders, with Shirley and Alfredo, had moved about 40 yards away. They were standing in a huddle arguing. Alfredo was insisting they give him back the contents of the mailbags he'd tried to steal. But Danny had had a few minutes to reflect on it all. He jabbed his finger towards Alfredo. "Listen, when we turned up, you'd already been captured. If we'd just walked away, you'd still be banged up with a sizeable portion of porridge in front of ya."

But Alfredo wasn't listening. "Ain't the point. We're fuckin' brassic and you took the piss."

Tall, slim, smiley-faced Bob picked up on Danny's point. "You 'eard what the man said, we did you a fuckin' favour. You'd be in deeper shit if it weren't for us."

Alfredo could do nothing to get the stolen property back. He was a fit and strong young man – a skilled boxer – but he was aware he couldn't take them all on, and he could hardly go to the police. All he could do in the end, would be to swallow it and just walk away.

The Raiders weren't happy with the situation either. Shirley knew they were significant thieves, and her husband had seen them at a railway station showing a particular interest in mailbags. It wouldn't take long for her to put two and two together. This young couple, both of whom felt aggrieved at them, had information which, in the wrong hands, could see them put away for a long time. The courts would be keen to make an example of the Raiders. This was a bad situation for all concerned.

Alfredo put Tony in his pushchair and pushed it from the cemetery with Shirley close by at his side. The Raiders remained in earnest conversation.

It took the young family 15 minutes to walk back to their flat. It was more than enough time to conclude they had stumbled across the identity of the infamous South Coast Raiders. It was a bad outcome for them; these were not men to make enemies of.

# Chapter 5

Victoria Station was always busy, but mid mornings were comparatively calm. A train was preparing to depart as Tom Wisbey, smartly dressed and carrying two dark green Harrods shopping bags, sauntered towards it.

Meanwhile, nearby, Danny Pembroke and Freddie Sansom, dressed expensively, walked separately towards the same train. Each had a first-class single ticket to Brighton. Each looked like a successful businessman. All walked to the first-class coach next to the coach containing the mail. The mail coach had an area in which the train guard travelled. As they boarded the first-class carriage, postmen loaded mailbags a few feet away.

The first-class passenger coach had several compartments and a corridor connecting it to the next passenger coach at one end and the mail coach at the other. Each passenger compartment had seating for six. The three Raiders entered the compartment next to the mail coach, sat down, raised their newspapers – the Times and the Daily Telegraph.

The large broadsheet newspapers hid them from the gaze of any passengers or rail staff that might pass. A few minutes went by, the engine noise built, the guard blew his whistle hard and the train jolted forward. Freddie had his head in the Times and a serious look on his face. "You know, I've got to like the Times."

Danny lowered his paper and exchanged amused looks with Tom. "Fuck off, you always read the Mirror at home..."

Danny continued. "I suppose now you've made a few bob you'll be wearing a cravat an' all."

Freddie gave a reasoned response. "Fuck off."

Danny pushed on. "Yeah and talking like Malcolm bloody Muggeridge."

Freddie responded in exactly the same way as he had done before. He flicked his paper straight and continued reading, but now with a smile on his face. They loved the banter.

Meanwhile, 20 miles south, a van pulled up outside a quiet country railway station. Inside were Roger Cordrey, Bob Welch, and Ted Harris who was driving. Ted got out and headed towards the station entrance. Inside the old station building the only sounds were distant birdsong and the loud tick of the booking office clock.

An elderly clerk sat behind the booking office desk filling in his football pools coupon. Ted, casually dressed, approached the counter and asked if the '38 to Brighton was on time and the clerk confirmed that it was. Ted made his way unhurriedly back to the van and drove away.

Ten minutes later, just off a deserted country lane , the van parked tight against roadside bushes,. They were in an area of isolated farmland with no houses or commercial premises for miles. The three gang members were now wearing overalls, and headed towards the bushes. Roger carried a duffel bag, and Bob held a pair of bolt croppers. They pushed their way through bushes until they reached a railway boundary fence. It was a simple three-wire strand fence, and Bob cut the wires in seconds. Roger was first through carrying his duffel bag and set off parallel to the railway lines some 50 yards away. Unlike the others who were hardened robbers, Roger had just one minor conviction for fraud committed years before. Though he now took a very active part in stealing mailbags, he had always lived the life of a hard-working, somewhat 'clerical', henpecked husband. And unlike the others, he was a quiet, reflective man and a boffin. Yet his intelligence, attention to detail, knowledge and skills made him the most vital member of the gang. He was a resource they protected.

Within three minutes, Roger had arrived at a low-level train signal on the trackside. It glowed green. He bent down beside it and rummaged in his duffel bag. Quickly, he got to work with a battery with wires attached to a red light, and a large black leather glove. He placed the glove over the green railway signal light. Then he switched on the red battery light he had brought with him. He covered the face of the unlit red railway signal with his battery powered red light, fixing it with two elastic bands. Roger then turned to the trackside emergency BR telephone. Once the train had been stopped by the false red light, irrespective of the cause, technical fault, malicious damage or robbery, the driver or his assistant (aka the fireman), would go to the nearby railway emergency phone and contact the signal box and raise the alarm. The emergency railway telephone at the signals was the only means of communication between the train and the outside world.

Roger knew when he cut the signal phone wires that day that a fault would be indicated in the nearest signal box. The Signalmen's Rule Book instructed in the event of a signal phone failure, the signalman must at once visit the signal concerned, or if more expedient, advise the BR Signal and Telegraph department for instructions. But Roger had chosen the location carefully, as he always did, and knew it would take at least ten minutes for the signalman to reach the defunct signal phone.

A few minutes earlier, Danny folded his newspaper, looked at his watch and tapped Tom's broadsheet paper. Tom stood up and removed a boiler suit from a Harrods bag, put it on over his suit, left the compartment and positioned himself in the corridor to keep watch.

Meanwhile, Danny and Freddie quickly donned their overalls too. Tom gave them a swift nod; the coast was clear. All three pulled on stocking masks. Danny emerged from the compartment and, using a standard railway issue twenty-one key, unlocked the door to the mail coach.

Inside, the mail coach an elderly guard was sitting in his chair and reading the Daily Sketch while eating a corned beef and pickle sandwich. His world was about to collapse, he would never feel the same about his work, or corned beef sandwiches, ever again.

Tom took a hammer from the otherwise now empty Harrods carrier bag as Freddie quietly unlocked the door to the mail coach. Within a second, all three masked raiders rushed in and at the guard. They were shouting loudly, almost out of control, 'pumped up' by the adrenaline, high on their own mixed emotions, exhilarated yet fearful. Tom raised the hammer above the petrified old guard. The old man, still holding a half-eaten sandwich, raised his hands to cover his head. As he did so, he got down on his knees and he began to whimper.

Tom barked at him. "Quick, on the deck, face down. Face down."

The guard was very keen to comply.

Danny and Freddie were already amongst the mailbags, examining each one looking for those with the tell-tale 'high-value' labels. Tom tied the guard's wrists and ankles as Danny reminded him. "Lock the fucking door."

Tom quickly locked the door through which they had entered and then helped find the loot. Within a few minutes they were ready to leave. Danny looked at his watch. "Get ready."

Each of the robbers found a fixing and held tight. Within seconds, the driver, having just passed a green signal at top speed, suddenly faced a red. Assuming an emergency he put every effort into stopping the train in the minimum distance. He applied the full force of the brakes, the steel wheels screeched across the metal rails and many yards passed the false signal. The loud screeching and force of inertia seemed to last forever, then the train stopped violently.

Danny immediately threw open the external mail coach doors on the south side and scanned the trackside and adjacent fields. There they were, emerging from the shrubs and trees, 50 yards away, dressed in overalls and nylon masks and running towards them. Danny grabbed a heavy mailbag and threw it down onto the trackside. Immediately the others followed suit.

The passengers must have wondered at the sudden and violent application of the brakes. Several had been thrown to the floor. Some were now opening the train's drop-down windows and peering out. Some on the south side of the train also saw the figures in overalls running from the bushes towards the train.

Within two minutes, six men wearing stocking masks were making off with mailbags. Some of them were carrying two. None of the passengers, nor the driver, ticket inspector, or driver's assistant attempted to stop them. Soon the Raiders, sweating and aching, pushed their way back into the bushes and the hole in the fence and ran to the waiting van.

As the robbers pulled away, they removed their overalls and changed into casual clothing. About ten minutes later, behind a vacant building on an old industrial site, the robbers' van pulled up behind two waiting saloon cars. Tom got out of the van first. He looked around quickly and established all was still and silent. He knocked loudly on the side of the van to signal the others and went swiftly towards the waiting cars. The other Raiders climbed from the van.

Tom removed ignition keys for both waiting cars from where they had been hidden beneath the offside front wheels. Then he opened the boot of both cars and removed a full can of petrol from one. Behind him the other robbers were moving mailbags, transferring them to the waiting vehicles' boots. Within seconds the boots were closed again. Danny returned to the van and opened both the windows. Tom was waiting, petrol can in hand. The first of the high-powered saloons left with half the bags and three of the robbers. Bob Welch sat in the other car with the engine running and his fingers drumming eagerly on the steering wheel.

Tom emptied the petrol can inside the seating area and the back of the van where overalls and stocking masks were now piled. He threw the can in too. Then he briefly checked and saw Danny was climbing into the front passenger seat of the other getaway car and ready to go. From the front passenger seat of the remaining getaway car, Danny looked in the rear-view mirror. He saw Tom throw something into the back of the van then turn and run towards him. Danny leaned over and threw a rear passenger door open. Within a few seconds, Tom was inside and the door was closed again. Bob pulled forward 50 yards and stopped. He studied the scene through the rear-view mirrors and they waited. A few seconds later the abandoned van burst into flames. They drove away calmly.

That morning, a tatty old van had been parked for hours outside Shirley and Alfredo's flat. Inside the van the windows were steamed up and the air was filled with blue tobacco smoke. The two occupants didn't seem to notice. The driver, a big, heavily built, ginger-headed man in his thirties, took out two more cigarettes. He lit one and threw the other onto the lap of the scruffy, fat, middle-aged bald man sitting in the passenger seat. The fat man put the cigarette to his lips. "Got a match, Ginge?"

Ginger looked through the inch-gap opening in the top of his window and spotted Alfredo emerging from the block. His Irish accent was strong. "Yeah. Your face and my arse."

With that, he climbed out of the van, lit his own cigarette and threw the match to the ground. He saw Alfredo approaching accompanied by Shirley and little Tony in his pushchair. Ginger slammed the van door shut and moved forward. His grubby companion hurried to catch him up.

Shirley and Alfredo were side by side but lost in their own thoughts. Then Shirley froze and grabbed Alfredo's arm. The imposing figure of the red-haired man was approaching them, closely shadowed by his sidekick. Alfredo pushed Shirley's arm away and took a step in front of his wife and child protectively. The two men came up close and Ginger straightened up to his full height, then looked down at Alfredo. "Mr Green wants to know where his money is?"

Alfredo matched the bigger man's pose, he didn't fear for his personal safety. "I need a bit more time."

Ginger took a deep drag on his cigarette and blew it out fast. "Your time's up, pal. Pay up or else."

Alfredo's face hardened. "I'll get it, but you gotta wait. I ain't got it yet."

Ginger flicked the cigarette away and pointed at Alfredo.

"Simple, it's gonna cost ya. Green says you don't owe him £300 anymore. Now it's £325, and it'll cost you another pony every week 'til it's paid in full."

Alfredo held Ginger's gaze. "Tell him what I told you, he'll 'ave to wait."

There was a pause then Ginger looked past Alfredo at Shirley and Tony. He licked his lips. "Your missus, pretty, I mean she could earn…"

Alfredo tensed even more. "You leave my fucking missus out of this."

The big Irishman grinned. "Your fucking missus. Yeah, that's what I was thinkin'."

Alfredo made a move towards him. Shirley stepped forward and grabbed Alfredo's arm. Tony started to cry. Shirley pleaded. "Alfredo, no. Please, no."

The two heavies sniggered and walked back to their van. Shirley held on to Alfredo, determined not to let him loose. They slammed the van doors shut and Ginger wound down a window. As he started the ignition and put the car into gear, he shouted to them. "Be back before the end of the week. Money or grief… and fuckin' your missus, it's up to you."

Alfredo broke loose and ran towards the van, but before he could get close it pulled away.

After the buzz of the job that day, and having had a close look at the loot, the Raiders had gone their various ways. That evening, at Walthamstow Dog Track, another robber, Buster Edwards, had joined Danny and Ted. All three were South London boys and had known one another since childhood. A race had just finished. Each of them tore up their betting slip. Danny and Buster smiled resignedly at each other.

Danny leaned forward. "Okay, Buster. What's it all about?"

Buster seemed keen to tell him. "We've got somethin' special lined up, and your firm's invited in."

Ted enjoyed the success of the Raiders and felt no need or desire to change anything. Buster was irritating him. "We're doin' all right, Buster. We ain't lookin' for work."

But Danny had a different view. "Let's hear him out."

Buster ignored Ted and focused on Danny.

"Look, I can't say too much until I know you're in. But it'll be worth at least fifty grand apiece, none of it traceable. It's right up your street an' all – mailbags."

Buster checked their faces to judge the reaction. Ted was frowning with suspicion. "Who else is in? Who's setting it up?"

Buster shifted uneasily on his feet, looked towards Danny and hesitated. "Well. I ain't supposed to say. Not until you say, yeah."

Danny looked as if he might be interested. "Fifty grand minimum each? Unbelievable. But we ain't gonna get involved with some mystery, are we, Buster?"

But Buster knew Danny would trust him. "Listen, I wouldn't be involved meself if they weren't reliable people, would I?"

Danny was nearly convinced, but Ted wasn't giving any ground. "Okay. Who is it then?"

Buster shifted his weight again and lit a cigarette. It gave him a few seconds to think.

Ted sensed the hesitation. "Who is it?"

"It's Gordon Goody."

Ted and Danny knew Goody. He had a strong reputation as a tough, reliable and experienced robber. But Ted now seemed even more suspicious. "No it ain't."

Buster was getting riled. "What ya mean?"

"If it was Goody you wouldn't be fuckin' around, you'd a told us straight away."

Buster thought about Ted's comment for a few seconds before taking a slow drag of his cigarette. "Look, don't say I said, but it's Ronnie and Reggie."

Danny smiled. "Ah, 'the ugly sisters'. Well they ain't up for it, Buster. We'll all get nicked or end up havin' a tear-up with 'em."

Ted nodded, his suspicions vindicated. "So you know the answer, Buster, fucking no."

But Buster didn't want to walk away. "You don't think me or Gordon would be involved if it didn't look right do ya?"

Ted was now a picture of cynicism. "They've found out we're makin' a few bob and are lookin' for a piece of it. It's all bollocks."

Buster looked from one to the other. "Well, they ain't gonna like it."

The implied threat was enough to finish the conversation. Danny answered with finality. "Nah. Like Ted said, Buster, fuck 'em."

Later that night, perhaps knowing the twins wouldn't take kindly to his opinion about them, or perhaps simply because it's the way he was, Ted was feeling angry with the world and was a little drunk. He was still in Walthamstow and, having left the dog track, had gone straight into the nearest pub. It wasn't one of Ted's usual haunts and he was on his own. The two men standing at the bar next to him were in high spirits, laughing and joking. Ted would have found that irritating enough, but irritation quickly turned to anger when one accidentally spilled beer on Ted's shirt. Ted reacted. "You clumsy bastard."

The stranger, a well-built man in his late twenties, knew it was his fault, and was still
smiling at whatever had caused the banter with his friend. "Accident mate, sorry."

But of course, the apology wasn't enough for Ted. "You fuckin' will be, fucking prick."

The stranger's friend chimed in. "He said he's sorry. What the fuck's wrong with you?"

Ted exploded in rage. He smashed his glass on the bar and thrust it into the beer spiller's face. A jagged gash opened. Before the spurting blood had reached the floor, Ted had grabbed the other man by a lapel and butted him, breaking his nose. Within seconds, the other locals had joined in and Ted was fighting against many. He was fighting for all he was worth, knowing if he went down the resulting injuries would be significant.

Ted retreated towards the exit as he threw punch after punch at the advancing locals, but they were surrounding him. Then the landlord fired one barrel of his shotgun into the wall. Everyone froze, and only the moans of the injured were heard above the sound of Del Shannon on the jukebox. In the seconds after the explosive noise of the shotgun blast, while everyone around Ted froze, he turned and bolted out of the door. He was soon anonymous on the busy evening street. When anger gave way to rational thought, he became angry with himself. Why, he wondered, was he becoming more impatient and more unpredictable? He knew those around him had noticed this increasing tendency to lose his temper. Where would it end? What could he do?

# Chapter 6

As usual when the South Coast Raiders met at Bob Welch's club on business, and they never met frequently at any single place, they arrived at intervals and entered one by one. They used the private entrance in a back street, it gave access to Bob Welch's private office at the back of his nightclub. Roger had been first to arrive at about 9.30 pm and now, 45 minutes later, they were all assembled. Tom, Ted, Roger, Bob, Freddie and Danny were sitting around in easy chairs, sipping whisky. Ted had fresh cuts and bruises on his face, and his knuckles were swollen, torn and bruised. He had said nothing about the incident in the pub and was looking even less sociable than normal.

Bob's office desk had various bottles of spirits on it, including a partly consumed bottle of Glenfiddich. Each of the gang had rested a whisky glass on a spindly coffee table next to each of the easy chairs. The meeting was in full flow.

Roger held out a necklace for each of the robbers to value. "Go on, have a look at it."

Tom leaned across towards him and took the piece and examined it. Freddie pointed vaguely towards Ted's battered face and took a sip of whisky. "What happened then, Ted?"

Ted looked up as if mystified. Freddie pointed to his own face, "Your kisser, what happened?"

Ted shook his head. "Fuck all. Nothin'."

Danny ignored the exchange, but no one welcomed anything, such as an unnecessary punch-up, which might draw attention to any member of the gang. Danny took five envelopes from his pockets and cut across the conversation. "Seven thousand, five hundred divided by six. That's £1,250 apiece."

Now everyone immediately forgot about Ted's injuries, they were all focused on the share-out. Danny passed an envelope to each of them. They all tore the envelopes open eagerly and started checking the contents. "Trusting bunch of bastards, aren't ya?" Danny said, smiling.

There was no answer; every man was fully occupied. Danny picked up his whisky and took a very small sip. None of them looked up or stopped counting for a second. This was the best part of the job. Getting together to enjoy the pleasure of the share-out, a drink, a laugh and to reflect on the success. Most of them were perfectly relaxed. Bob, Roger, Freddie and Tom finished counting and stuffed the money into their pockets. Ted was different. These days he seemed to live his life in perpetual misery and on the edge of violence. His reliability was unquestioned, and they knew him to be as hard as nails and entirely focused on his job. He would never grass and would always stick to the plan. Yet each of the robbers had noticed, though they had not discussed it, Ted's decline into more immediate violence.

Roger was the other gang member who never seemed at ease; his mind was constantly churning. He always had anxieties about what could go wrong with the next job, or about his next bet on the gee-gees or dogs. And if those things weren't occupying his mind, then the difficulties of his marriage were. But at this moment he was contemplating the bundle of notes in front of him and the value of the necklace.

But a knock at the office door interrupted the fun of the share-out and the banter. Bob gave a short sharp verbal response which left little doubt he did not want to be disturbed. But the caller had other ideas.

"Bob, it's me, Winnie. Is Ted in there?"

Ted shouted back. "Fuck off home."

Winnie was 17, about 15 years younger than his brother and had lived all his life in his shadow. Winnie's existence centred on simply hanging around his big brother and picking up the crumbs from his ill-gotten gains. In the last couple of years, he had done some fetching and carrying for the gang as well. By and large, they trusted him. Winnie was a bit simple, a liability perhaps, but a pleasant, helpful and unassuming one. Winnie was on the fringes of the gang, too feeble to be a member, too dim to understand fully what was going on, but well-drilled and too terrified of his brother to say anything about the gang to anyone.

Tom spoke up. "Let him in for fuck's sake. Give him a drink."

Bob cursed, rose from his chair and unlocked the door. Winnie took a few tentative steps into the room with all his usual lack of confidence. He scanned the room with a daft, wide smile on his face. There were no spare seats. He stood by and watched the gang with his fixed smile directed at no one and everyone.

Danny glanced up at him. "Don't stand there like a spare prick, Winnie. Get yourself a scotch."

Indifferent to the new arrival, the gang continued with their drinks and the matter in hand. Roger was keen to get the jewellery issue finalised. "What d'you think, for the necklace, Freddie?"

Freddie kept a straight face. "Well, 50 quid."

Danny smiled. "Be serious, Fred."

Freddie shrugged. He wasn't interested.

Roger felt the stones between his fingers. "I'll give a grand."

They all knew it was worth much more, but there would be the hassle of selling it. Most thought it better to let it go to their regular fence, a pal of Tom's.

Roger made his final offer. "All right, 1100... Anyone else interested?"

Ted waited a few seconds. "Twelve hundred."

Roger looked pleased at the outcome. "Okay, well, if no one else is offering more... it's yours for £1200, Ted."

Ted, straight-faced, put his envelope with £750 pounds onto a coffee table, then opened his wallet and counted out another 450. Roger gathered the total and divided into six equal shares and pushed one towards each of them. Then, Winnie chimed in, grinning. "That's good, Ted, worth £4,000, you said."

Ted's mood went instantly from annoyance to anger. Winnie's outburst had exposed Ted as having spoken to his brother about their work, and secondly, it implied he was taking advantage of his awareness of the true value of the necklace by offering much less than he knew it was worth. Ted shouted back. "Shut your fucking gob."

His brother shrank. "I only said..."

But he didn't get to finish the sentence before Ted got to his feet and shouted. "Shut your fucking gob or I'll fucking shut it for ya."

The jovial mood was gone, Ted had done it again. Now, no one was smiling. Ted took the necklace and went to the whisky bottle on the desk. He put the necklace down, filled his glass and returned to his seat. He pointed at Winnie. "You keep your mouth shut about my business, got it?"

Winnie looked as if he was going to cry. His voice dropped in pitch and volume. "Sorry, Ted."

A few seconds passed, then Danny turned in his chair. "Get yourself another drink, Winnie. Then go and find a bird, eh?"

Winnie smiled meekly and approached the bottle of scotch. As he did so the others began to talk amongst themselves again, though the mood was subdued and Ted sat silently fuming.

Less than two minutes later, Winnie sidled away from the desk and towards the office door. "If you don't mind, I'm gonna shoot off." No one took much notice, and the conversation continued uninterrupted. The door closed behind him.

A few minutes later Danny explained he was going home. He returned his empty glass to the desk, straightened up, fastened his coat and turned towards the door. It was at that moment Ted realised he had lost track of the necklace. He jumped to his feet, stared at the coffee table in front of him and rummaged in his pockets. His eyes examined the carpet and the deep chair he had occupied. Then he remembered taking the necklace to the desk when he last poured himself a drink. He rushed to the desk, but there was no sign of it. Ted turned back to study the faces staring at him. "Some fucker's nicked me necklace."

Danny shrugged and took a final sip from his glass, put it down and moved towards the door. Ted moved to block his path. "Turn out your pockets, come on."

And that's how it started. The row quickly escalated to a fight. Ted came off worse: superficial physical injuries and a deeply wounded pride.

An hour later, as Roger approached his modestly furnished house in suburbia, he thought about the bitterly disappointing events of the evening. What should have been a few hours of camaraderie had turned into a nightmare. The team was now in serious disarray. What could they do about Ted? He was becoming a significant liability.

All the lights were out and the place was cold. Roger's wife had already returned home from wherever she had been and gone to bed. Roger could still smell her perfume. She, and their home, saw little of the wealth which had slipped through his fingers. Roger was a compulsive gambler who felt compelled to spend the money he didn't hand to the bookies or croupiers, on luxuries for his wife, such as the most expensive perfumes and jewellery from Garrard or Tiffany.

But he completely failed to understand all she wanted was for him to be by her side in their home. Their occasional minor disagreements had become major, more frequent and bitter. They were firmly stuck in a cycle of growing negativity, misunderstanding and alienation.

Hungry, Roger went into the kitchen. He put the kettle on and went in search of sugar, but there was none. It didn't matter, he'd skip the sugar. He found the breadboard and some cheese and butter and searched again, but there was no bread. He found a packet of Ritz cheese biscuits. Then he remembered the caviar he had bought for her. Beneath an insect net in the larder, he found the open tin of caviar he had bought in Harrods a week earlier. He had thought his wife would enjoy the treat, but instead she said she thought it disgusting. Her comments were designed to hurt him, and they always did. She lived a life of disappointment, just like he did.

Meanwhile, Ted had given the theft of his necklace a great deal of thought. Drunk, he staggered to Winnie's small one-bedroom flat. The block of flats, the landing, everything was in darkness. Only the light of the moon lit the scene. Ted knocked hard and shouted loudly. "Open the door, you little bastard."

Nothing stirred. Ted knocked hard again. A few seconds passed, a light went on inside, the door opened a few inches. Winnie peeped through the crack. "What's wrong, Ted?"

But his words were interrupted as Ted's boot struck hard against the front door. It hit Winnie hard in the face and sent him down onto the linoleum floor. Ted pushed inside and closed the door behind him. Then he pulled his brother to his feet and punched him hard in the face. The blood flew from Winnie's split lips and he reeled backwards into the sitting room. Winnie's legs had lost their ability to hold his weight and he crumpled onto the floor.

Ted flicked on the sitting room light and looked down at his trembling brother. "Where's me necklace?"

Winnie couldn't speak through the blood, pain, fear and torn lips. Ted had never been angrier. Winnie had stolen from him, and as a result he had wrongly accused Danny and lost face in the fight that followed. Ted was now shouting at the top of his voice. "I'm gonna do you proper this time, you useless little bastard."

Ted grabbed Winnie by the collar and pulled him to his feet. Winnie had suffered many beatings from his father in earlier years and over the same period by his brother too. But he had never been more terrified. He forced out one inaudible word. "Please."

In response, Ted punched him in the face again, knocking Winnie backwards towards the kitchen. Ted went after him. "I'm gonna kill ya, now where's the necklace?"

Winnie gasped and spluttered. Blood ran from his mouth, he could hardly form the words. "Under my bed."

Ted punched Winnie square on the nose. Blood spurted, Winnie dropped to his knees crying, his head was swimming, his vision blurred. Within seconds, Ted pulled his brother to his feet in order to land another heavy blow. Winnie turned his head away and tried to make himself small and to cover his beaten face with his hands, but all to no avail. The beating continued.

At some stage Winnie ended up on the floor next to the kitchen drawers. Ted pulled him up to his feet yet again, now Winnie was barely strong enough to stand. Ted stopped hitting him and glared into the beaten and bloodied face. "You've always been like a fucking anchor. Well, no more."

A heavy thumping noise on the wall interrupted. The next-door neighbours had had enough of the din. It distracted Ted for a moment, he glanced towards the wall and another potential enemy to deal with. Aware of the distraction, Winnie opened the kitchen drawer and through tear-filled eyes, grasped the handle of a kitchen knife. Ted glanced back at Winnie, saw the knife in his hand and sneered in derision.
Winnie, crying, pointed the knife at Ted. The older brother laughed. "You ain't got the balls."

Ted lunged to strike again and, in that moment, Winnie pushed forward with all his weight and remaining strength. Ted gasped. The knife entered between shoulder and heart and penetrated deeply. He grabbed Winnie in an effort to stay on his feet, and the younger man saw an expression on the other's face he had never seen there before: shock and fear.

They slid to the floor held together, the knife lodged firmly in Ted's upper chest.

About 20 minutes later, Winnie, frightened, confused, badly beaten and covered in blood, stumbled in the darkness to a neat terraced council house about a mile away. All the lights were out. After some hesitation, he knocked on Danny's door and waited, seconds passed. The net curtain in the front window moved slightly. A few seconds later, Danny opened the door, allowing light to flood out from the hall.

For several years, ever since the money had started to role in from the mailbags, Danny had put some energy into rekindling his late father's small scrap business. To all intents and purposes, it was his job. There were no obvious signs of wealth, no flash cars and no big talk.

Danny looked Winnie up and down before whispering. "What the...? What happened?"

Winnie was nearly crying. "It's Ted, I think I've killed him."

Danny opened the door wide and ushered him in. Upstairs, Danny's two young daughters were sleeping soundly. His wife was used to unusual happenings at strange hours and had already gone back to sleep. But his son climbed out of bed quietly and listened from the bedroom door. Danny pointed Winnie into the sitting room and kept his voice low. "Dead?"

Winnie looked a complete mess; he was covered in blood. His lips, eyes and nose were all bloody and swollen. With difficulty, he began to explain. "He was gonna kill me, Danny."

Danny shook his head. A few seconds later the sitting-room door opened and a boy of about eight looked around the door. "Dad?"

Danny looked towards his son and spoke gently. "Go back to bed, Danny. Go on, before you wake your sisters up."

The little boy gave Winnie a long look and went back to bed. Danny watched the sitting-room door close and turned back to his visitor. "You sure he's dead?"

Winnie shook his head and continued his story. Before he could finish, Danny cut in again. "Anybody see you? You told anybody else?"

Winnie shook his head and mumbled. "No, come straight here?"

Danny nodded. "Call an ambulance, did ya?"

Winnie shook his head again. Danny leaned forward in his chair. "Good. Right, he's still lying on the floor then?"

Winnie swallowed and nodded slowly. Danny thought for a moment. "Is there anythin' at your place that you don't want Old Bill to find?"

Winnie looked surprised at the question. "No... Don't fink so."

Danny nodded and spoke hurriedly. "What about the necklace? You had it didn't ya?"

Winnie looked away and nodded.

Danny studied the bloodied face and clothes. If Winnie were to be seen in the street by the police in this condition, questions were bound to be asked. Danny got to his feet. "Where's the necklace then?"

"Under me bed."

Danny. "You'd better get cleaned up. Come on, let's get it sorted."

Ten minutes later, Danny and Winnie were in Danny's van heading back to Winnie's place. They parked 100 yards away, just in case the police were already on the scene. They found the flat exactly as Winnie had left it. Inside, Ted was semi-conscious and the colour of a corpse. He was lying propped up against a kitchen cabinet. The knife still protruded from his blood-soaked shirt. Winnie kept his distance, still frightened of him despite his condition.

Five minutes later an anonymous '999' call for an ambulance ensured he was soon hospitalised. His time with the Raiders was over.

# Chapter 7

It was just after 9 am and the Assistant Chief Constable (ACC) Operations was, as usual, in his tidy office inside the very orderly Transport Police Headquarters, Park Royal, North West London. As usual, he was in full uniform and sitting behind a big desk in a spacious office. On the wall behind him were pictures of himself on various training courses, a framed certificate in Criminology and a photograph of him meeting the Queen as she was about to board the Royal train.

Standing in front of him, very close to his desk, was a man of much the same age, but bigger, fatter and more threatening in his manner. The Detective Chief Superintendent (DCS) was being politely reprimanded, and he didn't like it a bit. Obviously agitated, he addressed his boss. "Mail thieves are one thing, but that isn't exactly the only crime we face is it?"

His boss took a deep breath and leaned forward, "Course not John, no one is saying otherwise. But the point is this. The world is looking at us, and they are focusing on our... no, your inability, to catch these so called South Coast Raiders."

Now the DCS worked himself into a barely disguised rage. "It's just the bloody newspapers making it up."

The ACC opened a file of papers and ran his fingers down the page. "Well, according to the Post Office, the number of high-value mailbag thefts from stations and trains has never been higher."

The DCS didn't hesitate. "Well, what do you want me to do, put every bugger on the mailbag team? I'll need more men. We're working flat out already."

The ACC nodded. "Just let me know how many additional officers you need to solve the problem and I'll get them. But do it now."

Within 24 hours the instructions went out across the country to each division of the Force instructing numbers of men proportionate to the size of the division be selected for immediate secondment to Force Headquarters (FHQ).

The following Monday, Detective Constable Roy Walcott walked up the approach to New Street Station, Birmingham, carrying a tatty suitcase. At his side was his wife of 20 years.

Roy had always seen his job as simply a means of bringing in a steady, if fairly meagre income. He wasn't ambitious, his family was his whole life. Work was simply a means to an end. His wife and children thought the world of him and completely shared his priorities.

But Roy was a detective constable, and his detective inspector had told him they needed him for a few weeks down at FHQ. Roy had reacted to those unwanted instructions the way he always did, with resignation. He wouldn't argue, there was no point.

When Roy and his wife arrived on the platform, the old London, Midland and Scottish Railway engine was limbering up and clouds of smoke were belching into the air. They slowed as they neared the train door and Roy touched his wife's arm affectionately. "It won't be that bad love, I'll ring ya as often as I can and I'll be home every week"

His wife gave a nervous smile.

Roy climbed aboard, put his suitcase to one side, pulled the window down to waist level and leaned out. His wife reached up and touched his face. "Look after yourself, and be careful won't ya?"

Roy smiled. "There ain't nothin' for you to worry about, give us a kiss then."

His wife leaned up and kissed him on the cheek. Further along the platform the guard waved a green flag, blew his whistle and stepped aboard. The train chugged slowly into motion.

Roy was one of 50 experienced, uniformed and detective officers from around the country who that day found themselves London bound.

# Chapter 8

Danny and Roger appeared to be successful businessmen, each smartly dressed in suit, tie and overcoat, trilby hat and carrying a briefcase. They were at Waterloo station in the early evening like many thousands of similar looking men. Sometimes they masqueraded as businessmen, or tourists, other times as Post Office workers or railway men. Their appearance always changed according to the needs of the job in hand.

Tonight, they were calculating the amount of time that mailbags, after being loaded onto a particular train service, were left unguarded before the train guard arrived. But Danny had something else on his mind too.

An empty train approached slowly and noisily, smoke billowing from its chimney. As soon as it had stopped, waiting passengers boarded. Three postmen, who had been chatting together while waiting with a loaded barrow, moved the barrow to the mail coach doors, opened them and began throwing the bags aboard.

Roger's newspaper was folded to expose a crossword puzzle. He glanced at his watch again and made more furtive notes on the crossword. Within three minutes the postmen had finished their work and were walking away, keen to find a cup of tea, or a pint or to go home.

The mail coach doors were, as always, left wide open for the attention of the train guard, but he was nowhere to be seen. It was over five minutes before he sauntered onto the platform. Roger made a note. Danny took his eyes off the mailbags and looked at his accomplice. "I've told Ted he's finished."

Roger nodded. Danny continued. "We're gonna need a replacement." Roger nodded again. "I know, but who?"

Danny hesitated. "Well, I been thinkin'. You know that business at the funeral? The young boxer kid?"

Roger was suddenly very interested. "Yeah. You told me. Well if you think he's right."

Danny continued, knowing if he could convince the much-respected Roger, then the rest of the gang might well agree. "We know he's up for it, I don't think he's got form, he's got the bottle, he seems to know how to keep his mouth shut, and apparently, he can look after himself. Plus, his missus, I know her family and she knows the score."

Roger looked back towards the mail coach thinking hard. He watched the guard walk straight by it without a glance. He paused. "If you think so Danny, I mean, whoever we take on it's going to be a risk. We could give him a try."

Danny. "And to be honest Rog, I don't like the fact that as it stands, he's got the hump with us and a good idea what we're up to."

The following morning, in an old and poorly lit boxing gym in South London, faded fight posters were fixed with yellowed sellotape to walls which had not been painted for years. At some time in the distant past, someone had made a botched attempt to paint the place red, white and blue. But the paint had long since discoloured, chipped, stained and faded. The place smelled of sweat, leather, liniment, decay and damp.

In the ring, two middleweights were trying to hurt each other more than they should have. Elsewhere, others were focused on their own performance. The speed ball, light bag, both heavy bags, rubber mats, a few weights, medicine balls, and skipping ropes, all were in full use.

There was no referee, a coach outside the ring was only half watching the two men inside it. No one else paid any interest to them, or so it seemed. No one was talking. Thuds, grunting sounds and heavy breathing filled the room.

Danny was standing at the back of the gym watching the two boxers and waiting for it to happen. Then it did, the three-minute bell rang out loudly. Everyone stopped exercising immediately. Danny went quickly to the ring and called to one of the sweating and bruised fighters. "Hey Alfredo, you got a minute?"

Alfredo's body was running in sweat and he was breathing heavily, his face flushed with exertion and light bruising. He looked down at Danny and paused. Then he climbed out of the ring without speaking. When they had last parted it had been on poor terms. Nothing had happened since to make Alfredo feel less aggrieved. He approached Danny with no hint of his feelings, he stared impassively, sweat running down his face. Danny studied him, then Alfredo spoke. "So, who are ya today then? DS Watson or Danny Pembroke?"

Danny ignored the remark. "Look, been thinkin'. I understand the way you feel... if you're still skint and need a hand perhaps we can work somethin' out."

Alfredo visibly relaxed a little, his shoulders dropped. "What you got in mind?"

Danny smiled. "Have your shower, I'll be waiting in the 'caff' across the road."

A few minutes later Alfredo was in the café, his hair still wet from the shower. He was sipping frothy coffee and watching Danny stir a mug of tea. Alfredo concentrated on the words of the man who sat opposite.

"You can come an' work with my firm, see how it works out."

But Alfredo was concerned, 'Could he trust them? Was it another stroke? Would they rip him off?' Alfredo stared at Danny levelly and spoke slowly. "Well, you know it really ain't my game don't ya?"

Danny smiled. "Yeah, well that was kind of obvious. Anyway, you want it or not?"

Alfredo's expression, giving little away, hadn't changed. "What about the money you owe me?"

Danny sighed. "Forget it. You'll soon make it up, much more an all."

Alfredo leaned back in his seat. "That bunch you work with, not exactly welcomin' are they?"

Danny stopped smiling. "You weren't on the team then was ya? Anyway, you want it or not?

Alfredo kept his enthusiasm in check. "Yeah."

Danny reached into his jacket pocket and took out his wallet. He removed a bundle of fivers and tenners and counted silently. Then he pushed the money across the table. "Okay, get yourself some decent clobber, and there's a few bob on top. Don't get nothin' flash. When you come out to work you gotta look like a successful businessman. You understand, nothin' too flash?"

There was about £200 on the table. Alfredo studied it. It was more than enough to pay the rent arrears, buy a little more time with the loan sharks, and get some decent clothes. He stuffed it into the pocket of his worn Wrangler jeans.

Danny watched him eagerly pocket the money, then looked around the quiet café. "If you look like shit, the world'll treat you like shit."

Alfredo was listening, keen to learn. Shirley had told him Danny's family had always had money but no one knew how they came by it, and most knew not to ask. Danny continued the briefing. "If you look like you're worth a few bob, people will treat you with respect, that's the way it is."

Alfredo nodded, Danny continued. "So, the way you're dressed now. You gotta stick to that sort of gear, same as always, when you're at home and in the local boozer and that. But when we're workin' it's different."
Alfredo nodded again, finished his coffee in one gulp and leaned in closer. "Okay. When we likely to, you know, go to work?"
Danny's voice dropped a little. "Seven tonight."
Alfredo allowed himself a smile and nodded. "Good."

Danny leaned back in his chair and drained his mug. "That gives you time to do a bit of shopping. And don't tell Shirl any more than you need too. That way she can't drop a bollock. She'll understand, she knows the score."

Danny couldn't help but like the boy. He had shown some courage in standing up to them when he thought they were policemen and again at the funeral. He was also a good-looking young athlete and like himself, a father and a determined breadwinner. But still Danny wondered, if he would make a decent thief.

Alfredo, gym bag on his shoulder, headed straight for the shops via the Tube. He resisted the temptation to buy high fashion items in Carnaby Street and followed Danny's instructions. Within 20 minutes he was in Sloane Square and on his way into Peter Jones department store. By 11.30 he was back at the flat with carrier bags of clothes including a new dress for Shirley and the ingredients for their favourite Italian meal. Shirley had not seen him since 7.00 that morning. She had assumed he had gone from the gym to the Labour exchange looking for work again. The broad smile and new clothes took her by surprise.

Alfredo put the Camp coffee to the back of the kitchen cupboard, rinsed the cafetière that hadn't seen the light of day for many months, opened the newly bought ground coffee and made a pot. The aroma filled the small flat.

Ever since he had arrived home, Shirley had bombarded him with questions, but he had just smiled and told her to wait until the coffee was made. Now they sat together, he was smiling broadly and she was trying to reciprocate. He told her all about his meeting with Danny. She listened in silence.

Alfredo had expected Shirley to be immediately excited and quick to show a smile. This, after all, was a fast route out of their financial mess. But the best she could muster was a gentle, tolerant smile.

Shirley reminded him she had always fought to keep away from crime. Her father had missed too many of her childhood years, too many Christmases, holidays and ordinary days while behind bars. She told him again about the many dodgy 'uncles', the whispering, the false promises and the secrets she had been sworn to keep. She told him she remained determined to create a different sort of family environment for young Tony. And she could also sense Alfredo's nervousness at the prospect of committing serious crime, though he was clearly doing his best to conceal it. But she also said she understood he was only agreeing to steal to save them from homelessness. After all, their situation was dire. She suggested he could keep looking for a proper job, while he continued to prepare to return to the ring.

Alfredo felt the deep sorrow in her words and could see the worry on her face. He agreed without hesitation to every word she uttered. And when she had finished, he kissed her gently and sat with her for a while.

After a few minutes he went to the bedroom and dressed up in his crisp new white shirt, dark blue suit and maroon tie. She told him he looked like a film star and they held one another and laughed together for the first time in a long time.

# Chapter 9

It was late afternoon, the ACC (Operations), the DCS and Detective Inspector Aldridge stood with their backs to the bar in the in the canteen area. It was the biggest open space at The British Transport Police Headquarters.

In front of them on wooden bar seats and metal canteen chairs were the 50 secondees. Most had suitcases with them, having arrived from as far north as Newcastle, and as far west as Cardiff. None of them had ever worked in London before. Many of them had impenetrable regional accents.

The ACC looked out across the audience with pride. He had given the DCS exactly what he had asked for, surely now the South Coast Raiders would be caught, and there would be no more threatening phone calls from the Minister of Transport, aka 'Bloody Marples.'

Ernest Marples was a former Post Master General and hated the railways. As Minister of Transport, he had quickly proven to be a nuisance to the bosses of British Rail. More recently, the long series of serious mailbag thefts had given him a big stick with which to beat the railway bosses and the Transport Police too. Marples might have learned a little about the Post Office as the responsible Minister of State. But he had not had the time, or perhaps the inclination, to learn about the railways. But he thrashed away with his big stick anyway.

The DCS looked out at the inexperienced bunch of no-hopers, clodhoppers and over ambitious secondees. "Oh well." He thought. "If they fail it'll be Aldridge's fault, he can't say he hasn't been given the resources."

Aldridge smiled too, but some people can't smile in a warm way even when they try. Aldridge was one of those. He smiled with his lips, but his eyes remained lifeless. Soon he would be rich beyond his dreams. He looked out at the men he now had responsibility for and did some quick calculations- 'Fifty blokes, on two shifts of 25, 12 noon-8 and 4–midnight. Staggered rest days. Put three on each vulnerable train, accompanied by a London man, obviously. I can cover over 30 trains a day. They could hardly expect me to do more.'

As long as he kept control and appeared to be doing all he could, they would never suspect him.

# Chapter 10

At Charing Cross station, Alfredo, smartly dressed in his new outfit, bought an Evening Standard from a vendor and waited outside the bar on the concourse. The evening rush hour was tailing off, but he was far from alone. Scattered across the concourse were men and women variously waiting for late trains, for friends arriving for a night out in London, and of course, their chosen commuting companions, particularly those of the opposite sex.

Danny arrived with Roger at 6.55pm. Roger was carrying an empty suitcase. Alfredo had never met Roger or even heard his of him. They shook hands. Danny described Roger as the brains and told Alfredo he knew of no one else who knew so much about the railways and how to stop trains. Alfredo studied Roger as Danny continued. "Roger knows all the different types of mail coaches, guards' brakes, signals, the lot…"

Danny continued as they bought tickets and walked to the platform. He made it clear to Alfredo, if he wanted to know anything about their business, Roger was the one to ask. Alfredo now looked slightly in awe of Roger and was keen to learn.

Their evening's work should have been simple, and the loot would, as always, be shared amongst the entire team, even if, as tonight, they needed only five participants.

Three of the gang would board the train and sit in the first-class compartment at the front next to the mail coach containing a guard's compartment. They knew from their observations the guard would leave his compartment within a minute of departing Charing Cross.

Once the guard had left, two of the robbers would unlock the mail coach with a railway issue '21' key, rifle the bags and put the loot into their suitcase. The robbers would re-lock the mail coach door and return to the passenger coaches. Meanwhile, the third robber would follow the guard down the train. If the guard turned back towards the mail coach before his accomplices had time to finish, he would detain the guard for as long as necessary and by any means available, but preferably by brains rather than brawn.

At Chislehurst, the robbers would decamp and make their way to two waiting cars.

Everything started as expected. The young train guard, who didn't look old enough to shave, left the mail coach almost immediately. Danny put his broadsheet newspaper down, moved out into the corridor and checked the guard had disappeared down the train. Danny nodded to his accomplices before leaving them to follow the guard. Without speaking Roger left the compartment and approached the mail coach door. Alfredo's mouth had gone dry and he could feel his heart racing. He picked up the empty suitcase and followed.

Roger unlocked the mail coach and they both entered. Alfredo pushed the door closed behind him and was instructed to relock the door from the inside and leave his key in the lock. This would ensure they could not be taken by surprise. But Alfredo's hands were shaking so much he couldn't get the key into the keyhole. He fumbled and cursed himself. Eventually he managed it. By then, Roger was busy in the mail stowage area. Alfredo rushed to join him.

Roger had located a high-value bag. He pointed to the numbers in black print on the manila cardboard label tied around the neck of the bag. "That's what you're looking for, the number in heavy print."
Alfredo nodded and picked up the search. Roger slit the pale canvas mailbag. Inside were many loose letters and a small, 14 inches by 14 green canvas sack fastened at the neck. Roger opened the suitcase and threw in the green inner bag. Alfredo watched.

Roger continued the routine, Alfredo copied. Both were fully engaged in locating mailbags with the right code, slitting them open and removing the green inners bags. They worked efficiently and without further talk.

Danny had positioned himself perfectly about two-thirds of the way down the second passenger coach. He stood in the corridor smoking and glancing at his newspaper. He could clearly see the corridor along which the guard would return before the end of the journey. This was simplicity itself.

In less than ten minutes, Roger and Alfredo emerged, re-locked the mail coach door and moved down the first-class carriage. Alfredo entered an empty compartment and sat down alone. Roger, carrying the heavy suitcase, moved on through the train to find another first-class coach. On the way he passed Danny without a word being spoken. Danny walked back up to the first-class coach and found an empty compartment too, then he got back to his newspaper.

Five minutes later, the train arrived at Chislehurst. Danny, Roger and Alfredo all alighted separately and started to make their way to the ticket barrier. However, the ticket inspector, a small man wearing an overcoat which was at least four sizes too big for him, for no apparent reason, got off the train and approached Roger purposefully.

Danny and Alfredo could see what was unfolding. Roger appeared a little flustered. He was searching frantically for his ticket but couldn't find it. It was also obvious he didn't want to put down the valuable and incriminating suitcase.

But trying to search all his pockets without putting the suitcase down made him more jittery. "It's here somewhere. I had it a minute ago, honestly."

The smug face of the ticket inspector said it all. 'You were travelling first-class without a valid ticket, now you are wasting my time looking for a ticket we both know does not exist.'
"Take your time sir." He said sarcastically.
Roger shrugged nervously. "Look, I seem to have lost it."
The ticket inspector pointed to the suitcase. "You sure it ain't in there?"
Roger wasn't sure if the ticket inspector was making an attempt at humour, knew more than he should, or was trying to be helpful.

Danny and Alfredo still couldn't hear what was being said, but judging by appearances, things could seriously unravel at any moment. They saw Roger shake his head solemnly. The ticket inspector spoke again to Roger, but with the sound of the locomotive it was impossible for Danny or Alfredo to hear. Alfredo moved closer. The ticket inspector opened his notebook. Alfredo could now hear the conversation. The little man looked up at Roger, and in his most officious tone instructed. "You'll have to pay the full first-class fare, otherwise I'll have to report you to the police."
Roger put the suitcase down reluctantly and felt in all his pockets again. "I've lost my wallet as well."
Now the ticket inspector was certain his early conclusion was completely accurate. He smiled in contentment. "If you can't verify your name and address, I'll have to call the police, they have the power of arrest for this."

Meanwhile, Tom Wisbey had left a parked getaway car and as planned, appeared on the platform ready to act if needed. He was standing just 15

feet away in the door to the waiting room. Danny closed in on the scene from the other direction and Alfredo was now only a few feet from Roger. The ticket inspector looked pleased with himself. "So, what's it to be?" Alfredo closed in and held out his own ticket to Roger. "Excuse me, I believe you dropped this on the train, I saw you get off and..."
Roger took the ticket from him. "Thank you, I thought I'd lost it."
Alfredo smiled charmingly. "You had."

The ticket inspector looked at the smartly dressed young man and doubted himself. Roger handed the ticket over to the ticket inspector who examined it in less than a second. He punched it and handed it back, then glanced at his pocket watch. "Thank you sir, if you will excuse me."
He moved his little legs, that were draped by the oversized coat, quickly back towards the waiting train.

Danny and Tom joined them, Danny spoke first, only just loud enough to be heard above the train. "Everythin' alright Rog?"

The guard blew his whistle, the engine noise built. Roger raised his voice a little. "Lost me wallet, might be in the mail coach."

The train juddered forward. Danny, Tom and Roger's heads swivelled towards the train as it picked up pace rapidly. The implications were obvious to Alfredo. The contents of Roger's wallet would no doubt provide a direct route to his front door. Alfredo tapped Danny on the arm urgently and spoke quickly. "I get nicked, you look after me family right."
Danny looked puzzled. "Yeah, why?"

At that moment the last carriage moved past them, Alfredo turned without speaking and sprinted hard to reach it. Danny called after him but Alfredo couldn't hear above the sound of the engine. The train was still accelerating as Alfredo threw himself against the rearmost passenger door. One foot landed on the running board, the other missed completely. If he fell now, it might be to his death. He instinctively grabbed a door handle and pulled himself close to the door. But to open the door with one hand, with his own body in the way, and against the motion of train, was almost impossible. But there was no alternative. With every second, the train gained greater speed it became harder and more frightening.

It took him about 20 seconds to climb inside, but it seemed like minutes. The rear carriage was empty and Alfredo needed time to get his breath, tidy himself up, brush the dust from his clothes and most of all, to calm down. He was sweating profusely, not from exertion but from fear. Then he began to make his way to the front of the train and the guard's brake.

As he progressed through the carriages, he congratulated himself on his quick thinking. After all, he thought, if Roger got nicked the gravy train would abruptly stop running. On the other hand, even if he, Alfredo, got captured and kept his mouth shut, Shirley's money worries would be over. The Raiders would look after her. So either way, he was on a winner. There was no doubt in his mind, tonight's events would mark him out with his team as a quick-witted, bold, team player.

Halfway along the train he encountered the little man in the oversized overcoat again. Perhaps the ticket inspector didn't recognise him, or perhaps he assumed Alfredo had only got off the train to return the ticket he'd found, but in any event, he simply asked to see Alfredo's ticket. Alfredo thought quickly and explained it was in his luggage further up the train. The little man adopted his, 'I've heard it all before look' again, and told Alfredo he would have to see it before Alfredo left the train. Alfredo nodded solemnly and moved on. Alfredo entered the buffet car and was relieved to see the guard drinking tea and playing cards. Alfredo moved further towards the mail coach and the first-class carriage he had recently vacated. As he approached the mail coach door, he took the key from his pocket, took a deep breath and within a second was back at the scene of the crime. He relocked the door from the inside and left the key in the lock, as taught.

He began the search. He had no idea when the next station stop was due, but assumed he would have plenty of time. After all, the train had only left the last station a few minutes ago. But the train slowed, and Alfredo immediately sensed the change of pace of the 'clackety-clack' of the train on the rails. He stood up quickly and frantically looked out from the dirty window. The train was arriving at Petts Wood. He looked at his watch, only five minutes had passed since Chislehurst. He searched as fast as he could, his eyes scanning urgently for the wallet. The train came to an abrupt halt, he was thrown forward. He heard voices outside.

Then he saw it, a black leather wallet, covered in dust. He heard the door to the mail coach being opened by the postmen on the platform a few feet to his left. He bolted for the door through which he had entered and slipped through. Each of the first-class compartments in the adjoining coach had their own door onto the platform. Alfredo went straight to the nearest, pulled the window down and peered out.

The postmen were no more than 12 feet away from him and engrossed in conversation. Somebody called Alf Ramsey had apparently just been made manager of the England football team. Alfredo closed the window again, his heart was racing, he moved down the coach and got off. He opened the dusty wallet as the 'the coat with legs' approached. Hands shaking, he removed the ticket from the wallet and handed it over. The inspector examined it very closely. "It says Chislehurst Junction, you'll have to pay the extra."

Alfredo took a half-crown from his pocket and paid. The 'coat' gave him his change, and re-boarded. All was well. Now all Alfredo had to do was await a return train to London. He had saved Roger from arrest and would be a hero with the rest of the gang. He smiled to himself, he could hardly wait to join the others. Ten minutes later he was on a train back to Charing Cross and even more keen to meet with his buddies and take the applause.

Bob had been waiting near Chislehurst Junction station with one car, Tom and Freddie with another. Both cars, as usual, had been stolen that day and their registration plates changed. Naturally, the new registration plate numbers would be identical to those allocated to cars of the same make, model and colour as the stolen ones. It was routine for those Raiders who had been active on the train to travel in separate getaway cars. So by the time the gang had entered London, even the duty getaway drivers knew all about Alfredo's death-defying leap onto the side of the train. They dumped both stolen cars within walking distance of the District Line, their keys left in the ignition. Others would steal them both within hours. Then each made their way to Tom's betting shop. It was not yet 8.30pm Less than two hours' work which would, typically, earn each of them at least six months' national average wage, and sometimes very much more.

Tom and Danny got a cab for the last part of the journey. They had the suitcase with the goodies in, Danny was dropped off with the suitcase just around the corner from the betting shop, just in case the balloon had gone up and Old Bill was waiting. Then the cab dropped Tom near his shop. He unlocked, had a look around, re-locked the doors and strolled back to meet his pal. The other three members of the team arrived within a few minutes. They didn't meet here often. They didn't meet frequently at any single place, and never met collectively in one another's houses.

Every one of them had some sort of front for their income. Danny was still notionally running a scrap metal come rag and bone business with a small yard and lock up premises. He went there most days for an hour or two. It kept up the front, gave him a break from the house, and gave him time to read, think and occasionally meet Roger to discuss plans.

Roger was ostensibly a florist with a shop in Brighton. Freddie described himself as a builder and drove a van advertising it to the world. And if anyone asked him to do a bit of work, he was always too busy, or he provided such an expensive estimate for the job as to guarantee it would be declined. Tom had his betting shop of course, and Bob had his nightclub.

Tom opened the scotch and put the kettle on for Danny's mug of tea, his usual preference. The buzz of the job was wearing off a little, though there was still adrenalin in their veins keeping them a little high. It was usual to share the afterburn by having an hour of piss-taking and leg-pulling. Tonight, Alfredo was the target, but there was, as they used to say, 'No show without Punch.' They would have to await his appearance before the fun could really start. As Bob put it with a grin. "We'll either see him tonight, or before the magistrate tomorrow."

But there was also business to be done. They opened the green bags and examined the takings with anticipation and pleasure. The haul comprised jewellery, blank chequebooks, 'self-employed' National Insurance stamps, new driving licences, new passports and some postal orders. There was little cash. It would all have to be fenced, and the team regularly used one of Tom's old pals. It would take him a week or two to turn the goods into cash.

Just after 8.45pm Alfredo arrived with a self-satisfied smile on his face. The mood wasn't quite as Alfredo had imagined, and it puzzled him. One or two of the robbers looked as if they were trying to conceal some amusement. Danny had a sort of parental look about him. Roger looked slightly embarrassed.

Tom, smiling at Alfredo, was the first to speak. "Tea or scotch?"

Alfredo looked around the room, everyone was looking at him. "Tea please."

Alfredo grinned again, though not with the same confidence. Tom poured a mug of tea from a half-full pot keeping warm on a single ring electric stove. He added milk, and a couple of sugars from a Tate & Lyle bag. He picked up his tea keenly and took a long drink. "Got it." He announced proudly and took the wallet from his pocket with a flourish, and lobbed it over to Roger, who just about caught it.

Roger looked unimpressed. "Thanks, but you shouldn't 'ave."

Danny was frowning. "No, you drew attention."

Alfredo raised his voice. "Hang on, if the postmen had found the wallet under the fuckin' mailbags, they'd a put two and two together for certain. Old Bill would be knocking' on Roger's door right now for fuck's sake."

Tom's smile was now very wide. Bob Welch couldn't help himself. "Fuck me, we never thought of that, Moriarty."

Freddie had been watching the exchange with pleasure. He shook his head in mock desperation. Now Alfredo looked a bit confused. Roger asked the question like a father who suspects his son might just have discovered where he keeps his contraceptives. "Did you actually look in the wallet?" Alfredo didn't know what to make of the question and now felt defensive. "I had to use the ticket."

Roger could see he hadn't grasped the point. "Yes, but did you go through it?"

Alfredo now seemed both defensive and baffled. "No, ain't my business." Roger handed back the black wallet without opening it. Alfredo looked inside. It contained a few pound notes, nothing more.

Alfredo raised his voice. "So I was wasting me fuckin' time? Leapt on that train, nearly killed meself, I could 'ave got nicked, an' all a complete waste of bloody time."

The others, apart from Danny, laughed out loud,

Danny was smiling. "Listen Alfredo, never carry anythin' that would help Old Bill if you got a tug. Just money and a house key if you have to. And fuck all else."

Then the barracking really started. They all got stuck in... the running at the train... leaping on to the side, etcetera. Alfredo knew the only way to diffuse it was to join in, to mock himself, so he told them how he nearly got captured at Petts Wood. He stayed an hour, laughing at himself and playing the fool, but in truth he couldn't wait to get home.

Before he left, knowing Alfredo was short of cash, the gang let him have, as part of his equal share, the relatively small amount of cash stolen that night.

Alfredo made his excuses and left. First a visit to his favourite local Italian shop, it might still be open. The whole Italian family who ran it seemed to live in the back of the shop, granddad, granny, mother, father, two aunties and six children. You could be served by any one of them on any day of the week, day or night, or so it seemed. He bought panettone and champagne. Tonight, Shirley would smile for the first time in months. He had big news for her. He would get about another £500 from the night's work in the next two weeks, once they had sold the goods. It would pay off the back rent and the moneylender.

The clock showed 2.45am, little Tony was fast asleep. The needle on the old second-hand record player was a bit scratchy, but Dean Martin's voice sounded silky smooth. The panettone was nearly half eaten, and now Shirley and Alfredo were on the last of the champagne. They were sitting on the battered old sofa, Shirley was sitting sideways with her legs on Alfredo's lap. She spoke softly. "Been great tonight, ain't seen you as relaxed since you done your leg."

Alfredo sipped the last from his glass. "Same with you Love, like your old self."

Shirley smiled, they sat quietly, enjoying the warmth of each other's feelings. Then Shirley's mind wandered back to practical matters. "So we'll be almost straight in a couple of weeks. Don't seem possible." She paused as she thought about how the path to the future she wanted was now visible. "A couple of jobs, that's all, just put a few quid away, so long as you're right careful."

Alfredo wanted so much to keep the Shirley he had found again. "Yeah…you're right Shirl, for sure."

A contented silence fell.

A few minutes later Alfredo asked. "You heard of this bloke Roger?"

Shirley smiled. "Roger? The only Roger I ever knew was Dodgy Roger, used to sell horsemeat as beef down the market, think he's dead now."

Alfredo smiled back and shook his head and spoke slowly. "That ain't 'im Love, Roger's a brilliant bloke. Knows everythin' about the railways and plans everythin' with Danny."

But this wasn't something Shirley wanted to think about or needed to know. "Yeah, well best you keep lookin' for a job." She said softly.

But Alfredo pushed on, keen to express his appreciation. "You know Shirl, with two keys that any railwayman can get, Roger says we can get to any mailbags we want."

Shirley raised for eyebrows in mock astonishment. "Fancy that."

Alfredo now seemed to be talking to himself. "Yeah, called a 'T' key and a '21' key."

"How romantic." She allowed herself to smile.

Neither of them wanted the mood spoiled and Alfredo grinned back. "Yeah… let's have an early night."

Shirley finished her drink in one. They walked to the bedroom, little Tony was still sleeping soundly.

It would be the last passionate evening they would have for many months. The champagne would prove to be much more expensive than either of them could ever have imagined.

A few hours later, Alfredo left Shirley in bed and crept out before 7.00am, the chilly morning felt good and he felt positive. He saw everything in a new light, or rather the light he remembered from perhaps a year earlier, before he had broken his leg. Then, life at home was full of happiness and a promising career in professional boxing was taking shape.

They had been poor but managing to survive, the accident had finished that. Since then the need to borrow money from back-street lenders had filled him with shame. The inevitable threats that followed non-repayment at extortionate interest rates had preyed on the woman he loved and shamed him.

As he made his way to the gym, he sighed with relief and smiled, now he would have enough money to pay off the loan shark and they could forget Ginger and the 'slug' who helped him. Training was going well once again and his muscle tone and timing were returning. He enjoyed the training, the hard work, the feeling that his body was getting back to peak fitness. But best of all he loved the boxing, the challenge, the danger, the need for complete focus and of course, the anticipation of success.

He was walking on air when he left the gym, his body and mind were fully in-tune, confident, strong and relaxed. He had already decided to go shopping for something he had missed a great deal since his marriage, a bean grinder and fresh coffee beans. Both were a staple of his childhood growing up in the family's Italian café in Clerkenwell.

He bounded up the steps to the flat, shopping bags and gym bag in hands. But as he walked the landing leading to his flat he saw the front door ajar, and was full of foreboding.

# Chapter 11

It was a night of mental torment for both of them. All night Alfredo had tossed and turned. Sleep had been impossible. He knew Shirley was awake too, lost in her pain, fears and loathing, her eyes held firmly closed in an attempt to shut out all she could.

Over and over it turned in his head, if he won the physical battle against Ginger and his slimy friend, their boss would send other enforcers. Yet neither he, nor Shirley, could report the rape to the police. Old Bill were the last people Alfredo wanted asking questions. One thing he knew for certain, he could not do nothing, and whatever he did would have repercussions. Shirley and Alfredo were sharing a bed, both alone, awake and silent. Tony was awake too but determined to make his presence felt.

Both parents were fully washed and dressed by 7.00am. But she was still not talking. Alfredo tried to put his arm around her, but she brushed it away. She knew he would seek immediate revenge and warned him. "If you go, then don't come back."

He looked as if he were in agony. "I love you, but don't ask me not to be a man."

Shirley snorted. "So, you get killed, or nicked, how do you think that works out for me and Tony then?"

Alfredo didn't answer or even look in her direction.

She tried pleading. "At least speak to Danny, see what he says."

Alfredo took this as a slight. He didn't need to seek any other man's permission or direction. He knew what he needed to do. "Look, I don't need to speak to anyone."

Shirley went from pleading to rage. "Alright. Get your things together and fuck off back to your mum and dad. I'm sick of you. They'll be pleased to 'ave ya back, that's for sure. They always hated me anyway."

He glared at his wife and shouted. "You can't stay here on your own. What's wrong with you?"

She picked up the bag of coffee beans and threw it against the door. "I ain't an idiot, I'll find somewhere, now just fuck off."

Shirley grabbed her packet of Park Drive filter cigarettes from the coffee table. It was empty, and she threw it down on the kitchen table in frustration. "I need some fags."

Alfredo sensed the erupting volcano had finished for the moment, his tone became conciliatory, he put his hand on her arm. "We're gonna stick together. Pack a bag for the three of us. We'll meet at two o'clock at The Bonneville."

The Bonneville was a café in Clerkenwell where they had often met years earlier when they were dating. Shirley pulled away from him. She put on her topcoat and a headscarf to help to hide some of the injuries to her face. "I need some fags. Look after Tony for ten minutes, will ya?"

She didn't wait for an answer; she grabbed her purse and left.

Normally, Alfredo would give in to his wife, even if an argument had to ensue first. But this time it was different and he would not compromise. He watched her leave, picked up his son and with his free hand collected a suitcase from the bedroom. By the time Shirley returned, Alfredo had dressed little Tony, put him in his folding pushchair and started packing a suitcase. He told Shirley to finish the packing. Out of character, she silently obeyed. Perhaps because of exhaustion or frustration, perhaps because all her confidence had been stolen.

Having left the suitcase in the sitting room for Alfredo to collect later, they made their way to the Tube, then separated. Alfredo entered the station and Shirley and Tony headed towards the bus stop.

Less than 30 minutes later, Alfredo entered his parents' café. Of course, everything was exactly as it was the last time he visited. It was always the same – the sound of Italian music, the smell of fresh coffee, the aromatic warmth from the kitchen and the chill of his father's glance.

In Alfredo's eyes, his parents' world was unchanging: the café, their friends, their conversations, and they both always looked the same, did the same things with the mood between them fixed at best at mild irritation.

His mother beamed, she always did when she saw him. But this morning Alfredo wasn't in the mood to placate anyone or show deference. He ignored his father and approached his mother purposively. As he did so, he took a small brown paper parcel from his pocket, "Just returning dad's tie, I'll take it up."

His mother smiled even more broadly. "Oh, don't worry about that, just put it anywhere, come and have a coffee with me."

But Alfredo didn't answer, and his pace didn't change. He walked to the back of the café, climbed the stairs and went to the bedrooms on the first floor. He returned one minute later and left without speaking further. His mother stared at the door as it closed behind him. His father ignored the visit completely.

Alfredo emerged at Holloway Road tube station about 20 minutes later. There was a little greasy spoon café right next to the entrance. Unnoticed, Danny was standing outside leaning against the red-tiled wall drinking a mug of tea. He saw Alfredo stop on the pavement nearby, he had been here just once before in desperation to collect the loan.

Perhaps Alfredo had stopped to check he was heading in the right direction, perhaps to calm himself. Danny studied him, placed his cup on the café window ledge, walked over and touched Alfredo on the shoulder. "Alright then?"

Alfredo stared back, startled. "Danny...what you doing 'ere?"

Danny shrugged. "You're part of the team, son. So, what's the deal?"

Alfredo thought for a moment. "Shirley."

Danny nodded. "Worried 'bout ya."

Alfredo looked angry. "What she tell ya?"

Danny didn't hesitate. "Loan. Couple of Green's ginks knocked her about, pushed their way into your place, turned it over, nicked some stuff."

Alfredo paused, thinking hard, trying to read Danny's expression. Did he know more? Did he know they had defiled his wife? Alfredo took a deep breath. "This is something I gotta settle meself."

Danny nodded. "Yeah sure. But not on your own."

Alfredo shook his head. "Thanks but just stay 'ere. I gotta settle it meself."

Danny. "Listen, I'll lend you the money."

Alfredo started to move forward. "No. It's gone too far."

Danny put his arm on Alfredo to stop him. "You think you're gonna waltz in and take these geezers on, they're gonna be mob-handed. I'll come with ya. It's your show, I'll keep my gob shut, watch your back, that's all."

Alfredo stopped and thought for a few seconds. "No. If I hurt 'em bad then you'll get nicked an all."

Danny removed his arm and forced a smile. "I weren't planning on either of us of getting nicked."

Alfredo thought long and hard, he stared down the street, then back at Danny. "No. You stay here."

Danny shrugged. "No. I'll either walk three paces behind ya', or with ya."

Alfredo didn't respond, he just set off. Danny followed three paces behind.

A few minutes later Alfredo recognised the premises ahead of him – 'Green's. Turf Accountant.' The exterior was painted emerald green and the name had been picked out in gold lettering. Alfredo pushed the door open and walked in.

A long desk ran the width of the small brightly lit shop. On top of the long desk, metal bars ran to the ceiling, completely separating the premises into two distinct areas. A small gap below the iron bars and above the long desk enabled punters to pass their betting slips and money through to the three men who were taking the betting slips and cash from the other side.

On the punters' side of the shop, a narrow, chest-high ledge ran around two sides of the room. Above the ledge, pin boards held newspaper pages displaying details of all the various horse races of the day, the runners and riders and the horses' form. Chalkboards fitted to the bars over the long desk displayed the latest odds on the forthcoming races. A radio gave a live commentary on each race.

There were about 12 men studying form. Some were merely running their fingers down the lists in the newspapers on the pin boards. Others were studying their own copies of The Sporting Life and other papers.

Away from the punters, on the other side of the divide, behind the bookie's clerks, Ginger and the fat man were standing with two others. One of them, another fat man, perhaps in his early fifties, was smoking a cheroot and wearing a blue striped suit and bright green tie, a green tartan waistcoat and a pocket watch.

No one noticed Alfredo. On both sides of the shop, the opportunity to gain unearned wealth consumed everyone. Alfredo walked to the middle of the shop and took in the entire scene. He spotted those he had come for and approached the dividing bars. He stared through waiting to be seen.

Danny entered and made his way directly to the newspapers pinned on the walls. He picked up a pencil from a ledge and ran a finger down a line of runners.

About ten seconds later, the fat man noticed Alfredo. He nudged Ginger and nodded towards the visitor. The Irishman looked across at Alfredo and sniggered. He turned to the man in the tartan waistcoat and said something inaudible. The man in the waistcoat smiled. "See if he's brought it all, if not..."

The Irishman cut in. "For sure boss."

Ginger opened a barred metal gate which separated the two parts of the shop and walked into the gateway. As he did so Alfredo approached him, The Irishman smirked. "Okay. How much you got?"

Alfredo took one pace forward, put his hand inside his coat and pulled out a Second World War .38 Italian Beretta semi-automatic pistol. It was a compact and powerful weapon with a barrel just over three inches long. Alfredo straightened his arm, the weapon was now only two feet from Ginger's chest. It all took place in half a second.

There was an explosion, the force of the bullet sent some of Ginger's jacket, shirt, string vest, ginger chest hair, pale skin, ribs, lung, and spine out of the wide exit wound in his back and through the open gate and onto the jackets and trousers of Ginger's associates.

Before anyone had taken in the enormity of what had taken place, Alfredo stepped across the fallen body and through the open gate. Another explosion of sound, this time it was the bald, fat man who got it. It was another bullet to the chest. But this time the victim had a moment to understand what was coming.

If the fat rapist had had the time he would have screamed, but he only had the opportunity to open his mouth slightly. Instead, his eyes expressed his terror. The force of the blast threw his him against a metal filing cabinet. He slid down, leaving a wide smear of blood on the cabinet behind him. He slumped on the floor, twitching. Alfredo immediately pointed the gun at the man in the waistcoat.

Everyone else in the shop had been shocked and frozen by the first roar of the weapon and subsequent events. The bookie's face had turned white. Alfredo spoke slowly, calmly, and with certainty. "You know why, and you'll get your money. But come near my family again, and you'll get the same."

Alfredo took two steps forward, pushed the barrel of the gun against the waistcoat. "You understand?"

The boss's cheroot was on the floor where it had fallen from his mouth a second earlier. He nodded vigorously. Alfredo took a quick look around him and backed up into the public area. His arm still outstretched, he swept the gun in an arc around the room, staring at each of the witnesses, but no one made eye contact. He backed up to the door and left.

No one moved in the shop for a few seconds, then all the punters headed out as quickly as they could. No one wanted to be any part of this.

No one wanted to be a witness in a gang killing, no one wanted to take sides, it could only bring danger.

In addition to Danny, three of the other punters had a special reason to depart swiftly. Three of the men holding up newspapers, or facing the wall studying form, were new to the premises – Tom, Bob and Frankie Fraser. Frankie was in his late thirties, not very tall, not very powerfully built, yet he had the well-deserved reputation of being as tough, pound for pound, as any villain in London.

There's an old saying, 'It's not the size of the dog in the fight that matters, it's the size of the fight in the dog', and Frankie was full of fight. He was a freelance, happy to work for almost anyone, provided the money was right and they knew what they were doing. But Frankie had his friendships and alliances and Tom had been a friend of his for some time. Frankie's principal employer was Billy Hill.

Tom had asked Frankie to come along that morning, just in case, and Frankie had been happy to help out. It seemed nothing very much would need to be done. Tom, Bob and Frank had come variously armed with a hammer, a small axe and a short club. They knew their threats of violence would probably be enough, and they certainly hadn't signed up to be part of a conspiracy to murder. Yet if they were identified as Alfredo's back up, that is the charge they would face. They were far from happy, after all they were well known 'faces' and no one more so than Mad Frankie. Anyone present might easily identify them to the police.

Alfredo didn't run from the shop, he walked briskly away. First, he would dodge down a few side streets and make his way on foot towards Islington. Then he would catch the bus back south of the river. But before he had gone 30 yards, Danny caught up with him and tugged the sleeve of his jacket. "This way."

Danny led him across the street and around the corner. A Ford Zephyr was waiting with Freddie at the wheel. Danny got into the front, Alfredo in the back. Freddie drove away gently. Danny, visibly angry, turned to face Alfredo. "Take your socks off."

Alfredo looked mystified. "Why?"

Danny wasn't in the mood to explain. "I said, take your socks and shoes off."

Alfredo did so.

Danny was still turned around awkwardly in his seat. "Now take the rest of the bullets out of the shooter, and point it at the floor."

Alfredo showed no emotion. He took the gun from his pocket and followed the instructions given. Freddie could hardly believe what he was hearing and looked horrified. "Shooter? What the fuck happened?"

Danny ignored the question. Actions were now more pressing than explanations. Danny watched Alfredo closely as Alfredo did as he was told. Freddie hadn't seen Danny white with rage very often and was very keen to know the cause. "He ain't used it, 'as he?"

Danny ignored him again. "Now use one sock as a glove, and wipe your prints off the shooter with the other one. Then the same with the bullets."

Both Danny's liberty and his income were in serious jeopardy. If Green retaliated, Danny would have to either support Alfredo and get dragged into a war, or abandon him. If he abandoned him, there would be bad blood with Shirley, and Christ knows what she would do. He knew beneath the calm exterior she was volatile and unpredictable, just like her dad.

On the other hand, if the police arrested Alfredo, or Green murdered him, Danny would have to find another replacement for Ted. And Shirley would still be dangerously unpredictable.

Danny watched Alfredo comply with the instructions, then continued. "Now put the gun and the bullets into the socks."

Then he added. "Why the fuck did you do it?"

Alfredo shrugged. "Look Danny, I told you I didn't want you there, didn't I?"

Freddie was still playing catch up. "He ain't used it, 'as he?"

Danny took the heavy socks and turned to Freddie. "Drain, Freddie."

Freddie slowed right down, turned into one side road, and then another before pulling over. Danny opened the car door, walked a few paces and dropped the socks and contents down a road drain.

Again, they pulled gently away. Agitated, Freddie still wanted an explanation, he looked at Danny and Alfredo, now he demanded. "I said, what happened?"

Danny shook his head. "He done two of 'em."

Freddie. "Fuck me. Done 'em in? Old Bill are gonna be all over this for fuck's sake."

Danny didn't want any more drama than necessary. "Listen, the last thing Green needs is Old Bill poking about in his business."

Freddie calmed down a little. "What about the boys?"

Danny lit a cigarette and offered one to Freddie. "They didn't show out, Billy the Kid 'ere didn't fuckin' need 'em."

Alfredo looked calm enough. He leaned forward. "What's all that about the boys?"

Danny didn't bother to answer, he had important questions to ask. "Nothin', where did you get the shooter?"

Alfredo's teeth were chattering, his pulse racing and his knees knocking, but he was trying his hardest to conceal it. "Italian Army issue, my old man's. Souvenir... the War."

Danny thought about that. "What's your old man know?"

Alfredo. "He don't even know I've had it."

Danny had one more question. "Used it before?"

Danny knew ballistic tests on the bullets recovered from the bodies, or the wall and cabinet behind the bodies, would reveal unique striation marks. As individual as fingerprints, the police would compare those striation marks to others on other bullets recovered from other shootings. If Alfredo was suspected of any of those crimes, then the road would lead straight back to him, and then to his associates.

Alfredo. "No."

Danny nodded. "Where you been keepin' it?"

Alfredo leaned back in his seat. "The old man's thinks it's still under his bed."

Danny grunted. Seconds passed. They were all deep in thought. Then Alfredo spoke. "Would you drop me at my place please, I've got some clothes to pick up."

Danny told Alfredo to dispose of the clothes he was wearing as soon as he reached the flat. They all knew that Alfredo and his family would have to leave the flat immediately, just in case Green sent other men. he told him to screw the electricity meter and run the taps in the kitchen and bath and to leave them running before abandoning the place. Then he gave his last instructions. "Leave the front door open and call me once you're clear and away from the area. Then call me."

Freddie dropped Alfredo near the flat. Alfredo hurried in, tore off his clothing and put it in a brown paper bag. Then he quickly dressed, and using a hammer and screwdriver, broke open the electricity meter and pocketed the shilling coins. Within seconds he was in the bathroom turning on the taps. Next the kitchen ones. Then he picked up the suitcase and brown paper bag of clothing and, leaving the door slightly ajar, he left.

It would seem to those who later entered the flat, that someone had burgled it for the sake of the TV and the contents of electricity meter. It was a common experience. The authorities would assume the thief left taps running in some random, malicious act. More importantly to Alfredo, it would render the place 'temporarily uninhabitable,' and mean the provision of emergency housing.

Later that day, Alfredo met up with Shirley and Tony. He had important news. While they waited for the council to find alternative housing, Danny said they could move into a guesthouse owned by Danny's trusted mother-in-law, Penny.

# Chapter 12

Penny's guesthouse wasn't bad at all. Shirley and Alfredo didn't sleep well on that first night of course, but it had nothing to do with the accommodation. The guesthouse was on one of the quieter roads in Dulwich, a big terraced Victorian place. In one vital way, the new accommodation was perfect, for no one in the area knew them. They would be safe.

They had two adjoining rooms and were the only guests. Penny was terrific. She was in her sixties, caring, funny and generous.

Shirley hadn't slept at all that first night and had watched the dawn arrive, heard the clatter of the horse's hooves as the milk cart came to a halt outside the bay window below. She had heard the dull clink of full bottles of milk being placed on the doorstep and the high-pitched clash of the empty returned bottles being snatched up hastily as the milkman raced to finish his round.

Later, still wide awake and with tortured thoughts running through her head, she heard the early buses and other traffic. She didn't know her husband had yesterday murdered two men, but she could see and feel the sweat on his skin and on the bedsheets.

She had heard his worried murmurs, heard him grinding his teeth, and felt the movement of his constant shifting. To her great relief, whatever he had done to punish her attackers had been achieved without harm to himself. But she could not escape her fear at the potential consequences.

Alfredo got up at 7.00am, bathed and shaved. He was subdued and hardly spoke. Shirley would not ask what had happened, and she knew even if she did, he wouldn't tell her, he would not burden her with the truth.

At about 7.30am, 'Dreadful,' as Penny was affectionately called by her son-in-law, called up the stairs. "Shirl, I got some eggs on. You want a cuppa?"

Shirley called back a thank you, picked up the sleeping Tony and left the bedroom. Alfredo followed behind a few seconds later. Dreadful and her new guests were still sitting at the kitchen table having breakfast when an old van pulled up outside. Danny got out from the driver's side and his wife, Iris, from the other. Penny got up immediately and went to the front door.

On her way in, Iris, who was in her early thirties, gave her mother a quick peck on the cheek. Dreadful held the door open and smiled at her son-in-law. Danny remained on the pavement. "Dreadful! How are ya love?"

Dreadful. "Same as always, tea's on."

But Danny declined, he was keen to speak to Alfredo alone. Iris took the message back inside and within a few seconds Alfredo appeared, still pulling on his black leather jacket.

In the kitchen, Iris had poured herself a cuppa and settled down for a chat with Shirley. They had never met before, Danny had asked Iris her to spend the morning with her, but Iris had no idea why. So Iris simply allowed Shirley to direct the content and pace of the conversation. Iris knew of Shirley's dad and remembered often seeing Shirley with her mum when Shirley was just a kid. They talked about mutual friends, familiar places, their shared ambitions and worries. And of course, Shirley eventually asked about what had gone on the day before, but Iris had no idea.

They were engrossed for hours talking about the big issues they both faced, but also about Alfredo's family and the problems between them. Lunchtime arrived and the conversation continued. Three pots of tea later and it was approaching 4.00. An entire day of talking, only punctuated by serving Tony's needs. By teatime, Shirley had a friend, a friend who urged her to reach out to her husband's mother. Shirley knew the advice was sound.

And so began a firm friendship. During the following days, weeks and months they met frequently. It made Shirley feel less isolated and helped clarify and validate her mixed emotions.

# Chapter 13

In addition to when they were out working, the Raiders all met together about once a week. Every man was otherwise free to enjoy his days and nights as he chose.

On this night, just two days after the shootings, Alfredo was at the guesthouse and completely unaware of a meeting being held just a couple of miles away. Freddie had called the meeting. Freddie lived in Brighton and having no base in London, this was his chosen venue, an upstairs private bar of a quiet pub, away from prying eyes and straining ears.

The landlord was worldly enough never to ask questions unless invited. He hardly knew Freddie, and knew none of the other members of Freddie's 'SW Camping club' at all, and that suited everyone. The private room had previously received few bookings, and the landlord was pleased to get the business. At Freddie's request, the landlord had installed a jukebox. The gang used it simply to prevent conversations being overheard. A handwritten note was pinned to the outside of the only door, 'Private Function.'

The jukebox had been fed with several sixpences and Danny, Freddie, Tom, Bob and Roger sat around an old wooden table. In front of them were the remnants of five pints of brown and mild and the remains of a large plate of cheese and onion, ham and mustard, and beef and pickle sandwiches. The Raiders had been talking and arguing for too long.

Roger looked exasperated. "I see your point Freddie, he's high risk." Roger studied the faces of the others.
Tom took a sip of brown and mild. "Well. He's got the balls, we know that… I like him."
Freddie examined a sandwich. "Ain't a matter of likin' Tom, I just don't want to get nicked 'cos of him."
Tom looked a bit agitated. "S'not what I'm sayin' Fred. I mean he's okay, he can handle himself and he's bright."
Danny had been listening and studying each member of the team. "And we do need another hand an all. If it ain't him, we're back to where we was."
But Freddie would not be persuaded so easily. "He's unpredictable, we can do better."

Danny had already decided, but knew Freddie needed to put his case. So Danny let the discussion run for a minute, then asked. "Who you thinkin' of then, Fred?"

Freddie cleared his throat and tried to appear nonchalant. "Well, I dunno... one of me brothers maybe."

Roger answered quickly but evenly. "We talked about your brothers before Fred, trouble is they're both so well known."

Danny saw the opportunity. "That's another advantage, the kid's got no form."

Freddie felt his chance slipping away. "Nah Dan, we gotta find somebody else otherwise we'll all end up in the nick."

Danny had heard enough. "Tell you what, see how it goes. We'll run with Alfredo for now. If you think of anybody who'd suit better, let us know Fred."

# Chapter 14

It had been two weeks since it happened. Shirley still had nightmares about it all and couldn't stand Alfredo even putting his arms around her. Alfredo still woke up in the night sweating and thinking about the awful attack on his wife, plus the look in the eyes of the men he shot in revenge, their blood on the walls, the overwhelming shock of the noise of the gun being discharged, the sickness in his stomach, the fear in his heart, and of course, the potential consequences. Now, the young couple were each lost in their own anxieties as they headed towards his parents' café.

Alfredo looked down at Tony all wrapped up and fast asleep in the pushchair, then he studied his wife by his side. He stopped 30 yards short of Luigi's. "You sure 'bout this?"
Shirley looked determined. "Yeah. It's the only family we got."
Alfredo was nervous. "I don't want no scenes, you know what my old man's like."
Shirley didn't dwell for a moment to consider her husband's words. "Ain't right keepin' Tony away anyway..."
Alfredo cut in. "Yeah but if the old..."
Shirley wasn't listening. She pushed the pushchair a little faster. "Come on, we've already discussed all this."

Alfredo caught up with her and a few steps later, pushed the café door open so she could enter easily with the pushchair. The smell of fresh coffee provided the perfect welcome. In the background, Perry Como was singing in his native Italian, 'Toselli's Serenade' (Dreams and Memories).

Alfredo's father wasn't present, but his mother was behind the counter. There were a couple of women drinking coffee together and a middle-aged man sipping a mug of tea and reading a newspaper. Alfredo's mother looked up as soon as they entered and a broad smile spread quickly across her face. Shirley smiled back instinctively, but Alfredo looked unsure.

Alfredo's mother came from behind the counter, wiping her hands in her pinafore. "How wonderful to see you."
Alfredo's mother kissed Shirley on both cheeks, kissed Alfredo, and bent down and set her warm eyes on her sleeping grandson. She kissed his

forehead gently, unfurled his little fingers and held them tenderly. She was beaming.

Alfredo looked around for his dad. "Where's dad, mum?"

His mother didn't look up, her eyes were still fixed on Tony. "Doctors, it's just *'indigestioni'*, indigestion, nothing."

She had hardly completed the sentence before Alfredo's father came through the front door. Alfredo went to meet his father, intent on speaking before his father said anything to hurt Shirley. "Dad, Shirley thought you'd want to see your grandson. Thought we'd leave him here with you for an hour, if you want?"

Alfredo's father studied his son's eyes for a moment, then his attention moved to the little stranger in the pushchair. The little boy had woken up, his eyes were glowing, and he was smiling innocently. Alfredo's father could not resist. "You leave him, *'certemente'*. We look after."

Alfredo smiled and turned back to his wife and child. Two minutes later, he and Shirley were walking down the road without their son. Shirley thought it a small step towards a proper relationship with the nearest thing she had to parents.

# Chapter 15

Within a few days, outside Bob's nightclub, the Krays made their first move. Bob Welch was a tall, slim, light-hearted, carefree club owner with money in his pocket. And he spent it freely on casinos, fine clothes, expensive wines, champagne, fabulous holidays, the best restaurants, and of course, women.

On this day he had a long lunch at Olivelli's restaurant, rubbing shoulders with theatre and entertainment types and watching his female companion stare in wonder at the famous British singer, Frankie Vaughan, sitting at the next table.

Frankie was the British 'Dean Martin', though more Jewish than Italian. Frankie was enjoying many 'Top 10' hit records, such as 'The Green Door', 'Tower of Strength', 'Give Me the Moonlight' and 'Garden of Eden'. And when he called over and said how nice it was to see Bob, and smiled at the girl at Bob's table, the young woman was lost for words.

There followed a long champagne-filled lunch, Bob and the young woman spent a few hours in bed at an expensive West End hotel before having dinner. From there, Bob dropped her off a few minutes' walk from her home. She just had time to get bathed, changed and peel the potatoes before her husband got home from working a late shift.

After dropping her off, Bob stopped for a couple of snifters before driving to his club. He employed a manager and used the club to justify his wealth. Though it also helped serve his need for socialising with friends and the occasional secret 'business meeting.'

It was just after 10 pm when he parked outside the front of his club. As he climbed out of his sports car, a figure moved out of the shadows and called. It was a tough guy called, 'Battles' and in these professional circles his face was known across London. "Hold on. I got a message for ya."

Bob smiled, completely underwhelmed, and walked casually towards the club entrance where Battles now waited.
"Battles, how the devil are ya?"
Battles moved into Bob's path and was clearly not in the mood for banter, but then again, he never was. "You listenin'?"

Bob took another step forward, right up close into Battles' space, then he pulled a mockingly serious face. "Come inside, be my guest, what you fancy? Glass of milk? A rub down with the Sporting Life? A young boy perhaps?"

Bob sniggered, pleased with himself.

But Battles' only concern was delivering a message, "Buster says you boys don't want to work with the twins, is that right?"

Bob didn't appear at all worried. "Danny made it clear didn't he?"

Battles' face set hard, he glared at Bob. "Well, the twins told me to explain, so there's no misunderstandin'."

Battles paused…"Unless your firm signs up tonight, tomorra' some of you are gonna be put out of action for a few months."

The smile disappeared from Bob's face. He leaned forward. "Well, here's another message for ya'. Gert and Daisy can just go fuck themselves. Tell 'em that."

Battles looked almost pleased at the response. He knew what the repercussions would be and would enjoy inflicting some pain on this man. He spoke with relish. "I'll tell 'em word for word."

Bob wasn't moved, he nodded almost casually. "Good. And tell 'em we'll be in the Palmerston all through lunchtime tomorra, tell 'em to come over if they've got the fuckin' bottle."

Battles couldn't wait to get back to East London to deliver the message. He drove straight to the Regal billiard hall and joined the twins who were seated at a table and watching the games. Battles was soon in animated discussion describing his encounter.

Reggie lit a cigarette. "He'll fuckin' pay for that."

Reggie turned away from Battles and called to Buster, who was in the middle of a game a few yards away. Buster finished his shot and sauntered over.

Reggie frowned at him. "Put a few blokes together, you, Bruce, Big Jim Hussey.... how many you gonna need? Eight? Ten?"

Buster looked uncertain, he glanced at Battles before studying the twins. "What for?"

Ronnie stood up and took a pace closer to him. "Tomorra, get over to the Palmerston and sort out Danny Pembroke, and the rest of that team. Give 'em a fuckin' good hidin'."

Buster had known many of those South London men for many years. He had never acted as an enforcer for the Krays, nor did he want to create a major problem with people he liked. He shifted his weight from one foot to the other. "Hold on Ron, ain't it best if us what's gonna work with 'em, keep away from it? I mean if we're gonna end up workin' with 'em we don't want any bad feeling between us do we?"

Ronnie, who was the more unpredictable of the two, hardened his face. "Just do as you're fuckin' told."

Buster took out a packet of cigarettes and offered them, but the twins waved them away. Buster lit a cigarette. He was generally his own man, an 'independent', he didn't rely on handouts from the Krays or anyone else. "If they're gonna get a good hidin' it's best if others do it."

Reggie looked as if he wanted to speak but was trying to choose his words. Ronnie was obviously getting steamed up and Reggie didn't want to witness his brother's loss of control.

That was certain to happen if Ronnie thought he had been seen to make a basic tactical error. Reggie spoke first. "'Listen Buster, they'll do what they're fuckin' told and be well paid for it."

Ronnie nodded.

Reggie continued. "Now finish your game, and we'll continue this in a minute."

Buster took another drag of his cigarette and sauntered away. Reggie looked around signalling to Ronnie no one was within earshot. It was important his brother was not seen to have made a mistake or to have backed down. Reggie spoke quietly. "Buster will do whatever you tell him. But I been thinkin', Buster might know 'em too well, be reluctant to see 'em get a good smackin'. We could send others instead and Battles' raring to go."

Then Reggie smiled to lighten things a little. Then he added, "And how would it play out if it all went wrong and Billy got to hear? No point in risking it, is there?"

Ronnie lit a cigarette and took a deep drag. "Alright, as long as no fucker here thinks we're runnin' some sort of bloody democracy."

The following lunchtime at about noon, Alfredo, like dozens of other punters, strolled into Tom's betting shop as usual. Alfredo made out a betting slip and handed it over to Tom with the stake money. Tom made eye contact and indicated that he wanted a word with him. A couple of minutes later Tom left his shop via the front door, Alfredo followed at a distance.

Tom's Vauxhall Cresta was parked around the corner. Three minutes later they drove off together. Tom explained about the approach from the Krays and how they wanted the Raiders to be part of a bigger team to do 'something big'. Tom said all the Raiders were against the idea. The Krays were ponces, they thieved off thieves. They didn't know how to conduct themselves and were untrustworthy and unpredictable. The Raiders were doing very nicely and weren't, Tom explained, prepared to be bossed by people who, "Didn't have a fucking clue about anything."

They drove a short distance to a back street near an old-fashioned pub, The Palmerston. Inside, the record 'Telstar' played on a jukebox, it was completely at odds with its surroundings. The place hadn't changed much in 50 years, and most of it since Victorian times.

Danny, Freddie, Bob and 'Mad' Frankie Fraser, were sitting together, Tom and Alfredo joined them.

Most thought Frankie had gained the name, 'Mad' Frankie, after feigning mental illness whilst in prison. But anyone who knew him might have easily concluded it was because of his fearlessness, ferocity, and his ability to take extreme physical pain without hindrance. Billy Hill had long since recognised Frankie's value in striking terror into those who might otherwise cause him inconvenience. Frankie was a freelancer, but he was frequently called upon to help Billy, the man he was most closely associated with. But Frankie was also close to Tom Wisbey (and eventually married his daughter!) .

Frankie gave Alfredo a hard look before lifting his glass to him, Alfredo nodded back, someone brought more drinks over. Alfredo didn't recognise Frankie from their brief encounter at the shootings and wondered why he had been greeted with a glare. hard look.

Other men were standing together in small groups, talking, drinking and chatting amicably. Some were sitting at tables playing cards, some were playing darts, others were laughing and joking. It was a happy, busy, normal lunchtime pub scene.

A stranger walked in from the street and looked around. He strolled to the bar and spotted the Raiders. He bought a pack of cigarettes and left. His visit had been noticed, it had been expected. About three minutes later, a local man shouted across the bar from the front door. "Here they come, three cars."

Everyone fell silent for a few seconds. Then in unison they returned to their socialising.   As a single lone group, Alfredo, Tom, Danny, Freddie, Bob and Frankie moved so that they stood with their backs to the bar. Danny and Tom stood half a pace forward.

Twelve men, led by Battles, walked in slowly, taking in the scene. They moved at a slow pace towards their prey as the drinking and socialising continued all around them. Then the visitors took out and brandished knives, small axes and other weapons. The pub fell silent, and a gap opened up in their path towards the Raiders waiting at the bar. All conversation, card games, darts, drinking, and laughing froze. Only The Tornados playing 'Telstar' seemed oblivious to the sudden drop in temperature.

Battles sneered and called out loudly. "Now you fuckers are gonna learn some manners. Frankie moved from the Raiders' at the bar and went to Battles' side. Battles tipped his chin and nodded at him, Frankie nodded back. Battles gripped a small axe. "Right let's go."

Battles took half a pace forward before Frankie smashed a fist into his stomach and another to his head. And all hell broke loose. Everyone in the bar joined the fray. The visitors were suddenly being attacked on all sides, surrounded, outnumbered and out thought. In much less than a minute of furious fighting, all the visitors were on the floor bleeding and moaning, but the attack on them was continuing. Danny raised both his arms and shouted loudly. "Alright, they're done. Hold up."

The locals pulled back, one or two put a final boot in as they did so. Danny pointed at the bloodied men on the floor. The place was now quiet again. "As for you fuckers, stay on the deck unless you want some more." Danny's eyes shot to Tom. "Make sure none of 'em moves."

Tom nodded and, wielding a hammer, walked to the middle of the fallen men.

Bob walked behind the bar and returned with a knife and a long length of tow rope. "Right. I'll string Battles up first. Let the rest watch."

Bob made a noose and measured out the rope while looking up at the ceiling as if to find a place to fixing for the rope. Battles had no reason to think he wasn't about to be topped. Holding a scalp wound which was bleeding profusely down the side of his face, he appealed to Danny. "For fuck's sake Danny."

Danny completely ignored him while Bob continued the preparation for the lynching. Seconds passed, Battles tried again. "Danny, for Christ's sake."

Bob spotted a metal arm supporting a big old shelf eight feet off the floor. He threw the noose over and prepared to slip it over Battles' head. By this time the East London men were looking extremely nervous. Tom and Bob dragged Battles over to the rope. Battles put up a fight, determined not to go to the slaughter quietly.

Eventually, subdued by several stomach punches, the noose was placed over his head and Bob, standing about four feet away, pulled the rope tight. Battles stretched up, on tiptoes and gasped for air. He was completely at the mercy of his captors. Agonising seconds past before Danny walked right up close and stared into Battles' eyes. "You come near any of us again and we fuckin' will, you understand?"
Battles nodded. Danny shouted at him. "I can't fuckin' hear ya."
That was enough to get Battles speaking loud and clear.

Battles and his injured gang gradually eased themselves up off the floor and skulked out as quickly as they could. The locals jeered and mocked as they left. Danny signalled to the barman – drinks all round. The Raiders grinned at one another. Alfredo had been useful in the fight and was congratulated by Frankie.

They all wanted to share again the fun they had just had, and it looked as if the gang were about to enjoy a 'session'. But Alfredo knew he had other duties. He bought his round of drinks of course, and supped, chatted and laughed for a while, but he was home within 30 minutes.

By 2.00pm Shirley was getting restless. She had expected her husband back more than an hour before. Alfredo got home as quickly as he could, but as he anticipated, he was met by Shirley's disapproving look. She frowned at him. "You been ages, thought you were comin' straight back from Tom's?"
Alfredo looked frustrated. "Yeah I couldn't, the boys had a job to do urgent, sorry Shirl."
Shirley's tone didn't change. "We're gonna be dead late at your parents' place ain't we? Your mum will have done us dinner. Don't look good, does it? S'pose they'll think it's me?"
Alfredo now understood the reason for her mood. "We ain't too late, I'll tell 'em it's my fault. Come on, let's get goin."
Shirley stood up. "So where you been?"
Alfredo wanted to keep it light and to move on as soon as possible, "The Palmerston, come on, better get Tony ready."

Shirley was far from satisfied, "You been on the piss while I'm waiting here?"

Alfredo sat down and tried to relax and lighten the mood a little, hoping his wife would do likewise. "Someone had sent over a few blokes to cause some trouble."

Shirley was anxious, and this news didn't help. He had her full attention. "So what happened?"

Alfredo told her the minimum. He downplayed his role as much as he could. But slipped up, he mentioned the Krays and Frankie Fraser and how he, 'seemed a decent geezer'. Shirley took it all in quietly, then let rip. "So now you're enemies of two dangerous nutters and made a friend of Mad Frankie Fraser, what the fuck's happening?"

Alfredo was taken aback and couldn't get a word in, she went on and on.... "Doin' a bit of quiet work with mates of me dad is one thing, publicly embarrassing the Krays is another."... "You got a death wish or what?" She was in full flow.

"Frankie Fraser's your best mate now, so next he asks you to help him out in return. What you gonna do, tell him to fuck off?"

On and on she went. Eventually Alfredo interrupted. "Listen, what d'you want me to do?"

But Shirley wasn't ready to calm down, wasn't ready to discuss anything calmly. She made it abundantly clear he was not, at any price, to become known to the Krays as a friend or enemy, and similarly, Frankie Fraser. Without another word being spoken, the trip to Alfredo's parents was cancelled.

That day, Alfredo learned a lesson the Raiders had preached to him. 'Don't tell your missus anything you don't need to.'

The next day, Shirley took Tony to see his grandparents, and over the next few weeks she got into the habit of doing so. It was clear everyone enjoyed the experience. Tony's grandparents loved to see him. His granddad was keen to do as much as he could to introduce little Tony to Italian ways, Italian food, the Italian language and his Italian heritage. Tony was too young to understand a word of it, but it didn't seem to matter.

Meanwhile, Alfredo's mother looked on at the two of them and felt her heart go out to her husband. He was more animated and more full of life than she had seen him in years. Shirley took an interest in the lives of her in-laws, and she found it a distraction from the issues constantly preying on her mind.

# Chapter 16

Professional caution demanded the crimes carried out by the South Coast Raiders, their location and their modus operandi, changed constantly. They thought through every aspect of their work meticulously. For them, it wasn't just a matter of getting away from the scene safely with the stolen goods, it also mattered that the police had little chance of identifying any links or patterns. That is how they stayed undetected for years.

It was a bright, fresh morning. Alfredo worked hard in the gym, had a big breakfast afterwards at a café nearby before wandering into Tom's betting shop. It had become a habit to have a little flutter and then go home for lunch and listen to the results on the radio. After a short wait in the queue, Alfredo handed Tom the pound note stake money and betting slip, Tom checked the bet, stamped the slip to indicate the time, date and a unique betting slip number, stamped a printed receipt and passed it back to Alfredo. Then Tom leaned forward and got Alfredo's attention, and spoke quietly. "It's on for tonight."

Alfredo left home at 10.00pm dressed in black trousers, a pair of old black leather shoes, white shirt and a light three-quarter length topcoat. Freddie had supplied the trousers and shirt. The moment he left home to go to work, as always, his pulse started to race a little. He went straight to the Underground and after 35 minutes he got off the Piccadilly line train at Osterley.

A few minutes later he met Danny. Danny had dressed in similar black trousers and white shirt over which he wore an old tweed jacket. They looked like two ordinary working men, which is more or less what they were.

They walked a few minutes from the station to a quiet side street where a stolen saloon car, a blue Hillman Imp, was waiting. Both were already wearing gloves. Alfredo had by then learned that to wear gloves while working was essential. The gloves would remain on their hands until the job was done, and they were well away from the crime scene and vehicles used.

The Hillman had enough power to reach 60mph, but only with a good deal of effort. It had barely enough room for two adults, and it was noisy and uncomfortable. They had not chosen it for pace or space, but for anonymity, being conscious of the need to avoid the attention of the police, or anyone else. Soon they were on the A4 heading towards Slough. Danny drove at a conservative speed, a typical Hillman Imp driver perhaps, considerate and cautious.

They parked in Petersfield Avenue, a quiet residential street of mostly terraced houses, three minutes' drive from Slough railway station. At one end of the road were a couple of small commercial premises with yards and a piece of waste ground. Roger and Danny had chosen the location about two weeks earlier, but Alfredo had not visited it before. Danny checked his watch and removed a pack of sandwiches from the glove compartment. "We got ten minutes, fancy a sarnie?" Alfredo accepted the offer.

They sat in the dark eating and talking. Danny sounded relaxed, but Alfredo found it hard to talk naturally, his mind was fully occupied with the task ahead. The conversation was stilted, Alfredo seemed unaware his contributions comprised one-word answers and the odd grunt. He was, after all, still relatively new to the business and still thought himself simply playing the part of a thief.

About ten minutes later they set off on foot towards the railway station. They didn't go onto the platforms, but just walked the route they would soon follow again later – Mill Street, Railway Terrace, then along the side of the station and across the bridge to the other side of the station, then along Brunel Way. The roads were empty, no one noticed them. Everything looked right.

Danny checked his watch again, 12.34 a.m, they began the quiet walk back to the car. While they were away, Freddie had parked an old Post Office van on the waste ground a few yards from the Hillman. He had bought it via the Exchange & Mart magazine for cash under a false name. It still had all the official Post Office markings. Freddie had done a good job on the clapped-out engine and it would be good for a few miles, more than enough for their purpose.

Danny spotted the post van and took the Hillman Imp keys from his pocket and passed them to Alfredo. "Just unlock it and leave the keys in the ignition."

Alfredo nodded and did as he was told. Meanwhile, Danny walked to the waiting van, took the keys Freddie had placed close to the front offside wheel, and unlocked the rear doors. He climbed in and held the doors open, Alfredo quickly joined him and they closed the doors behind them. Danny switched on the internal light, took off his jacket and placed it in a waiting empty bag. Folded neatly on the floor of the van were two postmen's uniform jackets, ties and peaked caps. Within five minutes, both men looked just like any two of the thousands of ordinary postmen at work across the country that night.

The engine started first time, and they drove at a sedate pace down to the railway station.

Meanwhile, just one and a half miles away, Tom and Freddie were also busy. Another Post Office van, but rather newer, also destined for the railway station, had to be stopped.

There was just one unlit road between the Slough Post Office Sorting Office and the main railway station. Ensuring this one short street had no functioning streetlights was, they joked, the trickiest part of the operation. At first light about 18 hours earlier, Freddie had shot out each of the twelve lights with an air rifle. Now, under cover of darkness, Freddie and Roger waited for the real Post Office van to approach. There would be no reason for the postmen to be on their guard, after all, they were not carrying any mail; they were simply on their way to collect it.

The mail van driver turned into the quiet dark street, behind him other car headlights followed, but he didn't notice. No sooner had the Post Office van turned into the unlit street, its headlights lit the scene of a very recent traffic accident. A man had been knocked off his bicycle. He was lying motionless in the road. A car, no doubt the one responsible, was stationary with its sidelights on and the driver's door ajar. The accident completely blocked the road.

Quickly slowing down, the post van stopped a few feet short of the scene, its headlights lit things brightly. The car driver was facing away, bent over his apparently unconscious victim who was face down in the road.

As the post van stopped, Tom turned the dark corner with car lights off and parked. He approached the stationary van out of sight of the driver and his rear-view mirrors and rammed old rags firmly into the exhaust pipe. Now the internal combustion engine could not exhaust and the combustion chamber would fill with fumes. No air could enter the chamber, and without oxygen, there could be no combustion.

The post van driver's colleague had hurried across to where Freddie was bent down next to the apparently unconscious Roger. "What happened?" Freddie, wearing what they called in those days, a 'car coat' with its huge imitation astrakhan collar turned up, peak cap and spectacles, looked sideways at the postman. "He drove straight off the pavement, straight in front of me."

The worried postman responded. "He needs an ambulance?"

Freddie nodded.

The postman turned back towards his van. "Hang on, I'll get a radio message sent."

The postman started the short walk back to the van. As he neared its doors, Freddie called out loudly. "Hang on, come back, quick."

The postman did as he was asked. Roger seemed to have regained consciousness, Freddie looked down at him," Where's it hurt?"

Roger took his time. "I think I'm alright, just a bit shocked."

Freddie enlisted the postman's help in getting Roger to his feet and clearing his bicycle from the road. It mattered little to the postmen they had been delayed, after all, trains were often delayed. The train would have to or if the train guard wanted to he could unload the mail onto the platform himself.

Eventually, reassured he was uninjured, Roger apologised to Freddie for causing such trouble and thanked the postman for stopping to help him. Handshakes followed, then Roger mounted his bike and cycled off. Freddie walked back to his car. Within seconds, the road was clear again and the postmen could be on their way to the station. But as Freddie drove off the post van moved a feets forward and stopped and try they did, it simply would not start.

Meanwhile, Danny and Alfredo collected a barrow from its usual resting place near the cigarette machine on Platform 1. They wheeled it near the spot where the guard's brake normally stopped. Two minutes later the 'down' train stopped right on schedule. Within a few seconds more, the guard had opened the guard's compartment doors to give access to the mails. The two uniformed men worked quickly and soon had more than a dozen bags off-loaded and onto the barrow. No one watched, it was all so routine. Within a few minutes they loaded the mailbags into the post van, and pulled away. By this time the train guard had waved his green flag, blown his whistle, and the train had left the station.

Ten minutes later another post van arrived at the railway station. The occupants fully expected to see the bags lying on the platform, thrown there by a cursing train guard. But there were none. Perhaps, they thought, there were simply none for collection that night.

# Chapter 17

Alfredo entered the public telephone box near the flat and took four pennies from his pocket, lifted the receiver and dialled. The phone was quickly answered. He pushed button 'A' and heard the four coins fall. A woman's voice answered. "Green's Betting shop."
Alfredo didn't introduce himself. "I need to speak to Green, it's urgent."
The woman responded curtly. "We ain't open yet."
But Alfredo knew Green was the sort of man who didn't keep business hours – his own or anyone else's. "I need to speak to him urgent."
The woman didn't give it a moment's thought. "He's busy."
Alfredo's tone hardened considerably, and it got her attention. "Well, he won't be too busy to take this call, so get him."
Now she was taking things more seriously. "Who wants him?"
Alfredo had his answer ready and it was guaranteed to get results. "The bloke what done his ginger bastard and his fat mate."
There was silence for a few seconds as the woman took the message in. Alfredo heard the receiver being put down on the desk, then muffled voices, then the sound of the moneylender bookie. "You got some fuckin' nerve."
Alfredo didn't want a conversation. "Listen, your money plus 20% is in a baked bean tin, in a brown carrier bag next to a bin near your shop... outside Fancy's sweet shop."
Green. "And you think that's it?"
Alfredo expected the threat. "Take your money. Anyone comes near me or my family again I'll blow a hole in you."
Alfredo hung up.

# Chapter 18

They stayed at Dreadful's guesthouse for longer than expected, it was two months before the council offered them a two-bedroomed flat, it was on the second floor of a 1930s-built block in Clerkenwell, the area in which Alfredo had been born and raised, and a short walk from Luigi's.

They moved in as soon as they could. They both loved the new place. It was on a back street, a bit quieter and less densely built-up than their last. Alfredo was now more than flush enough to pay for new furniture for the whole place. He was happy for Shirley to choose it all, and he knew she would love to. Most importantly for Shirley, the flat and the area had no negative connotations.

Though Shirley had recovered enough to want to furnish the place herself, she still had nightmares. She still felt tired for most of the day, and she really wasn't interested in doing much other than sleeping. When she tried to sleep, she couldn't. The flat therefore remained sparsely furnished.

The weeks went by and her energy and motivation remained low. As a result, she didn't maintain their home the way she always had, and she felt guilty her son and husband were less cared for. Her mental state deteriorated again, and she felt worthless.

She made an appointment to see the doctor with the sole intention of getting a chemical fix. The next morning Shirley sat in the waiting room feeling anxious. She felt he was bound to ask her why she needed the pills. What could she say? After being in the waiting room for half an hour, the receptionist called her name.

The middle-aged man sat smoking and reading. He didn't look up, but he heard her open the door and close it behind her. Without looking up, he waved her towards a chair.

Shirley didn't tell the doctor the cause of her sleeplessness and anxiety. She simply couldn't face telling him about the rape, it was too demeaning and painful to describe to anyone. And of course, she couldn't tell him her husband had committed murder, and that she was terrified there might be a knock at the door. Nor could she explain her husband was now a robber, and she certainly couldn't tell him about her concern over the Krays. So instead, she just talked about her symptoms – she couldn't sleep, she was crying all the time, angry, sad and bad-tempered. She worried to death about everything and cared about nothing. Shirley was about halfway through her third sentence before the doctor looked up from his desk for the first time, he looked at her over the top of the spectacles perched on his nose. "I've written you a prescription."

The doctor stood up, her cue to leave. She took the prescription from him and he lit another cigarette and mumbled something as she turned to leave. She didn't hear what he said. Within seconds she was back in the waiting room, the entire process had taken about one minute. But she left with her Valium prescription, convinced this would be the answer.

But the Valium didn't recreate motivation, it didn't return her energy, and it didn't clear her mind. She could sleep, but the nightmares still interrupted. And during the day she didn't really feel better, just sleepier and less aware of everything.

Yet after a while, and with the help of her in in-laws and Danny's wife, Iris, gradually the darkness lifted. Alfredo now saw the occasional smile and glimpsed the old Shirley. Once again, the couple enjoyed talking together at length. Their conversation was generally about sharing the pleasure of young Tony's development, or the budding relationship with her in-laws, or simple family small talk.

Alfredo persuaded her to do some furniture shopping with him. It was the first time they had ever bought new furniture, let alone a flat full, and not a bit of it was bought 'on tick'. They bought most of the larger items in high-class shops, but Shirley still enjoyed reading the Kays and Empire mail order catalogues, and so they bought smaller items there. In a way, the mix of expensive indulgence and the cheap and commonplace, represented all aspects of their lives.

Alfredo's job, like those of his associates, involved long periods of inactivity. These were punctuated by a few hours of high concentration observing mailbag movements at railway stations, listening to briefings by Roger or Danny, taking part in the planning of a job, and of course actually stealing mailbags. So far as spending time supporting his wife and child were concerned, and training hard to get back to a life of professional boxing, Alfredo's working hours were just about perfect.

On this afternoon, Alfredo was fiddling with an expensive TV with a huge, 26 inch screen. To be more precise, he was trying to find the best location for the indoor aerial. Tony was in a bouncy walker and jumping up and down, gurgling and laughing. Meanwhile, Shirley was reading the instructions for the new refrigerator. It was a device she had never used, and she knew no one else who had ever had one.

"I love the new place." She found herself saying.

Alfredo didn't stop what he was doing to look at her, but smiled to himself. "Good, you seem much more like your old self."

Shirley thought for a while. "Yeah, still not sleeping great though."

She paused for a long time...then she added. "I saw it in The Evening Standard, ages ago, the bookies, what you did."

Alfredo put down the indoor aerial and went over and held her in his arms. "Didn't think you knew."

It was a tender moment, the first sign Shirley could again trust a man to put his arms around her. The first time she could feel stubble against her neck and face again without being transported back to that awful day.

Alfredo took the opportunity. "And you know if Old Bill were goin' to come knockin' they'd 'ave done it by now."

Shirley nodded. "The Standard said it was an attempted robbery."

Alfredo. "Yeah, no surprise there."

Shirley looked at young Tony blowing raspberries. "You think Green might still come after  you?"

Alfredo looked into her eyes. "It's just business to him Love, and I've given him all his money back including interest, it's finished."

She held him for a while. "Heard any more about that ruck in the Palmerston?"

Alfredo shook his head. "Nope. Ain't heard or seen Mad Frankie either."

Shirley kissed him lightly on the cheek. "I do love you, you know."

# Chapter 19

Most of the approaches to the main railway termini in London have Victorian railway arches. Many have now been modernised and provide offices, restaurants, shops and other respectable, even fashionable, businesses. But in the 1960s they were mainly run-down, rat-infested, sooty places, typically occupied by scrap metal dealers, second-hand furniture shops, dodgy storage facilities and grubby small-scale engineering outfits.

The Raiders held the keys to one of the many railway arch premises around Waterloo. Inside, Roger was sitting down and holding a mirror to his face. He looked frustrated, concerned, annoyed even. Standing next to him, Bob held a small box of white powder and attempted to brush some onto Roger's face. Tom, Danny and Alfredo were standing nearby, laughing and making wisecracks. But Roger had had enough. "Look this isn't some sort of bloody game. If this doesn't look right, I'm gonna get nicked. It ain't bloody funny."

That evening, at Basingstoke railway station, Alfredo, well dressed in a smart, heavy, woollen overcoat, tweed trousers and brogues, was carrying a suitcase. By his side, a porter pushed a wheelchair. In the wheelchair, an unrecognisable Roger Cordrey was silent, ashen faced, limp and seemingly semi-conscious, old and ill. He wore a trilby and dark glasses and a heavy scarf was wrapped around his face and neck to protect him from the cold. A blanket covered his legs.

The porter pushed the wheelchair to the mail coach. This was the usual place in which wheelchair users would have to travel. The coach was of the type entirely separate from the guard's coach and passenger coaches. The guard had no access once the train was moving.

The mail coach doors were wide open and postmen were throwing mailbags in. The train guard stood by watching the postmen at work and spotted the wheelchair approaching. He knew well enough the passenger carriage doors were not wide enough for wheelchairs to board. 'Disabled' passengers had to travel in the mail coach even though there was no heating.

The porter pushed the wheelchair to within a few feet of the mail coach and turned to the very well-dressed Alfredo. "We'll just have to wait a bit 'til the postmen have finished, sir. Sorry about the delay."

Alfredo simply nodded. He had learned to keep his mouth shut as much as possible.

Within seconds, the postmen walked away from the train with the few bags they had removed for local delivery. The guard boarded and made a space amongst the pile of mailbags. Without speaking, he got back onto the platform and went to the front of the wheelchair. The porter was still holding the wheelchair handles. He glanced kindly at Alfredo. "Dad is it?"

Alfredo permitted himself one word. "Yes." But he said it clearly, it was not his usual 'Yeah.'

The porter nodded at the guard and they lifted the wheelchair, and Roger, aboard.

Alfredo took a shilling from his pocket and handed it to the porter as he boarded. The porter touched his cap and made off down the platform. Alfredo boarded with his suitcase.

Two other well-dressed men noticed the porter in passing. Both were already seated on the train. They were in separate first-class carriages, Danny in one, Tom in the other.

The guard stepped down from the mail coach onto the platform and glanced back inside. "Where you gettin' off sir?"

Alfredo gave a gentle smile. "Woking."

The guard nodded. "See you at Woking then."

The guard slammed the doors shut, moved a few feet down the platform, blew hard on his whistle, waved a green flag and stepped up into a small, separate guard's compartment. The train juddered forward belching grey smoke.

Roger immediately removed the blanket, scarf and dark glasses and got out of the wheelchair. Then he removed his overcoat and instructed Alfredo. "Make sure you leave the bags tagged 'Woking' alone. And get that overcoat off."

Alfredo began to take his coat off. "Why?"

Roger was already at work and didn't look up. "Postmen at Woking will take the Woking bags off, if we've done 'em they'll see."

Alfredo was removing his overcoat. "No, I mean, why the overcoat?"

"Bags are covered in dust, it'll be all over your coat and show out."

Both men had by now removed flick knives from their pockets and were examining labels and slashing open selected mailbags.

About 20 minutes later, at a quiet platform at Woking station, two postmen were sitting on a trolley on a quiet platform, waiting. It was getting dark. On the station concourse, a few passengers were coming and going. Others were waiting to meet friends, Bob was amongst them, car keys in hand.

On the platform, the postmen heard and saw the train approaching. It slowed to a halt and gave out a loud 'hiss' as the driver released the air brakes. Passengers flung the train doors open and hurried for the exit. But Tom took his time alighting, and then sauntered slowly down the platform towards the exit. Just like many other passengers, he carried a suitcase. Then he stopped, put his suitcase down, took a note from his pocket and appeared to study it.

By then, the train guard had walked the short distance to the mail coach, unlocked it with a standard BR 'T' key and beckoned to a porter. Within seconds, the guard and porter boarded, and within a few seconds more, Alfredo with suitcase, and Roger, wrapped up and carried by wheelchair, were on the platform and ready to leave.

Without speaking, Alfredo gave the guard a shilling. The porter wheeled the chair clear of the waiting postmen and set off towards the concourse. Alfredo followed a pace behind.

A couple of coaches away, Danny stepped off the train and watched events. Tom was standing ahead of the approaching wheelchair, closer to the platform barrier. He still looked to be reading a note. The porter pushed the wheelchair past Tom. Tom then nodded at Alfredo and appeared to ask him a question. Alfredo stopped and put his suitcase down. He answered briefly. Tom nodded, picked up his suitcase and walked on.

Alfredo picked up the other suitcase and caught up with the wheelchair and porter. Danny followed at a discreet distance.

Less than a minute later, the wheelchair had reached the ticket barrier. The ticket inspector on duty there held out his hand to inspect the tickets. Alfredo handed them over and gave the porter a shilling. The porter grunted and headed back towards the train.

But just as the ticket inspector was punching the tickets, behind them, back down the platform, a commotion had started. The postmen and train guard were hurrying towards the ticket barrier shouting and waving their arms. One of the postmen shouted to the ticket inspector. "Keep 'em there, the mail's been done."

With suitcase balanced on Roger's knees, Alfredo attempted to push the wheelchair through the barrier opening onto the concourse. But before he could do so, the ticket inspector shut the extending metal gate and turned to Alfredo. "Would you mind just waiting a minute, sir?"
But it wasn't a question.

Roger stayed calm and continued in role perfectly. But Alfredo could feel his stomach churning, his heart pounding. He tried hard to look calm. The postmen and entourage had nearly reached the barrier, and other postmen and rail staff had joined them. Several passengers had stopped to watch the excitement.

As the running postmen and guard reached the barrier, one of the postmen looked at Alfredo. "Mind if I ask you what you've got in the suitcase?"

Alfredo was trying hard to continue to play the part. "What do you mean?"
"Sorry sir, but it seems someone has interfered with the mailbags."

Alfredo was agitated, and therefore managed with ease to look and sound indignant. "What's that got to do with me?"

Danny was now just a few feet from the scene, watching, judging, ready. A few feet further away, Bob was likewise.

Another postman chimed in. "You were the only ones in there."

The older postman had now recovered his breath and pointed at the suitcase. "Basingstoke bags were done, so it must have been…. just show us what's in there, then."
Alfredo had been tutored well. He didn't rush to show the contents. "We haven't done anything."
The postmen were now more confident of the outcome. "Open your suitcase then!"

The guard looked at his fob watch. "I can't hold the train up. I'd better get going. I'll report it to the railway police at Waterloo."

One of the last postmen to join the little group then spoke for the first time. "We've already dialled 999. The police will be here shortly."

The guard turned and hurried back towards his train. The imminent arrival of the police changed things. Alfredo flicked the brake on the wheelchair and placed the suitcase on the platform. The railway staff and postmen gathered in close. Alfredo opened the catches and lifted the lid completely. Then he stood back. Instantly the youngest of the rail staff bent down and looked closely, moving the contents around, but there was nothing unusual to be found. Then a postman bent down and looked again. Alfredo watched it all in silence with an air of effrontery. The postman stood up and shrugged, mystified.

Alfredo said nothing but bent down and closed the suitcase. He placed it back on Roger's knees and turned towards the closed gate. A helpful and impeccably dressed first-class passenger, a man in his thirties, pushed it wide open for him. Rail staff and postmen were left talking quietly amongst themselves.

Alfredo headed off across the short concourse towards the exit and car park. Danny strolled after him. But before Alfredo got halfway across the concourse, the bells of an approaching police car were clearly audible.

Bob, who had been watching the proceedings at the platform barrier, rushed to Alfredo and took the suitcase. Now they could move more quickly. But the sound of the bells stopped before they had gone more than a few feet. The police car had arrived. Two uniformed constables rushed by them towards the waiting postmen and railway staff.

Outside the railway station, the blue rotating lights of the police car lit the scene. Bob, Alfredo and Roger made their way as quickly as any innocent people might, towards their waiting car. Fifty yards and they would be safe. But within seconds, they heard shouting behind them. They half-turned, a policeman emerging from the station, shouted loudly. "Hey, stop, police, you with the wheelchair."

Now they abandoned pretence, wheelchair cast aside, they rushed to the car. Bob, clutching the suitcase, quickly unlocked a rear door, then the driver's door and dived into the driving seat. By then Alfredo and Roger were in the back and their door secured. The engine burst into life. But before Bob could put the car into gear the two constables were upon them. One quickly wrenched open the driver's door and shouted in Bob's face. "Turn the engine off, now."

At that moment, they heard a police siren approaching, Bob and the constable swivelled towards the approaching police car. It slowed down and came within a few feet of them, Danny was driving and grinning widely. Sitting next to him, Tom had covered his lower face. Danny wound the driver's window right down, and switched the siren off. The blue flashing light continued to light the car park.

The policemen had momentarily believed reinforcements had arrived. But they now realised the horrible truth. They had allowed their police car to be stolen.

Danny slowed the police car to less than walking speed, just a few feet away. The officers got only a glimpse of the driver as he called. "Just goin' for a spin. Back in a bit, boys."

Danny revved the engine. The two constables forgot all about potential mailbag thieves and rushed towards their car, after all it was only moving at walking pace. But as the officers neared the car, Danny accelerated gently, switched the flashing lights off, and increased his speed just enough to keep the officers interested for a few seconds. It was all the distraction needed. Then he drove away.

In those few seconds, Bob drove away too. He drove for about half a mile, then took two more rapid turns into a quiet side street. The headlights of a parked car flashed once, it was Freddie. Bob pulled up in front of it, ready to abandon the stolen car.

Danny drove about half a mile and parked the police vehicle in a quiet spot. Danny and Tom separated and within five minutes, one was travelling by cab, the other by bus. Both made their way to nearby West Byfleet, where both joined a slow train to Waterloo.

It was several hours before Alfredo got home. He knocked gently, Shirley was waiting, wide-awake behind the heavily bolted door. She let her husband in quietly. He kissed her on the cheek and headed straight for the breadboard. "They think of everything Shirl." he began.

But Shirley didn't pick up on his comment. She was used to him wanting food as soon as he got home and she stood beside him as he went about making himself a sandwich. In the past, she would have made his late-night supper, but the habit had died with the sudden exit from the old flat. She knew he would want coffee and began making enough for both of them. But she wore a solemn expression. Alfredo hadn't noticed, he was fully engaged preparing food and reflecting on the considerable abilities of his teammates.

Shirley touched his arm. "I took Tony over to your parents' place this afternoon."

Alfredo looked up with a smile. "Good...Everything alright?"

Then he noticed Shirley looked concerned. She spoke softly. "Your dad's had a heart attack. He's in St. Mary's."

Alfredo stopped cutting bread. "Is he gonna be alright?"

Shirley looked away. "Your mum told me they said it's too early to know."

Alfredo digested those words, then looked at his watch. She read his mind. "Better not disturb him now. See him in the mornin', better for both of you."

Alfredo nodded. "What about Mum?"

Shirley took a deep breath and nodded gently. "I told her to come over here, but she said she wanted to be at their place. Open the caff as usual and that." Alfredo understood, the café had been precious to his parents for as long as he could remember. "Yeah. I'll pop in and see mum first thing, then dad. Come with me?"

Shirley nodded sympathetically. Alfredo completed his sandwich and transferred it to a plate. The fresh coffee was about ready. He grabbed two mugs from the cupboard. "We really scored tonight."

Shirley nodded again, but this time it expressed mild irritation, he was talking about stealing again. Her tone hardened a little. "You still lookin' for a regular job?"

Alfredo had become sensitive to the negative implications of a certain tone of voice, and the tone of his own response showed it. "I'm putting enough together to get back boxing properly. I ain't gonna take any old shit job, I can tell ya that."

Shirley's tone hardened further. "Too good for a shit job now then?"

"Listen. I was doing what I had to. Now I've got a choice."

Shirley sniffed and moved away. He looked down at the sandwich. His mood had been completely flattened. She went to the bedroom and sat on the side of the bed, holding back the tears.

Alfredo sat down in silence in the sitting room. He was thinking about his dad when Shirley roused him. "You ain't heard anymore from the Krays then?"

Alfredo responded wearily. "No, I told you, that's sorted."

Then he saw the vulnerability and fear stress portrayed in her eyes, her face and her posture. He cuddled her tenderly.

# Chapter 20

Ronnie and Reggie were in dinner suits as they descended the steps of a Knightsbridge casino and approached the waiting chauffeur-driven limo. Billy sat in the back facing forward. They climbed in and sat opposite him as the car pulled gently away.

Billy wasn't dressed for clubbing, he was still working. He wore a smart dark blue suit, white shirt and red tie, thrown casually on the seat beside him were a trench coat and trilby. He took a deep drag on his Capstan Full Strength cigarette and gave the twins a hard look. Reggie could see the mood and knew the reason. "It weren't our fault Billy. They didn't want to know."

Billy glared at him. "You got a knock back and then got your arses kicked." Ronnie looked as if he would explode with rage. "Well, they'll fuckin' regret it." But Billy didn't want regrets. This wasn't about the Krays ego, or anyone else's, it was a question of recruiting and managing the right team. He now wondered if the Krays were up to it, "Look, just back off now, leave it to me. I'll sort it."

Ronnie felt slighted and mumbled something inaudible as he looked out of the window. Reggie wanted to make sure they hadn't just been sacked. "What we gonna do then Billy?"

Billy took another drag and blew the smoke to one side. "I'll do it. Another way. If you get a call from a geezer called Black, he works for me. Give him anything he wants. Understand?"

Neither twin had never heard of Black, Ronnie glanced through the window. "Who's he then?"

Billy's mood lightened. "What you don't know can't hurt ya Ronnie. Like I said, everythin' needs to be as tight as a duck's arse... watertight."

It had been a very long evening for DC Roy Walcott, sitting in a second-class compartment with a complete stranger. Officially, they were 'doing observations.' That simply meant watching, and hoping one or more of the South Coast Raiders would walk by their carriage mid-journey, on their way to the nearby mail coach.

The detectives' only additional duty was to note whether the mail coach was visited by the train guard, and to make notes on whether, if, as on some train services, the guard's quarters were within the coach carrying the mail, and for how long the guard left the mails unattended. All this information was fed back to the CID clerk at Force Headquarters in order, ostensibly, to identify those mail trains which were most vulnerable to attack. Of course, such information was helpful in prioritising observations, but for Aldridge it had a very different purpose.

That evening, both officers quickly read and re-read every inch of their own newspaper, the Daily Mail and the Daily Mirror, then swapped and read the other's too.

The Post Office Investigation Department had highlighted this train service as regularly carrying a good deal of high-value mail, just like about 50 others running every day. The detectives had been told this mail train service had been attacked before, but then again, they all had.

Roy's companion was a Newcastle man, on attachment, just like Roy. But 'Geordie' was ten years younger and the most opinionated man Roy had ever met. He seemed determined to make sure Roy not only fully understood his thoughts on every subject, but that Roy should completely agree with them. Only when it came to the untrustworthiness of senior officers were they truly at one.

The mail coach in question was in the middle of the train and had a passenger aisle running its length. It could be accessed freely from either side. The mail 'cage' separated the bags from the passenger aisle. There was a small guard's compartment at one end, though the guard could only be relied upon to be there when the train entered a station.

Two more detectives were in a second-class compartment on the other side of the mail coach. They had no means of communicating with Roy and Geordie, other than by meeting face to face. They did this occasionally, meeting for a cigarette near the coach carrying the mails, or by taking it in turn to meet in the buffet car for a cuppa.

The detectives' plan was simple and had executed countless times over the years. In the event of a potential thief being spotted heading towards the mail coach, the detectives would wait a few minutes to give the thief, or thieves, the time and opportunity to get well into their work before descending on them. Sometimes the plan worked, but not very often, and not tonight.

This routine, copied on numerous trains every day, was the British Transport Police (BTP) strategy to catch the Raiders, and as per the intention of its chief architect, it stood no chance of doing so. Roy and

Geordie had heard whispers that Aldridge's London detectives arrested innocent men, and opportunist thieves, and then convinced news reporters they were members of the South Coast Raiders. But as Geordie pointed out, the deception could never last, for the major thefts were continued.

By the end of the shift, Roy knew more about Geordie's forceful views on corrupt policemen, freemasonry and the evils of people from Sunderland and why keeping cats is a terrible idea, than he really ever wanted to know. No mail thieves were caught.

# Chapter 21

It was just after 9 a.m at a parade of shops near Brighton seafront on a pleasant morning. You could clearly hear the seagulls just a street away. Inside the small florist shop, Roger was taking payment for a bunch of flowers from a very satisfied customer. He thanked her for her custom and gave her a penny change. She smiled and left. Roger hurried from around the counter and back through a door connecting the shop to the storeroom, where Alfredo was waiting. Roger carried on where he had left off a few minutes earlier. "As I was saying, it depends, there are at least four different sorts of mail coach and..."

But again, the shop doorbell interrupted the lesson. "Sod, it. Hold on a minute."

Roger went back into the shop, pulling the back-room door almost closed behind him. A middle-aged man carrying a thin leather briefcase was waiting to be served. Roger hurried around the counter and smiled. "Morning sir, can I help you?"

Aldridge's expression gave nothing away. "Mr Cordrey is it? Roger Cordrey?"

Roger was a little surprised. "Yes, what can I do for you?"

Aldridge pulled a pair of handcuffs from his pocket. "You're nicked. You know why."

Roger froze. Aldridge walked calmly around the counter and handcuffed him. Then he went to the shop door and turned the 'Open' sign on the window to 'Closed' and locked the door.

Without speaking, he emptied Roger's pockets onto the counter. Roger was trying to conceal his panic, his mind was racing. "Can I make a phone call?"

Aldridge shook his head. "Don't be fuckin' silly."

Aldridge glanced around the shop and spotted Roger's jacket hanging on a peg. He emptied those pockets too – fags, lighter, address book and wallet. He put all of Roger's personal effects into his leather briefcase. Aldridge had a cursory look around the shop and then shoved Roger towards the store room. "Show me what's out back."

Roger tried to resist. "There's nothing back there."

Aldridge pushed him again. "Suddenly I'm very interested..."
Aldridge pulled Roger by the arm towards the back-room door, shoved him in and followed. His eyes flicked around the room – a few boxes of flowers, a locker, a sink, kettle, tea, milk, sugar, a pair of wellingtons, mop and bucket, pine disinfectant, Ajax powder, rolls of string, a pair of scissors, a pile of tissue paper, a sash window slightly ajar.

A few hundred yards away, Alfredo ran into a public telephone box. He dialled frantically and pushed the pennies home. At the other end, Danny's wife, Iris, answered. She told Alfredo, Danny was out. He told her to get a message to him urgently. "No racing at Lingfield today." She knew what it meant. She swore and replaced the handset.

That same morning Shirley and Tony had headed off to the café as they had done every day since Alfredo's father's heart attack. She had quickly adopted the habit of helping her mother-in-law and had developed a useful role and routine. Waiting on tables, cleaning and washing dishes and filling in on the till as necessary, she was a real help. Her mother-in-law did the cooking and food ordering duties and had come to enjoy the presence of her daughter-in-law, and of course, her grandson.

Alfredo's father was still hospitalised. His wife visited daily and was perhaps a little too keen to describe how smoothly things were going in his absence. Alfredo visited his father regularly too, and it was clear his father enjoyed his company. The bond between them, once strong, was growing again.

Alfredo's father had already convinced himself it was his duty to encourage little Tony towards an understanding of the Catholic faith, and thereafter along the path within the Catholic Church. He also dreamt of the day when Shirley would worship the Holy Mother of Christ. Alfredo's father had for the first time, found a way to be free to enjoy the return into his life of his son, and the involvement of his grandson and daughter-in-law. His mind at ease, and he was now very much looking forward to returning to the café.

Later that morning, Aldridge sat Roger down in an interview room in a South London police station. The room smelled of carbolic soap and stale cigarette smoke. Three scruffy chairs, one damaged table and an old green filing cabinet were the only furniture. Aldridge was relaxed, confident, he knew his agenda.

He sat opposite his prisoner. "Okay. Now's your chance to come clean."

Roger looked about nervously, he was unused to such surroundings. "I think I should get a solicitor."

Aldridge looked irritated. "What, like on the movies? Grow up for fuck's sake."

Roger looked away. Aldridge pushed on. "So you deny forging somebody else's name on a number of cheques?"

Roger didn't understand, and it showed on his face. "Cheques?" "Yeah cheques, what did you think you were in here for?"

"Err...Well I don't know... I haven't done anything wrong."

Aldridge leaned forward. "Well, if you ain't signed any dodgy cheques you'll be happy to give me a handwriting sample for comparison purposes, won't ya?"

Roger looked perplexed. "Comparison with what?"

Aldridge seemed to be losing his patience. "Look, a handwriting expert will compare your handwriting samples to the signatures on the dodgy cheques. If you didn't sign 'em you got nothing to worry about. Except we both know you did."

Roger's mind was racing, he couldn't recall signing any cheques. Whenever they had stolen bank cheques or travellers' cheques, the gang sold them on. He had never signed a dodgy cheque of any sort, but his head was far from clear.

Aldridge opened his briefcase and removed several sheets of plain paper. He put them on the desk in front of Roger, unlocked the handcuffs and put a biro in front of him. "We'll soon see. Just give me a sample of your signature at the top of the paper."

Aldridge pointed impatiently at the pen. "In capitals first, your full name, then usual signature."

Roger obliged. Aldridge picked the page up and studied the writing carefully. Then he folded the page once and handed it back. "Now sign it again there, at the bottom. I need several samples."

Roger did as he was told, and Aldridge inspected the signatures again. Then he put the sheet with the handwriting sample to one side and put another clean sheet down. "Same again, your normal writing."

Roger signed the second sheet and Aldridge began to fold it. "Why are you folding it?"

"So, you can't see how you signed it last. Don't want you copying some dodgy signature to cheat the expert, do we?"

Roger was keen to get the whole nonsensical process behind him. He hadn't signed any dodgy cheques. It was ridiculous. But he felt vulnerable. He wanted to get the process finished and get out of there before there was any talk of mailbags. He signed six sheets of paper in the same fashion. Aldridge examined the signed pages and put them to one side. Then he handcuffed Roger again and breathed out slowly and fully, entirely satisfied. Aldridge took out a cigarette and lit it casually. Roger watched. "Can I go now then?"

Aldridge smiled thinly and studied the signed pages in front of him. "Go? That's a long way off. Now, your confession."

Roger looked puzzled. "What do you mean?"

Aldridge sniggered. "I mean these blank pages you've just signed, top and bottom. Give me ten minutes, they'll be a fully signed confession."

Roger sat up straight in his chair and raised his voice. "You can't do that I haven't signed any cheques."

The tone of Aldridge's voice dropped, and the pace slowed. "It ain't about cheques. It's about mailbags Roger. You'll get ten years apiece."

Roger couldn't believe he had been so totally taken in. "Oh, Jesus Christ."

Aldridge said he knew the names of all the gang: Tom Wisbey, Danny Pembroke, Bob Welch, Freddie Sansom and Ted Harris. He was also keen to explain that once those men discovered Roger had grassed, Roger would be lucky to live long enough to stand trial.

Alfredo got back to South London from Brighton as fast as possible. He was fearful the police had all of their names. Had the rest of the team already been arrested? Was Old Bill waiting at the flat, or keeping watch, waiting for him to go home so they could pounce? What would happen to Shirl' and Tony if he went to prison? He might get ten years. Would she wait for him? Little Tony would be nearly a teenager before his dad was free.

He had no choice, he would have to take a chance and hope the police were not yet at his flat. He would take a train north, disappear for a few days. But before doing so he had to meet with the rest of the gang. That was the contingency plan. But more immediately he had to get his emergency money and some clothes from the flat.

It took him nearly two hours to get to south London from Brighton, and his mind had been racing. How would Shirley cope on her own? She was still nothing like back to her usual self and always on the verge of tears or anger. She wouldn't sleep if he wasn't there.

As he climbed the stairs to leave the Underground station, he felt so unsure of himself, lost. What if the police were waiting at the flat? Now he wished he had gone straight to Luigi's. After all, he had no previous convictions and so it was likely to take the police some effort to find him there.

He wanted so much to speak to Shirley, but he couldn't phone her at the café and ask her to go home to meet him. She would be in a state of panic and the police might be waiting. If so, she would walk straight into a storm. No, he just had to push on as first planned.

As he left the Underground station, he saw a lad of about 15 who lived down the landing from him. Alfredo introduced himself and offered the lad 'ten bob.' All the teenager had to do was go straight to the block of flats and knock repeatedly at Alfredo's door. He was then to report straight back. The boy agreed to do it and rushed off. Alfredo waited impatiently.

Within a few minutes he returned. He said there was no answer at the door and no sound of anyone inside either. Alfredo paid him and went to a telephone kiosk to phone Shirley, she would be at Luigi's. His mother answered the phone and told him Shirley was already on her way to pick something up from the flat. He rushed home.

Once inside the flat, he went straight to the kitchen and pocketed the emergency £50 he had hidden under tea leaves in an apparently unopened Typhoo Tea box, then he rushed to the bedroom and threw a few clothes into a holdall. He could not afford to wait around, the police could come knocking at any second. He dashed back to the kitchen and wrote a cryptic note and propped it against the electric kettle. "Go to Luigi's straight away. I'll call at 9. Love you XXX."

Suddenly there was a noise outside. Alfredo tensed. There was no escape. He turned quickly and snatched up his holdall. A thought rushed through his head, 'hide behind the kitchen door.' But before he could move, the front door opened. And the sweetest sound he had ever heard filled his ears. "You tired? Come on, mummy cuddle you. Go bye-byes."

Alfredo let the tension go from his shoulders and stepped out from the kitchen into the sitting room, holdall in hand.

Shirley was lifting their son from the buggy. She looked up, surprised to see him, "What's wrong, what's goin' on?"

"Roger's been nicked, gotta scarper."

114

Shirley's voice stayed calm. "Shit. When will I see you?"

"Pack a bag, you're coming with me."

"Where we goin'?"

 "Don't know yet."

Shirley was devastated. Suddenly all their dreams were shattered, and just as her life seemed to be straightening itself out. Suddenly they were in a worse position than they had ever been.

But of course, the Raiders had a plan in the event of one of them being arrested. The coded message 'no racing at Lingfield' was just the first signal. Anything more said on the phone might be of value to any policeman listening in. One key part of the plan was if any member got arrested, no one went home. Alfredo had already transgressed.

Five minutes later, Alfredo with holdall in hand and Shirley and Tony by his side, was making his way along the street. She would take Tony back to Luigi's and wait while  Alfredo met with the other gang members as formerly agreed.

Once again, Shirley and Alfredo had no idea where they would spend the night.


The Horse and Groom pub in Sudbury was far enough away from their usual haunts for none of the locals, civvies or police, to recognise any of the Raiders. By the time Alfredo got there the other five had already assembled. He found them talking quietly at a table in a recess. The pub had been well chosen, they could not be easily seen or overheard, and they could see the bar and the entrance.

Alfredo didn't take time to order a drink, he was too desperate to hear the news. He didn't expect to see Roger sitting there sipping a pint. No one spoke to him, they were all too busy listening intently to Roger. Alfredo placed his holdall down next to his associates and took a chair from another table. The bar was almost empty. Roger was speaking in a loud whisper, Alfredo sat down and leaned in.

"… 15% and he gives us information on what trains to hit and makes sure Old Bill isn't about."

Danny nodded, thinking hard. "And you never seen him before?"

Roger shook his head. "No. And I don't know his name, or what nick he's from."

Tom. "Must be Sweeney." The others paused to think, Alfredo was bursting to find out what had happened. "You been bailed Roger?"

Roger glanced at Alfredo and shook his head briefly, then looked back at Tom. "Don't know, but somebody's given him all our names including Ted's."

Alfredo was frantic. "What's happened?"

Danny put his drink down and met Alfredo's eyes. "Copper had Roger over, knew all our names, wants a regular cut."

Alfredo. "How come?"

Freddie didn't appreciate the interruption, they were all desperate to know exactly what had happened and to analyse it fully. He glared at Alfredo. "For fuck's sake, that's what we're tryin' to sort out."

Alfredo was still playing catch up. "So you're not nicked, Roger?" Roger glanced briefly at Alfredo and once again briefly shook his head.

Bob Welch lit another cigarette and threw the open pack on the table, Freddie took one, and they shared a match. Bob took a drag. "Well there ain't many who could write a list of the people round this table, is there?" Danny shook his head.

Alfredo broke the silence. "Perhaps it was Ted, I mean he's not earning now, is he?"

Freddie was suddenly angry and glared at Alfredo. "Ted grass? No fuckin' way."

Roger went on. "No it couldn't be Ted, the copper put his name in the er confession thing with the rest of us. Well, except Alfredo."

Alfredo looked more puzzled. "Confession thing?"

They all turned to study the one man whose freedom was not, apparently, in jeopardy. Alfredo still looked completely confused. "For fuck's sake, what's happened?"

Danny informed him. "The copper knew all of our names, threatened to nick us all except for you, unless he gets a regular cut."

Freddie started jabbing his finger in Alfredo's direction and raised his voice. "Pretty obvious what's happened ain't it?"

Alfredo couldn't let this pass. He got to his feet and matched the tone and volume. "You sayin' I grassed?"

Freddie straightened in his chair. "Yeah. I fucking am."

Then he got to his feet too. Danny raised his arms. "For fuck's sake, quieten down you two, and sit down."

He looked around cautiously, then he continued. "I'm trying to think."

But Alfredo and Freddie continued to glare at each other. Danny touched Freddie's arm. "Let's get it right. Let's think."

Tom spoke slowly. "There ain't many who know, it's got to be somebody close."

Bob had a different take. "Perhaps it don't matter. If he can give us a steer and make sure we don't get nicked?"

Danny had been thinking about the likelihood of Alfredo being responsible. And if Freddie was right, then there would need to be very serious repercussions for the young man. Then something occurred to Danny, "Freddie, if Alfredo grassed, why would he be sitting here now? Why did he put a warning call in to my missus?"

Freddie shrugged his shoulders. Danny pushed the point home. "We don't know who gave that copper our names, there's too many unanswered questions to start lashing out, but we'll find out, for sure."

The mood settled, though the tension between Alfredo and Freddie remained clear. The gang talked it all through time and again, but resolved nothing. Alfredo phoned the café before he left Sudbury.

Alfredo stopped to pick up fish and chips on the way back to the flat. When he arrived, Tony was being fed. Ten minutes later the couple were enjoying their supper in traditional fashion – eating from newspaper pages, covered in salt and vinegar, without knives and forks and accompanied by a mug of tea.

Alfredo had decided it was best to manage his wife's fears about the events of the day by giving her an abbreviated version of the truth. He told her the outcome would make them fireproof. Of course, Shirley wasn't satisfied with a shortened account, less still with Alfredo's assertion that it was all for the better. She smelt a rat, or rather two rats, "It's too much of a coincidence, first the Krays try to muscle in, now this. Don't it strike you as odd then?"

Alfredo had not even considered a link. He stuffed a couple of chips in his mouth while he thought about it. He ate them and took a sip of tea, no doubt believing if the Krays were behind it, the Raiders would have figured it out as quickly as she had done. "Yeah, I mean I thought about it, but it ain't likely to be connected is it?"

Shirley finished a chip and shook her head in frustration.

# Chapter 22

Aldridge had never been to the British Museum before. Now he was alone in the Reading Room, sitting at a desk that faced a wall, glancing at the pages of a large volume he had taken from one of the old wooden shelves. A few minutes later, Billy Hill sauntered in, removed his trilby and smiled. It was his default expression. Both felt out of place.

Billy. "Good morning, Mr Black? How are you?"

Aldridge nodded and smiled, then looked around at the old reading room. "Why 'ere', Billy?"

Billy rested his trilby on the desk. "How many Old Bill or 'faces' come in 'ere?"

His grin widened, then he got to the point "Now. Is it sorted?"

Aldridge nodded. "Definitely. I got 'em all eating right out of my hand."

Billy thought about those words. "Good. But you mean 'my hand' don't ya?"

Aldridge didn't want to offend and responded quickly. "Yeah course, your hand, I only meant..."

Billy interrupted. "If this goes bandy, we'll both be in Shit Street for the rest of our lives."

Aldridge nodded solemnly. "Yeah."

Billy let the seconds pass while Aldridge took in the key message. "So everything's got to be right, got to be certain, no loose ends. I need the Raiders fully on side. If they ain't, I need to know."

Aldridge nodded gravely. "I know that Billy."

But Billy wanted Aldridge to slow down a little, to think about it all properly, he studied the detective. "There are three sorts of blokes Dennis, them what know, them what think they know, and them what know they don't know. The dangerous ones are them what think they know... So, what sort are you?"

Aldridge took out a packet of cigarettes, removed one and offered them to Billy.

Billy shook his head and looked around the room, giving a clue that smoking in here probably wasn't the best way to avoid attention. Aldridge hurriedly put the packet away.

Aldridge tried to save a little of his dignity, "I'm the sort of bloke who you've been relying on for a long time Billy."

Billy nodded in amusement. "Alright… Now, this bloke Cordrey, what's he like?"

Aldridge physically relaxed. He let the air go from his lungs, "Well he ain't a villain. More like a, I don't know… a clerk, or something."

"He knows you're railway police?"

Aldridge was keen to show how smart he had been. "Nah. I thought the less he knows the better. He just knows they're all fuckin' nicked unless they follow orders."

A few days later. The Raiders were at their various day jobs, Roger was in his florist shop, Danny was enjoying a morning mug of tea at his yard. Freddie and Bob were sleeping off the effects of a very late night following too much champagne and bedroom exercise. Tom was at his betting shop. Alfredo was giving Tony his bottle. Things had returned to normal. Almost. Roger was unpacking another box of flowers fresh from Covent Garden. The phone rang, he finished unpacking before lifting the receiver. It was Aldridge. "Roger. It's your new best mate. Get a pen and paper, I've got somethin' for you."

Roger instantly recognised the voice, he pulled a pad and pencil from beneath the counter. "Ready."

"Next Tuesday, the 20.15 Victoria to Brighton. Fifteen minutes before it's due in Brighton. Do it then. You'll have 12 minutes. The guard who's rostered always returns to the brake just seconds before Brighton. Be well clear of the brake by then. Got it?"

Roger scribbled a note and repeated the details back, then added. "You shouldn't be talking on the phone."

Aldridge laughed. "There's only one firm interested in you, and its mine. Now listen, I'll get to know every item that's nicked, so don't try and short change me."

Aldridge put the phone down.

# Chapter 23

The following Tuesday, the train left Victoria on time and was now on the final part of its journey to Brighton. It was dark outside and a single Victorian-style glass lamp above every seat lit the first-class compartment. Roger, Danny, Alfredo and Bob appeared to be City types returning home after a long day. Danny checked his watch. "Okay, let's go."

Alfredo moved out of the compartment and looked down the corridor. All clear, he turned and nodded to the others. Each of the others took a suitcase from the overhead racks and moved swiftly out of the compartment and towards the door to the mail coach.   Danny unlocked the door using a standard BR 21 key. They all entered except Alfredo who stood guard about halfway down the coach.

There were two piles of mailbags, each about four feet high. The gang set about their work, sorting the bags, slitting them and putting the high-value green inner bags into the suitcases. Roger moved a bag and exposed a foot sticking out beneath the mailbags. "Shit. It's a body."

Immediately they stopped work and stared down at the unmoving lower leg. Danny spoke. "Cover it back up. Let's get finished."

Then a groan was heard from beneath the bags, the foot moved, a drunken Scottish football supporter emerged from beneath the mailbags and got to his feet. "Wort you's fuckin' doin? You mess with me and I'll 'ave ye, ya' fuckin' Mormons."

Roger looked at Danny. Bob laughed, Danny laughed. Then Danny struck the drunk hard, just once. He went down fast but had a soft landing. Now he was unconscious again. Bob couldn't resist comment. "Cheeky fucker. Mormons!"

Danny, entirely focused on the job in hand, glanced at his watch. "Come on. Let's get finished, three minutes."

But Bob had an idea which amused him and he was determined to share it. "Hold on."

Bob bent over the drunk and stuffed a railway BR 21 key into his trouser pocket. Then he stuffed some registered packets in the drunk's jacket. Danny was already back at work. "What the fuck you up to, Bob?"

Bob returned to slicing open mailbags, he grinned and looked up.

"Teaching that fucker a lesson and confusing the enemy."

The Raiders quickly finished filling their suitcases and left the mail coach. This time they left the connecting door to the passenger compartment unlocked. The guard, returning soon, would soon discover the culprit.

# Chapter 24

The money was flowing in, the Raiders were making big money on a regular basis. The recent successful attack on the Brighton train had continued their good fortune. Of course, they all lived well. But the extent to which each exposed their wealth varied. Danny always drove his old van. His modest house remained ordinary. He avoided any show of wealth around his family, the street he lived in and the local pubs. But further from home, he enjoyed something of the good life. He sometimes spent evenings out in West End clubs and casinos, and took his family on occasional holidays to Brighton. On the other hand, Bob always drove an expensive new sports car, wore expensive clothes, drank the finest champagne, ate at top restaurants and gambled freely at the casinos.

Gambling was a pastime they all enjoyed, all but Alfredo. But for Roger it was an addiction. Going to the races together very occasionally, usually horses, sometimes the dogs, with their families, was the only time that wives, apart from Roger's, and girlfriends met. Roger never brought his wife to any occasion where he might gamble, or where other gang members, or their partners, might be present. She hated his gambling and the company Roger kept, and it seemed, their very lives together too.

Today, on this sunny autumn afternoon at Epsom Races, they were all gathered, except of course for Mrs Cordrey. Danny, Tom, Alfredo, Freddie and their wives, plus Bob and Roger, enjoyed a good deal of laughter and banter, booze and betting. Their mood was shared by the sizeable crowd around them. It was a happy, carefree scene.

Roger smiled and looked down at his betting slip. He had placed a big bet on an outsider and it had finished second, but it was a good 'each way' bet none of the others had made. They all saw the look of satisfaction on his face.

Shirley hadn't felt like dressing up and going out. It wasn't her thing anymore. But Alfredo was so keen to take her to Epsom, and Iris had been so encouraging too, that she had gone along. To her surprise, she was enjoying herself. Iris was an attractive woman in her thirties, but Renee, Tom's wife, who she had not met before, had the shape and face of a model and was as generous and kind as Iris. Freddie's wife was attractive and fun too. Shirley loved the company. But at about 3.45 pm Danny looked at his watch and quickly ended the light mood. "Time to go to work."

Iris took the hint and addressed Tom's wife, Renee. "What you fancy in the 4.30 Ren?"

The two alpha females moved away from their husbands, Shirley followed with Freddie's wife. When the women were a few yards distant, Danny turned to Roger. "You better get mobile Roger, see you at Chipstead."

Roger nodded and headed off through the race course crowds and across the fields towards nearby Tattenham Corner railway station.

The Raiders went to their waiting cars. Aldridge had told Roger to meet him alone at Chipstead station at 4.30 to hand over his cut of the Brighton job. The Raiders intended a very unpleasant surprise.

Aldridge was the one factor in their operations causing them concern and he had to be put in his place. After all, he was effectively now controlling them, and they didn't even know his name. They had no reason to think he wasn't just another crooked chancer, another bent cop, another villain they could easily get the better of.

They planned to force him into a car at the quiet rural station of Chipstead. They would take him somewhere remote, search him and rough him up a little, just to show who was actually running things. His warrant card would show his name, rank and station and he would probably have a driving licence in his pocket with his address too. Intimidating this man, making him as vulnerable as they were, was absolutely necessary to their own continued liberty.

Roger entered Tattenham Corner terminus station, its prime purpose was to serve Epsom racecourse. The London Bridge train was waiting to depart and was already busy with people heading back to London, but Roger found a quiet carriage. The train set off exactly on time.

Tadworth was the next stop and when the train was just one minute away from stopping there, Aldridge approached Roger, they had underestimated Aldridge's planning. The train began to brake.

Aldridge. "We're gonna have to disappoint the boys, Roger. Get off here."

The train was coming to a halt. Roger didn't argue.

The platform at Tadworth, another rural village, was completely empty. There was no waiting room or station office. The railway lines and station had been cut deep into the Surrey countryside and had high banks on either side. The two men were completely isolated and unseen from the nearby road. Roger took an envelope from his pocket and handed it over. Aldridge didn't bother to examine it. He placed it straight into his jacket pocket.

Aldridge then explained a big mailbag job was being put together, worth well over a million, and the Raiders would take part. They would each get a 'whack' of at least £50k, probably more.

Roger felt overwhelming distrust and dislike, but didn't know how best to react. "But you might be setting us up, we don't know anything about you. What nick you from? Or even your name."

Aldridge stayed calm. "It's a sweet piece of work. No one's going to get nicked. The people setting it up know what they're doing."

Roger wasn't pacified. How could he be? "But you might be setting us up, we don't know anything about you."

Aldridge continued. "You don't need to. You can call me Mr Black."

Roger pushed on with the questions. "Who else is involved?.... When will it come off?... Where?....How?...

Aldridge didn't provide any detail, but he did tell Roger the Krays were 'in' and there were a few months before it would take place. But he also reminded him of the alternative...

"Or you can all go to prison for a very long time, I've got more than enough to nick the lot of you right now."

Aldridge had given no more away than Billy had instructed. Roger was deflated. "Look. They won't work with the Krays."

Aldridge, or rather Billy, had anticipated the reluctance. "Most of you have got a missus and kids. You got to think about your families, you understand?" Roger's mind was still racing. No one had foreseen the threats to their families.

A train approached from the other direction heading back to Tattenham Corner. Aldridge had to cross a steep footbridge to catch it, either that or travel towards Chipstead, and Aldridge had no intention of doing that. He spoke quickly. "Tell 'em to do as they're told – and get rich."

Thirty minutes later, at Chipstead, Roger updated the Raiders. They weren't used to being outsmarted or kept in the dark. They argued amongst themselves and failed to agree what to do next.

# Chapter 25

The Raiders had been planning this job for months. It had nothing to do with Aldridge, and he wouldn't be getting a cut. They were at their premises under the railway arches and it seemed they had shut the problem with the Krays out of their minds. Tom, Danny, Alfredo, Bob and Roger were all wearing overalls and standing around a large wooden crate, all but for Alfredo were grinning. The crate was a four-foot cube and exceptional in only one way. One side had a large, hidden removable panel that could be secured from the inside. All four vertical sides were clearly marked 'Fragile. This Way Up.'

Danny. "What's wrong with ya? You'll be fine Alfredo, honest."

Alfredo looked concerned. "Seems dodgy to me. I mean, six hours?"

Tom mocked him a little. "Don't be such a fucking tart. Torch, bottle of pop, bottle to piss in, sarnies, fuck me it's practically a day out..."

Bob chimed in. "And you can spend the day playing with yourself, like at home."

They all laughed, except Alfredo.

They heard a lorry stop outside, then the driver's door slammed. Their premises had a large metal shutter door with a smaller door set into it. Within seconds, Freddie came in through the smaller door and banged it shut behind him. He hurriedly picked up some overalls from an old wooden chair and began changing. "Sorry I'm late lads, missus, you know."

The others nodded back at him as Freddie quickly did up the buttons on his overalls and called to them. "Everything set, lorry's ready. I been thinkin', we gotta try to sort Black. Get hold of him, give him a good hidin."

Suddenly they all looked exasperated, the smiles disappeared. Danny turned back to Alfredo. "In you go then."

Alfredo reluctantly climbed into the crate and secured the secret panel behind him.

They carried the heavy wooden crate into the back street and onto an old flatbed lorry. Freddie drove it to a railway goods yard at nearby Waterloo. The porters who unloaded the lorry placed the crate in the goods shed, the porters who brought the crate from the goods shed to the platform, and the porters who loaded it onto the train, all turned the crate over. First this way and that, and then that way and this. And with every ninety-degree turn and change of direction, sandwiches, bottles, torch and Alfredo were churned.

When Alfredo had first been enclosed, the air inside the box was still cool and as fresh as any in the back streets of the dirty capital. But within minutes of being sealed in, the temperature started to climb. It was two hours before porters loaded the 'express delivery' crate onto the goods train. There it nestled against other boxes until Alfredo heard more muffled voices as postmen threw in mailbags. Then the goods wagon's doors were slammed shut.

Alfredo hadn't reckoned on the heat, the lack of air, the complete absence of light, the disorientation, or the claustrophobia. Now, waiting for the train to depart, nearly four hours after being concealed, he could hardly breathe. The air was stifling hot and stale.

The crate was well made, but on the flatbed lorry some light had still entered. However, once the crate was under the roof at the goods shed, all light had virtually gone. Now, in this unlit goods wagon, the blackness was impenetrable.

Eventually, he heard a muffled whistle and felt the train lurch forward. The goods train was soon heading southwest at full-steam. By now he didn't know which side of the crate had the secret door, but managed to find it at the third attempt. He pushed hard to open it. But the door moved only an inch, mailbags and other goods had been loaded against it.

Alfredo pushed hard, but now he had little oxygen in his blood and felt weak and sick. He put his back against the opposite wall of the crate and his feet against the panel and pushed hard with both legs and stomach. The panel opened about ten inches and stopped firmly. It would open no further.

Alfredo somehow squeezed out through the gap. He stretched and took in the cool air. Roger had told him where he would find a switch for the coach lights. He looked at his watch. To his relief, he saw he had an hour to work without interruption. Using his Stanley knife, he cut the tie of the first of the high-value mailbags.

He found a total of eight high-value green canvas inner bags and one red; he hadn't seen such a red bag before. He slit it to find bundles of tightly packed banknotes of various denominations. He carefully re-tied every outer bag and put the unopened coloured inner bags inside his crate. Finally, he looked around the coach – everything appeared as he had found it. Again, he looked at his watch. He still had plenty of time before the train arrived at Southampton Goods station. He was in no rush to lock himself back in.

That evening in a scruffy little warehouse on a back street near the docks at Southampton, the other Raiders were playing cards and drinking tea. The expected delivery was overdue. Roger looked at his watch. "Think something's gone wrong?"
Tom looked up. "If he'd been nicked, Old Bill would have been round here by now, I mean even Old Bill can read a fuckin' delivery address."
They all smiled. Bob joined the fun. "On the other hand, perhaps we should wait down the road a bit, just in case."
They all grinned.
A lorry slowed down outside and stopped with the squeal of badly maintained brakes. The driver's door creaked open and slammed shut. Only seconds passed before they heard a heavy banging on the shutters. Freddie opened the old metal inset door, an elderly driver stood outside and held papers on a clipboard. "BRS. Got one for ya, express delivery."
Tom and Freddie helped remove the crate from the truck and carried it in. Within a minute the crate was safely inside and signed for, the warehouse door closed and the driver back at the wheel.
Inside the warehouse the gang was fussing around the crate, keen to get Alfredo and the goodies out. Danny knocked on the side of the crate. "Alright Alfredo? You..."
But before he had finished the sentence, the panel on the side of the crate opened and Alfredo started to climb out, naked but for a pair of 'Y' fronts. "That was fuckin' 'orrible. I ain't ever doin' that again. Never, fuck it."
Of course, it amused the rest of them, but they had a more pressing matter, Bob had already pushed past Alfredo and was dragging out the stolen property. Roger directed Alfredo to a sink where he could wash off some of the dirt and debris. As he ripped off his filthy clothes, Bob Welch called, "How come you slit the money bag?"
Alfredo called back, "The red bag? I never seen one before, didn't know what it were."
He turned on the tap and used a rough bar of light brown, strong-smelling soap to wash the grime from his face and hands.
Bob hadn't finished, "You're supposed to bring 'em back unopened."

Alfredo was washing eagerly, and his face was covered in soapsuds. He already felt like the fall guy and didn't take kindly to the implied criticism. He turned and shouted back. "Listen, it could a been a bag of turds for all I knew."

Bob was enjoying himself, but Alfredo couldn't see the grin.

"Turds? Christ knows what you're talkin' about. Fuckin' 'turds'?"

Alfredo was by now thoroughly agitated, "Go fuck yourself."

Bob and Roger loaded the suitcases as Freddie and Tom broke up the wooden crate. Within a few minutes, the crate was no more than a pile of pallet wood piled outside in the scruffy back yard.

The gang divided into pairs and left the warehouse at two-minute intervals. Within an hour they were all, separately, at Southampton's main passenger station awaiting various trains to London.

The railways, and even the buses and Tube trains, provided the most anonymous way to travel. Consequently, whenever they could, the gang travelling separately, used the trains to make their escape. The alternative, to travel by car, risked that the police would see a bunch of likely lads travelling together as a sign of something amiss. Caution and the avoidance of unnecessary risk was everything.

They planned to meet again the next morning, at Danny's yard.


It was nearly midnight before Alfredo approached his flat. Over the months, Shirley and Alfredo had developed an early warning system, a potted aspidistra in the bathroom window. Visible from the road at the back of the flats, in the event of the police calling while Alfredo was out, and possibly lying in wait inside or out, Shirley would pop to the bathroom and move the plant from the centre of the window to one side. So that night, before entering the flats, Alfredo went to the rear of the block and checked the aspidistra was still where he hoped it would be. Then he made his weary way up the stairs. Shirley had, as always, bolted the front door. She was awake of course, and the clock seemed to her to get louder and slower as the minutes and hours dragged by.

Alfredo knocked gently. She rushed barefoot to the door and called out softly. "That you?"

Alfredo answered, and she unbolted urgently. He closed the door quietly behind him for fear of waking Tony, she put the sitting room light on and studied him. How tired he looked. She picked a piece of remaining debris from his hair affectionately and smiled. "Remember when you always came home dirty?"

He smiled back. "A million years ago."

Shirley had a winsome look in her eyes. "Innocent days."

Alfredo nodded his head slightly. Shirley and Alfredo were at one. Nothing more needed to be said. She took a deep breath. "Run yourself a bath, I'll make some tea."

Alfredo thought about how much he loved her.

# Chapter 26

Most people don't set an alarm clock unless they have to be at work at a specific time. Given the amount of free time professional thieves have, setting an alarm clock is therefore unnecessary and generally avoided. Most coppers, like most of the population, therefore seem to think villainy results in lying in bed until at least 9 a.m. Business meetings after dawn, and before 11 a.m seem generally assumed to be virtuous simply by their timing. But whether you are a professional mail thief, or a professional investment banker, alarm clocks do have to be set if you are taking your profession seriously and have business to attend.

The following morning Danny arrived early at his yard. It was on a back street and small, about forty yards by sixty. A six-foot wooden fence encircled it and barbed wire ran along its top. The only entrance was via a tatty wooden double gate, wide enough to let the horse and cart pass, as indeed it recently had. 'Pembroke & Son. General Dealers' was painted on the gates about 50 years earlier, and referred originally to Danny's grandfather and father. Danny's father had died a few years since. His horse had more recently gone the same way. Now the only transport on show was an old, hand-painted Morris van.

Canvas covered piles of old scrap metal, building materials and various types of 'tat' were scattered about. Very little of it had moved in years. Various small interesting items decorated Danny's office in a large wooden shed.

The Raiders arrived separately on foot and in good time. The gates, locked behind them, shut the world out very effectively. If the police, or any nosey parker, wanted to enter, it would not be easy or quick.

Danny had lit the Rayburn stove early, and now the shed was warm and tidy and the seating comfortable. The stove had burnt the last of the green bags and was now aglow with ashes. A large pot of tea was brewing.

The 'Trojan horse' job had been another very profitable day's work. The mood was light, and they were enjoying a little more fun at Alfredo's expense again, this time about his experience in the box.

Alfredo asked more about the red canvas bags. Roger explained they were used for transferring money between banks, in this case to the tune of £7,000. In total, they had made in excess of £20,000. However, the pleasure of reflecting on the Trojan horse success was short lived. Roger was still smiling, but he let the smile fade on his lips. "You know we need to decide as a group what we're gonna do, the Kray business isn't going to just go away."

Danny leaned back in his seat and listened. Over the weeks since Chipstead, each of them had dissected a thousand times what Roger had told them about the encounter.

Freddie was still keen to track down the bent copper, 'Black', and sort him out. Tom reminded him of the confession, but Freddie wasn't listening. He seemed convinced if they could just reach the copper, they could beat him into submission. Bob reminded Freddie, Black wasn't alone, he had the Krays behind him.

But Danny had an additional thought. "I think they're just frontin' it for somebody."

Danny, Freddie and the other gang members looked towards Roger. Roger took a sip of tea as he responded to Danny. "It doesn't make much difference does it, Danny? If the Krays are running it, or just involved, we're still cornered, aren't we?"

Danny leaned forward. "Well, it makes a big difference. 'Cos if the twins ain't behind it, whoever the real boss is, he might just know what the fuck he's doin'."

Everyone was lost in that thought for a few seconds. Tom poured some scotch into his mug of tea. "There ain't many who could put this together?"

Danny had already wondered who it might be. "Billy Howard? Billy Hill?"

Roger cut in. "The copper said the train would carry a million or more. There's the gold trains up from Southampton, and some of the TPOs must carry that much."

Alfredo was amazed at the sums being mentioned. "Fucking 'ell."

Danny continued. "Tell the copper we're in. Then we watch points, find out what we can, have a drink with Billy Howard and Billy Hill, put a few gentle feelers out.

Bob nodded in agreement.

Danny looked at the others present, "You alright with that Tom, Freddie?"

In the afternoon, while Tony was having an afternoon nap, Shirley and Alfredo were enjoying a late lunch together, beans on toast, followed by some posh desserts from Harrods. They were half listening to the radio programme 'Go Man Go' on the BBC Light Programme. Money was flowing now and life was easier. Alfredo finished a mouthful of toast and beans. "...And within a few months we'll be set for life, only the best for you and Tony."

Shirley sensed Alfredo's expression of great confidence and certainty were concealing something he was much less certain and confident about. She put her fork down, "'Set for life?' How come we're gonna be so rich so quickly then?"

Alfredo wanted to reassure her. "Well, there's somethin' really special comin' up."

Shirley stopped eating. She looked concerned. "What?"

Alfredo realised he had put his foot in it, right up to his waist. "Danny says best not tell anyone anythin' they don't need to know... that way they..."

Shirley interrupted. "Listen, I'm not anybody."

Alfredo tried to backpedal. "I didn't mean..."

Shirley pressed on. "So come on, what's it all about?"

Alfredo sat back in his seat, putting a little distance between them. "Trains, mailbags, the usual...we're waitin' to find out a bit more."

Shirley didn't like it. "Waiting for who?"  Alfredo had nowhere to turn, but wanted to avoid a return to hostilities. "The people runnin' it?"

Shirley's voice dropped and slowed. "People runnin' it'. She said contemptuously. "What fuckin' people?"

Alfredo felt the contempt and reacted. "I told ya. I can't bloody say."

Every word Alfredo uttered made Shirley feel more excluded, less in control, more at risk, more anxious and fearful. And the more she probed and pushed the angrier Alfredo became. After ten minutes of bad temper, angry words and recriminations, Shirley had found out the Krays had got their way, and were pulling the strings of a bent copper.

Shirley told Alfredo everyone knew the Krays were ruthless bullies who would inflict serious injury just for the sadistic pleasure of doing so. They lived off the backs of shop and club owners by getting money for 'protection'. The practice was, of course, simple blackmail. In addition, Shirley knew very well about the Krays' deserved reputation for stealing from thieves, as well as the credible rumours about the rapes and disappearances of young men who they had taken a shine to. She told Alfredo the twins had corrupt friends in the Met who survived because the Krays threw the little fish like Alfredo to them to feed their arrest numbers.

132

But no matter how hard she tried, Alfredo would not back off. In reality, Alfredo couldn't back out of the job, nor did he really want to. He told himself yet again, Shirley wasn't being herself, she was being illogical. But the greatest affront was to his masculinity. All in all, he was determined to see the job through.

By the end of the evening, Alfredo seemed to have got what he wanted, Shirley had accepted he would be working with the Krays.

But he didn't know Shirley as well as she knew him. Her decision, reached months ago, to balance the scales in favour of his committing a minimal amount of crime with known associates, had now been well and truly outweighed. The fears, anxieties and depression following her rape had made her more dependent on Alfredo than she had ever been. Thus, she could not have been more determined now to keep him safe to look after her. That meant extricating him from his new life at any cost.

# Chapter 27

By 5.30pm most of the British Transport Headquarters CID staff had either gone out on observations, or gone to the pub to buy each other two hours' worth of booze. But on that night, all the lights were still on in the large CID squad room. One lone detective remained. He knew less about mailbag thefts, London gangsters and London itself than any other detective in London. He was busy reading the many reports on mail crime which had been allocated to his team for investigation.

The phone rang, DC Roy Walcott lifted the receiver and heard the sound of pips – a public telephone kiosk. He heard the coins drop. Then he spoke, his voice heavy with his pronounced Birmingham accent. "Good evening, this is the British Transport Police, Headquarters CID. Can I help you?"

Shirley was nervous, but she knew what she had to do. "Is that the Railway Police?"

"Yes. Good evening."

Shirley spoke quickly. "I got some information for ya. There's a big mail job bein' planned."

Roy reached for a pen. "Who am I speaking to?"

Shirley felt her first flutter of concern. "Never mind about that. This is just between me and you, right?"

Roy knew all about practical jokes, he'd experienced more than enough of them over the years. He suddenly remembered taking a phone call years before detailing the theft of a suitcase from a 'Mr L E Fant.' Perhaps those cockney bastards were taking the piss again. Those 'cockney bastards' being his London based colleagues.

Roy sighed heavily, suggesting to the caller he knew it was a hoax. "Yes, you and me, in complete confidence, my lips are sealed."

Shirley didn't hesitate, she spoke quickly. "Right meet me straightaway, on your own, anyone with ya I'm gone."

If this was a joke, then the actress was remarkable. "Come where? When?"

Shirley had it planned, she didn't intend to allow anytime for a team of officers to organise any sort of surveillance. "I'll give you 20 minutes. The Fountain at the Elephant."

Roy's mind wandered. "L E Fant."

Shirley waited… "You 'ear me?"

But Roy was baffled. "Elephant? Fountain? What elephant? What fountain?"

Shirley took a deep breath. "For fuck's sake, The Elephant & Castle in South London. There's a boozer called The Fountain, in Elba Place. Be there in twenty or I'm gone."

Roy felt unsure. What if it wasn't a joke? It sounded real. "I can't be there in that time. I've got to find it in the London A-Z map book. I'm at Park Royal, North West 10. I don't even know who you are, you might be wasting my time."

Shirley hadn't expected the ignorance, or the reluctance. She thought for a few seconds. "London Brighton train got done a few weeks ago. 'Part from other stuff, a box of weddin' rings on their way to Samuel's in Brighton got nicked, Check it."

Clearly, whoever this woman was, she appeared to know at least one fact most people, including Roy, did not. "Give me an hour. How will I recognise you?"

After this brief exchange, Shirley was certain she would recognise whoever filled the 'size 10's.' "Don't worry, I'll recognise you. You got 45 minutes, be on your own."

Shirley put the phone down.

It took Roy nearly an hour, but by then he had checked his A-Z map, located the file on the Brighton job and found a list of property stolen that night. He had also handed the keys to the CID office to the night security man on the front desk and made the long journey from north London to the Elephant and Castle. He found The Fountain a few minutes later. The place was straight out of Victorian times with two small separate bars which shared a circular serving counter. The place seemed empty. Behind the bar, an old lady was polishing glasses. She barely looked up when Roy entered. She smiled. "Hello Love, what can I get ya?"

Roy wandered across to her while taking in the scene. "Err, we spoke on the phone, half a bitter please."

The barmaid's eyes flicked up from the over polished glass, then she turned away and reached for a half pint glass. "Don't think so sweetheart. I'd have remembered."

She pulled the half pint and placed it on a well-used bar towel. "Seven pence please darlin'. Try the snug."

Roy spotted the half-glazed door separating the bars, he put seven pence on the counter, picked up his drink, thanked her, and headed towards it.

The snug was empty but for Shirley sitting in a corner. She had come straight from home, her hair was a mess and she had no make-up on, but she wore an expensive topcoat and shoes. Roy went over. "Excuse me, did we speak...?"
But he didn't finish the question. "Yeah, sit down."

Shirley had to be careful. She knew only too well most professional villains were in league with the many corrupt police officers in the capital. She knew she was taking a massive risk. Her experience had taught her that most detectives would do whatever they needed to earn a few extra quid. Shirley felt she had to know a bit more about this stranger before she took the irretrievable step. "You a Geordie?"
Roy wondered if she had ever travelled outside of London. "Brummie. What's it all about then?"
But Shirley wasn't satisfied. "How long you been down 'ere?"
Roy didn't understand why she was questioning him. "What you want to tell me?"
Shirley. "I said, been in the smoke long 'ave ya?"
Roy took the line of least resistance, his default position. "Not long, why's it relevant?"
"It's relevant because it means there's less chance you're in anybody's pocket." Shirley took a good-sized gulp of her vodka and orange.
Roy wasn't offended. "I'm not in anybody's pocket, except perhaps me missus."

Shirley's hard expression didn't change. She finished her drink and Roy offered another, Shirley shook her head. "No thanks, you check it out did ya? The rings and that?"
Roy nodded. "Let's start with your name."

He took out a notebook and placed it on the small table, then he reached for his biro. Shirley looked horrified. "Put that fucking thing away. And you ain't gonna get me name, ever."
Roy could see the concern on her face. He put pen and notebook away and dropped his voice. "A young Scotsman was arrested for that job. You know him then?"
Shirley looked puzzled. "You must have nicked the wrong bloke."

Roy shook his head. "Well, I didn't nick him. But he was caught red-handed. So, who else was involved?"

"I ain't sayin'. I ain't a grass, and if they found out I was talkin' I'd get a good hidin', you understand?"

Roy nodded, but really hadn't grasped the situation at all, he continued. "McNish, John McNish. That was the name of the young Scotsman. You know him?"

Shirley said she had never heard of anyone called McNish. She studied the Brummie. He seemed so unworldly, so unlike any London detective she had ever met. But she had to trust someone. "It's about the Krays."

Roy looked at her. He wondered if she was having a nervous breakdown. She was obviously talking from her heart and she was deadly serious. But she didn't seem to want to tell him anything. Perhaps she was some sort of fantasist. Her hands were shaking and she looked terrified and angry. He had just spent nearly an hour travelling here. He wondered whether to cut his losses and head back to his digs.

Roy's response surprised her. "Who?"

Shirley thought he must have misheard. "The Krays, the twins, Charlie an all as far as I know."

Roy took a sip of his half pint. "Charlie who?"

Shirley couldn't believe it. She shook her head. "The twins' older brother. You must have heard of 'em? Surely to Christ?"

Roy was completely unimpressed and unconcerned. "Why's that then?"

"Cos they run the East End and think they run the West End and South London an all."

Roy was getting an inkling. "So, known criminals are they then?"

Shirley's patience was being stretched. She resorted to sarcasm. "Yeah, that's it, 'known criminals'."

Roy nodded. "So you're saying the Krays stole the mailbags from the Brighton train"?

And so it went on for another 30 minutes. But at the end of it, Roy understood Shirley's position. Shirley was informing on the Krays to prevent a more serious crime being committed. She was doing it solely because the commission of such crime would, she thought, result in someone she loved getting seriously hurt, or receiving a long prison sentence. She didn't want reward money, she didn't want revenge, and she certainly didn't want public thanks. This made her very credible. It convinced Roy this was no act, but she could of course, still be wrong.

Throughout the meeting, perhaps because she had put herself in danger, perhaps because Roy was such hard going, whatever the reason, Shirley made it plain what she thought of Roy's apparent lack of savvy. The meeting ended on exactly the same note as it had started. As Roy emptied the last of the small beer and stood to leave, he asked a final question. "So, what are the Krays' full names?"

Shirley's tone remained the same. "Just ask anybody who knows their arse from their elbow..."

As Shirley travelled home she wondered about the wisdom of what she had done. The copper seemed like a decent enough bloke, not exactly Fabian of the Yard, but unless he was as good an actor as Tony Curtis, he wasn't connected to anything dodgy. Anyway, he was all she had, and he had learned nothing about her identity or Alfredo's.

The next morning, DC Roy Walcott got into work well before 9.00 a.m. He was surprised to see several of his colleagues had already arrived. Some had started work in earnest, but most were joking, drinking tea, waiting for their guvnor (inspector) to appear.

Roy had plenty on his mind and was keen to speak to the guvnor at the earliest opportunity. But for the moment he was talking to Joe, the old CID clerk. Joe had seen many flash detectives come and go – some on promotion, some in handcuffs, some having learned a bit of humility, and several as useless alcoholics. Joe wasn't easily impressed anymore. He was sixty-four and due to be compulsorily retired before the year was out. In the meantime, he was still keen to do his job to the best of his ability.

In the weeks Roy had been there, Joe had been trying to show him the system as best he could, but for some reason, this morning, Joe found Roy keener than ever. Joe answered yet another question from him. "Yes of course, we keep files on all known mailbag thieves and suspects, and an MO index too. I'll show you it all later."

Roy was listening keenly. "Thanks Joe. By the way, are the rosters done for next week yet? I need tell the missus what days I can get home."

Before Joe could answer, the guvnor, Detective Inspector Aldridge, entered. Without looking at anyone, he sauntered across the room and called out loudly. "Morning Girls."  One or two detectives responded. Roy went straight over to him. "Morning sir. Okay if I have a word?"

Aldridge tapped a desk with his rolled newspaper. "Kitchen Brummie, speak while you make me a cuppa."

Aldridge headed off towards a small kitchen tucked away out of sight, Roy followed. Once in the kitchen, they were alone. Aldridge tapped Roy on the shoulder with his rolled newspaper. "I already told you. Don't call me sir or guvnor. It's Den or Dennis. If we're doing obs. and somebody hears you, the job's blown."

Aldridge used his rolled newspaper to point at the kettle. "Tea. Milk and two."

Roy put the kettle on and searched for the packet of Brooke Bond tea.

Roy didn't like to call the inspector by his Christian name. He had never called an inspector anything but sir, and as for guvnor, it was a London expression. Besides, using a Christian name implied friendship and Roy made his friends slowly. He found the packet of tea and put three teaspoons in the old brown china teapot. "Can I ask you about the Krays?"

Aldridge smiled. "What about them?"

Roy was impressed. "So you've heard of 'em?"

Aldridge was still smiling. "Heard of them'? I'd have to have had my head stuck up my arse for the last five years... So, what about them?"

Roy warmed to the subject. "Well, I was speaking to someone last night who said they'd been doing mailbags."

Aldridge kept an even tone. "That's complete bollocks. Somebody's taking the piss out of you. Who was it told you?"

Roy tried to convince him. "I don't think it was a piss-take, I think they were serious."

Aldridge. "I said, whose fillin' your head with shit?"

But Roy wasn't completely stupid and knew an informant shared was an informant lost. "A bloke I met in a pub."

Aldridge found it impossible to countenance the very idea that this daft Brummie, who couldn't find a handkerchief in his top pocket, could possibly know anything about his most important secrets. He studied Roy and pointed at the tea. "Knew you were on mailbags did he?"

Roy wasn't keen to be questioned further. "Yeah."

Aldridge nodded. "Want a drink for the info did he? Buy him a drink did ya?"

Roy saw how to steer the conversation. "Yeah."

His inspector nodded. "What boozer was it?

Roy knew the right answer to close things off. "Near Waterloo, full of porters and postmen."

Aldridge nodded and sniggered, his theory confirmed. "My advice, don't buy him any more beer, Brummie. And by the way, remember, always best keep your mouth shut and look a fool rather than open it and remove any shadow of doubt."

Aldridge pointed at the waiting mug. "Now, pour the fuckin' tea before it's cold."

Roy turned his attention to the milk, which was keeping cool outside on the window ledge. He pulled the sash window up and as he reached for the milk, Aldridge offered a bit more advice. "And don't think you can claim that beer back on exes if that's your game."

Later that day, in a small meeting room at British Transport Police HQ, two men in cheap but tidy suits, Post Office Investigation Department (POID) officers, were sitting with Aldridge. One looked like a librarian, the other a maths teacher. They were not police officers, had no powers of arrest and had received no recognised detective training. However, they were experienced and reliable postmen, intelligent, hardworking and very knowledgeable about the workings of the Post Office. Every member of the POID had developed some detective skills through experience, some more than others.

The one who looked like a maths teacher made a suggestion to Aldridge, after all it's all he could do, he was not in a position to insist. "I think we've all got to up our game before we're all in real trouble."

Aldridge could hardly bother to look at him. He took a drag on his cigarette and looked out of the window. "Yeah, the papers ain't helping, all this talk about South Coast Raiders."

The 'librarian' chipped in cautiously. "Papers aside, there's a real problem, Dennis, high-value mail thefts never been more frequent."

Aldridge wondered how much longer he would need to stay in this conversation. It was valueless. "You don't need to tell me that. My blokes are working flat out."

The 'librarian' changed tack. "Will you be able to make the security review meeting next week?"

Aldridge was supposed to attend these monthly liaison meetings but found them irrelevant. They were fine for talking about security systems and looking at the printed analyses these blokes loved preparing, but of little value in helping to catch thieves.

"Maybe." He managed to say, but his lack of enthusiasm was clear.

The 'librarian' frowned. "It's just that it's an important one, the new high security TPO coaches are ready for use and…"

Suddenly Aldridge was interested. "New coaches? What's so special about them? When they coming in?"

# Chapter 28

On Billy Hill's instructions, the Krays met Danny and Tom in the basement bar of their recently acquired Glenrae Hotel on the Seven Sisters Road, in Finsbury Park, North London.

The hotel was extremely useful for clandestine meetings, and the police seemed, as yet, to be unaware of its existence. It was around midnight, and the first meeting since the Raiders had agreed to participate. No one else was present, Ronnie was acting as barman. Danny took his first sip from a mug of tea. "Didn't know you had this place."

Reggie had taken his blue pinstripe jacket off to reveal a slightly sweaty white shirt. It was undone at the neck, a red and white spotted necktie had been loosened, and the bright red of the tie matched the colour of the braces now on show. Reggie peered back at Danny. "Nobody does. We're makin' sure we keep it that way until the job's done."

Tom, like the twins, was sipping a scotch. "Meeting in club hours is a good idea. You thought about early mornings an' all?"

Reggie walked towards the jukebox and spoke over his shoulder. "Yeah Tom. If we need to, we will. Whatever we need to do to keep things tight. There's a few things we gotta tell ya'."

Ronnie's tie and shirt were still fastened, he sat on a stool behind the bar weighing up the two guests. Ronnie and Reggie didn't yet know much about the planned robbery, just the very limited information Billy had chosen to share.

Billy made sure, in the interests of security, that he only told the twins, at every stage, exactly what they needed to know and no more. But Billy had decided Danny and Tom now needed to know a little more. How else could he take advantage of Roger's technical knowledge during the planning stages? Billy also wanted them to be reassured they would only be working with seasoned professionals.

The twins' instructions were to pass all information and instructions on to the Raiders as their own. Billy's name must never be raised.

Reggie walked back from the jukebox, Roy Orbison sprang into voice. Reggie moved between Danny and Tom. "Look, we want to tell you a bit about the job. It's a TPO but don't let it go no further at the mo'. Second, your team ain't big enough so we're gonna share the other names with ya' and third..."

The twins were very close to one another, in every sense, but both felt the need to be heard on equal terms. Ronnie interrupted from behind the bar. "The whole team needs to get some practice at working together, know what I mean?"

Danny took in Ronnie's words carefully, then exchanged glances with Tom. Danny put his mug on the bar. "Well yeah, err, we'll 'ave to talk about how the takings are gonna be divvied up."

The twins had expected the issue to arise, or rather Billy had. He knew very well the Raiders would not share the proceeds of their crimes with the Krays any more than absolutely necessary.

Tom looked uneasy. "It's just the one practice job, right?"

Reggie nodded and put his hand on Tom's shoulder as if they were old friends. "Yeah. We supply the information, you supply the technical and half the manpower, a dummy run. We'll plan it together, using your bloke, Roger."

Danny was waiting for the right moment to ask. "What about Mr Black?" The twins immediately looked at one another in silence. Danny noted their reaction. "So, work for you does he?"

Ronnie responded. "Yeah, anyway, you don't need to know nothing more about him."

Danny nodded his head. He had found out what he needed; the twins hadn't sent him, if they had, they would have wanted to rub a little salt in. And if they hadn't sent the bent copper they weren't running the job. It gave him reassurance. He paused and reflected. So did the twins.

Danny changed the subject. "The first job, what cut you want then?" Reggie smiled. "Me and Ron, we'll share a single whack." Danny and Tom exchanged glances. They spoke almost simultaneously. "OK."

Tom and Danny asked about the big job but learned nothing more. The twins ran through the names of those they would work with: 'Buster' Edwards, Gordon Goody, 'Big Jim' Hussey, Bruce Reynolds, Charlie Wilson and so on, there were no surprises. Tom and Danny knew most of them.

# Chapter 29

It was one of the most unwelcoming nights of the century. During February 1963, the country was in the grip of arctic weather, and being hit by freezing winds, heavy snowfalls and sub-zero temperatures. Drifts of snow were 20 feet deep in places, much of the country was cut off, and the sea in many ports had frozen solid. Much of the Thames was iced over. No one travelled far unless compelled.

Again, Aldridge had deployed all 50 drafted officers to travel on specially selected mail trains. In addition, as usual, Aldridge's London detectives were divided to supervise activities. But there were still not enough officers to provide observations on even 30% of the potential target trains. So as long as Aldridge managed his resources carefully, there was very little chance of Billy Hill's plans being spoiled.

By 8pm the detectives travelling on trains in and out of Euston Station had stood down after a long, cold day. Shortly after,14 empty burgundy coloured London, Midland and Scottish (LMS) Railway coaches pulled into the station. Each passenger coach comprised six passenger compartments with six seats. In addition, there was a sleeping car and, at the very rear, a parcel/postal coach and guard's compartment. This train was to form the 8.40p.m Euston to Holyhead passenger service carrying high-value mailbags bound for Ireland. The train was known as 'The Irish Mail."

On this night, because of the awful weather, the Holyhead bound train was unusually quiet.

Not long after leaving Euston, now a few miles northwest of London, as the train chugged across open countryside thick with snow, the robbers were already at work.

In the first-class restaurant, Freddie Sansom and another robber, both dressed elegantly, were sitting at a table sipping wine while waiting for their first course to arrive.

Uniformed stewards buzzed around the few passengers who wanted dinner. The size of the potential tips had become increasingly important as the number of passengers taking dinner was small.

Meanwhile, right at the back of the train, in a dimly lit mail coach, accessed from the passenger coaches, Danny, Tom, and Alfredo, all dressed

144

in overalls, were cutting open mailbags and placing the green inner bags into a large holdall.

By now, Alfredo had taken part in many mail thefts, but working with a bigger team that included strangers made him nervous. "How long we got?" He asked.

Danny was his usual unperturbed self. "Plenty of time."

But things don't always go according to plan. The information supplied by Aldridge, via Hill and the Krays, indicated the train guard would be out of the mail coach for well over an hour. This had been established by the observations of Aldridge's team and duly reported back as required. Those observations provided the perfect means to establish the actual working patterns of the train staff. it was Aldridge's suggestion to Hill to test the combined new team of robbers.

It had been noted by Aldridge's team that the ticket inspector and guard worked in unison. They always began checking tickets the moment the train departed Euston. Each time they had been observed, the two had started checking tickets together at the front of the train. They always took at least an hour to work their way back checking every passenger ticket before getting to the guard's compartment within the mail coach at the back of the train.

On this evening, Guard Howell was being assisted by his colleague, acting Ticket Inspector Thomas. The routine they followed was the usual one. Working together, starting at the front of the train, the guard set off first and knocked heavily on each compartment door, then threw it open sufficiently noisily to wake any sleeping passengers. Then he loudly asked passengers to have their tickets ready for inspection and moved on. The ticket inspector followed up a few seconds later, and quickly checked the tickets passengers held ready before moving on swiftly to other freshly roused passengers. This process saved the ticket inspector, valuable eating, drinking and card playing time.

But on this freezing night, when those with any sense, and any choice, would delay travel, passengers were few. The ticket inspector and guard moved swiftly towards the rear of the train. Examining tickets tonight had taken barely 20 minutes.

Bruce Reynolds and two more of the gang, Gordon Goody and Buster Edwards, were sitting comfortably in the first-class compartment at the rear of the train right next to the mail coach. They were there to prevent by whatever means, anyone interrupting the work of their accomplices next door. They were confident they had about another 40 minutes before any ticket inspection.

However, a heavy tap on the glass in the compartment door indicated that things were different tonight. The door was immediately pulled open. Guard Howell, a man of similar age to the robbers, happy to be early, spoke loudly to get their attention. "Evening, tickets ready for inspection please."

The robbers exchanged concerned glances. Guard Howell turned towards the mail coach, knowing Ticket Inspector Thomas was only seconds behind.

Bruce Reynolds looked at his watch. Guard Howell moved towards the mail coach door. Reynolds stood up quickly as the guard removed a '21 key' from his pocket. If Reynolds did not act decisively now, then within a second things would go irretrievably wrong.

As Reynolds took his first pace towards the unsuspecting guard, the ticket inspector called out from behind him. "Tickets please."

Reynolds spun around, Ticket Inspector Thomas, big, well-built and over 15 stone, was right up close to him with one foot in the compartment's doorway where Goody and Buster were still seated. Fortunately for the robbers, the Raiders team had, as normal, left the key in the lock on the inside of the mail coach door. Guard Howell struggled to get his key into the keyhole.

Reynolds checked his pockets and turned towards the ticket inspector. "Oh where did I put it, sorry about all this, I know I've got it somewhere."

Ticket Inspector Thomas gave the tall, elegantly dressed man time to search his pockets and instead turned his attention to the men inside the compartment. "Tickets please gentlemen."

Reynolds obligingly moved aside into the corridor to allow the ticket inspector to move into the passenger compartment. Within half a second, behind the ticket inspector, Reynolds signalled to Goody and Edwards, they immediately understood. Reynolds pushed the ticket inspector hard in the back. Ticket Inspector Thomas tumbled forward over the outstretched legs of Goody and Edwards. As he landed on the compartment floor Goody and Edwards set upon him with coshes. Reynolds immediately attacked the guard just a few feet away, who had been still facing the mail coach door and struggling to unlock it.

At that moment, the entire future of the gang and the planned major robbery was in jeopardy. If any other passenger, or steward, had seen the beaten and bloody railwaymen, the emergency cord would have been pulled and the train would have screeched to a halt. In the middle of the countryside, at night, in arctic temperatures, with over three feet of snow on the ground, lost and without transport, or lighting, probably miles from the nearest road and without means of communication, capture would have been very likely. Reynolds rapped furiously on the mail coach door.

Danny heard the knocking, but didn't think for one moment things had gone so wrong. Tom and Alfredo continued ripping open bags. Danny was irritated at the interruption and shouted. "What ya' want?"

Reynolds knew every second exposed them to additional risk of detection. "It's Bruce. For fuck's sake open up."

Danny put on a stocking mask and signalled to the others to do likewise, then quickly unlocked the door. The train guard, bleeding and semi-conscious, was pushed in. Then the ticket inspector, in the same state as his colleague, was dragged in by his ankles.

The opening of mailbags stopped. All eyes were on the injured. Danny was almost speechless. "What the fuck's happened?"
Reynolds was agitated. "Had no choice, they come back early."
Danny looked around urgently and pointed at a pile of torn mailbags. "Put 'em on the bags. "Tie 'em up, we still got work to do."

Alfredo felt sick at the sight of ordinary working men beaten senseless. This was the first time he had seen violence inflicted in the course of crime. Now, for the first time, he fully realised the nature of the work he was involved in, and he felt ashamed.

Reynolds, Goody and Edwards dragged Guard Howell and Ticket Inspector Thomas to the pile of ripped mailbags and threw them on top. They quickly tied their wrists and ankles with nylons they had brought as stocking masks. The ticket inspector's head was still bleeding profusely.

The two injured men barely conscious, whimpered in pain and fear. Gordon Goody put his hand in his jacket pocket and removed a handgun. He leant over the two injured men and shoved the barrel into one face and then the other. "Listen. Stop your fucking noise. I'll fuckin' blow you away if I 'ear another fuckin' murmur. Got it?"

A few seconds later, Alfredo heard one of the injured men groan, Danny's words echoed in his head, 'Never use more violence than you got to.'

Miles away, another part of the plan was falling into place. Bob Welch and two other drivers, had gone in separate cars to Hemel Hempstead

Station to check the time at which the target train passed by. They had a good vantage point in an empty car park overlooking the quiet station.

Once Bob Welch saw the train pass through, he would rush to a nearby telephone kiosk and relay the information to Roger, who was waiting with an accomplice at a phone box a few miles north near Tring.

Once Roger had the positive news from Bob, he and an accomplice would hurry to the railway signal and change the green light to red and then fix the signals emergency phone. It was a simple process. Roger had again brought a battery powered red light of the right shape and size. When the moment came he would cover the official green signal with a leather glove, and illuminate the red battery powered light.

Yet it was vitally important Roger timed the change of signals accurately. If he was too early, he would accidentally stop the preceding train. The target train would then be held at a distant signal. To prevent that happening, the Raiders always made sure the target train was on time and close to the right section of track before interfering with the signals.

On this occasion, the robbers on the train would need three large saloon cars for the getaway. This was the Raiders' first attempt to stop a TPO, though they had on many occasions stopped lesser mail trains at signals. There were 14 robbers involved that night. Not because the job required it, but because Billy was determined these men would get to know each other before the big event followed six months later.

As Bob Welch waited for the train to pass by Hemel Hempstead, things on the train were going terribly wrong. In the first-class restaurant car, two of the three stewards were washing up and completing their paperwork. The other steward, young Michael, just 21 years old, was still serving when a young soldier in uniform approached him.

The only two remaining diners, Freddie Sansom and another robber, were lingering over their coffees, listening and watching. The steward looked at the soldier. "Sorry, first-class passengers only, but I'll be round to second class a bit later with the tray."

The soldier shook his head. He looked concerned. "No. Sorry. We don't stop at Crewe do we?"

Young Michael felt sorry for the man in military uniform. "Sorry mate, next stop Holyhead."

The young soldier looked crestfallen. "Is there any chance you could get it to stop at Crewe?"

Michael wanted to help, but was powerless. "I don't know, don't think so."

The young soldier could see he might have to accept an undeserved Army punishment for being late. "The bloke at Euston told me it stopped at Crewe. If I'm late back I'll be in real trouble."

Michael couldn't do anything. "Best you speak to the guard."

Michael looked at his watch. "He should have been here by now."

A few feet away, at a first-class dining table covered in white linen, Len Tappy, the most senior steward on board, completed his paperwork, put his pen down and drained his coffee cup. He had overheard the exchange and told the soldier he would walk to the back of the train with him and explain to the guard. Behind them, Freddie and his sidekick heard it all.

Len and the soldier headed off. Freddie and Jim drained their glasses and followed a coach length behind.

Now there were no passengers left in the dining car, Michael went to the kitchen area where the third steward was still cleaning. Michael prepared to take refreshments to the passengers travelling second class. As he did so, he explained what had taken place to his remaining colleague.

Perhaps just to avoid further cleaning, perhaps just to escape the dining coach for five minutes, the other steward told Michael he was going to join Len. So, two coaches behind Freddie Sansom and his accomplice, another steward headed towards the rear of the train.

Inside the mail coach, Alfredo stopped slitting bags and checked on the injured and bound railway men. One of them was face down in the mailbags with blood bubbling from the corner of his mouth. Concerned he might suffocate, Alfredo rolled the more badly injured man onto his side. Reynolds noticed. "What the fuck you doin?"

Alfredo responded in a similar tone. "Just checkin' on these fuckers."

Chief Steward Len and the soldier moved swiftly through the train and were well ahead of those who followed. Len knocked hard at the mail brake door. "Hugh. Open up, it's Len."

The robbers froze. Danny moved silently towards the door, Alfredo followed close behind. Danny unlocked the door in a flash and pulled Len into the mail coach by the lapels. Len understood within a split second and pulled back hard enough to create sufficient space to take a mighty swing at Danny. Danny avoided the punch. Len had all his body weight behind it and lurched forward. Alfredo, keen to get in on the action, and standing right up close behind Danny, had no sight of the punch arriving. It landed on Alfredo's nose. Danny immediately elbowed Len sideways before pummelling him with his cosh. But the soldier was determined to take the robbers on. Perhaps he thought it would be two against two. He struck Alfredo another heavy blow, Alfredo was knocked back into the mail coach and the soldier followed in.

So now the soldier was in the mail van he could see he was in the presence of a dozen violent men and three badly beaten railwaymen. He made for the doorway, desperate to reach the emergency cord situated over the passenger door a few feet away. But Alfredo was equally determined to stop him and a fight ensued in the narrow doorway of the coach. In that very confined space the soldier could only be attacked from one direction.

Yet Alfredo's fight in the doorway lasted no more time than it took for him to regain his senses. He parried another heavy punch from the soldier, feigned a body blow, and as the soldier dropped his guard, Alfredo struck him a clean punch on the jaw. The soldier fell backwards into the passenger coach.

Behind the soldier, Freddie and another robber were approaching fast from the rear. They scooped the soldier up easily and within seconds he joined the other prisoners tied hand and foot. Two of the robbers were shouting loudly, out of control. One of them threatened to kill the young soldier, it was pandemonium. The robbers' brains were in overdrive, having to capture so many members of the train crew had not been contemplated. Perhaps that was why the robbers forgot to relock the mail coach door.

Who knows why Alfredo thought of it. But the second he did, he moved quickly to lock it, but at the very moment at the moment he reached for the door handle, a third steward entered. He breezed in as if he were the last to arrive at a terrific party. But this was not an experience the like of which he, or any of his colleagues, had ever imagined. He had trouble processing the information his eyes fed him – right in front of him stood a stocking masked figure, behind were other robbers, blood, torn mailbags, colleagues beaten and tied. He was terror struck.

Alfredo had also been taken by surprise and had frozen. The steward turned to run, he needed to escape, raise the alarm, pull the emergency cord.

Alfredo sprinted down the passenger coach and caught up with the steward before he reached the eyes of a single passenger.

Who knows what that steward thought was going to happen to him. But he wasn't going to be passively escorted back to the mail coach. The ensuing fight was short and furious, and Alfredo's opponent bled heavily as he was dragged to join his colleagues.

Alfredo had inflicted harm on others before. As a boy growing up on a council estate in south London, fights were commonplace. And he had been boxing for 11 years and seen blood flow from his opponents many times. But this was different. His stomach churned. He hated it.

Alfredo's prisoner, beaten, bloodied and tied, was dumped with the others. Alfredo watched.

Meanwhile, young Michael Carey, the twenty-one-year-old steward still in the restaurant car, was wondering where on earth everyone had gone. He had to find out so he locked the dining car and kitchen and headed down the train.

Inside the mail coach, order had been restored and the robbers' search for high-value mailbags continued. Seventeen high-value 'inners' had been found so far, and the robbers' holdall was nearly full. They were working in silence, each alone with their thoughts. Alfredo's nose was still bleeding and he could feel the swelling and pain from his injured lips. The light was poor, but he could clearly see the mixed blood of others and his own on his clothing and skin. He felt disgraced, dirty, inside and out.

With the bleeding prisoners fully subdued and silent in fear for their lives, things had gone quiet, the train was making the only noise apart from the occasional 'rip' of a mailbag.

Then the unimaginable happened. Another knock at the door. Then a muted voice. "Is everything OK?"

Young Michael had no idea where all his colleagues had gone or what they might be doing, but there was nowhere else they could be. Alfredo and the rest of the gang immediately stopped work again. But before any of the South Coast Raiders had time to think of the best response, one of their accomplices shouted. "It's alright it's the police, now fuck off."

You didn't need to be a very experienced villain to know the remark was truly stupid. Alfredo's heart raced, he knew more trouble was certain to follow. Some others made furious gestures at the offender, but it was too late. He had said the words, and the response wasn't long in coming.

Within 20 seconds, every robber was thrown to the floor with the force of inertia. The emergency cord had been pulled and the train brakes firmly applied. Alfredo was first back to his feet. The train was still moving but now at barely more than walking pace. Alfredo wiped the condensation from a small window and stared out, but he could see nothing but blackness. He rushed to the other side of the coach and looked out. It was the same, no street lights, no car lights, no light from buildings and no moonlight. He felt panic rise in his stomach; outside was a frozen wilderness. He felt lost in all senses.

Yet he knew to escape the train now was his only chance. He turned from the window towards the nearby external doors. It was now or never, he would have to jump before the train actually stopped, and other passengers or the driver or his 'mate', showed an interest in events. With luck, Alfredo thought, he could get far enough away from the train not be seen when it stopped.

In that moment, he detected a flash of light pass by the window. He turned his attention to the window again and forced his face tight to the glass. He glimpsed a signal box as the train passed by. Then he saw street lights, the train was still moving forward, but it was approaching a station. Alfredo called to the other robbers, they turned away from their captives. Two robbers struggled to quickly fasten a bulging holdall, while others raced to place loot in their coat pockets.

Seconds later the train stopped, members of the gang jostled to throw open the doors. Suddenly they were free. Alfredo barely noticed the station name, Hemel Hempstead. They ran blindly to the exit. It was an unscheduled stop, and the train driver and station staff still had no idea what had taken place.

Bob Welch and Roy James were sitting together in Bob's car enjoying a cigarette while waiting for the train to pass through. Something had gone wrong. Roy James climbed from the car and returned to his own. Both getaway drivers started their engines.

The robbers rushed from the station exit. they saw two cars flashing their headlights, Danny shouted. "This way, quick."

The high-powered saloon cars were quick off the mark before slowing to pick them up. The ten men and large bulging holdall didn't fit easily, even into a Mark 10 Jaguar and a Humber Sceptre. Danny threw himself into the seat next to Bob Welch. In the back, Alfredo scrambled in on top of three others. This was the lead car, the other followed close behind. Danny's first words to Bob, "Phone box."

In the time taken for the station staff to understand what had taken place, to phone the police, and for the police to get a vehicle to begin the journey to the station, the robbers had gone. They hadn't raced off like madmen. To race away was simply to bring unwanted attention.

It took 3 minutes later, for the getaway cars to reach a phone kiosk. Danny made a swift call to a waiting Roger Cordery, and they agreed a rendezvous. The two getaway cars drove off, one minute apart. Less than ten minutes later, just as the first uniformed constable arrived at Hemel Hempstead station, the robbers were more comfortably divided amongst four cars.

On the journey south, Tom passed a bottle of whisky around the car. Alfredo poured a good amount into a handkerchief and wiped the blood from his face, ears, hair and hands.

Thirty minutes later they were in North London. It was about 10.30pm but it seemed to Alfredo the night had been endless. Each man was dropped off quickly and quietly, singly or in twos.

The plan was for everyone to make their way to the Glenrae Hotel. But Alfredo, who was the most injured and bloodstained, easily convinced Danny he should go straight home. He borrowed Roger Cordrey's overcoat and scarf to cover his blood-stained clothing and took a cab the last leg.

As always, he stopped a couple of hundred yards from his home, though he couldn't wait to close the front door behind him. He approached the block of flats wearily and cautiously. First, he went to the rear. All was silent. The only noise was the crackle of the icy pavement beneath his feet. He looked up, the light was on in the bathroom and the aspidistra was 'centred', all seemed well.

Alfredo made his weary way up to the flat hoping she would be asleep. He didn't want her to see him like this. He knocked gently on the bolted door. She called softly. "That you?" His lips were puffy, he took a deep breath and tried hard to sound normal, but it was impossible. "Yeah, me Love."

She hesitated, then unbolted in silence. There were no lights on in the small hallway, and it suited Alfredo perfectly. He kicked his shoes off and undid Roger's overcoat, keen to get stripped and washed. He tiptoed across the sitting room and almost reached the small hall on his way to the bathroom before she spoke again. She had switched the television off an hour before and was now sitting alone in the dark with only her anxieties for company. She called gently. "You alright Love?"

Alfredo didn't want to worry her, and he didn't want her nagging him either. He turned back to the sitting room. "Fine, just let me get washed." But before he could escape to the privacy of the bathroom, Shirley flicked on the sitting room light. She stared at him, her hand went to her mouth, she frowned with lack of comprehension and started to shake. Fresh blood was smeared between his nose and mouth, his lips were torn and swollen, he had dried blood in his eyebrows and sideburns, one of his eyes was bloodshot and puffy. The open overcoat was not his, and beneath, she could see blood on his shirt. The small amount of colour she had in her pale face drained. Alfredo took it all in before he spoke wearily. "It's OK, I'm alright."

He tried to escape to the bathroom, but she stopped him. She held his arms, looked at his damaged face and examined his damaged hands and his blood-stained clothes. Her stomach turned over. She had never been more concerned about her husband and their future. Her heart was racing and her mouth was dry. He let her hold him without resisting.
"What happened?" She whispered.
"Nothin', just a bit of a scrap, everything's okay, honest."
Shirley shook her head. "Scrap? Who with?"
Alfredo looked away. "I was workin', weren't I?"
Her voice was still calm, worried. "This big job? It's over then?"
He could hardly bring himself to answer her. "No. It was a sort of dummy run."

Shirley could see Alfredo was not only hurt, but seemed somehow disappointed, and it scared her. But it wasn't disappointment, it was shame. Now she was certain, Alfredo's life of crime had to stop right then and there. They had paid their debts, had a well-furnished home, a few bob in the bank and enough money to buy a house. But more than that, she was terrified he was being swept away to his own destruction and the end of their lives together.
She spoke gently. "Dummy run? Is that a joke?"
Alfredo managed a pretend smile.

# Chapter 30

Meanwhile, concealed in the basement bar at the Glenrae Hotel in North London, the mood of the gang members was mixed – anger, exhilaration, relief and self-congratulation. Unspent adrenalin was still coursing through their blood. Within a few minutes the robbers were all seated with a drink – whisky, tea, beer.

The twins were eager to find out how the rehearsal had gone. The mood of the gathering was clearly very mixed. Yes, the outcome had been good; they had all escaped arrest and made off with a decent profit. But the Raiders could barely keep their anger in check. The shock of the early return of the guard and ticket inspector, the extent of unnecessary violence, the number of prisoners they had to take, the shock discovery at least one of the combined team was carrying a gun, and threatening to use it, the idiocy of someone pretending to be a policeman, followed by his shouting, "Fuck off."

It was only as a result of extremely good luck the train stopped at a station rather than in the frozen, snow-laden fields. It was all so nearly a disaster.

The Raiders made all these points strongly, and two sides quickly formed. None of the Raiders had been responsible for any of the above, and the guilty parties did not like the criticism.

The Krays were incapable of playing the role of mediators, but the situation forced them to become referees. Keeping the combined team together and under orders was, after all, their primary function. It now seemed a very difficult task indeed.

The errors were of two sorts: those of individuals during the robbery, and those which arose from poor planning. The Raiders made it clear, if the Krays had set the job up they had to account for the poor planning. But of course, that was impossible. They had no idea how any of the planning had been done. All they could do was bluff and bluster. Eventually, Reggie suggested they postpone the debrief until everyone had calmed down. He suggested they concentrate on sharing the loot.

The robbers and the twins sat around an open area in the bar, a table was hurriedly pulled away to create a space and the holdall, and pockets were emptied into a pile.

The jewellery, cash, blank chequebooks, savings stamps, and other items of monetary value formed one pile, legal documents, items of personal but little intrinsic value formed the other. The latter would be incinerated in the next couple of hours.

The twins were keen to hold on to as much of the loot as they could in order to do the 'fencing'. But the Raiders had no inclination to trust them, after all, the Raiders had their own very secure means of selling items on. Tom explained he had a reliable contact who had proven very effective at turning virtually anything into cash.

Finding a trustworthy, reliable fence who was not a police informant had been vital to them. But the more the Raiders insisted their man would get the best price for virtually anything, the more the twins dug their heels in. Tom offered a suggestion. "Look, I'll take all the jewellery and see what my bloke thinks. You take the chequebooks and stamps."

Perhaps because the poor planning had made them seem incompetent, but for whatever reason, the twins now seemed determined to show their authority.

Reggie rejected Tom's offer. "No offence Tom, we'd rather deal with your bloke face to face. Bring him over."
But Tom wouldn't expose his fence. "He don't work like that."

It seemed they had reached an impasse. There was a natural break while Reggie went for a fresh bottle of scotch. But opening a fresh bottle didn't deliver a solution. In the end, fed up with intransigence, the Raiders persuaded the Krays to split the property immediately.

Alfredo was mentioned more than once. It was a name the Krays had not heard before, and in the end they asked the obvious question.
Danny responded evenly. "Yeah, he's been working with us a while."
Ronnie nodded. "Better bring him over so we can have a look at 'im."
Danny felt protective towards the young man, especially around the twins. "No need. He's one of our firm and sound."
Reggie chimed in. "We don't know him. Bring him over, what harm?"

Danny knew a refusal would create more problems than it solved. He shrugged. "Alright, I'll tell him."

Once the twins were on their own again, Reggie, as instructed, phoned Billy's flat in Marylebone. Billy had been out for the evening with Lady Docker, a close friend and famous socialite and he had only returned an hour before to await the call. When the phone rang he was drinking tea and listening to his record player. The call was brief and followed a security routine Billy insisted his professional contacts complied with. Reggie didn't announce himself, he simply said. "It's me."
Billy's answer was similarly brief. "Okay."

They both hung up. Billy put on his heavy Cashmere overcoat, trilby, gloves and scarf and left the flat. It was freezing. He walked past two public kiosks and entered the third. Meanwhile, in the East End, Reggie got dressed against the weather and went to a phone kiosk. Within a few minutes, the phone rang at Reggie's end.
"All OK?
"Sort of. They got the result but nearly scored a couple of own goals."
"We need a meet?"
"Yeah. They got a few beefs."
"Alright, lunch tomorrow, same place as last time. I want to know it all."


The following day, the twins gave a full account and described all the Raiders' complaints.

Billy had already made it plain to the Krays, the valuation and division of the loot on the rehearsal was trivial compared to the big prize awaiting. The most important thing was to learn lessons in time for the 'big one'. Now, to his annoyance, he found himself reminding them.

Billy told the Krays to pass the message that all other jobs were to be put on hold. After all, it was now vital none of the train gang got captured.

In reality, the planning errors put at Billy's door truly belonged at Aldridge's. That same day, Billy explained to Aldridge very clearly, that his lack of foresight had nearly cost them all very dearly. Aldridge knew he had been lucky to escape punishment, if it had come, it would have been quick and extreme. But for now, Billy needed him.

# Chapter 31

Surrounded by the furniture and fittings of a well-equipped office, dressed in smart blue suits, ties and shiny shoes, the twins were sitting in leather easy chairs sipping tea from bone china cups and talking about business opportunities. Interrupted by a knock at the door, 'Bomber', a hugely overweight man of about 50, poked his head in. "Excuse me Ron, Reg, that Alf Reed bloke is 'ere."

Ronnie smirked at Bomber, and glanced at his brother. "Who?"

Bomber suddenly looked nervous and shifted the weight on his feet.

Ronnie grinned. "Keep him downstairs for now and send in that ponce, Hewitt."

Bomber nodded and left.

Reggie chuckled. "Fucking 'Alf Reed', I told him, Alfredo."

His brother shook his head. "Bomber's got a heart of gold, his mum told me. She didn't mention he's as thick as pigs' shit."

They sneered, both the twins finished their tea simultaneously and moved to office chairs behind a large desk.

There was another knock at the door before Bomber pushed it open and ushered in a middle-aged man who had the manner and dress of a bank clerk. Bomber left without speaking.

Ronnie and Reggie looked up from their chairs, smiling. Hewitt stood nervously by the door waiting for instructions. Ronnie pointed casually to a vacant seat facing the desk. "Come and sit over 'ere and take your jacket, shirt and tie off."

Hewitt's expression changed, now he looked terrified. "Oh Ron, can't I just stand 'ere?"

The smile vanished from the twins' faces, Ronnie frowned. "No. I fuckin' told ya, or are you goin' wind me up?"

Hewitt moved slowly to the vacant chair and sat nervously on its edge. Visibly shaking, he pleaded. "No, Ron, sorry, I got the money ready, just gotta collect it. Can I get it now?"

Ronnie took a Senior Service cigarette from his silver cigarette case and offered one to Reggie, he declined. He studied Hewitt as he removed a cigarette lighter from his jacket pocket. Ronnie's eyes were fixed on the man opposite. At last he lit the cigarette and blew a perfect smoke ring. "Too fuckin' late now my son. It ain't the money, it's the principle." Ronnie was building himself into a rage. "Do you know anythin' about leadership?"

Hewitt was shaking and sweating. "No Ron."

Ronnie mimicked, "'No Ron'. Well, if you're leading people, they gotta know you means what you says, otherwise ya fucked. I'll tell ya, anythin' else results in ill-discipline and fuckin' disorganisation. And you can't run a firm like that, can ya?"

The sweat was running down Hewitt's face. "I'm sorry, let me go get the money."

Ronnie's expression was of someone staring at vomit. "You're fuckin' clueless. If we let you take the piss, what you reckon other people gonna think?"

Hewitt didn't answer. Ronnie stood up and moved around to the front of his desk, Hewitt was sitting in front of him. "Did you fuckin' hear me?" Hewitt was terrified. "Don't know Ron."

Reggie sat back watching with amusement, Ronnie looked ready to explode. "Don't know? Course you fuckin' do. You must think I'm some sort of cunt."

Hewitt was trembling and sweating, his eyes fixed on the carpet in front of him.

Ronnie moved closer. "I told you five minutes ago to get your shirt off. But have ya? No. Still you ain't learned to do as you're told."

Hewitt slowly got to his feet and reluctantly removed his jacket and tie, both fell to the floor, then he began unbuttoning his shirt. It was drenched in sweat. Ronnie didn't like the slow pace, he was too excited, his pleasure and excitement building too rapidly. "Get your shirt off now or I'll have you bollock naked."

Hewitt seemed to revert to infancy. He stood with his shoulders drooped, staring at some point on the floor and started to cry. Ronnie picked up Hewitt's tie and walked towards the door and opened it. He shouted out. "Bomber, get Alfredo up 'ere now."

Within seconds Alfredo entered wearing the sort of smile you might when going for a job interview. But it transformed when he saw the back view of a half-dressed man and heard the sobbing. As Bomber closed the door behind Alfredo, Ronnie studied the necktie, walked around to Hewitt's back, placed it over Hewitt's head and tightened it around

Hewitt's throat. Hewitt's hands instinctively went to his throat to pull the tie clear of his airway. But Ronnie's strength was much the greater and his grip immoveable. Hewitt's fear of imminent death overcame his fear of the twins and he struggled violently. Hewitt's eyes bulged, his white face turned red, the sweat ran even faster down his face, arms and his back. He couldn't get air into his lungs, his legs began to buckle.

Ronnie released the tie and began beating Hewitt with his fists, Hewitt slumped to the floor and curled up in a ball. He was crying, gasping, urinating and bathed in sweat. Ronnie took a pace back and studied the man on the carpet. Alfredo was standing as if paralysed. Ronnie turned to Alfredo and smiled benignly. "You must be Alf Reid then?"

Alfredo looked completely confused with it all. The twins laughed hysterically like madmen, but Alfredo's senses were fixed on Hewitt. Reggie spoke almost inaudibly. "Don't worry about him. He ain't dead."
His brother picked up on the comment. "In fact, he'll be a better man for the experience."
Reggie responded to his brother, ignoring Alfredo. "Yeah, whether he lives or dies."
The twins laughed again. Hewitt was still in a ball on the floor whimpering, eyes closed firmly, still shaking with fear and shock.

Ronnie went to a table and poured three glasses of scotch. He took one to his brother, and a second to Alfredo. He studied the contents of his own glass, then looked up at Alfredo. "So, Alfredo. We've heard all about you. Danny and the boys rate you, that don't come cheap."

Alfredo tore his eyes from Hewitt and was trying to get back into 'interview' mode despite Hewitt. "Thank you."
Ronnie took a sip. "They tell me you're a useful middleweight?"
Alfredo found himself saying. "Nothing special."
Ronnie patted Alfredo on the shoulder. "Modest. I like that Reg. Handsome bastard too."

Ronnie's eyes remained focused on Alfredo's face for several seconds before he turned to Hewitt again. Ronnie pointed with his glass of scotch. "This turd let us down. You have to be able to rely on people. Know how important that is Alfredo?"
Alfredo nodded. "Definitely Mr Kray."
Ronnie liked Alfredo's courtesy. "I'm Ronnie, that's Reg."

Alfredo glanced politely at Reggie, and returned his gaze to the other twin. "Yes, Ronnie."

Ronnie nodded with approval. "We gotta know we can always rely on you to follow orders Alfredo."

By now, Alfredo would have agreed to follow the orders of the devil himself. "For certain you can."

Ronnie put his whisky down and picked up the discarded tie again. "Good, but words is cheap."

Ronnie handed the tie to Alfredo. "So, your turn."

Alfredo looked at Hewitt on the floor, then at the stretched tie in his hands...

# Chapter 32

The four hundred acres of Regent's Park were snow covered and icy, the trees and shrubs looked forlorn. Apart from the odd dog walker, the park was virtually empty. Roy and Shirley were sitting on a bench wrapped up warmly against the freezing conditions. Roy had brought a flask and sandwiches. Since he had arrived in London, Roy had been busy learning about how the mailbag team went about its work, and about London and its policing habits. But more recently, he had been secretly researching the information Shirley had provided.

He had done weeks of observations with his colleagues; they had arrested a train guard, and a postman, and a homeless man who had stolen a mailbag from a mail barrow at Victoria station. But they had come nowhere near the Raiders, and the high-value thefts from the mail trains continued.

Over the last few days, the violent Irish Mail train robbery had created a growing stir. The newspapers had splashed stories about it across their pages, and the pressure on the mailbag squad to get results had grown yet again. Aldridge made it known to his detectives he was protecting them from their bosses, who were insisting heads would roll unless they quickly solved the mailbags problem.

According to Aldridge, the BTP bosses didn't have a clue about anything. "They can hardly find their way home on their own" … "They couldn't find their own arses using both hands" … "They couldn't find a whore on a summer's night at Kings Cross."

But, apart from the hassle, and having additional officers, life within the mailbag squad had continued very much as always. Of course, it didn't matter to Aldridge. Once the 'big one' was over and he got his share, he intended to see out his time in the Force and a few years later retire on full pension and disappear into obscurity and a very luxurious retirement. Alternatively, if he got blamed for the 'big one' it would give him the perfect opportunity to 'resign as a matter of principle.' That would suit him even better.

The latest theory, as instigated and encouraged by Aldridge, proposed the South Coast Raiders, who sections of the press were also calling, the

Red Light Gang, were not responsible for any great number of the thefts. Instead, encouraged by the numerous newspaper reports indicating how easy it was to steal mailbags, numerous individuals and small gangs were now operating,

Roy hadn't been immune to such propaganda. Just because Shirley had given him reason to believe she had inside knowledge about the Brighton job, he had no reason to conclude she really had access to vital information about another, bigger, crime. And even though she had inside knowledge of the Brighton job, it had not led to any further arrests. Afterall, there was overwhelming evidence against the young Scotsman, and Shirley had admitted she had never heard of him.

But the Irish Mail train robbery had changed things, and Roy wondered if this was the big job Shirley had been talking about. Suddenly her information made some sense.

As they sat on the park bench, Shirley was preoccupied too. Thanks to the newspaper reports, she was now well aware of who and where Alfredo had been fighting that night in late February. She now knew whose blood it was all over his clothes when he arrived home, and she knew armed robbery carried a life sentence.

Roy thought about the woman sitting next to him. "We're all working twelve hours."

Shirley seemed completely unimpressed and just nodded.

Roy went on. "Gang robbed the Irish mail train. Suppose you seen it in the papers?"

Shirley nodded lightly, as if it was nothing to do with her or anyone she might know.

Roy took another bite from his sandwich. Shirley was keen to change the subject, "From what I'm told the job is going to be worth over a million quid."

Roy smiled. "Don't sound right, I don't think there's a train carries that much. Even the Irish Mail had nothing like that."

Shirley didn't like being taken lightly. "Listen, do I strike you as a bloody idiot?"

Her sudden change of mood brought Roy to his senses. "No."

Shirley spat back. "Well check it out then."

Silence prevailed for a minute while both recovered from the outburst. Roy took another bite of his sandwich. "Got any names, likely dates, anything?"

Shirley. "No. But I will. You know who the Krays are now then?" She smirked at him, determined to stay in control.

Roy finished his sandwich. "Yeah I always knew."

Shirley smiled. "Yeah right."

# Chapter 33

Usually, the Raiders would not meet together socially, especially in the West End, or South London. They knew for every successful thief there were at least a hundred locals who would tip off the police. The reasons varied: money, revenge, jealousy, spite, piety, or even a sense of public duty, but the result was the same irrespective of motive.

Tonight Freddie, Danny and Alfredo were making an exception. They were going to meet in a famously fashionable West End nightclub and casino. Freddie and Danny had dressed as expensively and stylishly as their fellow guests. They drank Krug Vintage champagne like lemonade on a hot day. They picked at caviar hors d'oeuvres and placed individual bets of a hundred pounds and more.

Fully immersed in the scene, they were unrecognisable as common thieves. It all intoxicated the robbers, in such company they were part of another world. Danny and Freddie were standing together at the roulette wheel. Freddie looked at his watch. "Said I'd meet Alfredo at Binxie's 'bout now."

Danny saw no pleasure in remaining in the casino without company. "Yeah? Why's that then?"

Freddie was watching the spin of the wheel. "He promised the Krays he'd pop in their place and have a drink."

Danny wasn't following his logic. "And?"

Freddie sipped champagne and smiled conspiratorially. "I told him not to drag the bastards back 'ere with him. Told him to tell 'em he had to leave 'cos he was meetin' me at Binxies. Twins ain't exactly welcome there are they?"

Danny smiled and nodded. "You bringin' Alfredo back?"

Freddie finished the glass. "That's the plan. Better go. See you in half an hour."

At about the same time, in a posh flat in Marylebone, Ronnie was sitting up in bed with a slim, olive-skinned teenage boy next to him. Both were naked. The boy was lying on his side, facing away from the older man. Both looked unhappy. Ronnie was smoking a cigarette. Agitated, he looked at his

Patek Philippe wristwatch. "You might just as well go. Yeah, go on, piss off out of it, I'm fuckin' bored. Go on, fuck off before I crown ya."

Almost in tears, the teenager climbed out of bed, picked up his clothes and walked to the bathroom. Ronnie jumped out of bed, took his clothes from a wardrobe and dressed quickly - smart dark suit, fresh shirt, tie, and black shiny shoes. He went to the mirror, checked his appearance, smoothed down his hair and left without speaking.

Meanwhile, Alfredo arrived at the Krays' club in the West End. He knew he could not decline the invitation indefinitely. Better, he thought, to pay him a quick courtesy visit and get it over with. But of course, Ronnie had other ideas.

Reggie welcomed him like an old friend. He took him to the Krays' table, champagne was quickly served. They sat together and chatted. Alfredo was nervous, he didn't like the company and was aware he had already looked at his watch too often. There was a Blues singer called Long John Baldry performing, and he didn't sound at all bad. But Alfredo couldn't relax and enjoy it.

Ronnie arrived from the flat at Marylebone and came straight to the table. He smiled at his twin and Alfredo, and sat down close to his guest. "Good to see you, Alfredo. How are you?"

The twins played the attentive hosts for a while and Alfredo started to relax a little. Alfredo managed a smile, Ronnie felt a surge of sexual excitement.

The two waitresses were instructed to come by their table once every few minutes, and they never failed to do so. They were well motivated with carrot and stick - good pay and harsh punishments.

Within a minute, Ronnie had ordered a fresh bottle of Dom Perignon. Within another minute, the waitress had opened the chilled bottle and Ronnie was passing a glass to Alfredo.

It was easy for Ronnie to do it, after all, there was no reason for Alfredo to be watching closely, he had no reason to. Ronnie dropped two little pink tablets into Alfredo's drink and beneath the bubbles in the half-light of the club they seemed to dissolve immediately.

Alfredo was keen to lose his nerves, keen to be good company for a short a while before making his excuses and leaving for Binxies. He downed the champagne as if quenching a thirst. Ronnie smiled and graciously poured him another. Reggie left the table, there were people arriving he wanted to welcome personally.

A few minutes later, Alfredo felt was suddenly overcome with tiredness, he could hardly keep his eyes open. Soon the room seemed to be spinning, the music seemed distorted and was fading. Ronnie studied him closely. "Hey, you alright Alfredo?... Alfredo?"

Alfredo tried to respond, but he couldn't form the words. Ronnie helped him to his feet.

Alfredo was vaguely aware of being helped along a short corridor, then into a room marked private, then across an office. He began to lose consciousness. He was dragged on through an unmarked door and onto a bed where he lay on his back, completely unconscious.

Ronnie locked the door of this his most private room. The walls were painted a dark shade of red. Large, framed, black and white photographs of naked boys and young men filled three of the walls. The bed was at least six foot six inches wide and had a large mirrored headboard. The wall opposite and the ceiling were entirely mirrored. Opposite the bed, just inside the door, a drinks cabinet displayed various spirits, mixers and three spirit glasses. A bottle of champagne had been opened, covered, and placed in an ice bucket. Three chilled champagne flutes awaited use.

Ronnie smiled, removed his jacket and looked down at Alfredo. Ronnie took the cigarettes and lighter from his jacket pocket and placed them on the drinks cabinet. Then he continue to undress, slowly.

His excitement was already evident when, naked, he went to a record player and moved its arm to the record spinning on the turntable. Within a second, Louis Armstrong sang, 'Mack The Knife.'

Ronnie licked his lips, stared again at the young man on the bed, lit a cigarette and took a deep drag. He went to the drinks cabinet and poured himself champagne and took a sip. From the small wardrobe, he removed a camera tripod and set it up at the foot of the bed. Then he went to one of the bedside tables, opened a drawer and removed a camera.

Another sip of champagne, and he fitted the camera to the tripod and returned to the bedside drawers and removed four long pieces of red silk and a tub of Vaseline. He removed Alfredo's jacket, shoes, socks, and tie and took photographs. He took Alfredo's trousers off, leaving him naked but for his 'Y' fronts. "Mack The Knife" had ended and the record player now generated only a repetitive 'click....click.' But Ronnie was oblivious, totally engrossed in his passion. More photographs, another sip of champagne. Then he knocked the long ash from the cigarette which had been wasting on an ashtray, and took another quick drag.

Ronnie brought a deep red velvet footstool from the corner of the room. He pulled Alfredo's body to the edge of the bed and placed the stool in the centre. Then he rolled Alfredo onto the low stool. He was now face down with the stool supporting his hips. More photos, a final drag and he extinguished the cigarette.

A light knock at the door. Ronnie was expecting it, and opened it quickly. A distinguished-looking man in evening dress, perhaps sixty years of age, smiled and nodded as he entered . He spoke with an aristocratic drawl. "Oh Ronnie dear, you've started without me."

Ronnie smiled back. "No, just a bit of preparation, that's all."

The elderly man smiled as he stared at his victim and started to undress. Ronnie poured him champagne. Naked, the newcomer moved closer to the unconscious young man in front of him. He ran his hand over Alfredo's calf. "Where did you find him? He looks delicious."

Ronnie didn't answer, he was busying himself. The old man took another sip of champagne. Both men moved onto the bed.

Less than a mile away, Freddie was getting fed up with waiting. He had only agreed to come to 'Binxie's', a 'spieler' (a drinking club and unlawful gambling place), in order to help Alfredo out. He looked at his watch. Alfredo had practically begged him to meet him tonight, and now he hadn't even bothered to show.

Freddie was all dressed up with his pockets full of cash and more than ready to have some fun. He was about to abandon Alfredo and get back to the casino when he spotted another well-known South London 'face.' Freddie hadn't seen this man since his release from prison, and he was delighted to have someone he respected to drink with while he waited. Jack Mullins was in his late fifties, a legend, and the son of a legend of the same name.

They shook hands, exchanged pleasantries and immediately started to take the piss out of each other. Jack asked what Freddie was up to. Of course he didn't mean 'professionally', that would have been inappropriate. Freddie talked about Brighton and his brothers, then mentioned he was working with some local boys at Jack's old game. Jack looked amused. "Which game is that then?"

Freddie scratched his head and smiled back. "Well Jack, they reckon you've emptied more fuckin' sacks than Father Christmas."
Jack smiled. "You got the wrong bloke Fred."

Freddie smiled back and changed the subject. "How long you been out? GBH weren't it?"

Jack was enjoying the banter. "All I done was slap this geezer across the 'ead with a bunch of flowers. Five years I got. Justice? I ask ya!"

Freddie was happy to play along. "Five years? Hit him with flowers? Seems harsh."

Jack had told the joke a hundred times before. "Yeah, well they were in a concrete pot!"

They both laughed.

Jack Mullins had been stealing mailbags all his life and had never been caught. He'd been found in possession of property stolen from the mails and pleaded guilty to handling. He had been locked up for 'causing grievous bodily harm', 'wounding with intent' and illegal bookmaking. But neither Old Bill nor the Post Office investigators had ever known the truth. Perhaps it was because Jack always worked alone, always kept it simple, always used caution and always kept his lips sealed.

Freddie looked at his watch. "S'posed to meet one of the team in 'ere, he ain't showed."

Jack was interested. "Anyone I knows?"

Freddie shook his head dismissively. "Nah, young Italian kid. Got invited over to Gert and Daisy's place down the road, he wanted an excuse to get away sharpish, knew they wouldn't follow him in 'ere."

Jack nodded wisely. "That pair of bleeders? Wise boy."

Freddie took a sip. "Course. You had a run in wiv' 'em didn't you Jack?

Jack smiled, "No, we didn't have no 'run in', they tried to come it and I fucked them off out of it... So you ain't worried about this young lad then? With the Krays I mean."

Freddie thought for a moment. "I s'pose I'd better walk round. Make sure he's still a virgin."

Jack gave a devilish grin. "Just let me finish me gold watch and I'll be wiv ya."

Back at the Krays' club, Reggie had noticed the absence of his twin and was starting to get a little nervous. The twins knew one another's appetites intimately, and also the amount of impetuosity each was capable of. Reggie couldn't stand it any longer, he had a quick look around the public part of the club and there was no sign of Alfredo or his brother. He walked briskly to the private office and found it empty. More concerned now, he went to the private 'lounge'. The door was locked. Reggie knocked. "Ronnie, it's me, open up."

Inside, Alfredo was still unconscious, silk scarves now bound each wrist and ankle to the four corners of the bed. More photos had been taken, more champagne consumed, on the gramophone 'The Platters' were singing softly, 'My Prayer.'

Ronnie was behind the camera and the old man, naked but for a leather hood and mask, was in a state of arousal on the bed next to Alfredo. In his hand he held a Stanley knife.

Ronnie called out to his brother. "I'm busy. See you later."

The old man took the Stanley knife and gently cut through both sides of Alfredo's 'Y' fronts. Then he gently exposed Alfredo's buttocks. Ronnie took more photographs.

Reggie raised his voice. "Ronnie, I needs to speak to ya right now."

Ronnie ignored it.

Reggie was agitated. If Alfredo was raped or injured, a bust up with the Raiders was sure to follow, and then a war with Billy, a prospect too awful to contemplate. "You got Alfredo in there?... Alfredo?...Alfredo you in there?"

But Ronnie only had ears for the gentle harmonies of the Platters. Reggie shouted. "Ronnie let me in."

Still there was no response. Reggie waited a few more seconds, he was sweating now and his mind was racing. He threw himself against the door and his momentum carried him into the room. "Fuckin' hell."

Ronnie, standing naked, turned and took a pace towards his brother menacingly. "Fuck off... Burstin' in?.. Fuck off."

But Reggie could see a disaster unfolding. "Have you gone completely fuckin' mad?"

The old man, frightened by the turn of events, immediately concealed his 'excitement' and climbed off the bed, he tore his mask off and got dressed as fast as he could.

Reggie glanced at the old man as if he were of no significance, then back at Ronnie. He gestured towards Alfredo. "I don't fuckin believe it. Why him for fuck's sake? Ain't there plenty of others?"

The old man fastened his handmade black leather shoes and got his jacket on as quickly as he could. Ronnie, glowering at his brother, looked as if he was trying to decide whether to attack. Reggie kept up the initiative and started to untie Alfredo. "Help me get him dressed, we gotta get him out of 'ere."

The Platters continuing to sing softly, unaware of the change of mood, they now sounded as if they were mocking those who could hear them. Ronnie picked up the partly drunk bottle of champagne and smashed it down onto the gramophone.

The old man, now looking like a Lord again, albeit a sheepish one, darted out of the door as fast as he could.

Reggie, struggling to get Alfredo's trousers up, snapped at his brother. "Help me, come on quick."

Ronnie just sat down on the bed in silence, for some seconds he was completely motionless, then he reluctantly moved to help his brother.

They had put away the camera, tripod and other items, and were just finishing dressing Alfredo when Freddie and Jack Mullins appeared at the bedroom door, neither was hardly able to believe the scene. Ronnie was wearing only his pants. Alfredo was still unconscious on the bed, almost completely dressed now, the twins were putting on his socks and shoes.

The twins looked up in silence while Jack and Freddie looked around the room and absorbed it all. Jack was the first to speak, and he did so slowly, seriously. "Fuck me, looks like a 'Ginger's wet dream."

Reggie's mind was still racing. What explanation could he offer? Freddie looked at the twins with undisguised disgust and anger. "What's wrong with Alfredo, why's he in 'ere?"

Ronnie ignored both visitors and set about getting the rest of his own clothes on.

Reggie took a quick look at old Jack, but addressed Freddie. "Oh, he got pissed, thought he might want to sleep it off."

Jack was quite happy to torment the twins, in fact he was relishing the situation. "Sleep? Looks like you were up to somfink else. Wonder what? Cards was it? 'Pairs' was it? 'Find the Lady'?"

Ronnie lurched towards Jack, but his brother held him back. Old Jack wasn't intimidated, he still thought himself about thirty, and fighting fit.

Freddie studied Alfredo. He had his suit, shirt and tie on, but the buttons on his shirt were not fastened properly, his shirt wasn't tucked in and he was completely unconscious.

Freddie pulled the young man up off the bed and without speaking carried him 'fireman's lift' style towards the door. He quarter turned in the doorway to address the twins. "I don't know what the fuck's been goin' on but..."

Then he shook his head and left. Jack, grinning, followed closely behind. Ronnie shouted threats and cusses at old Jack, but Jack just laughed. suddenly Freddie, Alfredo and Jack, were gone.

# Chapter 34

6 a.m the next morning in East London, the only other people on the streets were milkmen and paperboys. At the local police station, this was the time the night shift arrived back and signed off duty. The early turn shift (6-2) were about to have their usual briefing from the night sergeant. Afterwards the beat officers would mooch out and find a free breakfast somewhere. No policeman was thinking about criminal activity at 6 a.m.

At their hotel, the Krays, Danny and Roger were sipping tea. Danny had called the meeting. Neither Danny nor Roger knew what had taken place with Alfredo the night before. But in any event, neither would have noticed any change in attitude from the twins, they were their normal, abnormal selves. Roger was explaining why the meeting had been requested. "They're introducing these new security vans for the TPOs."

Reggie didn't seem at all impressed by Roger's knowledge, or the fact he had brought this new information to their attention, especially at 6 a.m. "For fuck's sake. Is that it? What do you expect us to do about it? You're supposed to be the expert."

Danny wasn't going to take this bullshit. Didn't these two understand this news had a significant impact on their ability to break into the coaches? "Hold on Reggie, Roger's makin' an important point."

Both twins glared at Danny. But Danny's remark emboldened Roger to continue. "See they've been made of wood up to now. If they've put metal bars in and strengthened the doors, it'll make a difference."

Reggie's mood changed quickly. He nodded, lit a cigarette and provided an obviously false smile as if tolerating an idiot. "We'll look into it Roger." Ronnie turned to Danny. "Where's the others?"

The question was clearly designed to see if Alfredo or Freddie had said anything about the events of the night before. Danny responded. "I expect the lucky bastards are still asleep. No point in coming round 'ere mob-handed was there?"

Alfredo missed his gym session that morning and slept until gone ten. By the time he woke, Shirley had already taken Tony to Luigi's. Alfredo found himself lying in the sitting room behind the sofa. He opened his eyes to a bad headache and an unquenchable thirst, and wondered what he was doing there. He stood up with difficulty, his head was swimming, he was mystified as to why he was still wearing the clothes he had worn when he went out the night before. He had no recollection of what had happened.

Shirley had been less than sympathetic when Freddie carried him in at about midnight. She had asked Freddie to dump Alfredo where he later woke. Freddie had offered no explanation, and Shirley had asked for none.

Alfredo kicked his shoes off. Unsteady on his feet, he dragged himself to the bathroom and ran a deep bath. As the bath was running, he splashed cold water on his face and the back of his neck. He felt awful. Memory loss was a new experience, and he didn't like it.   Alfredo thought hard. He was supposed to have visited the Krays, but couldn't remember if he had. He wasn't sure why, but he felt confused and soiled. Alfredo began to undress, intending to drop all of his clothes right where he stood and dumping them in the bin as soon as possible.

First, he took off his wristwatch and noticed a piece of red silk had been trapped in the strap fastener. He gave it only a moment's thought before being distracted by the red welts around his wrists. He thought hard but no possible explanation came. Then he removed his jacket and tie. As he began to unbutton his shirt he noticed the buttons were in the wrong buttonholes. He thought perhaps in a drunken state he had undone his shirt and failed to fasten it again properly. He put his curiosity aside and undid his trousers. They fell to his ankles, but so did his 'Y' fronts. He picked them up and saw they had been slit completely through on both sides. A sweat broke out on his forehead, he examined them again, more closely, and thought hard. What possible explanation could there be? He kicked his trousers clear of his ankles and took off his socks. He noticed red marks running around his ankles too. What could it all mean? What could have happened to him?

He didn't have the long bath he had intended; he felt compelled to find out what had happened the night before. His mind searched hard to find answers but only found more questions.

By 11.45 that morning he was at Luigi's. Shirley was brusque with him. But he established how and when he had arrived home. He went upstairs and phoned Freddie in Brighton. "Hello Freddie. Just called to say thanks for lookin' after me last night."

Freddie was surprised to get the call. "It's alright."

Alfredo got to the point. "So what happened?"

174

Freddie now understood why. "Fuck knows, you got completely pissed at the twins' place, I carried you out and got you back to your place." Alfredo thought for a moment. "I wasn't pissed."

Freddie didn't understand why Alfredo was questioning it. "Well you done a perfect impersonation of bein' completely fuckin' legless."

Alfredo didn't understand. "Somethin' happened... I dunno what."

Freddie really didn't want to know any more, but found himself pursuing the point. "What you mean?"

Alfredo had no more to offer. "Dunno, somethin's not right?"

Freddie tried to help. "Look, I found you out the back of the twins' club with 'em both. You were laid out. It were all a bit fuckin' queer to be honest ..."

There was silence for a few seconds, Alfredo was taking it in. "What else?"

Fred didn't want to elaborate, he didn't want to describe the bedroom, the mirrors, the pictures on the wall, Ronnie in his undies. "Dunno what to say...nuffin. That's it."

Freddie hated the twins but found all this business distasteful. He hated talking about it and wanted to say no more than was necessary. So he gave Alfredo no more.

Alfredo could not share the indignity of telling Freddie about the cutting of his underwear or about the marks of apparently being bound wrist and ankle. The implications were just too abhorrent, humiliating, belittling. If his worst fears were even partly true, he would feel compelled to inflict retribution. The targets and the timing could not have been worse, or the implications more enormous.

Alfredo told himself it was some kind of joke. After all, he would know if he had been buggered, wouldn't he? Or would he? Alfredo put the phone down and ran to the bathroom and vomited hard into the toilet bowl. Now he felt he carried a vile secret, something he could never share with another soul, and something he could not even properly contemplate. He knew he must bury his fears deeply, and put the matter out of his head forever.

Two nights later, Freddie was driving too fast late at night when he crashed into a car parked without lights. His injuries were serious. It was many months before he recovered, and by then, thoughts of Alfredo's humiliation at the hands of the Krays had been filed somewhere at the very back of his mind.

But for others it simply meant there was now a vacancy in the combined team.

# Chapter 35

Weeks earlier, Billy had suggested the twins go to Scotland to witness the loading of the Travelling Post Office (TPO) service they intended to attack. So, after the Alfredo 'incident' the twins travelled north and spent a couple of days in Glasgow. After all, they could hardly appear at Euston station and watch the TPO loading there.

Upon return to the capital they met Billy for lunch. Billy lit a cigarette. "So, how did you get on in Glasgow?"

Reggie nodded. "Yeah, alright. First time we been there."

Ronnie stubbed out a cigarette. "We had some haggis. Said they shot it special for us."

Billy smiled. "Sheep's offal. You know that don't ya?"

Ronnie looked appalled. "You're kiddin'?"

Billy's smile broadened. "No. Sheep's innards, bollocks, brain, eyeballs, anythin' all wrapped in sheep's stomach with some cereal mixed in with salt and pepper."

Reggie looked at his brother in disgust. "Oh fuck off Billy, you'll spoil me lunch."

Billy laughed lightly. "The jocks don't eat it ya know. Anyway, how'd ya get on?"

The twins nodded. "Yeah, useful … understand a bit more now."

Billy knew the Krays had never seen the inside of a mailbag, except perhaps when making them in clink. 'Nor could they distinguish a TPO from a Hornby train set', he thought.

He also knew their ignorance could easily create a credibility problem with the gang. He wanted the twins to understand how little they knew in the hope they would value those who actually knew what they were doing. Billy Hill knew the Raiders skills were vital, and Roger's in particular. If the twins failed to respect Roger's contributions, problems would undoubtedly arise. He also had to convey to the twins the importance of relaying information and questions from the Raiders quickly and accurately.

The twins told him that Roger had explained more secure TPO coaches were being introduced. Billy listened carefully and gave his instructions. "If that's right, it means a re-think. Fuck it. I'll find out. Tell 'em you're lookin' into it."

Billy took a sip of orange juice, picked up his fork and focused on his main course.   Reggie took a sip of red wine and put the glass back on the table. "That young Alfredo kid, looked like a shrewd move. Understand Ted Harris went mental."

Billy didn't even bother to make eye contact, he was now enjoying his main course. "Ted went mental? What you on about?"

Ronnie gave Reggie a furtive look. "Yeah, mental. They got shot of him, that's why Alfredo's on the firm"

Hill put his fork down. "Alfredo? Who the fuck's that?"

Ronnie thought the boss must have misheard. "Alfredo."

Billy looked across at Ronnie. "Yeah I heard, like I said, who the fuck is he?"

Ronnie and Reggie exchanged worried glances. Ronnie was unsure of his ground. "Replaced Ted. He's on the team."

Billy. "What fuckin' team?"

Reggie spoke. "Your team, our team."

Billy. "No he ain't."

Ronnie couldn't believe his ears. "Well, he was on the Irish Mail job, been part of the Raiders for months."

Billy was deadly serious and calm. "Can't have."

The twins very rarely knew something Billy didn't, and this something went to the heart of Billy's supposed immaculate planning. Ronnie couldn't resist pushing the point home. "I'm surprised you didn't know that Billy."

Billy was furious. His voice dropped in pace and tone. "What you know about him?"

Reggie answered whilst Ronnie was still taking it all in. "We think he's sound. Been with the Raiders since Ted Harris fucked up. Youngster, married, good middleweight. Seems to be a good lad."

Billy nodded. "Know where he lives?"

Within five minutes, Billy was speaking to Aldridge from a public telephone box. He told Aldridge to leave whatever he was doing and meet him immediately. One hour later, Billy and Aldridge were safely ensconced in a reading room at the British Library.

Aldridge didn't seem concerned. "Yeah I know they're supposed to be introducing new coaches, but it don't make no difference."

Billy spoke calmly, but the threat was obvious. "You should 'ave told me there might be a problem. What the fuck was you thinkin' about?"

Aldridge had screwed up and he knew it, but he also knew he could not admit it. "They been rabbiting about new coaches for over a year and..."

But he didn't get the sentence finished, Billy leaned forward in his seat and poked his finger. He spoke slowly, deliberately. "I've told you before. Fucking wake up. You find out anything that could affect my plans, you let me know straightaway. You got that?"

Aldridge nodded. "Yeah." He looked away from Billy's cold stare.

But Billy pressed on. "So, if these new carriages look as if they'll fuck us, you'll solve the      problem pronto like your life depended on it – cos it will."

Aldridge thought for a moment and stroked his chin. "Yeah, course."

Aldridge knew Billy had the power to have him fitted-up, or severely beaten, or killed. He wasn't a man he wanted to disappoint.  Billy's manner changed suddenly from glower to smile. "Right. Now is there anythin' else you ain't told me?"

Aldridge sensed a trap. He leaned back in his seat, thought hard, hesitated. "Don't think so, Billy, honest."

Billy smiled, "Honest? I know how honest you are."

He grinned. "And it ain't very. What about Alfredo?"

Aldridge looked confused and more than a little worried. "Who?"

Billy's smile vanished as quickly as it had appeared. "You tell me. You said you had all the Raiders onside. Now I find out you don't even know who's on their fuckin' team."

Aldridge responded too quickly. "You gave me the names."

Now Billy was in danger of really losing his self-control and whipping out the cutthroat razor he always carried. He had never done so on impulse before, but now came very close. Billy reminded Aldridge why he had been paying him. He told him to make sure Alfredo was "100% solid" or to get rid of him permanently.

It would have been easier for Aldridge to kill Alfredo than to guarantee his dependability, but Billy knew it. He reminded Aldridge the robbery required 15 proven, reliable robbers, and if he had to find a replacement, then Aldridge's task of checking on the replacement would be the same.

The Raiders had assured Billy that Freddie's car accident would not prevent his return to the team, but it had also clearly illustrated the lack of any obvious replacement.

179

Aldridge said he understood completely and apologised again. Then, determined to change the subject and end on a positive note, he added. "Been thinkin', it would save time on the big one to handcuff the driver and his mate instead of wasting time tying them up. I can put me hands on half a dozen pairs of handcuffs."

Billy studied Aldridge for some time. "Alright."

Before leaving, Billy threw a scrap of paper in front of Aldridge. It showed Alfredo's name, description and home address, he pointed to it. "Check him out. And let me know."

Within 30 minutes, Aldridge had contacted two of his trusted men. He knew they would keep their mouths shut no matter what he did, after all, he could implicate both in serious crime.

By 8.20 the following morning, all three were parked up right outside the entrance to Alfredo's flat. Aldridge was sitting in the driver's seat of a dark green Ford Zephyr, the two bent detective constables were sitting in the back.

It was a long wait. But late morning Aldridge saw a man in a tracksuit carrying a duffel bag, walking down the road and towards the car. He fitted the description perfectly. As he neared, Aldridge studied him. "That's my boy. Here we go."

The two detectives sitting in the back got out of the car and walked casually towards Alfredo, they seemed to engage in small talk. Then Aldridge got out too. Alfredo was just a few feet in front of him. Aldridge stepped into Alfredo's path. "You Alfredo Pantelli."

Alfredo stopped and gave him a hard look. "Who the fuck are you?"

Aldridge had long ago become accustomed to such casual rudeness, it was the norm. "CID." he replied.

Alfredo turned quickly, intending to run, but the other two detectives were now right there, so close they were practically touching him. Alfredo turned back to Aldridge. Aldridge's tone didn't change. "Say again, are you Alfredo Pantelli?"

Alfredo looked away. "Never fuckin' heard of 'im."

Aldridge punched Alfredo hard in the stomach, and it took him completely by surprise. He gasped in pain as the breath was forced from his lungs; he was doubled up and unable to get his breath. The other two detectives were now at Alfredo's shoulders.

Aldridge looked down at him. "Let's not fuck about, son. Have a bit of respect. Now, you Alfredo Pantelli?"

Alfredo took a few seconds to get his breath, but could hardly yet speak. He spluttered, "My name's Sam Costa."

Aldridge nodded. "Okay, Mr Costa. Where do you live?"

Alfredo still hadn't recovered, "I ain't sayin' nuffink."

Of course, Aldridge had faced this situation a thousand times before. "Well, I'm gonna take the keys from your pocket and check if they fit that flat up there. How does that sound?"

Alfredo almost managed to straighten up. "OK I'm Alfredo Pantelli, so fuckin' what?"

Aldridge punched Alfredo hard in the stomach again with the same result. One of the detectives grabbed Alfredo's wrists and within seconds they were handcuffed behind him. A few more seconds more and he was seated between the two detectives in the back of the car, the duffel bag with his gym kit had been abandoned on the pavement.

They drove for a few minutes and stopped near a Tube station. From the time of Alfredo's arrest, up to this very moment, no one had spoken a word. The silence continued. The two detective constables got out of the car and headed towards the Tube station.

Aldridge drove Alfredo to a derelict building on an abandoned industrial estate. There, he dragged Alfredo from the car and pushed him onwards until they were completely hidden from public view. He pushed Alfredo to the ground. Aldridge glanced around, the ground was covered in debris, broken bricks, old used building timber, one or two items of long abandoned clothing, broken bottles and a little household rubbish. He found what he was looking for and picked up a piece of wood, perhaps part of an old window frame. It was about two feet long, heavy enough to hurt, not heavy enough to break bones. He sneered down, Alfredo looked at the wood in Aldridge's hand and then into Aldridge's mean face, but said nothing.

Aldridge began beating Alfredo across the head. Soon Alfredo's face and scalp were streaked with welts, and blood from scalp wounds wet his hair and face. He showed no sign of pain at first, but as the beating became relentless, so he began to moan and flinch, his reaction to each blow became more emphatic.

Eventually Aldridge stopped. "Now, that's just a starter so you know not to fuck about... So, what you know about the Krays then?"

Alfredo's face was running in blood, his lips were split and blood covered his teeth and lips, but he spat out an answer. "Fuck off."

Aldridge resumed the beating, now slow and methodical, every blow aimed at soft tissue to inflict maximum pain. Soon the splashes of blood became more significant as the cuts on Alfredo's face and scalp became joined, extended and deeper. Aldridge stood back and admired his work, then he asked Alfredo again. Alfredo said nothing.

Aldridge removed the handcuffs and left him barely conscious amongst the debris. He drove to a telephone kiosk and made an anonymous '999' emergency call and requested an ambulance.

An hour later, in University College Hospital Casualty Department, Alfredo was sat opposite a nursing sister who was making notes on a clipboard. He had fresh stitches in his scalp and swollen face, his eyes were blackening and his lips were badly puffed up and split. Shirley was sitting next to him with young Tony on her lap. The nursing sister looked up from the clipboard. "Hold on a moment I'll get your prescription."

The nurse hurried off. Shirley turned to her husband. "What the bastard look like?"

Alfredo was finding it difficult to speak through his cut and swollen lips, he shrugged. And spoke inaudibly. "Dunno."

Shirley persisted. "Did he have any sort of funny accent?"

Alfredo wondered what on earth she was talking about and struggled to respond, but managed a twisted quizzical look.

Shirley. "Was he a Jock, or a Paddy, a Brummie, or what?"

Alfredo shrugged.

Shirley changed tack. "What you think he was after then?"

Alfredo tried a whisper. "Krays."

She thought for a moment. "Krays? How could he know you're connected to 'em?"

Alfredo shrugged and shook his head, then made a motion as if lifting a phone to his ear. He leaned in close. "Danny."

Five minutes later Shirley phoned Danny from a phone box just outside the hospital on the Tottenham Court Road. She didn't mention her name, her husband's name, or anyone else's. The message was simple and clearly understood. "My old man told me to tell ya' to have a drink with him tonight, said you'd wanna know the goin' at Lingfield is heavy. Said he'd see ya in the French House in Dean Street at eight."

The name and location of the pub were specifically designed to lead astray anyone who might listen without an invitation. They would recognise the pub, they knew it as a place that attracted both gangsters and 'wannabes.' None of the Raiders would ever go anywhere near it. 'The Grapes,' was another pub half a mile away from the French House, and was one of those pubs the Raiders had agreed as suitable for emergency meetings.

Then Shirley made a brief call to British Transport Police headquarters. She spoke to Roy; they agreed to meet at 5.30pm.

It was raining, and the small parade of shops provided just enough cover. Roy was standing well back in the doorway of a dry-cleaners shop that had closed about 15 minutes earlier. He had only been there a short while when Shirley arrived. "You bastard. You couldn't wait, could ya?" Roy hadn't expected the animosity. "What do you mean?" But Shirley had decided, to her it was obvious, Roy had somehow established her identity and it had led to him easily identifying Alfredo. It was therefore Roy who had questioned and assaulted her husband. It was obvious. 'All coppers are bastards.'

Shirley. "What do I fucking mean? Beat the shit out of Alfredo didn't ya. S'pose you thought he'd tell you everything, did ya?"
Roy shrugged. "Who's Alfredo?"
Shirley wasn't listening. "You found out who I am and it were easy then weren't it? Big mistake."
Roy shook his head. "I don't know what you're talking about."

But Shirley was meeting Roy for one purpose only, to let him know he had better back off immediately, or he would find out just who she could call upon to hurt him badly.

Shirley didn't need to involve the Krays, or the Raiders, her own family connections were more than sufficient for the purpose. But the more she threatened, the more belligerent Roy became. Shirley had worked herself up from righteous anger to blind rage. "I mean it. You nick Alfredo, or come anywhere near me or him again, and you'll have your legs broken. You understand?"
Her eyes were blazing. She turned to walk back out into the rain, Roy didn't finish his cuppa, but he gave it a couple of minutes before leaving himself.

# Chapter 36

The Grapes was quiet. It was on the verge of closing forever. A tatty old pub owned by a surly pair of old age pensioners who only ever had time to serve a few old friends. But its unpopularity made it perfect for quiet meetings.

It impressed Danny that although Alfredo had taken a severe beating, he had somehow kept his mouth shut and arranged, and attended, the meeting.

But it was clear the police knew Alfredo was up to something with the twins, and it was seriously worrying. It would mean Alfredo would be of little future use to them, and it might also mean perhaps the cancellation or postponement of the big TPO job. Danny would have to tell the twins immediately. Danny would also need to tell the rest of the Raiders tonight, they would need to be on their guard. After the short meeting in The Grapes, Danny quickly phoned around from a nearby call box.

He found Reggie at Valance Road, his mum's address. Danny spoke with urgency. "Listen Reg, we need a meet, got to be tonight."
Reggie was less than keen to take orders. "No, not tonight, we got plans."
Danny sighed. "I ain't being funny, but this ain't gonna wait."
There was a pause, "Err... okay, let's meet where we met last, but we'll have to make it quick, we're busy."

Danny understood the unspoken message, Reggie wasn't putting himself out. He responded evenly. "I'll be there by eight."

Shortly after 8.00pm Danny, Tom and the twins were sitting around a table in the basement bar of the Glenrae Hotel. The insistence on an immediate meeting had been treated by the twins as an intrusion, if not an impertinence. No drinks were on the table, or on offer.

Danny explained the TPO job might need to be postponed, the police seemed to know something, then he explained what had happened to Alfredo. "He took quite a beating. His head and mouth are full of stitches."

Reggie and Ronnie exchanged glances and seemed completely unconcerned by it all. Ronnie leaned forward and spoke calmly. "It weren't Old Bill."

Tom and Danny exchanged glances. Danny looked puzzled. "What's that mean?"

Reggie took a drag of his cigarette and spoke as he exhaled the smoke. "Look, we hardly know the lad, we had to make sure he was sound, would keep his mouth shut if Old Bill got hold of him. That's all, no harm done."

Danny looked disgusted. "You're completely out of order. The lad's so straight he don't worry he might be dropped, no he phones and says Old Bill's knocked him about and he might not be safe."

Ronnie shrugged his shoulders. "He ain't dead, is he? What's the fuckin' problem?"

Tom stood up. "The problem? One of our team has had a good hidin' from you that he ain't deserved. So who the fuck is next?"

Reggie shook his head. "Calm down Tom, I mean, why the fuck would we?"

But neither Tom nor Danny were appeased or prepared to be pushed aside easily. Tom raised his voice. "Listen, you're missin' the point. If you think you can just tear into any one of us, then you gotta know you're gonna have a fuckin' problem."

Reggie shook his head and tried to calm things. "Listen. What's done is done. Ain't no point in 'arpin' on about it Tom, it's done right? And it ain't goin' to happen again, I swear."

Danny had been thinking about the hold the Raiders had over future events. "Yeah, what's done is done, and the TPO ain't done yet, is it? So if this is how it's gonna be, perhaps there ain't gonna be any TPO job."

Ronnie, as usual, made a 'frontal assault'. "You won't fuckin' back out, the payday's too big."

Danny was certain of his ground and let it show, "Well, that's somethin' else you got wrong. You can forget the whole fuckin' thing. Find some other mugs, and do it quick, otherwise we might just do the job and leave you two fuckers out completely."

The twins looked alarmed. Suddenly they were being unfairly blamed for something they hadn't arranged, and which could cause a complete loss of face, a fallout with Billy, and perhaps expose their empire as being much less than invincible. The twins exchanged hurried glances.

Reggie was first to speak. "We all gets our orders Danny."

Danny saw an opportunity he had long been waiting for. "What does that mean?"

Reggie and Ronnie exchanged hurried glances again, but before they had the opportunity to close the moment, Danny pushed. "Billy Hill."

Ronnie responded without thought. "How the fuck d'you know?"

Danny was still obviously raging. "Up to recent, neither of you were into the mails. Suddenly you know all about 'em and plan to knock over TPOs.....had to come from somewhere else. I mean a job like this, who else?"

The twins looked both angry and bewildered. Reggie was the first to speak. "For fuck's sake. If he finds out we told ya..."

Danny continued. "Right then, we need to speak to the organ grinder."

This was too much for Ronnie. "You takin' the piss?"

Before Danny or Tom could react, Reggie interjected. "Listen chaps, if you just roll up and have a go at Billy, he ain't gonna take it, is he? He must have had a reason, let me speak to him first. See how the land lies, know what I mean?"

Tom ignored the twins and spoke to his mate, "Dan, we don't lose nuffin', and ain't lookin' for a tear up with Billy, are we?"

Danny nodded and answered Reggie. "We ain't gonna wait forever, we wanna know why knocking shit out of one of the team was a good idea, otherwise we're out."

The meeting with Billy took place the following afternoon in his offices in Warren Street, near where the Tottenham Court Road meets the Euston Road. His wood panelled office was well appointed in a tasteful mix of art deco and Victorian styles. An impressive antique desk and chair were positioned towards the back of the office. Armchairs and side tables were available towards the front of the office for more informal meetings. A young woman, a niece, served as a smart and efficient secretary. To all intents and purposes, this was the office of a very, very successful entrepreneur, which, of course, is exactly what it was.

The main difference between the nature of Billy's successful business and others, apart from legality, was the need for absolute secrecy and the need for extreme caution in all dealings. These were two of the many lessons Billy had learned the hard way. He was the youngest of 20 children, born into poverty, brought up in the worst of London's slums. He had learned from infancy, if he wanted a share of the cake, he had to grab it, and he had never stopped grabbing.

Billy's earlier 'professional errors' had cost him dearly. As a young teenager he was disfigured by electrified railway lines in making an escape from the scene of his crime (lack of planning). Later he was imprisoned for robbery and violence (owing to careless words and untrustworthy associates). As a teenager, his face had been razor-slashed and badly scarred (because he had failed to strike first). Above all, Billy was a man who learned his lessons.

Earlier that day, Reggie went on his own to meet Billy. He had only been to Billy's office once before, and he knew special rules applied there. Billy always behaved as if any dodgy conversation might be secretly tape recorded by the police. He would always have a gramophone playing as background noise, sometimes Sinatra, sometimes Mantovani, sometimes something classical. He would talk in riddles, use rhyming slang, nods, winks, written notes, etcetera. Was he paranoid? No, this wasn't an illness, it was his chosen method of doing all he could to stay out of jail, and it worked.

Billy seemed to accept with apparent calm, despite his absolute determination to stay one step away from the robbers, that the team somehow knew he was behind it all. Reggie tried to make it sound like a compliment. "They said only you were capable of putting this job together, Billy."

But inside, Billy was angry and cursing, not the twins, nor the team, but Aldridge. Once again he had caused a significant problem.

Billy had agreed to meet Danny and Tom that afternoon, but a meeting with two 'faces' so close to their joint involvement in a major crime was a big risk for him. It was against all his instincts. But he knew the job was now in the balance. He couldn't just brush them aside, for if the Raiders suspected that the planning was in chaos they would undoubtedly walk away. Reassurance was needed.

It was just after 2.00pm, the three of them sat in armchairs in a semi-circle. Each had a side table on which was served a cup of tea in a china cup and saucer and a side plate of biscuits. On the record player David Whitfield, backed by the Mantovani Orchestra, was singing 'Cara Mia.'

Billy had made a lot of money in earlier days stealing mailbags from the Brighton line, and the Raiders had inherited the work after he had moved on. Billy took a sip of tea.

"How's Freddie?"

Tom nodded, "Getting stronger, still limping a bit, but he'll be OK."

Bill smiled, "Good. You still takin' the sea air in Brighton?"

Tom and Danny exchanged glances. What was this a reference to? Perhaps Billy was reminding them he had control over them via Aldridge.

After all, the Brighton job was the first in which Aldridge had pulled the strings. Perhaps it was just a pleasantry?

Danny responded. "Occasionally, you?"

Billy picked up a biscuit and dunked half of it. "Yeah, I love Brighton, Danny, still got house there..."

He ate the biscuit before it could fall in a soggy mess and then stopped, looked around theatrically as if addressing a hidden microphone, then spoke up, ..."And let's face it, I mean...Brighton... got the best police force money can buy, and I should know, I got shares."

Billy grinned. His guests followed suit. Then he leant forward, lowered his voice and nodded. "What you was told yesterday was right, sort of anyway. I asked somebody from the opposition to make sure your lad was kosher, course bein' a fuckin' idiot he, well you know the rest...."

Tom took a sip of tea. "Why didn't you speak to us, Bill?"

Billy shrugged. "You know how it is. You do your best, if people would just use their brains for fuck's sake?"

Danny and Tom nodded in agreement. Then Danny answered. "Be much easier if we talked direct in future Billy."

Billy nodded, finishing the biscuit, "Easier yeah, but it ain't in our interests. We gotta be sure nobody can (Billy dropped his voice even more) ...link us."

Both his guests sipped and nodded. Billy went on. "And to be straight with ya', with a team this size, I wanna keep a bit of distance, know what I mean?"

Tom and Danny nodded again. Then Danny asked in whisper. "But why the twins?"

Billy kept his voice low. "If it went tits up and anybody's thought' of grassin' I want them to know the twins would be on 'em. I mean nobody on my firm could go near 'em, could they?"

Billy had said enough. He raised the volume of his voice and lightened the tone. "Tangiers? So, you wanna visit then?"

Danny and Tom smiled and shook their heads. Billy exaggerated his response. "Really? I mean, what could be nicer, the sunshine, the girls....?"

Billy looked at Tom, he drained his cup, smiled and nodded. "Might be a bit hot for me, but thanks anyway, Bill."

Billy smiled. "Fair enough. Anyway, want a top up? How's Renee, Tom?"

# Chapter 37

A few days later. It was after dark and Alfredo had again slept for most of the day. Danny knocked at the door and Shirley let him in. He didn't call often but needed to speak to Alfredo. His smashed up face looked even worse now the bruises had developed and it would attract too much attention for them to meet publicly. Danny and Shirley exchanged pleasantries, and she explained Alfredo was still asleep. But there was something she needed to speak to Danny about before waking her husband. "Dan, I'm really worried. Listen, I was dead grateful you took Alfredo on, but I'm really scared now the Law's onto him. I think you should drop him. It ain't no good if you all get nicked, is it?"

Danny hesitated, he hadn't foreseen this. "Look Shirl... we ain't gonna get nicked."

Shirley looked bemused. "What you mean? You saw what they did to him, they wouldn't 'ave done that if they weren't onto him."

Danny was torn, he knew Shirley had been traumatised by the rape and had been very insecure, fearful and unpredictable ever since. He knew she now relied on the constant company and reassurance of her husband. But somehow Danny needed to reassure her Alfredo was not facing imminent arrest, for Danny was not in a position to let Alfredo pull out. If Alfredo withdrew, others would view him as a security threat who needed to be 'dealt with'. And Alfredo would need to be replaced, but by whom?

Danny looked around and then leaned in towards Shirley. "Look love, we've had to involve a few extra people in somethin'. It's a big job and needs the extra hands. They don't know Alfredo, thought they'd get him tested. They got a bent copper on 'im. That's how he got hurt."

Shirley was frowning heavily. Danny continued "...To see if he would grass...Obviously we didn't know nuffin' about it, and I've had a right go at 'em..."

Shirley nodded. "Bastards. Who are they then?"

Of course, Shirley knew it was the Krays, but she couldn't let on to Danny, it would expose that Alfredo had told her things he shouldn't. Danny shook his head, "You know better Shirl... Look, he's gonna be alright, and the payday will be very good, I promise ya."

Alfredo appeared in the doorway leading from the bedrooms and leaned against the doorframe. He had come straight from his bed and was still wearing pyjama bottoms and a creased white 'T' shirt. Black blood and stitches patterned his scalp and face. His hair was matted and tussled. He just about managed through his swollen lips. "Right Danny?"

Danny put his tea down. "Blimey, even uglier than usual, she been knockin' you about again?"

Danny smiled. Alfredo tried to force a smile in return.

Shirley went to her husband. "Want a coffee love?"

Alfredo nodded. "Please."

Then he staggered across the room and carefully sat down opposite his visitor. Danny studied him. "Thought I'd pop in. I was just tellin' Shirl…"

Danny looked up towards the door to check Shirley was out of earshot. In the background he could hear the noise from the expensive new coffee machine as it burst into life. "It weren't Old Bill what done ya, it was the Krays what organised it. Used a bent copper."

Alfredo's face hardened, they had done so much to infiltrate his soul in the short time he had known them. He forced a question through his painful lips. "Same one that fitted up Roger, err…Black?"

Danny shrugged. "Could be. Listen, we had a meet yesterday, sorted a few things out, but one thing you gotta do is get an alibi organised for early August."

Alfredo nodded. Danny looked back towards the open doorway, Shirley was still out of hearing. "Listen, Gordon's got family in Ireland, says he'll go over a few days before the job, pop back here on a bent passport to do the business, then back to Ireland straight after. He'll spend a few more days over there, then travel back here on his legit passport as if he's been away all the time. Clever eh?"

Alfredo thought about it. Danny was keen to encourage him. "Be easy enough to get your photo put on one."

Alfredo shook his head. "No need, I got an Italian passport."

Danny confirmed. "And a British one an all?"

Alfredo nodded. "I'll get one sorted."

Danny sat back in his chair. "That sounds perfect. So, book yourself a couple of weeks out in Italy, first two weeks of August."

After a few days, Alfredo's headaches subsided and the muscular aches started to ease. Now it was time for him to get on with his life. He wasn't ready for the gym of course, so he went for a long run. Then he set off to Luigi's. Shirley and Tony were already there.

Shirley was cleaning tables, Alfredo's mum was cooking, and the rich, delicious aroma wafted across the café. Alfredo's father was sitting at a table reading a newspaper. Tony was in a carrycot on the table next to him. The atmosphere was warm. Italian music played softly, providing a lullaby for the little one. Alfredo's mother looked up from the cooking and wrung her hands in concern. She looked horrified at his appearance. Alfredo allowed his mother to fuss over him for a while, then he kissed Shirley lightly on the cheek and sat down near his father. His father gave him a relaxed smile and nodded. Alfredo smiled back. "You okay dad?"

His father lifted his hand towards Alfredo's face, "Si, everthin' good. Your missus say you runnin' and crash with bike?"

Alfredo nodded. "Yeah cyclist, it was my fault, didn't hear him coming, too busy running."
His father nodded.

Alfredo's mother arrived at the table and gently placed her hands on her son's injuries. "So sore! It looks terrible."

Alfredo explained the injuries were superficial and would soon disappear. His mother offered both men coffee. Then he explained to his dad he had decided to visit his family in Italy. He was planning to travel on Thursday, August 1st and spend time with Italian family members before Shirley and Tony joined him prior to the national holiday of Ferragosto on the 15th August. After all, there could surely be no better occasion than a national festival for Shirley and Tony to meet the extended family.

His father beamed and said he would write to his brother and make the arrangements. Then he remained silent for a while as if considering things, then he added he would talk to Maria, Alfredo's mother, perhaps they could close 'Luigi's' for a few days and travel out to Italy with him.

Alfredo nodded and thought quickly, then he said he didn't really want Shirley and his son left alone while he was away. Alfredo's father didn't ask why, but he had noticed the once very confident, strident young woman had changed. She had become hesitant, nervous, a little withdrawn even. He nodded, everything could be arranged. Shirley and Tony could stay in Alfredo's old room above the cafe until they all joined Alfredo in Italy.

But Alfredo had an additional message. He told his father if he liked Italy, then he, Shirley and Tony might stay there for an extended holiday and perhaps even stay indefinitely. His father confessed he had long dreamed of moving back home. He said if Alfredo and his family stayed in Italy, then he and his wife would sell the café and move back. But why, he asked, was Alfredo suddenly so keen? How could he afford to go? How could he afford to even think of taking Shirley and Tony out there for an extended holiday? Alfredo knew his father was an honourable and honest man. He also knew he had never been able to lie to his father convincingly. So he answered without lying. "I'm not gonna' tell ya dad. But there's nowhere I'd rather be with my family than in Italy, and that's the truth." His father nodded. He didn't ask him any more questions.

Later that afternoon, Alfredo visited an Army surplus shop near London Bridge. He left with a British Army issue khaki uniform tunic, trousers and socks.

# Chapter 38

Joe the CID clerk got his coat on. Time to go home. Again, Roy would be the only one left in the office. Roy was sure he could trust Joe to keep his own counsel. In fact, he was the only one in the building Roy trusted. For some strange reason, the inner circle of London officers protected their knowledge of mailbag thieves, so Roy took every minute they were alone to pump Joe for information. Following Shirley's comments, Roy was desperate to know if any trains transported a million pounds worth or more of valuables.

Joe's answer surprised him. "Many. I mean, there's all the gold that comes in from South Africa – then goes by train, Southampton Docks to Waterloo. Then there's the TPOs of course, apart from that there's..."
Roy interrupted. "Okay, Joe. I got the picture. Thanks anyway."
Joe grinned, buttoned up his coat and held out a key. "Getting quite a habit, don't forget the lights or I'll get a rocket from the security staff in the morning."
Roy took the keys and nodded. "Night Joe."
Roy returned to studying files but within seconds the phone rang. It was Shirley, and she was crying. "It's me. Can we meet?"
Roy spoke softly. "What's happened, Love?"
Shirley was sobbing. "I'm sorry, I don't know what to do."
Roy continued. "It'll take me half an hour, the café near here."

Roy put his files away, signed off duty and locked up. He dropped the keys in at the front security desk and headed off into the summer night. He got to the café where he had met Shirley several times, bought a mug of tea and a corned beef and mustard sandwich.

Shirley arrived and apologetically explained how she had found out he was not responsible for the assault on her husband. Roy took it in his stride and moved the conversation on.
Shirley had significant news. "Listen, I've just found out, it's a TPO, the Travelling Post Office."
Roy looked fidgety and unsure. "And you're telling me they had nothing to do with the attack on the Irish Mail?"

Shirley expected his suspicion. "Yeah. If that was the big job I wouldn't be 'ere would I?"

Roy thought about it, he didn't look convinced. Shirley studied him. "They ain't the only mail thieves out there you know."

Roy looked away, took another bite of the 'corned beef and mustard' and thought hard. "You sure? A TPO?"

Shirley looked at the mess he was making of eating the sandwich. "Yeah, and you got pickle on your cheek."

Roy nodded. "Well done. So, which one?"

"How many are there?"

Roy smiled. "Which cheek?"

Shirley looked up at the ceiling in mock annoyance, then pointed to the left-hand side of his face. Roy smiled and wiped it away. "Well, there's about 50 TPOs, I think, most are attached to passenger trains. Some of 'em don't have any passengers at all. Is it one of them?"

Shirley looked crestfallen. "Sod it. I don't know."

Roy was keen to keep her focused. "No, but it still helps. Honest. Do you know what part of the country?"

Shirley thought for a while. "Perhaps you already know enough. I mean, you know enough to scare 'em off."

Roy shook his head. Then he told her if this big job was going to be stopped, then he would need sufficient facts to persuade his bosses to take preventive action. But he pointed out he couldn't guarantee they wouldn't simply let the job 'run' in order to arrest the gang they had been chasing for so long. Roy offered an alternative. Roy told Shirley he had been giving the matter a lot of thought and he could see a way he could extricate her husband. As long as Roy had at least 24 hours' notice of the job, Roy would have time to arrest Alfredo on some fictitious charge and thus make sure he wasn't available to take part in the robbery. He would make sure Alfredo was released without charge after the train robbery had been carried out and the perpetrators arrested.

Shirley shook her head. It was an old trick, his fellow robbers would soon realise what had taken place and Alfredo would be hunted down as an informer.

They were in a predicament. How could they find a way of getting the job stopped without creating the potential for a trap? They both sat without speaking for several minutes. Shirley broke the silence. "Christ, I don't know."

Roy spoke as if he hadn't heard her, "If you got information about the Krays on something else, say some other robbery that don't involve your bloke, I could put that information to the Met and they'd be nicked and out of the picture, then the train robbery might be cancelled?"

Shirley hesitated. "No, Roy, here ain't nobody in the Met you can trust."

Roy nodded, and they sat in silence again.

Then Roy had another idea, "One other thought. What if we give the information to my bosses so late in the day they wouldn't have time to set a trap? Say on the day of the crime? I mean, they would have to try to prevent it then, wouldn't they?"

Shirley. "That don't work either. Your firm might not be able to scramble in a few hours but I reckon the Sweeney would."

Roy wasn't giving up on the idea so quickly. "I know, we could use the radio people. If you was to phone the BBC a few hours before and tell them..."

Shirley shook her head again. "No, they would go straight to the Met."

Roy promised to give it more thought and they parted company on good terms, which suited them both.

Roy spent weeks, whilst performing his normal duties and even when at home with his wife and kids, furtively trying to establish what this big TPO job might be. Now he was at his desk studying hard the open file in front of him marked, 'Irish Mail Robbery.' Elsewhere on his desk were a pile of train schedules and TPO movements.

Aldridge entered the CID office and casually approached. "Walcott. What you doin'?"

For no accountable reason, Roy felt as if he were doing something wrong. "Err, reading these files sir, err Den."

In the seconds between starting to ask the question and hearing Roy's answer, Aldridge had scanned the desk and knew exactly what Roy was up to. "You being funny? Who the fuck do you think you are, fucking Maigret? Listen, all you gotta do is what I fuckin' tell ya'. No more than that."

Roy hadn't expected the anger. "Sorry, sorry, yes sir."

Aldridge interrupted. "Just put that file and the rest of the papers back where you found 'em... And what you doin' with details of the TPO movements anyway?"

Roy picked the papers up. "Just trying to learn."

Aldridge was still angry. "It's lunchtime, piss off down the pub and have a drink with the lads, that's what we do round 'ere. Got it?"

Roy. "Sorry."

Before Roy could do more, the phone rang on his desk. He picked it up hurriedly, keen to end the conversation with his inspector. The sound of the pips in the call box was clear and loud. Aldridge stood close by watching and listening. "Transport Police Headquarters CID."

Shirley spoke loudly and with urgency. "Roy, we need a meet, today." Roy couldn't afford to let his inspector hear any of it. He turned away and dropped his voice. "Now's not a good time. Call me back later."
Roy pressed the handset hard against his head, determined not to let a murmur of Shirley's words reach Aldridge, Shirley ignored him. "I've got what you wanted. Meet me at the caff."
Roy couldn't risk putting Shirley off. They had only just repaired the last damage, "Ok, at six."
Aldridge interrupted. "Is that a personal call?"
Roy put the phone down immediately. "Yes Den, personal, sorry."
It was no surprise to Aldridge that Brummie was a poor liar.

An hour later, Roy was on his second pint of bitter and listening to five other detectives telling 'war stories.' Nearby, Aldridge was in a similar group. A nondescript man in his forties came into the bar, looked around, spotted Aldridge and hurried towards him. Aldridge saw him approaching and met him before the stranger got as far as Aldridge's drinking group. The stranger whispered something in Aldridge's ear and left.

Aldridge put his glass down on the bar and excused himself from the company. The stranger was waiting outside, they exchanged 'nods' and Aldridge followed him. Waiting 500 yards away, in a side street, was a limousine with darkened rear passenger windows. As Aldridge approached, the heavily built driver climbed out and opened the rear door for him. The driver strolled away from the car and Aldridge climbed in. Billy was waiting. "What's goin on? Somebody from your firm's been on to the Yard asking about the Krays."
Aldridge sighed. "Was it a somebody called Walcott?"
Billy nodded. "Yeah. Who the fuck is he?"
Aldridge was confident of his ground. He sighed again. "He's a nobody, a thick Brummie, his first time south of Watford, he ain't got a clue."
Billy wasn't convinced, "Sounds to me like that's exactly what he has got. Why's he ringing the Yard then?"

Aldridge bought a second or two by offering Billy a cigarette. Aldridge lit both. "Honest Bill, Walcott's harmless, thick as pig shit, there's no problem."

Billy took a long drag. "So why's he calling the Yard?"

Aldridge was still relaxed. "Somebody twigged him as a mug and told him all sorts of old bollocks while he bought them beer all night. It was a piss take."

Billy was still agitated. "Who?"

Aldridge shook his head. "Just some fuckin' postman lookin' for free beer."

Aldridge was determined to calm things down, he smiled. "And the postman told him he used to play centre forward for the Arsenal. Walcott believed that an all."

Billy's face was still hard set. "When was all this?"

Aldridge. "Months ago, when he first got transferred from Brum. He'd never even heard of the Krays. Honest Billy, He knows sod all, a fuckin wanker."

Billy stared at Aldridge without responding, judging the veracity of his words. Over the last few weeks, Billy had lost confidence in Aldridge, and Aldridge was on thin ice. Billy knew, despite his distrust of Aldridge's abilities, he still depended on him for the forthcoming robbery. "Well, idiot or not, he could still fuck things up. Do somethin' about it. Sort him out. Understand?"

Billy leaned across and pushed the limo door open. Aldridge took the cue and climbed out. Aware of the serious threat he now faced, and feeling he had made an escape and bought a little time, within a few minutes, Aldridge was back in the pub and thinking hard about his options.

By 5.35pm that afternoon, all of headquarters CID staff were variously, out on observations, on their way to a pub, or least likely, on their way home. Joe and Roy were still in the office, though Joe already had his jacket on and was ready to leave. A few minutes later they set off. Whenever Roy's duties permitted it, the two of them had fallen into a pattern of walking to the Tube station together.

Before they had got 50 yards from the building, Aldridge was on their tail. They reached a junction, Joe turned left to catch the Tube, and Roy went right. Roy picked up the pace, he hated being late, even when he knew the person he was meeting was less punctual. After another ten minutes, Roy entered the café.

Aldridge had watched him enter, now he stood back in a shop doorway out of easy sight and observed the café entrance, he lit a cigarette.

Roy went to the backroom where Shirley was waiting with two teas. She pushed one to him. She had taken the cup from the saucer and placed the saucer on top of the cup to keep the contents warm. Roy took a quick look around. The back room was otherwise empty, but he dropped his voice anyway. "Thanks, what you found out?"

Shirley dropped the volume of her voice too. She was keen to tell him. "The job's in about three weeks, a TPO somewhere in the sticks north of London but within a couple hours' drive."

Roy took it in, "Hmm. Well, they could rob it if it stopped at a station..." But he didn't finish the sentence. "No. They're gonna stop it at signals somewhere remote."

Roy sat quietly, listening intently as Shirley continued. "You ain't gonna like this bit, the Krays got a bent copper whose gonna fix it so the right coaches are runnin'?"

Roy looked puzzled and leaned in closer. "Bent copper? Right coaches? What's that mean?"

Shirley shrugged. "Dunno, something about metal coaches, I think." Roy didn't know what on earth this was all about. "Metal? The bent copper's going to fix it '. What's that mean?"

Shirley. "That's what I heard."

Roy looked confused and looked away. He sipped his tea. "This bent copper, Met is he?"

Outside, Aldridge shifted his weight from one foot to the other and lit another cigarette. As he put the matches back in his pocket, he saw Shirley and Roy leave and go their separate ways.

Shirley had a ten minute walk to the Tube Station. She didn't notice Aldridge, nor would she have recognised him if she had. He followed onto the Tube, and from the Tube station to her home and watched her climb the stairs to her flat. He saw her walk along the passage on the first floor and enter her home. Now he knew where Brummie was getting his information from, Alfredo.

But the sense of satisfaction turned sour as Aldridge felt the panic rise in his stomach. If Billy found out, then Aldridge, who had supposedly 'tested' Alfredo, would be dealt with swiftly and with finality. And not only had he slipped up with Alfredo, but equally badly, one of Aldridge's own officers would be the prime architect of Billy's failure.

Aldridge had to stop the flow of information immediately for the sake of his own life and obviously, Billy had to be kept completely in the dark about it. Aldridge tried desperately to think of an alternative, but none worked: he had to kill Alfredo that night. But first he had to think of a way of doing so. He decided that once he had tempted Alfredo from the flat, he would shoot him in the first back street they encountered.

Aldridge, like most seriously bent detectives, had easy access to all the necessary 'props' to fit someone up, including illicit firearms. Such weapons were 'pocketed' having been abandoned at scenes of crime, handed in by the general public, or found during the execution of search warrants and immediately disowned by the householder.

One hour later, in a public telephone box near Shirley and Alfredo's flat, Aldridge waited impatiently for someone to answer his telephone call. Eventually the receiver was lifted, Aldridge pushed four pennies home. "This is Mr Black, who's speaking?"
Ronnie had long since forgotten Hill's words, 'if you get a call from a Mr Black then give him what he wants,' Instead, Ronnie was, well, Ronnie. "This is Ronnie, who the fuck is it?"
Aldridge. "A mutual friend called Billy told me if I ever called you for help, you'd give it."
Ronnie's memory returned. "Oh yeah. Alright, what you want?"
Aldridge spoke slowly. "Call Danny straight away. Tell him to get a message to the youngest member of his team to come to your place in Eric Street, back entrance, straightaway. I'll ring you back in five minutes and confirm you've done it."

Ronnie wasn't keen to take orders from this 'mystery', and he thought Alfredo might well be very reluctant to attend another private meeting with him. "Don't think that's right, I ain't supposed to make contact like that."
Aldridge didn't quibble, he knew Billy's name carried more than enough weight. "It's urgent. And tell him to come on his own."
Ronnie. "What if he ain't there?"
Aldridge kept his patience. "Like I said, I'll ring you back in five to check."

Aldridge put the phone down impatiently. Five minutes later he called back and Ronnie confirmed he had passed the message to Danny.

# Chapter 39

Aldridge had never met Danny and had no means of recognising him, but at about 8.15 that night he saw him knock at Alfredo's door. Eventually, the door was opened and Danny disappeared inside. Fifteen minutes later, Alfredo and Danny emerged. Two minutes more and they were on the street and heading towards the Tube station. Aldridge cursed Alfredo was not alone, but still he had to see this through. Revolver held in his pocket, Aldridge, wearing a long mackintosh and trilby, followed.

In close conversation, Alfredo and Danny made their way down the two flights of stairs at the station and onto the station platform. Aldridge followed them down and it then occurred to him there might be the opportunity to push Alfredo under a train. He picked up his pace. The more he thought about it, the more the idea made sense. He could make it look like an accident, his own Force would investigate and he could monitor the investigation. There would be no awkward questions from Billy, no noisy guns, no attracting undue attention and an easy getaway.

He moved closer towards his intended victim but the platform was too quiet, he could not get close enough to Alfredo without a strong chance of being seen to push him, he needed either a crowd of people.

The Northern Line train made a noisy entrance and screeched to a stop. Alfredo and Danny boarded and Aldridge boarded one coach behind theirs. He stood near the adjoining door and watched them furtively from the next coach. As the train approached Borough he saw them prepare to get off. He did likewise. As they stepped from the train, Alfredo and Danny were still deep in conversation and oblivious to what was happening around them. They walked towards the exit sign with Aldridge about 40 paces behind them.

The exit sign led them through a short tunnel to the platform running parallel to the one at which they had alighted and which served trains travelling in the opposite direction. To Aldridge's relief, this platform was very busy, he quickly got closer without any risk of showing out.

A train announcement broke his concentration, 'The train approaching is for Morden, please stand away from the doors to allow passengers to alight. Keep clear of the doors, please.'

A crowd of noisy and excited partygoers, probably medical students he thought, was jamming the platform between his prey and the exit. This was his chance, Aldridge moved swiftly as the waiting passengers jostled towards the platform edge in anticipation of the train.

Avoiding the tight group of noisy students, Danny and Alfredo moved towards the platform edge and walked single file, Danny was a single pace ahead of Alfredo. Aldridge had now reached Alfredo's back, just two feet ahead of him. The train could be heard approaching. Danny and Alfredo were having trouble moving forward as the boisterous students shoved towards the platform edge. The students' eyes were on the tunnel entrance.

Alfredo was no more than 18 inches from the platform edge. Aldridge quickly checked, the students were closely bunched around and noisily engaged with one another.

The noise of the approaching train increased as it burst from the tunnel mouth. Aldridge took one last quick glance around and moved towards Alfredo's side. As he did so he gave Alfredo one firm, shoulder-to-shoulder barge and moved on. Alfredo fell down onto the bed of the track about four feet below.

The train was approaching at high speed. The driver saw Alfredo land awkwardly on the track in front of him and immediately braked hard, the brakes screamed, metal on metal, but it was too late to stop.

Aldridge didn't wait to see the inevitable results, he moved quickly onwards through the throng of people and headed for the exit just yards away. Within seconds he was out of sight.

Danny, walking one pace ahead of Alfredo, was completely unaware of what had happened and had walked several paces further.

One partygoer, a young woman, standing close to where Alfredo had fallen, screamed loudly. Danny turned, he saw the terror in her eyes and her hands at her mouth. Her eyes were fixed on the tracks in front of her. Immediately following her gaze he saw the stunned Alfredo. It would of course be impossible for the train to stop before causing Alfredo's death.

Alfredo was only making a feeble attempt to climb back onto the platform, death was moments away.

Danny screamed at Alfredo and reached out to him. He grabbed Alfredo's lapel to pull him clear, but Alfredo's jacket tore.

Now the train was just 30 yards away, distance it would cover, even with brakes fully applied, in less than three seconds.

Danny grabbed Alfredo's outstretched arm and pulled with all his strength. Alfredo's legs would not have cleared the train if he had not rolled on his side onto the platform.

He survived with less than a moment to spare. The train continued to screech as it came to a stop. The partygoers had been shocked into silence.

Alfredo climbed to his feet, his hands, clothes and face dirtied. Danny made some token effort to brush him down as Alfredo seemed to whisper a prayer. The train doors opened, but the waiting passengers were still mesmerised by what had happened. The young woman who had screamed, went close to Alfredo. "I saw what happened, a man barged you, I saw him, he deliberately barged you, it was awful."

Alfredo was still in shock, Danny pushed in. "What man?"

The young woman looked around and down the platform. "He's gone now, he was about 50, tallish, wearing a long coat."

A young man, perhaps the young woman's boyfriend, put his hand on her shoulder. "Better call the police."

Alfredo nodded, but Danny was thinking otherwise. "Look, it was probably just an accident Love."

The train guard rushed from the rear of the train and was keen to make a Federal case out of it. But Danny would not allow Alfredo to stick around long enough for officialdom to get involved, too many questions would arise. Danny tugged at Alfredo's arm. They moved off the platform and out of the station. And into a nearby café. Alfredo was silent, lost within himself.

The place was virtually empty. Danny studied Alfredo and ordered two teas. They sat down as far from the counter as they could. Alfredo was staring into space, unblinking. They remained in silence for a while, each alone with their thoughts. Then Danny posed the big question. "You think it was deliberate?"

Alfredo was still white with shock, and his face and clothing were still smeared in black dust. Eventually he responded. "I felt a definite shove, it weren't no accident."

They sipped tea in silence for a minute, then Danny spoke. "That bookie Green making a point, or Gingers, or Fatty's, family?"

Alfredo nodded. "Yeah."

Danny scratched his head. "Well ...you gotta think they might try again. What you gonna do?"

Alfredo took another sip from the white mug. "... a few days and I'll be out the country."

Danny nodded.

Alfredo. "Must have followed me from the flat?"

Danny studied his tea. "No point in you going huntin' for Green, right?"

Alfredo looked slightly offended. "No. It's Shirl and Tony I'm worried about."

They finished their tea and Danny explained to the proprietor that his friend had fallen badly and asked if he could get cleaned up. A half-crown secured a smile and washing facilities. Danny told Alfredo it was best not to mention any of this to anyone else, it would only raise issues that best remained buried.

Alfredo went straight home. Danny phoned Ronnie and told him they wouldn't be able to make the meet, Ronnie didn't seem to care.

Within 30 minutes, Alfredo was back home. At first, he tried to bluff it with Shirley, he tried to tell her it was just a strong 'feeling' they should go to Italy straightaway. He tried to tell her there was no pressing reason why they all had to leave the flat that very night, why he had to go to Italy on the next available flight, and why he wouldn't leave her and Tony alone in the flat for a second. But of course, it was impossible. So, Alfredo told her a diluted version of the truth. "I think it was just an accident, some drunk, but no point in taking any chances."

Shirley didn't believe that either, but neither did she make a fuss. She guessed it was the bookie. She knew they had to leave immediately.

Alfredo was in the bedroom putting a few clothes in a suitcase. Little Tony was asleep on the bed. Shirley was watching her husband, preoccupied, worried, but trying not to show it. She kissed Alfredo lightly on the cheek. "I'm gonna miss ya."

Alfredo looked up from his packing. "I know. I'm gonna miss you an' all."

Shirley put her arms around him. Alfredo kissed her neck. "You'll be alright at Mum's, you ready to go?"

Shirley nodded, forcing a smile, "Yeah, all ready. I like it there and Tony loves it. When will I see ya?"

Alfredo thought for a moment, still reluctant to add anything to what he had already told her. "August."

Shirley nodded. They stared into one another's eyes and kissed tenderly. Shirley spoke softly. "When you get back, we can meet here on the night before the job. No one will know, and if Green come looking for you here, he'll be long gone by then."

Alfredo squeezed her gently, "Sounds good."

Then Shirley added the punchline. "But I got to know what day in August you're coming back. If it don't I ain't gonna be here am I?"

Alfredo was doing everything he could to assuage and comfort his wife, he sighed. "I'll be home Bank Holiday Monday, the 5th August, once it's dark."

Before closing the door behind her, Shirley had to have one more good look at the home she had created.

Their first stop was Luigi's to settle Shirley and Tony, then Alfredo, new passport in hand, headed for Heathrow.

# Chapter 40

Aldridge got to work early the next morning, but instead of going directly to the CID offices as usual, he visited the Force Headquarters Information Room.

The Information Room staff logged all significant crimes and incidents from across the nation's railways, docks and the London Underground. Aldridge knew personally every member of the Information Room staff and sometimes spent 20 minutes having a cuppa with them. He could rely on them to know what was happening across the force, as well as antics of senior officers. This morning he casually enquired about the last night's events.

Amongst the reports was one relating to a 'one-under' on the Underground at Borough station. The constable who attended in response to a call from a member of the public had made enquiries and concluded the near fatality was accidental. Details of the victim, who had not been injured, had not been obtained because he had left the scene 'before the arrival of police.' The log entry had been endorsed, 'N.F.A' (No further action). Aldridge cursed. Alfredo had to be permanently silenced as a matter of urgency, but Aldridge also had to get rid of Roy.

Just after lunchtime, Joe finished a brief phone call and approached Roy. "Sorry to interrupt Roy, just had a call from Aldridge, said tell you to go straight up to his office."

Roy had no reason to suspect what was coming. He'd been at HQ for just over six months and seemed to have been accepted. He hadn't proved himself to be brilliant, but he never expected to. Roy climbed the stairs to the floor above, knocked at Aldridge's door and waited. There was a terse. "Come in."

Roy walked smartly over to the front of the desk and waited to be, as was usual, invited to sit down. Aldridge was shuffling papers, he looked up at Roy with no hint of a smile or welcome, and there was no invitation to take a seat. "You've been posted back to Brum. Go back to your digs, pack your stuff. This is your last day here."

Roy couldn't believe it. "Why?"

Aldridge was perfectly calm. "Cos those are your orders. No point in you wasting any more time down here. Report for duty at New Street tomorrow at nine. That's it, off you go."

Roy knew he could do nothing about it, he couldn't even demand an explanation. He turned and walked towards the door. As he reached for the handle, Aldridge added, "Oh, and bring me everything you're workin' on. And details of any informants or info you've got. I want the lot before you go."

Roy walked back towards his office. He felt deflated, his head was swimming, he had experienced nothing like it before. And so far as he was aware, he had done nothing wrong. He found himself back at his desk, he opened his briefcase and packed his personal effects – a paperweight, a photograph of his family, pens, diary, then his phone rang. It was Shirley, she said they had to meet urgently. She sounded distressed, panicked. But Roy's priorities had now changed, he needed time to finish packing, to tell his wife he would be home from now on, to say his goodbyes, to get to his digs to pay what was owed for the week, collect his things, and of course to his train. He studied his watch. Shirley sounded so concerned, he agreed to meet her at 4.30pm.

Roy had digs near to BTP HQ in Park Royal. They had been on an 'approved' list handed out the day he arrived at FHQ. Roy's digs had only two things to commend them; they were close to his place of work, and they were cheap. The house was small, scruffy and cold. Roy's room looked out across a railway goods yard and the sound of shunting wagons continued 24 hours a day. He would be glad to see the back of all this, Aldridge, Force Headquarters, and London. Tonight he would be back in the arms of his family and in his own bed in his hometown.

Yet leaving in disgrace, for that's how it felt, left a bitter taste. He packed the few essentials he had brought with him, just toiletries and enough shirts and underwear to see him through the working week. Five minutes later, he closed the door at his digs and with suitcase in hand, made his way to the café. Both he and Shirley had significant news.

She told him all about the attack on Alfredo's life. Roy told her he had been posted back to Birmingham. They were both disheartened. He tried to show some interest in Shirley's news, though mentally he had already arrived back to Birmingham. Roy did his best to show interest. "You don't think the Krays were behind it, do you?"

"I don't know." She muttered.

But Roy was preoccupied with his fall from grace. "Why would I get posted, I haven't done ought wrong?"

Shirley thought for a while. "So who's decision was it?"

Roy looked down at his suitcase. "Dunno. But my inspector could have stopped it if he wanted to."

Shirley lit a cigarette, "So it was him then, weren't it?"

Roy didn't see where this was going. "Suppose so."

Shirley could see she might be onto something. "Do you think the two things are connected?"

Roy took a sip. "What two things?"

Shirley was impatient. "Jesus! You bein' transferred and somebody trying to kill Alfredo?"

The sight of large custard pies behind the counter, and the undoubted lift in his spirits they would provide, distracted him ."Err. No. Why would they be?"

Shirley was warming to a theory. "Well, we know there's a copper involved somewhere in this don't we?"

Roy tried to drag his eyes away from the pies. "No, we haven't got actual proof. Anyway, this will all be behind me in a few hours."

Shirley stubbed her cigarette out as if she was trying to kill a small animal. "Thanks."

Roy finally broke the spell the custard pies had held, "Sorry I didn't mean... I'm sorry I won't be able to help any more, that's the truth. Be good to get back to Brum, see me family every day, you know...That's all I meant."

Shirley softened her voice a little. "Don't know what I'm gonna do now. I can't go to the Met, it'd be a minefield. And I ain't been too impressed with your lot either."

Roy nodded. "Thanks. Me, you mean?"

Shirley didn't answer. "Can I have your phone number, just in case?"

Shirley's 'Park Drive' cigarette box was on the table in front of her. Roy wrote his office number there and glanced up at her. "What if I want to phone you?"

She had no intention of giving Alfredo's parents' number. She said nothing. Roy felt the need to make sure he could contact her if he needed to. "You must know somebody who has a number who could get a message to you?"

Shirley. "Okay, meet me in here at six. I'll work somethin' out by then."

Roy shook his head and looked at his watch. "Can't, I'll be on the..." Suddenly he looked panicky. "Oh shit! Forgot to hand over me files...Bloody well got to go back. That's me train buggered... all right, see you at six but not here, Euston Station cafeteria, by platform five."
Roy rushed off with his suitcase.

An hour earlier he was pleased to think he had seen this office for the last time. Now he placed his suitcase down by his desk, and sat down once more. The office was empty but for one person. Joe, as usual, was two-finger typing, spectacles perched the end of his nose. He looked up briefly, "Changed your mind?"
Roy smiled weakly. "No, forgot something."

Joe was already typing again. Roy gathered the Irish Mail Train file, various other crime files, maps, intelligence reports and TPO schedules from his desk. He put the papers back in order, typed up a covering note and carried it all to Joe. "For Aldridge, Joe."

Joe stopped typing and nodded briefly, then got back to his work. Roy had one more thing to say. "And thanks again for all the help Joe. You know you were the only one around here I trusted."

Joe stopped typing again, he took his glasses off and tapped the files Roy had put next to him. "I'll make sure he gets them, the dodgy bastard. It was him who made a fuss, said you had to go. It all happened this morning. The bosses decided over lunch in the mess. I've heard nothing like it in all me 42 years."

Roy didn't know what to make of Joe's comments. "So what you make of it'?"

Joe shook his head. "I dunno. I've seen a lot of so-called detectives pass through here over the years, and you're better material than most of them. Self-interest, bet your life on that."

Roy was thinking hard about those words when Aldridge sauntered in. He spoke to both of them like a long-lost friend. "Still here then Joe, time you were away. And as for you, Brummie, I thought you'd be home by now."

Joe didn't look at Aldridge, he didn't acknowledge him, he got back to his typing. Roy nodded. "Yes, sir."

Aldridge noted Roy had reverted from 'Den' to 'sir' and it amused him, 'So this was Brummie's pathetic effort at asserting himself', he thought. With a sickly smile on his face, he looked towards Joe. "Well, I'm away now Joe, got to see a man about a dog, don't forget to lock up."

As soon as the door had closed behind Aldridge, Joe stopped typing again and shook his head. "Bloody man."

The events of the last 24 hours ran through Roy's head, and he wondered why Aldridge had been so very desperate to get rid of him immediately. 'Never before in 42 years,' Joe had said.

Roy. "You lock Aldridge's office as well?"

Joe stopped typing and put the typed papers in his desk drawers and locked them. "No, does it himself."

Roy thought about it. "So what if he's off sick and somebody needs to get their hands on a file?"

Joe put his jacket on, then his trilby. "Security's got keys to every office. Anyway, I'm off."

Like many times before, Joe handed Roy the office key. They shook hands, Joe left. Roy had to think things through and stayed at his desk.

Meanwhile, Joe wandered down to the main entrance and out into the street. Aldridge hadn't got far, he was in conversation with another senior detective. As Joe passed by, Aldridge called to him, "Where's Brummie then?"

Joe called back. "Still working."

Roy picked up his suitcase, left the general CID office and left it unlocked. He went to a cleaners' cupboard near the stairs and hid his suitcase. Then he climbed the stairs to the floor above. The corridor was deserted. For the second time that day, he went to the door marked 'Det. Inspector', but this time he noted the room number, 'B310'. Then Roy made his way down to ground floor main reception area. There, an elderly security officer, bored out of his mind, was sitting at a desk with a flask of tea and his face in a Readers' Digest. The front doors to the building had been closed for the night, only the Information Room staff remained in the building, and they had their own entrance.

Roy approached the security man who was engrossed in a column headed, 'Humour in Uniform'. Roy held out the key. "General CID office. Sorry, but I forgot to lock it, would you mind?"

The security man didn't look up. "Suppose I'll have to."

Roy placed the key on the desk in front of the guard. But the man's eyes were still glued to his magazine. Roy needed a speedier reaction, "Sorry, but I won't rest until I know it's locked. Could you do it now...please?"

The expression on the security officer's face was clear, 'Who do you think you are? This is extremely inconvenient.' He sighed. "If it's so urgent, do it yourself."

Roy leaned forward. "Look, I'm really sorry but I've a train to catch to Birmingham."

The security officer hardly stirred, his eyes were still on the page. Roy's tone hardened. "Listen, the DCS has told me to be in Birmingham for 9pm on an urgent operational matter. I need to get the next train and I've got exactly twenty-eight minutes. If I miss it cos you can't be bothered, you can be certain the DCS will get to know."

That got the security man's attention. He sighed again. "Alright, alright, keep your hair on."

The security man stood up and made his way slowly past Roy, picking up the key from the desk on his way. As soon as his fat, shiny backside had disappeared up the stairs, Roy went to the key cabinet on the wall behind the security officer's desk. He quickly found the spare key for B310. Then he went to the foot of the stairs and listened hard. Not a sound.

Two minutes later, Roy was on the second floor and outside Aldridge's office. He felt scared, he had never before done anything like this. The corridor was still silent and he moved swiftly to unlock it, he took a deep breath and entered and locked the door behind him. He felt like a criminal. Meanwhile Aldridge, wondering what Brummie could be up to, re-entered the building via the Information Room.

Roy knew what he had to do and couldn't wait to get it over with. While his conduct wasn't actually illegal, it certainly was a huge breach of trust and a serious disciplinary offence. If he was caught he might well get the sack. He looked around the office - two large grey metal filing cabinets, Aldridge's big old wooden desk, a very heavy 'captain's chair' on one side of it and a more modest chair on the other, a coat stand, a picture of the Queen on the wall, some training course photographs and a plant pot.

Roy went straight to the filing cabinets but found them locked. He looked around the room again, went to the desk, sat in the captain's chair and looked down at the drawers, he pulled every one, they were all locked. He knew the culture of the Force well, and in many respects it didn't differ in London, Birmingham, Liverpool and Bristol. It was common to hide spare desk keys elsewhere in the office. Roy began a search, first under plant pot, on the top of the door frame, the back of the filing cabinets, under the heavy table lamp, on top of the frame holding the print of The Queen, under the heavy Bakelite telephone, on a ledge under the desk – and there it was, a single key. Roy quickly put the key into one of the top drawer. It fitted, and in a small box there he found a full set of cabinet and drawer keys. Three minutes had elapsed.

In the bottom right-hand drawer he discovered a small notebook with pages containing a list of dates, numbers and initials. Some appeared to be times of the day, other numbers might represent amounts of money, he couldn't tell immediately and had little time to contemplate. Might they represent illicit payments of money to Aldridge? Could the dates represent mail train attacks? Roy was torn, he couldn't possibly copy all the information the notebook contained, he would be there for hours. But neither could he ignore what might, on further scrutiny, be invaluable evidence.

On instinct, in defiance, or on impulse, Roy stuffed the little notebook in his pocket. He still had the filing cabinet and other drawers to search. He quickly relocked the bottom right-hand drawer and moved to the next one. There was nothing of interest, he relocked it and moved his hands towards the drawer above. Then he heard it, a movement outside the office door followed by a key being inserted into the door lock. Roy felt his heart pound and the sweat instantly break out on his forehead. He had no time to think. He dived under the big old desk. Roy's heart was racing and thumping in his chest. He heard the door close, sensed movement on the carpet just a few feet away, a second passed, he saw Aldridge's shoes beneath the vanity screen at the front of the desk. If Aldridge were to come around to the business side of his desk now, Roy would certainly be seen. Aldridge seemed to be hesitating.

Then Roy heard the desk phone being lifted from its cradle. "Hello. This is Detective Inspector Aldridge, has Detective Constable Walcott left the building yet?"
There was a pause... Then Aldridge spoke again. "Yes, the Brummie. Has he gone?"
Another pause. "You're sure?" ... "Okay."
The receiver was replaced.

A few seconds later, Roy heard the door close behind Aldridge and the key being turned in the lock. Aldridge had departed.

Roy couldn't wait to escape. He gave himself a couple of minutes for Aldridge to get clear and to try to calm himself. His mind was racing. What if Aldridge came back again? What if he was still in the building? He might be talking to the security man on the front desk, or in the CID office, or even in the Information Room. What if they found him and the stolen notebook in his pocket? He would be charged with theft, he might go to prison. Roy was still sweating, panicking. He had only just started searching, what else might he find? He would never get another chance. But he just couldn't stay there any longer, his courage had failed. He came from under the desk, quickly put everything back as it was, apart from the notebook, and hastily left the office. The corridor was silent.

He quickly collected his suitcase from the broom cupboard and hurried towards the Information Room. There he said a quick farewell to officers he hardly knew and got some odd looks in return. Then he left the building via the Information Room exit.

Running late, Roy met Shirley in a cramped, grim and crowded railway buffet at Euston Station. They found two seats on a table shared by a crying child and its mother, and a drunken vagrant. Neither Shirley nor Roy bothered to buy any refreshments. Roy was still agitated. He looked about furtively. "So, you got that phone number for me?"

Shirley leaned in close and spoke in an excited whisper. "Listen, the TPO. It's the first week in August, just after the Bank Holiday weekend."

Roy leaned forward and matched her posture. He took a quick glance at the drunk by his side who was in a quiet stupor and unlikely to be able to even recall his own name. "How do you know?" Roy asked in a loud whisper.

"I know." She said with certainty. Then, "What can we do?"

There was another pause while they both thought about the possibilities. Roy looked at his watch. "Don't know. Unless you can get Alfredo nicked beforehand, I think it's your only way out now."

Shirley had heard that option before, and it was no more appealing now. "No. I ain't doing that."

Roy moved on from Shirley's news, 'Been thinking. You might be right, my guvnor might be involved."

Shirley was eager to know more. She was keenly aware that in a few minutes, Roy would be gone for good and she would be on her own. If there was anything more Roy knew which just might help her then she needed to hear it now. "Go on."

Roy looked across at the woman sitting next to Shirley. She was totally engaged in trying to pacify her restless baby. Roy spoke slowly. "What if he was involved and found out about you and me? He'd have to get rid of me... and you an all...or get rid of Alfredo."

Shirley lit a cigarette and leaned in even closer. "If he's involved, he wouldn't want to get rid of Alfredo, would he?"

They paused for thought. Roy's thoughts went back to his hiding under Aldridge's desk, he pulled out the little notebook and opened it at a random page filled with notes. Before Roy had finished his glance through the pages, Shirley cut in. "What's your guvnor's name then?"

Roy looked up and made sure he could not be heard by others at the table. "Aldridge, Detective Inspector Dennis Aldridge."

Another pause, then Roy added. "I found this in his desk."

Roy put the notebook down in front of him. Shirley picked it up immediately and began to study it closely. The number '200' was written against every month for many months, bigger numbers were shown at irregular intervals. She noticed what might be a bank account number. Shirley was fascinated by it and couldn't take her eyes off the pages. "How long you had it? He know you've got it?"

Roy explained as Shirley studied. "I err, took it, borrowed it, from his office just now. Course he don't know."

Shirley had a firm grip on the book. "This might be the key. Mind if I keep it for now?"

Roy took a deep breath and another look at the others at the table, buried in their own worlds. He whispered. "Listen, according to the Larceny Act, I nicked it. Now you're officially receiving stolen property. So, let's not get pinched."

Shirley couldn't help but smile. "If it's what I think, he ain't gonna file a complaint, is he?"

Roy shook his head in frustration. He wasn't happy to trust the continuation of his employment and liberty to the care of Shirley. "Listen, you take that book and I'll deny all knowledge of ever seeing it."

Shirley ignored the comment. Her eyes were still on the pages. "It's him."

Roy was suddenly fearful Shirley might go overboard and take some massive action against Aldridge based on nothing tangible. He needed to calm her down. "There's a big leap there. All you got is a notebook with some numbers and some dates and places. None of it ties together. Don't go off half-cocked."

Shirley put the notebook in her pocket. "Don't worry, your name won't be nowhere near any of this, and I ain't goin' to do nothin' daft."

Roy was feeling more nervous by the second. "I think I'd better have it back, give us it back."

Shirley, leaned back in her seat and increased the volume of her voice considerably. "You want to take somethin' off me you'll have to fight me for it."

The drunk's eyes opened and he attempted to focus on what was going on. The woman sitting next to Shirley turned sharply, baby in arms, and stared first at Shirley, then at Roy. Roy swallowed hard. Shirley calmed her voice again. "So that's it then, I'm on me own."

Roy stared at the notebook, now firmly and irretrievably grasped in her hands, and simply nodded. "You were going to give me a phone number." She shook her head. "Been thinkin' about it, I can't, but I won't let you down, I swear. And it's Shirley by the way."

Roy looked at his watch, stood up and lifted his suitcase. They said goodbye in the noisy cafeteria. She didn't entirely hear what he said. By 10 o'clock, Roy was at home with his wife and children and glad to be putting his London experience behind him. There was no one on earth he could even tell about it.

# Chapter 41

That evening, just after dusk, Aldridge parked a nondescript saloon car 100 yards away from Shirley and Alfredo's flat. He steeled himself to kill Alfredo on his doorstep. And if the need arose, he would do whatever was necessary to anyone else who got in his way. The chosen weapon, a heavy kitchen knife, was concealed in his mackintosh. A gun would cause too much noise outside the flat, he could easily be seen or trapped on the landing or stairs. He pulled up the tall collar of his mackintosh and pulled the front of his trilby down to mask as much of his face as he could.

The street was quiet, and he got to the flats and up the stairs to the first floor quickly. The landing was silent. Every front door was recessed by about three feet. He stepped into the recess outside Alfredo and Shirley's flat and knocked the door. He gripped the handle of the long, heavy knife and pulled it from his coat, ready to stab whoever answered. But no light came on. He overheard no voices, no sound from radio or television. He waited impatiently and knocked again. After a few minutes, he returned to his car. Aldridge moved his car so no one could approach the flats without his being aware. Then he lit another cigarette, opened the car window and waited. The following morning, dishevelled and tired, he drove away.

Later that morning, Roger Cordrey was at work in his florist shop in Brighton, as he had been every day lately. His mind however, was rehearsing every aspect of the big job. The phone rang, it was Aldridge. "It's me, you expectin' company?"
Roger always felt uncomfortable at the sound of that voice. "No."

Aldridge hung up, and within one minute he entered the shop. Worried, tired and dishevelled, he forced a smile. "All set then?"

Roger was preparing a wreath. He looked up from his work, suspicious. He had not been expecting to see this face ever again. "Yeah."
Roger's eyes went back to the wreath. Aldridge tried to ask with apparent concern. "Seen Alfredo recently?"
Roger wasn't sure how to react, he kept his eyes fixed on the greenery. "Nah, he's not about."
Aldridge had an excuse for asking. "I heard that someone had a pop at him, Underground, weren't it?"

Roger's tone didn't change. "Yeah. But he's alright."

Aldridge. "Well, I hope he's safe. We need every hand...where is he?"

Roger kept his eyes fixed on his work. "Abroad."

Aldridge. "Good, he'll be safe then. Best he stays away until the last minute."

Roger replied without a second thought. "That's the plan."

At that moment Danny entered the shop. He had never seen Aldridge before and he stared at him, 'Old Bill' he thought.

Roger felt much more confident with Danny now present. "Danny, this is the copper you've been dying to meet."

Danny eyed Aldridge with loathing. "So....what you doin' 'ere then?"

Roger chimed in. "He's been asking where Alfredo is."

Danny glared at Aldridge. "Thought we was all makin' our own arrangements, so why you askin'?"

Aldridge. "I don't fuckin' answer to you Pembroke."

Danny opened the shop door as if to show Aldridge out. "Was there anything else?"

Aldridge walked out and Danny slammed the door behind him. Aldridge had got what he wanted.

# Chapter 42

Shirley spent that Friday evening in Alfredo's old bedroom above Luigi's, studying Aldridge's notebook very closely. After an hour she felt certain she had identified encrypted train times, probably mail trains, she thought. Some entries represented stations, she concluded. There were many, and all were abbreviated. Most of them were impossible to identify - MP, WSH, SC, and so on, but one or two others were more obvious – Vic, KX, Liv S. LB, CX, WTL, etc.

Elsewhere in the book she found those unique numbers repeated, though in reverse, with what might have been values e.g. 15,000, 4,800, 34,000 and so on. Every few pages contained different lists of text and numbers. By the end of the evening she was convinced all the entries were highly organised, systematically connected and unnecessarily encoded unless to hide illegality.

It was in the early hours that she awoke worrying that perhaps this was just the sort of information a detective investigating mail train thefts might keep. After painful minutes of self-doubt, and to her great relief, she remembered Aldridge would not have 'elaborately encrypted' information if he held it innocently. But she couldn't get back to sleep and went back to the notebook enthusiastically. At some point in the early morning light, she noticed what appeared to be a rolled piece of paper, just visible, hidden in the spine of the book. On it were written a mix of letters and numbers that appeared to be a bank account number.

The next morning, as Tony slept in a carrycot near his busy grandparents. Shirley was sitting in a quiet corner of the café in hushed conversation with an old school friend. Pat was known for her cheque kiting and hoisting (shoplifting) expertise. Pat looked at the rolled note bearing the bank account number. "Yeah, looks like a sort code with the account number in reverse.

Pat told Shirley the sort code would identify both the bank and the branch at which the account was held. Once Shirley had that information, Pat explained it would be easy for Shirley to find out more. She told Shirley to ring the general number for the branch and deliberately ask for the wrong department. Pat suggested Shirley might say she wanted a bank loan. Once Shirley was put through to the loans department she should say she'd been connected to the wrong one, and ask to be transferred to 'client accounts.'

Shirley gave her old school friend a quizzical look. Pat explained, if the call was transferred between departments, the person ultimately receiving the call, in 'client accounts,' would hear the ring tone associated with internal calls, and that was vital. Shirley had no idea how to establish the bank branch from the numbers shown. Pat told her this sort of information was available at public libraries. Pat would find out for her.

Shirley asked further questions and made a few notes. Twenty minutes later Pat left and

Shirley cleared the table and took the cups for washing. Her mother-in-law was keen to know what had been going on and asked politely about her new friend. Shirley didn't want to tell her mother-in-law lies, she had become fond of her, but she had no choice.

Later that day, Shirley was washing up when the phone rang. She rushed to the phone, it was Pat. Pat was brief. "I looked it up, Lloyds, Tottenham Court Road branch."

Shirley looked at her watch. She had no time to lose. But she could do nothing until Monday morning.

Monday arrived slowly. At 9.06 at the Tottenham Court Road branch, a well-dressed young bank clerk was typing at his desk when his phone rang. He could tell from the ring tone it was an internal call. "Client Accounts, Alexander speaking."

Shirley did her best to sound a little less 'sarf' London, "Good morning Alexander, this is Janet at Sydenham branch, not sure if we've met?" Alexander wasn't sure either. "Err, morning Janet, how can I help?" Shirley took a deep breath. "One of your customers, account number 47394409. Head Office is doing a special audit and for some reason they've sent the papers here by mistake."

The bank clerk thought this sounded like additional work. "Oh." Shirley pushed on. "I've tried to explain, but they are insisting they've got it right. You know what it's like."

Alexander understood very well how difficult head office could be. "Yes."

Shirley. "My manager says the best thing is for us to answer the query here. Be quicker. That okay with you Alexander? Or do you want to sort it out yourself?"

Alexander had no desire to volunteer to do work others were prepared to do for him. "No, that's okay. You can do it, thanks."

Shirley was nearly there. "That's alright Alex, just get me the account holder details and all payments in over £50 over the last 12 months."

Alexander sounded disappointed. Perhaps he was hoping to escape any additional duties. "That might be a lot."

Shirley. "Have a look, I don't think it will be."

Alexander, "Err...alright, I'll put it in the internal."

Shirley had been well briefed. "No. Do it now please, over the phone, I need to get this off my desk today, sorry but otherwise I'll have to send it all over to you, I'm busy myself."

That did the trick. Five minutes later Alexander was providing the information.

As soon as the phone went down, Shirley studied the information. The account holder, calling himself Mr Dennis Smith had been receiving £200 per month in cash payments. In addition, at irregular intervals there had been much larger cash payments in, the largest being £900. The balance stood at £5,000, the price of a nice house.

At first disappointed the account wasn't in Aldridge's name, she was now certain of her ground. Once she proved he was the true account holder, his deceit would help sink him. Dennis Smith's address was shown as 17 Sangi Avenue, Peckham.

Shirley made her apologies to her in-laws and went to the library. There, Kelly's Directory identified 17, Sangi Avenue, Peckham as occupied by a Mr Arthur Bloom. At lunchtime, Shirley and Tony took a bus ride to Peckham. She found 17 Sangi Avenue was a corner shop. An advertisement prominently displayed in the shop window read, 'Have your letters and parcels delivered here - two shillings a week.'

What could she do? She could hardly try to question Mr Bloom, for all she knew he was a crooked mate of Aldridge. Neither could she wait around outside for days in the hope Aldridge would turn up. She went back home.

That evening, once Tony was asleep, Shirley looked again at the information she had gained from the notebook and the bank. Most of the money had stayed in the account, but small amounts were regularly drawn in cash and there was the occasional payment out to just one other account. She had an idea. If she could show this second account belonged to Aldridge, then it would at least provide evidence linking him to several substantial payments from a bogus bank account. It would be enough for the police to launch a proper investigation. More importantly, it gave Shirley evidence with which to blackmail him. But how could she get his legitimate bank details?

Shirley was up early the next morning with a plan fresh in her mind. Before the café opened, Shirley, Tony and her in-laws had breakfast together. Her in-laws readily agreed to look after Tony while she went clothes shopping in preparation for the trip to Italy. By 8.45am she was outside a small solicitor's office in Catford, South London. The sign outside proclaimed 'Reece & Lunt. Specialists in criminal defence.' Reece was a bent, middle-aged solicitor who sounded as like an Old Etonian, which he might well have been. Reece was aided (and abetted) by a younger clerk who did mundane work and some less mundane, dubious stuff. The clerk had long since adopted the manner of a 'man-of-the-world', qualified solicitor. Now everyone assumed him to be just that. In reality, his only legal qualification was a Certificate of Secondary Education in Woodwork. It was a 'legal qualification' only in the sense that it was not actually, illegal. As for the other partner, Mr Lunt, no one had seen him in years.

Margaret was a gentle, honest and fair-minded middle-aged woman who did the admin, typing, made the tea and did everything else the legal eagles at Reece & Lunt could not be bothered to do or saw as beneath them.

Shirley's father had appreciated the 'cash in hand' relationship he had with Reece. It was also very useful to rely on Reece to get a bung to the right police officer without skimming too much off the top for himself. Shirley had visited frequently, but not for several years.

A bell announced Shirley's arrival as she opened the door, Margaret, busy typing, looked up and recognised her immediately. They exchanged pleasantries and Margaret enquired about Shirley's father. Shirley explained she needed to speak to Reece urgently. Within two minutes she was in his office, sipping tea. Shirley didn't tell him a lot, she didn't need to and he wouldn't have wanted to know anything he might later need to deny.

Shirley asked him if he would write a letter from an anonymous female to the chief constable of the British Transport Police. She said it was important to create the impression the letter came from a solicitor "more used to selling houses and doing wills" than dealing with crime. The letter was to be written on behalf of an elderly woman, a 'do-gooder.' Shirley asked that Reece's name, and the name of his practice, was kept off the letter, he was much too well known. Reece sat behind his large antique desk and listened with interest for a whole five minutes without speaking. He gave the occasional encouraging head nod, sipped his tea, frowned a couple of times and made a scribbled note.

When Shirley had finished, he sat back and smoothed the right-hand side of his face as if gently removing a cobweb. He remained silent for another few seconds. Then he spoke gravely. "We're old friends. I don't see why I shouldn't do this. You simply wish to keep your generosity and public spiritedness to yourself. I take your point about my own fame. And yes, I know just the chap to organise a cheque, he has a small practice in deepest Surrey."

Reece smiled. "The police will have never heard of him, land law and trusts, you see."

He looked down at his note and summed up. "I will compose a letter that will be sent under the name of a fellow professional, which asks that a reward payment of £50 be made to the officer named. Shirley nodded. Reece looked back at his note. "It will be delivered to the Transport Police Headquarters tomorrow ...all strictly in the interests of rewarding outstanding public service by one of their officers."

She knew he wouldn't disappoint, as long as she handed the 'readies' over and Reece had an excuse if one were ever needed. Reece continued to enjoy the sound of his own very polished voice. "And you know Shirley, because your father was such a long-standing and valuable client, not to say friend, my fee is just £25. Usual terms apply of course."

Shirley knew 'usual terms,' meant cash up front. Reece had a second thought. "Plus, of course the value of the cheque you wish me to organise, plus the inevitable admin fee my country cousin is bound to raise."

Shirley paid him the cash immediately. They spent five minutes drafting a letter. He promised to send it by special delivery that very day to his Surrey friend for signature and immediate onward transmission.

A few days later, the letter arrived at BTP headquarters addressed to the Chief Constable. Within an hour it was on its way to the Detective Chief Superintendent (DCS). The DCS sat behind his desk staring at the letter and cheque. There was nothing on his desk but his elbows, blotting paper, pen, two wire baskets and a black Bakelite telephone. The subliminal message, 'Here you will find cleanliness, self-discipline, functionality and lack of affectation.' But nothing could have been further from the truth, for in reality, it was all pretence.

The DCS had an awkward smile on his face. Sitting opposite him was one of the most successful detectives in the Force. The DCS was always slightly nervous of his operational detectives, perhaps because he himself had never actually been one for very long. He thought himself above them and secretly regarded them as being rather like police dogs. Both did a valuable and dirty operational job, but both were often noisy, vicious, and frequently left a trail of crap for somebody else to clear up. Neither were much good with a pen, and both were best kept on a leash and subject to simple, unambiguous, orders. He smiled suspiciously at the man sitting opposite. Aldridge smiled back, exposing his poor dental hygiene. The DCS peered down at the letter.

"...written by a lady, let me read part of what she says, *'The officer was of course unaware of my presence, but I watched the trial throughout and felt relieved when the jury announced the 'guilty' verdict.*

*I am sure had it not been for the diligence, intelligence and skill of Mr Aldridge, the perpetrator would not have been brought to justice.*

*One hears in the press these days of some officers, particularly in London, falling short of the high standards of policing we, as a nation, have come to expect. It is thus particularly gratifying to bring this instance of excellent policework to your attention.*

*Please pass my sincere thanks and greatest respects to Detective Inspector Aldridge, and please present him with the enclosed cheque for fifty pounds as a small token of my high esteem....* blah, blah, blah, ...

Anyway, the chief constable says you can keep it."

Aldridge was smiling and his brain whirring. "Very kind of all concerned boss. Anonymous eh?"

The DCS nodded and handed over the letter and cheque and stood up, which was of course his way of saying 'I have given you a precious three minutes of my valuable time, it's now time for you to leave.'

Aldridge obliged and stuffed the cheque in his pocket. It was only fifty quid, and these days that was not a lot of money to him, just about two weeks' wages. Still, money was the one thing you could never get enough of. Aldridge paid the cheque into his account the following day. It would be another three working days before it cleared.

# Chapter 43

Tuesday 30 July 1963, seven days before the planned major TPO robbery. Shirley had hardly slept. She waited for 9am before phoning the solicitor's office. Margaret told her she would enquire with Reece and call her back. It was 11.15 before Margaret did so and connected her to Reece. He told her he had just come off the phone to his contact in Surrey. The cheque had been paid into a Barclays account at Pimlico, held by a Mr Dennis Aldridge. Reece read out the details of the account and Shirley, with biro and scrap paper at the ready, wrote it all down. She immediately recognised the account number as the one that received payments from the dodgy Lloyds account at Tottenham Court Road. It was all she needed.

Now Shirley had to get Aldridge on his own, confront him, tell him she had damning evidence of his corruption. She would demand he leave Alfredo alone or else. Time was running out, but she had it all planned. She would place details of the evidence against Aldridge and an explanatory letter into sealed envelopes addressed to her MP and several newspapers. The explanatory letter would describe not only the evidence, and the fact the secret notebook was held by a friend, but also why she feared for her husband's life and her own. But she knew that unless she could reach Aldridge before he reached Alfredo, it would all be for nothing. As it stood, Alfredo would either be murdered, or participate in a crime that could see him imprisoned for the rest of Tony's childhood.

Shirley phoned Roy's old number at BTP HQ CID, confident someone there would get Aldridge to the phone. It was answered by what sounded like a kindly old man. Shirley asked to speak to Detective Inspector Aldridge. She refused to give her name but said it was urgent. The old man seemed to want to help but explained the inspector had not yet reported for duty that day. She rang again an hour later, and so on through the day. The old man kept his patience. In the end, he assured her Aldridge would almost certainly be in for duty the next day. The next day came, and by mid-afternoon she had made no progress. Aldridge seemed to have vanished and time was disappearing fast.

It seemed to Shirley she had three options. She could keep phoning the Transport Police in the hope of eventually reaching Aldridge. But what if he was off duty owing to illness? What if he had gone to Italy to kill Alfredo there? Perhaps he was on holiday, or on a training course? He might not come back to the Force until after the robbery, he might not come back at all. She decided she would have visit his home. She could get the address from the bank. They seemed easy enough to scam. She could also visit the corner shop run by Mr Bloom in Peckham again, and try to get his home address from there. She decided quickly, she would try all three. The 'in-laws' always seemed delighted to look after Tony if Shirley wanted to pop out for any reason, and that day was no exception.

After providing a quick alibi to her in-laws, she went to Peckham. The door of the small corner shop was open wide. From the other side of the counter an elderly fat man, wearing a discoloured vest and dirty grey trousers held up by a thick brown leather belt, looked down at her through tired eyes.

Shirley smiled. "There's a bloke what comes in here to pick up his private mail. He goes by the name of Dennis Smith."

She held his gaze, waiting and hoping he would engage with her, tell her something. But he didn't respond, not a word, not even a change in expression. Shirley went on. "I need to speak to him urgent. It's in his interest."

The old man shrugged. Shirley tried harder. "When you reckon he'll be in then?"

The old boy shrugged again. Shirley put her hand into her pocket. "Will you give him a letter?"

The old man stuck out his hand. Shirley took an envelope from her pocket and handed it over. Shirley repeated how urgent and important the matter was, but got no response at all. There was nothing more she could do, she thanked the shopkeeper and left. The shopkeeper threw the letter into a cardboard box near his feet. The letter simply told Aldridge to leave a contact number with his colleagues urgently, or find himself in prison.

Shirley got back to the cafe in time to phone the BTP HQ CID number again. The same kindly old man apologised and told her Mr Aldridge was taking annual leave and would not be back on duty until after the Bank Holiday. In desperation, she asked for his home address, but of course he would not give it.

She tried to phone Roy in Birmingham, an unhelpful man answered and told her he could not discuss anyone's hours of duty or whereabouts. Exasperated, Shirley she retrieved from her bedside drawer, the scribbled bank account information Reece had given her. But it was too late to do more that day, the banks were now closed.

The following morning, Shirley made another call, like the one she had made to 'Alexander' at Lloyds in Tottenham Court Road, and again found a bank employee eager to let someone else do his job for him. She soon established Aldridge's legitimate bank account at Barclays in Pimlico showed an address in Commondale, Putney.

It took her over an hour to get there, and when she got off the train she had a 20 minute walk. Commondale, she discovered, was a long road of old detached and semi-detached houses. Aldridge's was a tired-looking semi. The windows were dirty, the curtains drab, the paint faded and peeled, the whole place looked untidy and unloved. She knocked at the door but there was no reply. She went to the house next door. There were two old cycles leant against the outer wall, one had a wheel missing, the other a saddle. It was all very scruffy. She knocked and immediately heard a dog bark ferociously inside. A middle-aged woman opened the door about three inches. Shirley explained she was looking for the policeman who lived next door, but the neighbour simply said she hadn't spoken to 'the copper' in ages and promptly closed the door again.

So Shirley tried the house on the other side. A young housewife opened the door and tried to be helpful it seemed, but could only tell Shirley that Aldridge always 'kept himself to himself' and seemed to live on his own. She had no idea when he might return, she rarely saw him. Shirley returned to Aldridge's house, and posted the letter she had bought with her through his letterbox.

That night when she climbed into bed, she continued to rack her brain and to worry. Was Aldridge in Italy? What more could she do?

# Chapter 44

It was a warm late afternoon on Monday 5th August 1963, with less than 36 hours before the robbery, when Shirley returned to their flat for the first time in weeks. Shirley had spoken to Alfredo on the telephone occasionally and they always expressed how they missed one another. In the last call, Alfredo asked her to bring Tony to the flat that night, he had not seen him in weeks and missed him as much as he did Shirley.

Of course, Shirley couldn't begin to explain to him about Aldridge. It would quickly lead to questions about her passing information to Brummie. So Alfredo still believed that the bookmaker had been responsible for the attempt on his life and had no reason to think that this evening the flat would be a particularly dangerous place for them. After all, it had been weeks since he had been pushed under a train and even if Green knew his home address, he would surely have given up watching by now.

Shirley had, in their last call, suggested a posh hotel would be more romantic. But Alfredo wouldn't have it, he could not risk a public place for fear of recognition. If he was recognised, his alibi could be easily destroyed.

As her return to the flat now reminded her, Shirley loved their home. It was all so new, untarnished by bad memories, and of course, she had chosen everything it contained. She tried to tell herself the threat from Aldridge had evaporated, but the fear nagged at her. As she opened the windows wide, she reflected, this would be their last night there. Tomorrow she would return to Luigi's, and a few days later she, Alfredo and their son could be safe and sharing a new life in Italy. But one way or the other, the next 24 hours were critical.

The couple had long since discovered Alfredo was the better cook. But this evening she would prepare a special Italian meal, Braciole. Beef cooked with breadcrumbs, garlic, Pecorino, parsley, olive oil, white wine and tomato. He liked to enjoy it with Sangiovese, an Italian red wine. Shirley consoled herself. There was no reason to think Aldridge would be well-informed enough to know her husband would come home tonight. But she also knew if there were to be an attempt on Alfredo's life before the robbery, it would probably be before Alfredo met the other robbers tomorrow. And it might take place at or near the flat, after all, this was the place he would most probably visit, and Aldridge's only hope.

But already, Aldridge was nearby and ready to strike. He had no idea what time Alfredo would get home, or where they might meet, but he had seen Shirley enter the flat, and where she went, Alfredo would surely follow.

Shirley had the evening planned, she would feed Tony and put him to bed, then prepare dinner, tidy up and take a long bath before attempting to look her best. Fully prepared, she would then relax with a glass of wine, listen to music and await his homecoming. She knew Alfredo would have to stay in the flat and out of sight for the next 15 hours or so, and it pleased her.

Tony went to bed without any fuss. Shirley went to the bathroom, looked at the aspidistra still centred on the window sill and put the bathroom light on. Then unpacked the ingredients for the meal, took Alfredo's large meat knife from the drawer and began the preparation. Forty minutes later, she put the meal into the oven to cook slowly. She glanced at the wine she had used in the dish, most of it remained in the bottle. She poured herself a generous glass. Next, she would look in on Tony, then tidy up, wash up and lay the table.

She turned the transistor radio up a notch, Del Shannon was singing 'Runaway' and she loved it. The music took her back to when she and Alfredo were courting. The smell of the dinner slowly cooking reminded her of their first days of marriage. And there was more promise and anticipation in the air than at any time since they became engaged.

But a knock at the door interrupted her thoughts, 'It's Alfredo', she smiled broadly and ran to let him in.. She unbolted it in record time and pulled it open.

Aldridge took her by surprise. He forced his hand over her mouth and nose and pushed his way in. Easily forcing her to the floor, he trapped her arms with his knees, his gloved hands covered Shirley's nose and mouth. She was panicking, fighting for air. Aldridge was too strong for her, too heavy. She felt the light start to fade.

The flight back from Italy had arrived a little late, and Alfredo was keen to get home. He loved Italy, the food, the people, the weather, everything. And the next 36 hours would, with luck, make him rich beyond his dreams. A fabulous life awaited. All he had to do was see the TPO job through. And between now and then he just had to remain hidden. All was going according to plan.

Wearing a beard for the first time in his life, he took a cab from Heathrow. It was dark when the cab stopped 100yards from his home. He paid the cabbie, pulled his tracksuit hood up over his head and, holdall over his shoulder, he walked casually around to the back of the block of flats. He looked up; the bathroom light was on and the aspidistra was in the centre of the bathroom window. He smiled, all was well. He had been away from Shirley and Tony for weeks and the absence reminded him of how much he loved them both. He felt a thrill at the idea of holding her again. He quickly made his way silently up the steps and along the landing. He knocked on the front door and waited for Shirley to unbolt it. Nothing happened. He knocked again. Still no response. He pushed gently on the door; she had left it on the latch. He smiled in anticipation and pushed the door open. Both the lights in the small hall and the sitting room lights were out, the radio played Cliff Richard and The Shadows singing, 'Please Don't Tease.' The rich smell of his favourite meal filled his senses. Smiling, he closed the door behind him. Not wanting to spoil the mood Shirley had created he left the light switch untouched and having dropped his holdall in the middle of the sitting room, he went to Tony's bedroom and peeped in. tony appeared to be sleeping peacefully. He kissed his son gently and closed the bedroom door behind him.

Alfredo looked towards the bedroom in anticipation. The lights were also off, but the limited night light was sufficient for him to see the door was wide ajar. He said nothing but walked quietly to the bedroom door. The bedroom curtains were open, and the room was well lit by the moon and street lighting. All indications were that Shirley planned an evening of pleasure and was waiting for him in the bedroom. This was the 'old' Shirley. He smiled and without speaking, walked lightly into their bedroom, Shirley was in bed; the blankets pulled up high and covering her completely. Discarding his jacket, he sat on the bed and whispered to her, but there was no response. Alfredo took off his shoes, then stood and removed his trousers and socks. He turned and leaned across the bed to kiss her.

But as his face neared his wife's, Aldridge moved from behind the bedroom door, took two silent strides and struck Alfredo heavily on the back of the head with his truncheon.  Alfredo felt the searing pain and raised his hands to protect himself. As he did so, Aldridge raised the truncheon high again and brought it crashing down. In the half-light, Aldridge didn't immediately sense Alfredo's movement, this time Aldridge missed, Alfredo twisted and turned, and in desperation grabbed at Aldridge's clothing. Alfredo pulled Aldridge close so that he could not take another swing. They rolled onto the floor and separated. Alfredo got to his feet quicker and grabbed the truncheon, and with his free hand, punched Aldridge in the face. Aldridge lost his grip on the truncheon and fell back against the wall and the light switch. Suddenly the room was full of light. Alfredo now held the truncheon. But he was suddenly aware his wife had not moved at all, his attention was diverted to the bed. In that moment, Aldridge took a half a pace forward and delivered a heavy blow to Alfredo's jaw. Alfredo dropped to his knees. Aldridge punched him again and again and again. Alfredo lay semi-conscious on the floor. Shirley's body remained motionless. Aldridge, breathing heavily, stood over Alfredo. He had won.

All that Aldridge had to do now, once he had recovered his breath, was to finish it. Now it would be easy, and he would simply leave the bodies to be found in the days ahead. By then he would be long gone and very rich.

A heavy knock at the front door interrupted Aldridge's thoughts, he quickly turned Alfredo onto his back and handcuffed him. Then he put the bedroom light out, closed the bedroom door behind him, and went into the dark sitting room. Another firm knock at the door. Aldridge tensed and froze in the middle of the room. He listened intently. Then a voice from outside broke the silence, "So, I can go now then, can I?"
Silence.
"I said, is everything alright ... You two?"

Aldridge didn't know what to do, he had no escape. He didn't know how many were outside. If it was just one man, he might take him by surprise. His mind raced. Should he open the door and strike out? Perhaps whoever it was would go away if he remained silent. He decided if he got close enough to the front door, he could hear if there was more than one person, or hear whoever it was walk away. He took two steps before tripping over Alfredo's holdall and into Tony's 'infant walker'. Both he and the 'walker' crashed against the low coffee table that held the very expensive new TV.

Outside, Danny was a little annoyed and in a quandary. Earlier, he had agreed with Shirley he would discreetly make sure Alfredo was safe between leaving the cab and getting indoors. He and Shirley had planned that she, having opened the door to her husband, would wave down to Danny on the street. Then he would leave. But what, he wondered, was he to make of this? She hadn't waved, she failed to answer the door, and all the lights were out.

But the crash from inside the flat, followed by silence, changed everything instantly. Danny took a run at the door, and unbolted, it gave way easily. Aldridge had hurt himself and was cursing as he attempted to get up.

Danny quickly found the light switch. He could hardly believe his eyes. He pushed the front door shut behind him and turned back to see Aldridge, desperate to escape, charging at him. Alfredo had already taken most of the fight out of Aldridge, and when he tried to strike Danny, Danny easily parried the blow and hit Aldridge hard and square. Aldridge fell to the ground, spent.

Danny looked down at him with contempt, but a moan from the bedroom interrupted his thoughts. He bent down and grabbed Aldridge by his collar and dragged him to the bedroom. There he saw the semi-conscious, handcuffed Alfredo, and the unmoving body under the blankets. He looked down at Aldridge. "What the fuck have you done?"

Alfredo lifted his head. "Danny...Shirley."

Danny instantly threw the blankets back. Shirley had been beaten, tied, bound and gagged. He quickly removed the gag and untied her. Then Danny found the handcuffs key in Aldridge's pocket and unlocked Alfredo.

As soon as Alfredo was free, he went to Shirley, she held a look of terror, her face and hair were wet with sweat. She grabbed Alfredo and held him tight. "Tony, I'm frightened."

Alfredo held her tight. "He's safe, I just been in."

Shirley let go of her husband and without speaking and left the room.

Alfredo watched as Danny handcuffed Aldridge. "It's the copper that beat me up."

Danny grabbed Aldridge by his shirt. "What the fuck's goin' on?"

Aldridge didn't answer.

Alfredo shouted into Aldridge's face. "Why?"

Meanwhile, Shirley walked calmly into the kitchen where the large meat knife still rested on the kitchen sink. She picked it up. In the bedroom, Danny shook his head. "What's it all fuckin' mean?"

Aldridge said nothing.

Shirley walked slowly back into the bedroom with the knife held low by her side. No one noticed it. She was consumed by the rage burning deep inside ever since her rape, and driven by the constant fear for the life of her son, her husband and herself. Now, those powerful forces were charged by the evening's terrifying fear felt of another intruder, another rape, and murder. It had all, at this moment, led her to the point at which she knew exactly what she had to do next. She stared into Aldridge's face and without hesitation she lifted the heavy knife and drove it hard at Aldridge's throat. Within that same moment, Alfredo nudged Shirley's elbow, and the blade ripped into Aldridge's suit jacket before creating a superficial wound in his shoulder. The terrified Aldridge, hands still cuffed behind his back, cowered down in fear.

Danny looked on, astonished. Alfredo calmly removed the knife from Shirley's unresisting hand. Alfredo looked down at the policeman. "It's the bastard who beat the shit out of me, Shirl."

Danny added. "When you was away he turned up at Roger's, wanted to know where you was. Too interested."

Still in fear for his life, Aldridge had to extricate himself quickly. "I'm just following orders."

Then it dawned on Danny, and he closed in on Aldridge. "You pushed him under the rattler."

Aldridge shook his head. "No, not me."

Alfredo couldn't understand the puzzle. "Don't make sense. He's part of tomorrow's business, why would he or the twins want me dead?"

Danny. "Following orders? Easy to find out. I'll ring the twins, or perhaps the boss?"

Aldridge swallowed. "Listen, Pembroke, your mate here's a grass, got his misses to inform on ya. I been tryin' to stop 'em."

Danny. "Grass? These two? That the best you can do?"

Aldridge pleaded. "I'm tellin' you the truth, they're grassin' us up."

Danny shook his head. "And you got orders from who?"

Aldridge hesitated.

Shirley sensed the battle was almost won. "He's got his own agenda."

Shirley was full of loathing. "Let's just do him and get rid, no one's gonna miss this piece of shit."

Aldridge could see they might just do it. "Listen, you want the job to run tomorrow? Well I still got a part to play, you stop me and it's all over."

Danny poked him in the chest. "You're bluffin."

Aldridge stood taller. "Listen, you need me, whether you like it or not."

Shirley ignored Aldridge and addressed her remarks to Danny. "Listen, I got enough evidence on him, proof of a secret bank account, money paid in, we can prove he's bent if we need to. Easy."

Danny looked confused, "What you talkin' about?"

Aldridge made a twisted attempt to grin. "You don't even know who I am."

Shirley spoke calmly. "D/I Dennis Aldridge. Transport Police Headquarters, mailbag team. Also known at Lloyds as Mr Dennis Smith with an account at Tottenham Court Road with thousands in it. All from bungs and your cut of mail jobs. And you run the pony account from a shop address in Sangi Avenue, Peckham, I've been there."

Danny started to grin and shake his head, Alfredo looked perplexed. Aldridge's body seemed to sag in defeat. She looked at Danny, "One day I'll tell how I found out."

Then Shirley punched Aldridge in the face, he staggered backwards. "You ever make any trouble for me or me family there's a copy of everything I got on you with people who'll make sure you're nicked."

Danny's face hardened, but he remained determined not to reveal the name, 'Hill'. "It's obvious the twins don't know what you've been up to. If I tell 'em, you won't survive a week."

Aldridge now looked panic-stricken. He knew if the twins found out what had happened, they would report it all to Billy Hill, and Billy's patience with him was at breaking point already. Aldridge looked at Danny. "Alright."

Danny uncuffed him and handed him the key. "And course, needless to say, you ain't never gonna come near none of us. Any question any of us getting nicked, after tomorrow, and you get nicked an all."

Aldridge straightened up, placed the handcuffs and key in his pocket and picked up the truncheon. He took a final look at all of them, turned, walked across the sitting room to the front door and opened it. He was about to pass through the doorway when Shirley called out to him. He stopped and turned around. Shirley walked casually over to him and stopped in front of him, he looked down at her. In that moment she punched him again, hard in the face. He hadn't been expecting it and his head jolted backwards and bounced off the edge of the door behind him. It was a good blow. Shirley had five words left for him. "Now you can fuck off."

Alfredo and Danny walked Aldridge out of the flat, along the walkway and down the stairs to his car. He got into his car without another word. He drove off, he still had work to do if the robbery was to succeed. Danny and Alfredo walked to Danny's waiting car.

Danny whispered. "What a fuckin' turn up!"

Alfredo. "Shirley's been busy."

Danny. "What a girl she is!"

It had been quite a night. For some reason they shook hands, they had never done so before. The next 24 hours were going to be equally challenging.

Alfredo now had only a few hours to share with Shirley, he walked briskly back to the flat. Shirley was wide awake and had put the furniture straight in the sitting room and bedroom and tidied the mess. He expected her to be anxious, agitated, tearful. But she was none of that, instead she seemed a little high. She stopped tidying as soon as he entered. "OK. Let's get this sorted, finally."

Alfredo sat down without speaking, she sat opposite him. Shirley took a deep breathe. "So, one problem's sorted and one ain't. This business tomorrow, you can walk away now. Aldridge can't touch you. Neither can Danny. Let's just duck out now and bugger off to Italy, leave it all behind."

Alfredo sighed. "Alright. If that's what you want."

Shirley. "You mean it?"

Alfredo. "Yeah. I don't want to, but yeah."

Shirley. "You could so easy get nicked."

Alfredo shook his head. "No. That ain't right. The Krays have never been captured. They got people at the Yard who keep 'em safe. The Raiders ain't never been captured either, cos they're smart. There's a really good chance that tomorrow they will make a fortune. I want to be a part of that. For us."

Shirley said nothing, she was reflecting on it all.

Alfredo pushed on. "With what you got on Aldridge, I'm more fire-proof than ever. And as soon as the job's done I'm on a plane to Italy."

Shirley. "Well I ain't going to sleep tonight."

Alfredo. "But it'll be more than worth it."

Shirley nodded. "Be careful won't ya?"

Alfredo kissed her gently.

The meal was salvageable and the red wine tasted special. After the meal they sipped the wine and talked on for more than an hour, but neither raised the robbery.

Alfredo. "You got your passport yet?"

Shirley nodded and smiled. "Arrived couple of days ago."

Alfredo grinned back. "I have to go before it gets light, you know that don't ya?"

Shirley nodded again. "Where you goin'?"

Alfredo raised his eyebrows. Shirley understood. "Fair enough."

Alfredo sipped the last of his glass. "We got a bit of time yet. Next time I see you it will be in our new life."

Shirley touched his hand. He took her fingers in his and smiled. "You make quite a copper."

Shirley's heart missed a beat, "How's that then?"

Alfredo. "You know, finding out about Aldridge. How did you do it?"

Shirley took the last sip of her red wine. "That's a long and painful story, let's save it for now eh? How long we got? Come on."

She stood up and tugged at his sleeve. He understood.

# Chapter 45

Tuesday 6th August, Alfredo left the flat before first light and spent the first daylight hours of the day at Smithfield market. It was always busy at that time. All around, cafés and pubs opened to serve the special working hours of the hundreds of market workers. There was little chance of his being identified there, but beard, sunglasses and a deep tan from the weeks in Italy made it virtually impossible.

Large holdall in hand, he walked down nearby Charterhouse Street, turned right into Ely Place and entered St. Ethelreda's Church. He had never been there before, but knew it be one of the oldest churches in London. Within its ancient walls he found a place of deep tranquillity. Alfredo sat alone contemplating his life, and how it had reached this point. He prayed for God's understanding and forgiveness. An hour later he took a different route back across the market and waited for Danny outside the Red Cow pub in Long Lane. By now the rush hour was underway, and anonymity assured.

About ten minutes later Danny arrived on foot carrying a holdall. He nodded in acknowledgement and looked down at Alfredo's holdall. "Uniform fit OK?"
Alfredo. "No it's too baggy and too long in the arms and legs."
Danny grinned. "Totally authentic, then."

They walked the short distance to Farringdon Station, caught the Metropolitan Line and headed north. The train was quiet. It was early afternoon when they arrived at Aylesbury. Now just 15 miles from their eventual destination and way outside the Metropolitan Police area, no one would recognise them. Freddie was waiting in a Mark 10 Jaguar. It had been stolen that morning in Kent from another commuter station, and the owner was still at work in London and unaware.

In reality Freddie was still recovering from the car accident, but he was determined not to miss out on this chance of untold wealth. They drove in light traffic in the afternoon sunshine at a sedate pace towards Thame. Then they joined the even quieter B4011. The conversation was stilted and mostly about the route. All three seemed unable to talk and chat as they normally did. Each was understandably preoccupied by the events that lay ahead.

As they approached Oakley village, they turned right at Little London and followed a more minor road for about ten minutes before turning onto an overgrown private farm track. Alfredo looked out from his rear passenger window but could see no house or buildings, only hedgerows and the trees beyond. After a few hundred yards, Freddie pulled up outside a large, ugly, part rendered, part redbrick farmhouse and kept the engine running. All three studied the site, none of them had been there before.

The location of the robbery had been chosen by Hill on the advice of Aldridge. Acting on that information, Bruce Reynolds had researched the area, found Leatherslade Farm and arranged its purchase.

Alfredo looked at the drab buildings. Opposite the farmhouse were three large poorly maintained outbuildings made of breeze blocks and corrugated sheets of asbestos and tin. Nearby, a big, poorly maintained, garden shed and an old and dilapidated Nissen hut seemed to be entirely overgrown with brambles and weeds.

Alfredo's stomach turned over. He had little confidence in the combined team. The violent fiasco the February before was still fresh in his mind.

Danny turned to Alfredo. "Gloves."

Hill had instructed, via the Krays of course, that the stolen money should be taken immediately to this nearby hideout where it was to be quickly counted and divided. The robbers were to remain at Leatherslade Farm for a week or two, until the uproar had died down, but none of the Raiders liked the idea.

Freddie parked on rough ground to keep the drive free, more vehicles would soon arrive. He took a green canvas bag from the boot and Alfredo helped him cover the car. Then Alfredo saw Danny was heading towards the front door and hurried to catch up. Before they reached it, it was opened from the inside by Bruce Reynolds, several of the combined team had already arrived.

They sauntered in, keen to keep face and portray an air of quiet confidence. Those already present, some of whom were drinking from mugs and beer bottles, nodded and grunted. Alfredo noted they too were all wearing gloves as instructed. Bruce seemed to think he was running things. "Cuppa?"

Alfredo instinctively looked at Danny who responded for all three of them. "No thanks, gonna have a look around, drop the bags upstairs."

Reynolds walked to a chalkboard he had set up earlier. "I've allocated rooms. Danny you're in this one with Buster and Roy."

He was pointing to one of six rooms on the first floor. Then he pointed to a different room. "Alfredo, you're in here with Big Jim and John."

Danny smiled and nodded, "Thanks Bruce, but the Raiders will be in two of the rooms and you can divvy up the rest as you like."

With that Danny turned away but Bruce called to him. "Danny, it's important we follow orders to the letter. Now's not the time for dissent."

Perhaps because Danny was anxious, or perhaps because Bruce had played the schoolmaster once too often, but for whatever reason, Danny's patience left him. He turned. "Yeah. No dissent, I told you how it's gonna be, right?"

His raised voice attracted the attention of the others and their conversations stopped. Reynolds shut up, and the three Raiders climbed the stairs and found a room. There were three mattresses on the bare floorboards. It was hot, stuffy and stale. Freddie opened the bedroom window and fresh warm air improved things a little. They put the holdalls down and went back downstairs, where the various conversations in the large farmhouse kitchen had resumed. Gradually the rest of the robbers arrived in twos and threes.

A few years earlier, this farmhouse had been part a much larger farm, but it had fairly recently been reduced to a smallholding of about five acres. These days, another farmer ploughed the land close to the farmhouse. So it was not as unobserved as it first appeared. Farmer Wyatt, like most countryfolk, was always keen to take advantage of the slightest stimulation provided by even the smallest change. And activity in the old farmhouse was a cause for both study and conversation. In the busy streets of London, strangers vastly outnumber acquaintances. But the rural world is the very opposite; strangers are noteworthy.

That afternoon, while ploughing, Farmer Wyatt saw two Land Rovers in Army livery with green canvas roofs, an Austin Loadstar drop-side truck in similar colours, and several other vehicles moving down the poorly maintained track and into Leatherslade Farm. He thought he saw at least a dozen men too. This was big news in a place that could be excited by the sight of a strange cloud formation.

Ronnie Biggs was a stranger to Alfredo and the rest of the Raiders, and Alfredo watched as he entered and made a beeline for Reynolds, before announcing. "I'm bringing the driver in."

Bob touched Alfredo's arm, "Come on."

Alfredo followed Bob and all the other robbers as they disappeared upstairs. Only Reynolds and Biggs remained. Up to that point, the robbers had complete freedom of conversation and freedom of movement within the house. But now, a 'mystery' man known only to Biggs was to keep them company. 'Pop' was a retired train driver and had a vital role. But he was not a 'face' or even a regular villain. None of the gang was prepared to expose their face to him. After all, he would probably cough everything he knew if questioned and threatened by the police.

Biggs took Pop to his room upstairs and became his valet and minder.

Later, Alfredo helped unload the supplies and equipment from the heavy truck, foodstuffs – tinned food, dozens of eggs, fresh and evaporated milk, catering size tins of instant coffee, tea, as well as toilet rolls, soap and sleeping bags. But they also unloaded equipment such as overalls, several sets of handcuffs, as well as various weapons and balaclavas, a VHF radio and several walkie talkies (two-way radios).

The communications equipment was placed next to Reynold's chalk board. He had long since been nicknamed the 'Teacher.' Not because he was perceived as particularly wise or well informed, but because of his self-image.

Meanwhile, one or two robbers were engaged in touching up the Army vehicles' colours. Others had their heads under the bonnets and also checked the tyres etc. Once everything had been checked and put in its rightful place, it was back to the loneliness of their particular anxieties.

By 6.30 that evening in Glasgow, the high-value bags were loaded onto the Travelling Post Office, letter mail was still being thrown aboard. There was no particular security on the platforms, and any postman, railwayman, train spotter, thief or passenger could wander by and watch. At 6.50pm the train left Glasgow bound for many stops on its way to Euston.

Gordon Goody arrived at Leatherslade Farm hours late and dismissed his lateness lightly, merely saying the ferry back from Ireland, where he had created a false alibi, had been delayed.

The robbers anticipated that in the next few hours the job would be complete, the money shared and the long wait warmed by their new immense wealth. They had foreseen the danger of spending hours counting bundles of banknotes in view of the windows, it was light by 5 a.m. so that evening they shut each of the ground floor windows and closed all the ground floor curtains.

Some of the gang went to their rooms intending to get a nap before the action, but none slept. Others played cards, monopoly and darts. Roger spent his time reading, listening to the radio and chatting. But no matter what they did, there was no escaping the clock, or their nervousness. Alfredo had no idea how to spend his time and couldn't settle to any distraction, he just wanted to get the whole thing over with. But the more he focused on that wish, the more his watch seemed to slow down. Never before had he spent hours locked in the company of so many men who, with a few exceptions, he didn't like or trust. It occurred to him it would be like that in prison. An experience most of the others were very accustomed to.

Farmer Wyatt went to bed wondering what on earth was going on 'next door.' But nothing more would happen until confirmation was received that the TPO was on time.


The last stop before the attack would be Rugby at 02.12 and just 38 minutes later the train would be attacked. But that 38 minutes was insufficient time for the robbers to receive notification, get into their vehicles, drive to the intended scene of the crime, deploy and create a false red signal. So tonight the train would be three hours away when the decision was made whether to deploy. Hill had decided that if the train was on time when leaving Preston at 22.53, then the robbers should be in position to attack 15 minutes before it was due at the chosen spot. There was no phone at Leatherslade Farm, so instead the plan was to use the public phone kiosk in nearby Oakley village.

At about 20.45, Bob Welch and Danny left for the phone kiosk. It signalled the end of preparation and the start of the action. The village was quiet when they arrived, the sun had set 90 minutes earlier. They waited no more than two minutes before the phone rang and both quickly pushed into the box. Danny lifted the phone and Bob pushed his ear close to listen.
"It's off for 24 hours. Got it?"
Danny's nerves were taught. "What do you mean?"
Aldridge was calm, "The big money's tomorrow. Do it then. Tomorrow night. Got it?"

Danny knew the gang would interrogate him in their frustration, just as he wanted to interrogate Aldridge. But Aldridge put the phone down. They drove back to the farmhouse calmly, and by the time they arrived the rest of the gang were sweating and raring to go. Danny and Bob walked slowly into the farmhouse looking glum. "It's off for 24 hours."

Before Danny could say more, a groan went up. Danny added without enthusiasm. "The big money's tomorrow night."

The anti-climax was huge. Danny repeated word for word exactly what he had been told. Nevertheless, the questions came fast and furious, but all to no avail. Eventually things fell silent but for whispered conversations and snoring.

Wednesday 7th August. As the dawn chorus started, the robbers tried to sleep away the alcohol and the frustration. But farmers start their days early, especially in August. On this bright, warm morning, Farmer Wyatt, curiosity aroused, decided to work the fields close to the farmhouse and take a closer look at what was going on. He noticed several fresh vehicles had been covered with canvas, and scruffy drapes hung at the house windows. And all the windows were closed despite the heat. He thought it all a bit odd.

At various times thereafter and right up to noon, the robbers climbed from their beds, sleeping bags and mattresses. Everyone was still on edge and trying not to show it. They all knew the need to stay within the house and not to expose any conversation to the outside world by opening windows, but it made the farmhouse a hot prison. Some of the robbers were unusually quiet, like Roger. Some were laughing too loudly at things that weren't funny. Others were taking offence too easily.

While Alfredo was sitting in the kitchen having breakfast with Tom and Danny, Danny quietly pointed out that Gordon Goody seemed so very calm, and had remained his usual self from the moment he arrived. Alfredo quietly studied him. Goody had indeed breezed in late without an apology or fuss, and confidently settled in as if he had a grip on the whole situation. Danny told Alfredo he suspected Gordon was late not because of a delayed ferry, but because he had decided for himself to minimise his time at the farm. Tom nodded in agreement. Alfredo said he thought Gordon seemed to be his own man. Danny affirmed it. But Goody was also, like the majority present, willing to inflict serious injury without hesitation on anyone who got in his way.

While the robbers did their best to while away the time, Farmer Wyatt had created the perfect excuse to call at the house and made his way towards the front door. No one was keeping watch and the knock at the door caused a minor panic, followed by complete silence. Everyone stopped whatever they were doing and listened intently, worried glances flicked between them. Goody waved his arms wildly to get attention, it worked, all eyes were on him. Then he signalled to Reynolds to answer the door. Goody began to speak in a normal tone and volume. "Come on, time to puts the tea down. Let's get the job done."

One or two quickly caught on. "Yeah. Let's get back to it."… "Just finish me tea."

Reynolds opened the door. The farmer attempted see what was going on over Reynolds' shoulder and asked whether Reynolds was the new owner and if so, might he be able to continue to rent the field. Reynolds smoothly explained that he was part of a team of decorators renovating the farmhouse.

Farmer Wyatt thanked Reynolds and told him he would call back in a couple of weeks. But the farmer left reflecting that he had seen no ladders, or decorating equipment. He still had no explanation for the scruffy blackout curtains or the closed windows. What was it they were hiding from view? Don't decorators normally open the windows on sunny days? And what about that Army lorry, land rovers and other sheeted cars?

Danny spoke out, "If we'd done the job last night that bloke would have walked right into us counting tenners, or burning mailbags for fucks sake."

No one responded. Danny hadn't finished. "So tomorrow morning somebody's got to keep watch."

It occurred to Alfredo, that from the moment they arrived, Danny had remained himself; calm and rational, always thinking ahead and perfectly willing to make his point forcefully when he had to.

It was at about 4.pm the trouble kicked off, it had been simmering since 'Biggsy' arrived. As a result of the Irish Mail job six months earlier, there had been ongoing tensions between the two elements of the combined gang. But they all knew it was in their interest to keep a lid on it. However, Ronald Biggs, who was previously unknown to everyone but Reynolds, seemed completely unaware of the delicate relationship, and the effect his words and conduct were having.

Biggs was unknown amongst the London underworld. He had committed no crime, successfully or otherwise, to justify any sort of infamy or respect. He had committed various minor crimes which had resulted in several convictions. His last conviction had been for stealing a cycle. In short, he was an unskilled minor thief who was only present because of his attachment to his hero, Bruce Reynolds. Many of the gang already resented that Biggs was to receive a full 'whack', many thought he should only receive a 'drink'. After all, his job was simply, "Mind Pop.'

Most of the robbers had finished a midday meal, all out of tins, and were sitting around joking nervously with each other or playing cards etc. Biggs had been busy running up and down the stairs to answer Pop's calls for tea, requests to leave his room to go to the loo, ask umpteen questions, and to borrow a newspaper and then a radio. Biggs had been forced to act like a servant and clearly resented it. And when he wasn't being a servant to Pop, he was acting as chief ego inflater to Reynolds. It was all so very unmanly. And in this company, machismo was a requirement.

Eventually, his errand running and open and persistent fawning over Reynolds became the subject of knowing looks, half concealed smiles and hushed sarcasm. At first it went over Biggsy's head. But determined to elicit a response, some of the teasing became loud and blunt. Biggsy's answer was to find a different target for everyone's frustration. His eyes fell on Freddie who had remained quiet, and was dealing with the tension by reading a weekend newspaper, alone with his thoughts. But Biggs hadn't been part of this combined gang long enough to get 'clever' with any of them. And neither Freddie nor any other of the Raiders had ribbed Biggs directly. After all, they didn't know him.

Biggsy was well over six foot tall, well-built and reasonably fit. Freddie was less than five foot seven and not fully recovered from severe injury. Perhaps that fed into Biggs' calculation in his choice of victim. But it was a mistake. Biggsy showed his greasy smile and looked across at Freddie. "Reckon you'll be strong enough to climb the embankment then, son." No one spoke, and Biggs appeared to interpret the silence as encouragement. His smile widened. Freddie didn't take offence immediately, "Well, if you want to carry the bags for me, you can."

Biggsy sneered. "I don't reckon your legs' will hold up. Few months ago, you was supposed to be nearly dead. Course it might a' been your bottle had gone. Half-crown-sixpence was it?"

Alfredo was well aware of Freddie's rather direct approach to things, and looked around at the faces within the group. Gordon Goody was sitting back in an easy chair with his long legs stretched out and his head resting on the back of the seat. On his chest he cradled a glass holding the remains of a scotch he had been sipping slowly. He hadn't joined in the ribaldry.

Alfredo could see Goody was observing the exchanges and enjoying the event as it unfolded.

Freddie continued to think how best to put Biggs straight. Biggs concluded his wit had silenced the smaller man, and so, encouraged, continued to throw jibes. It was a spectator sport and the other robbers fell quiet and watched with anticipation.

Freddie took a little more verbal punishment, got to his feet and walked slowly to within a yard of where Biggs was sitting. Freddie spoke as if he was ordering a cuppa in a café. Casual, but clear, brief but formally polite. "Far as I can see, the only reason you're here, is in case Reynolds gets desperate for a blow job."

With that, everyone, including Goody, roared with laughter. Biggs got to his feet and looked down at Freddie. The laughter quickly gave way. Freddie looked up at him, "Your choice, in here or outside."
Biggs hesitated. Freddie didn't. "As I thought, full of piss and wind."

Then Freddie turned his back on him. It was another insult of course, it indicated he thought himself completely safe from attack. Biggs didn't know what to do or say, his bluff had been called.

Gordon Goody broke the silence. He kept a straight face and spoke slowly, sensitively. "Biggsy, don't worry about it. Forget it… Why don't you go upstairs? Bruce's up there, you never know, ask him, you might be able to do something for him."

There was more laughter, Biggs was speechless.  Goody added, "No. I didn't mean that, no I mean give him a hand… Well, when I say hand."
More laughter, Biggs walked out.

There was no change for the next eight hours – darts, monopoly, cards, radio, eating, drinking, laughing, piss-taking, arguing, trying too hard to relax. They tried to dream of a new life, but were overcome with anxiety about the remainder of the present one.

That evening, Bob Welch and Danny again left for the phone kiosk. Within a few minutes it rang. Danny snatched up the phone, Bob forced himself close enough to hear. "It's a go. It's well loaded."
Danny had rehearsed this moment 100 times, "Say that again."
Aldridge spoke more slowly. "It's a go. A full load and on time."
Danny put the phone down, Bob was grinning from ear to ear.

They drove back to the farmhouse calmly, but a little faster than they had 24 hours earlier. As they parked outside, men streamed from the house and towards the car. Danny got out quickly. "We're on."

They all went back inside, there was no wild excitement, just a sense of relief and heightened expectation.

Every member of the gang had been told to bring an Army uniform. Roger found an excuse not to do so, the rest had bought 'Government surplus' kit. All but one purchased the uniform of a private.

Well before midnight, the first to get dressed in uniform, Bruce Reynolds, appeared in the farmhouse kitchen dressed as a major. His beret displayed a fake SAS badge and he was clearly enjoying the rank. Other gang members noticed his self-elevation and preening, some smirked. Reynolds announced that the twins had asked him to have a final 'run through' once they were all in uniform and ready to 'deploy.' They drifted upstairs to get into uniform and amused at his use of the word 'deploy.' Reynolds went from room to room, "Muster downstairs for 00.15 hours."

Most of the gang were happy to let Reynolds play out his fantasy, but when he reached the room in which Tom Wisbey was, for the first time in several years, getting into army uniform, he received a different reception. "00.15? That's quarter past twelve is it?"

Reynolds didn't know if Tom was taking the piss or not but added. "Yeah. Ten minutes time." Reynolds quickly ducked out and went in pursuit of others to impress. Tom turned to Roger and grinned. "Major? In the SAS an all?"

Roger smiled. "I hope his uniform isn't tested under lights."

Tom added, "Course anyone who's actually done National Service would know the truck and Land Rovers ain't kosher, they got civvy number plates." Alfredo looked anxious again.

A few minutes later they were all, except for Pop, downstairs in the kitchen, dressed in khaki. 'Pop' was still in his room. Reynolds and Biggs had put chairs out in uniform fashion and cleared a space for the chalkboard. Major Reynolds was standing in front of it. The rest wandered in with mugs of tea and beer and some with a scotch, they were chatting, and some scratching at the course uniform material already irritating the skins of those who had never done National Service. With only a little encouragement they were all soon seated and listening. Bruce didn't waste a second before 'talking and chalking.' Tom nudged Freddie sitting next to him. Freddie made eye contact, Tom nodded towards the enthralled Biggs. sitting right in front of his master, Freddie grinned.

It was a hot night and the air was still. The thick, course khaki trousers were hot and irritated Alfredo's legs. One or too removed their uniform tunics.

Reynolds had two jobs. First he had to visit the signalman at Leighton Buzzard signal box. He had been promised 'a drink' to ensure that when the TPO had been stopped, he delayed notifying anyone for as long as possible. Second, Reynolds would walk a mile north from the signal box and await the approaching train. As soon as he spotted it, he would notify the others by walkie talkie.

The signals team, under Roger's leadership, would go to the dwarf and gantry signals 3,276 yards south of Leighton Buzzard signal box. Roger would climb the gantry, cover the green light and display a false red. Two others, having been briefed by Roger, would display a false amber signal, trackside at low level. Roger would also cut the British Railways telephone wires to stop the train crew of the stricken train calling from the nearby emergency railway phone.

The second team (of six), led by Goody, would wait at Sears Crossing, 1000 yards further south. That is how far the train would continue to travel once the driver had seen the false amber signal and applied the brakes. Once the train had stopped, they would overpower the driver and his assistant and install Pop. Then they would uncouple the unwanted postal sorting coaches leaving the numerous oblivious postmen behind, climb aboard the engine and Pops would drive it just two thirds of a mile south to Bridego bridge.

The third team (of six), Alfredo's team, led by Danny, would go straight to Bridego bridge. One of them would cut the nearby public telephone lines to prevent any call being made from the area. Then they would wait. Once the second team aboard the 'highjacked' train reached Bridego bridge, the combined robbers would smash their way into the TPO carriages and remove the fortune in used notes that awaited.

Alfredo's knees were knocking and his throat was dry. He looked at his watch, 12.50. Still half an hour to wait. Reynolds dished out the walkie-talkies. There were no questions. Everyone knew their role. Reynold's schoolteacher behaviour brought out the naughty schoolboy in all of them. Eventually, Reynolds looked at his watch and offered his last sentence, "OK. If there is nothing else. Let's go."

The gathering broke up into sub groups. Everyone picked up a balaclava and overalls to cover their uniforms. Alfredo checked his watch again. Only five minutes had past. He fastened his uniform and picked up overalls, balaclava and a metal bar.

Roger's team moved towards the door. Danny called out. "Good luck. See you later."

"And you." Someone called back, as if they might need all the luck in the world.

Two minutes later, Jim Hussey stood up. "Let's go eh Gordon?"

Goody nodded, Tom stood up and Alfredo stood up too. Tom mimicked a face of horror and turned to Alfredo. "Fuck me, you still don't know who you're with."

Alfredo lowered himself back into his seat promptly as the second team keenly approached the door. A minute later, Danny called out. "Right, let's get mobile."

Danny grinned at Alfredo, but Alfredo wasn't in the mood to smile at anything, except perhaps a cancellation of the whole thing.

As the third team moved out to the Army truck. Alfredo heard the regular, slow 'bip...bip...bip' of a walkie talkie radio close by.

It was a warm, moonlit night, Alfredo sat on the Army truck's fixed bench with his back against the truck's side, his gloved hands grasping his metal bar, overalls at his feet. There were three others in the back of the truck but he couldn't see their faces, but without speaking they shared their fears and hopes, as well as the engine noise, the smell of diesel, cigarette smoke, sweat, stale beer and whisky. The old truck noisily chugged on.

About 30 minutes later the truck slowed down. Someone up front called for everyone to keep still until the truck had stopped. The old truck manoeuvred back and forth three times before the driver was satisfied. Alfredo and the rest donned their overalls. One eager passenger too keen to alight tripped over outstretched feet, tools, and weapons and there was a good deal of cursing before any feet were on the ground. They had parked just off the road, right next to Bridego bridge. Alfredo looked around and breathed in the sweet, cool air.

Soon they were on the railway lines. Two of them set off to cut the nearby public phone lines. The remainder stayed on the lines near the bridge, amongst them. Alfredo looked around and took in the scene. All was quiet but for the sound of a gentle breeze. A few minutes later they were joined by the other two, public telephone wires duly cut.

Danny reminded them that a public road ran very close by and suggested they move a few yards north. After walking about 50 yards, Danny walked a few paces down the embankment and sat down, the others followed his lead. Now they were invisible from track and road. Danny removed a walkie-talkie from his boiler suit and studied it. They waited.

Aldridge had done his job well, and it had started about 18 months earlier. He realised then that the long running engineering works, which entailed the closure of some signal boxes on this stretch of the line, would mean a robbery could be committed with much less chance of interruption. Subsequently, it was Aldridge who monitored the TPO train movements to establish when the biggest haul would be carried. It was Aldridge who made sure, by the simple trick of stuffing screwed up newspapers into their air brakes, that the new high-security coaches were taken out of use just before the robbery. And it was also Aldridge who had monitored developments in police intelligence to make sure that the authorities remained blissfully unaware of Hill's plans. And even as the robbery was unfolding, he had not yet finished, he would continue monitoring the investigation, and when it came to the role of the British Transport Police, he would ensure that any 'promising' lines of enquiry were thwarted.

Reynolds drove one of the Land Rover along the B488 that ran parallel to the railway line towards Leighton Buzzard. He made his way on foot to the signal box and entered. The signalman was ready. Reynolds reminded him of the 'carrot and stick' he faced. Then Reynolds drove north until the road veered away from the railway. Reynolds parked the Land Rover and set off on foot towards the lines. There he settled and waited. About 15 minutes later he heard it and seconds later he saw it hurtling towards him, a Class 40 British Railways diesel electric locomotive hauling 12 Post Office coaches.

Alfredo's heart skipped a beat as he heard the crackle of the walkie talkie as it came to life close by. 'Bip...bip "This is it. This is it. This is it."...bip... bip...'.

His pulse was racing.

Danny spoke calmly. "Stay here for now. Let's wait until we get the nod."

Meanwhile, travelling at 60 mph and hauling 368 tons of locomotive plus 12 loaded carriages, Driver Mills and his colleague Mr David Whitby, unexpectedly caught site of the dwarf amber signal, then the red signal beyond.

Driver Mills applied the brakes evenly and noticed that beyond the amber and red signals, the signal lights ahead were green. 'Odd that', he mused. Railway signals operate in 'sections' and if one light goes red, then the remainder in that section should do the same. But it was not for him to reason why, the standard instructions were definite. He must stop.   His Assistant, Fireman Whitby, climbed down from the locomotive cab and made his way to the signals phone. But at the moment he saw that the phone wires had been cut he was set upon. At the same time, Gordon Goody, 'Big Jim' Hussey, Buster Edwards and Tom Wisbey attempted to climb aboard the locomotive.

Driver Mills fought hard, kicked and punched and held the bandits at bay. They simply could not climb the metal ladder onto the engine. One of them, we don't know who, ran around to the other side of the locomotive and climbed aboard unobstructed. Attacked on both sides, Driver Mills stood no chance. Within minutes of the train stopping, Alfredo heard the message. 'Footplate secured, Footplate secured.'

Those around Alfredo, congratulated themselves quietly, a half bottle of scotch was passed around, most had a nip, some had a mouthful. But, Alfredo couldn't focus on anything but survival. By now he had been two nights without sleep. The sweat ran down his face as he scratched at the thick army trousers sticking to his legs beneath the overalls.

About 1100 yards north, his associates had now finished uncoupling the locomotive engine and two high-value TPO carriages from the rest of the mail sorting carriages and the dozens of postmen working within them.

Danny looked at his watch again. It was a couple of minutes after three. "Be a few minutes yet."

This was the longest wait of all. No one spoke. Everyone was alone with their fears.  Alfredo watched one of the other robbers rise from their crouched hiding position. "I'm gonna walk up and wait on the line."
He climbed two paces higher towards the track before ducking down again. "Fucking train!"
Someone reminded him, "Don't you remember, Parcel train's due from London?"

A train rushed by heading north and towards the stricken TPO. A few minutes later someone spoke, "I just heard a motor stop, by the bridge I think."

Then a car door was heard to slam. Danny spoke. "Hold on here."

Within three minutes he was back. Bruce Reynolds had arrived with Pop and Biggsy. Pop had proven to be useless, completely incapable of driving the train. Biggsy and Pop remained in the Army Land Rover. Pop couldn't be left alone. More minutes passed. Then 'bip… bip… bip… "On way to you. On way to you over."' bip …bip …bip.'

Without speaking, Alfredo and the others emerged from their hiding place. For the first time, Alfredo noticed one man had a rolled white makeshift flag. At Bridego bridge the flag was unfurled and he watched the flag poles being forced into the ballast to display the train's intended stopping point. Alfredo's face felt clammy under the balaclava and could feel the sweat on his face and back.

"Listen." Someone near Alfredo whispered. And everyone kept still, held their breath and looked north. They could hear it coming, a slow chugging. 'Chuff…chuff…chuff…'

They stared hard into the moonlit night, and the chugging grew louder, then a torchlight shone out from the side of the driver's cab. Within seconds a huge engine roared into clear view, before quickly slowing to a noisy stop. The small locomotive cab was overcrowded with robbers and they climbed down eagerly.

Driver Mills, who was bleeding profusely from head wounds, was dragged down from the driver's cab. Handcuffed to Fireman Whitby with British Transport Police handcuffs, they were dumped on the trackside and threatened with further violence. The entire gang of robbers, together again now, split into two groups and headed to either side of the two burgundy coaches behind the loco. The few postmen aboard the lead coach had yet to suspect anything and were still working, They were in a sorting coach, and were examining postal addresses and placing packages in the right pigeon hole according to delivery area. That coach was linked via a door to the unstaffed storage coach.

The sorting coach windows were simply wide vertical glass slits, situated ten feet above the trackside and much too narrow for the robbers to use for access. The postal carriages looked strong, and were fitted with the sliding doors that were locked and sealed. But the doors to both coaches had glass windows from waist to shoulder height, each about 30 inches wide. Conveniently, a wide 'running board' ran along the 'threshold' to each door. Internal lights, necessary for the postmen to do their work, shone out brightly.

Inside the sorting coach. Frank Dewhurst, the very experienced postman in charge, concerned at the sudden stop and the noise outside, walked to the doors and peered down through the windows He didn't know what to expect, but he found the sight almost unbelievable. He turned and shouted. "It's a raid. Barricade the doors."

Now the prize was in sight and all the robbers' pent-up fear and desperation erupted in a final show of urgency and aggression. A frenzy of shouted threats was immediately followed by the crash of heavy blows of metal on wood and glass.

Inside the mail coach, the six postmen could hardly grasp what was happening. Frank Dewhurst grabbed a heavy mailbag and lifted it to barricade the doors. "Quick. For Christ's sake."

Immediately the handful of postmen followed suit and within seconds bags were being loaded against every door on either side of both coaches. Mike, a senior postman was in fear for his life. He had never imagined anyone could ever contemplate such a thing as this. 'What sort of men were these? Desperate men...willing to kill!'

Mike had led a blameless life. He, like his colleagues, was working long night duties to earn a little extra to enhance his modest family life. Now violent, armed men were breaking in and threatening his life. Mike and his colleagues had nothing to protect themselves and no means of calling for help. Everything Mike valued was about to be damaged.

In those seconds, Alfredo and another robber, Charlie Wilson, were lifted by eager arms onto the running board of the double doors. Without a moment's hesitation, using a metal bar and a pickaxe handle, they smashed the coach windows. Before Alfredo could do so, Wilson tried to climb through into the coach. At ground level, sledge hammers, axes and crow bars continued to smash at the lower part of the double doors. From the ground, the robbers shouted "Open up." "Open up or we'll fire." "Open up or you'll get it." "Get the guns."

More windows exploded into the coaches as other robbers began smashing other door windows to get aboard. The postmen cringed in fear of serious injury. So hyped up were the robbers, it seemed they were like a pack of hounds that had hunted a fox to its hide, now they were keen for the kill. The robbers poured in through the shattered doors, all around

Alfredo were moans of fear and screams of rage and threat. Alfredo watched and did nothing as Frank Dewhurst was beaten without cause. Other postmen were being struck repeatedly too, but none fought back. Alfredo pushed his way out of the coach and dropped onto the track. Danny was standing nearby and had already pulled one bag from the train. He shouted. "Come on, get the bags loaded."

Alfredo knew the next part of the plan, it had been discussed 100 times. He moved towards the embankment, as he did, he heard Danny shouting into the mail coaches reminding others there was not a second to lose. Within a minute, the robbers had formed a chain down to the truck and were in the process of removing the selected mailbags to the waiting truck.

Alfredo was handed another sack, he walked three paces down the embankment and passed it on and returned for another. As he faced uphill to receive another bag, he saw in the moonlight, two figures being manhandled along the embankment. They were handcuffed together and barely able to carry their own weight. The shorter one appeared to look straight into Alfredo's covered face. Alfredo guessed who they were. A few seconds later, as Alfredo turned to collect another mailbag, he heard the order for the two men to lie down on the embankment out of sight. He glanced across and saw the taller of the two men had halted and was hesitating, he seemed to be studying something just beyond the embankment. Alfredo stared for a moment, perhaps the handcuffed man was contemplating his poor balance before the descent, perhaps he wasn't well enough to negotiate the falling ground, perhaps...

Alfredo took hold of yet another bag and turned to face down the embankment towards the waiting truck. "Fucking lie down." He heard someone shout at the handcuffed men.

Alfredo thought he recognised, Biggs' voice and glanced over again. He saw the taller of the two handcuffed men shoved roughly down. His wrists, connected by handcuff, jerked at the man at his side. They both fell to the ground awkwardly, heads facing down the embankment.

The human chain continued to do its work briskly, mailbag after mailbag until finally a familiar voice stopped it. "Hold up lads, that's it. Let's get mobile pronto, like you just 'eard one of the Sweeney was up your missus."

A nervous laugh went up and work stopped immediately and the robbers headed towards their transport. But Alfredo had something else on his mind. It struck Alfredo that as surely as he could now see the fake Army truck lit by moonlight, so would the handcuffed driver and his assistant have done as they were forced down the embankment earlier. Perhaps that's what the taller man had been looking at. How easy it would be for them to give this information to the police. Should he do so quickly the gang might be arrested before they even got back to the farm. Within a minute, Alfredo and most of the robbers were in the truck and tearing off their overalls to show off their Army uniforms. Gordon Goody, still in his balaclava, poked his head in the truck. "Ok lads. Just be a minute."

His voice and manner were easily recognised. Alfredo reached out and touched Goody's arm, "When I was on the embankment I saw..." but as his lips were forming the words his brain was in overdrive and the message flashed up. 'He'll kill them.'
Alfredo hesitated. "I saw another train pass."
Alfredo couldn't see Goody's expression but his tone and words were clear enough. "Right, well we'll all a been in a fucking coma to miss it."

With that the engine of the old truck spluttered into life and Goody raced up front to the passenger door. Soon all three vehicles were a mile away. By now everyone in the back of the truck had removed their overalls and balaclavas, and some had undone their Army tunics. Confidence was growing, the worst was done, it looked like they had pulled it off, they were getting away.

Alfredo didn't know who was driving the truck or who was 'riding shotgun,' but one of them switched on the radio. Above the engine noise, the sound of Tony Bennett rang out. He was singing 'The Good Life.' Soon many of the robbers were singing along and delighted at the remarkable suitability of the song.

But Alfredo couldn't bring himself to sing, for him the lyrics had a tragic meaning–

'Oh, the good life, full of fun seems to be the ideal,
Mm, the good life lets you hide all the sadness you feel...

It's the good life to be free and explore the unknown
Like the heartaches when you learn you must face them alone.
Please remember I still want you, and in case you wonder why
Well, just wake up, kiss the good life goodbye.'

Would the good life include this feeling of 'sadness'? Was he being 'honest with himself'? In that moment he realised he would never again be 'free to explore the unknown'. And he had already experienced 'the heartache of facing things alone.'

Now it seemed, at the most pivotal of moments, Tony Bennett mocked him, "Well just wake up and kiss the good life goodbye."

At this moment, and for the first time in more than 24 hours, Alfredo thought about Shirley and little Tony, and tears filled his eyes. They would be torn from his life if things went wrong, and there would be no end to that threat. He thought back over the last 18 months, he had then been an innocent, an ordinary, honest husband and father. Wasn't it his sudden unearned wealth that had caused his wife's rape, and led him to murder? He and his wife now had more than enough money, yet their ability to live open and honest lives had been lost forever. He thought about his parents and how ashamed they would be and how concerned for his future. One day his son would be shamed too if the world ever discovered Alfredo's secrets. Alfredo thought about his sexual humiliation by the Krays, and how they had forced him to look deep into his soul on the day he had participated in torture. He was already guilty of the most serious crimes. Shirley had suffered beyond measure. And somehow, Tony Bennet seemed to know.

The truck slowed down and turned hard right into the private drive of the farmhouse. Alfredo looked at his watch, it was still dark but the luminous hands clearly showed it was just after 4.30am. There was no turning back.

Within minutes, the gangsters were hurrying to stack all 120 mailbags along the farmhouse's downstairs walls and stairs. Word circulated that their VHF radio had picked up a police message just after 4.30am indicating the police were aware of the robbery. Alfredo felt sure at least one of the handcuffed train crew had seen the army truck, and knew that the sooner he could get away the better. Then he was distracted by the sight of Buster Edwards kneeling down in front of some of the mailbags, Stanley knife in hand.

Everyone stopped and watched. Buster pulled out five sealed packages. He ripped one open and bundles of ten pound notes fell to the floor. A cheer went up.

Soon, seven pairs of robbers worked simultaneously, each took four minutes to open a mailbag and the packages within, and count the packs of £500. In total they opened 120 mailbags and 636 'high-value packets' within. They had a total of two million, six hundred and thirty-one thousand, six hundred and eighty four pounds. There was no argument about the division. Each of the 15 men present, Goody, Wilson, Reynolds, White, Biggs, James, Daley, Edwards, Hussey, and the Raiders – Danny Pembroke, Roger Cordrey, Tom Wisbey, Bob Welch, Freddie Sansom and Alfredo would get an even 'whack' of £141,000.

That left three further 'whacks' for Hill, Aldridge and the Kray twins (who had agreed to share a 'whack' between them). They calculated it would leave about £60,000 to pay 'Pop' and a couple of other helpers, including a particularly helpful signalman.

On that morning, Thursday 8th August, 1963, before the gang had finished counting, senior British Transport Police detectives from Force Headquarters were at the scene of the crime. Detective Inspector Aldridge had much to do. After all, his bosses were relying on his considerable 'mailbag squad' experience to get results.

Meanwhile, at the farmhouse, the robbers continued to play close attention to VHF radio, and as the minutes and hours passed, the number and intensity of police messages as they continued to grow. All around them were discarded Scottish bank notes, empty mailbags and debris.

Now the robbery was over, but Reynolds had an extra task. Driven by Roy James in a high-powered saloon, travelling on quiet country lanes, he delivered three of the equal shares to a disused airfield just two miles away. There, he handed them to the pilot of a small plane waiting to fly first to Essex. At his first stop, the pilot handed over two shares (one for Aldridge and one for a 50-50 split between the Kray twins). Then he flew on to the south of France and handed the third share to Billy Hill.

The two combined teams had concluded their work and the partnership was over. Now, the only thing the Raiders shared with the rest, was a mutual dependence on non-incrimination and the need to escape with their loot forever.

Though it was planned to use the truck and Land Rovers to evacuate the men and equipment once the heat had died down, every man was now free to take his share and follow his own getaway plan. Alfredo had intended to go on the truck, in civvies of course, and be dropped off to catch a train to Birmingham. But now he feared the police would be on the lookout for Army transport. He took Danny to one side. "Dan, you still shooting off straight away?"

Danny knew what was coming, "Yeah. Me and Tom."

Alfredo knew the rule about three in a car, but still asked. "Mind if I jump in with you?"

Danny studied him for a moment, "You'll have to ride in the boot with the take."

Alfredo nodded enthusiastically and 20 minutes later, two very smartly dressed men drove away, a third was cramped in the boot. They drove to Oxford, ten miles west.

As the other robbers contemplated the amount stolen, BBC Light Programme broke the news of the robbery to the nation. News of the robbery spread quickly. By 9.15am every national newspaper in Britain, and the BBC, were hungry for more information and were sending reporters to the scene.

Alfredo took a train from Oxford to Birmingham where he had rented a flat. In the 1960s, before the currency controls of the 1970s, in the days when international terrorism was no closer to Britain than Cyprus, British customs had no reason to search parcels being sent abroad. So, once in the flat, Alfredo split his £141,000 into 20 packages and addressed each to himself at his relations' home in Italy. By noon, all the money was back in the custody of the Post Office, this time on its way to Italy. That evening, Alfredo flew back on his Italian passport.

Back at Leatherslade Farm, things were getting increasingly tense, couped up together, the robbers now felt like sitting ducks. It seemed the robbery was the sole focus of the radio, updates were being given every hour. Many members of the press were at the scene and in the surrounding villages, and policemen were reported to be everywhere. The robbers were facing a huge effort to find them and it involved the combined powers, investigative, financial, and persuasive, of the two local constabularies, the British Transport Police and the Metropolitan Police, plus British Rail and The Post Office and every newshound from the local and national press. Already, local and national politicians had expressed both outrage and determination to do everything possible to catch the culprits.

This level of response had not been foreseen, and the robbers realised as long as they stayed at the farm with the stolen money, mailbags, Army vehicles, balaclavas and the mountain of other evidence, they were extremely vulnerable to any nosey neighbour or local policeman. By late evening on the day of the robbery, the robbers at the farmhouse were doubting the wisdom of remaining. Yet most stayed put.

The next morning, national concern had turned to international interest. Senior politicians and senior police officers were being interviewed on the radio every five minutes. The front pages of national newspapers had only one story, and it wasn't going away soon.  Yet still they remained at the farmhouse glued to the radio. That day it was announced that the police were to start an immediate search of isolated farms and buildings within a 30 mile radius of the robbery. Members of the public in that area and beyond were asked to be on the lookout and to report anything suspicious without delay.

Now even the dullest robber realised they must escape the farm as soon as they could. First, they would burn whatever evidence they easily could, paint the Army truck to disguise it, and wipe any fingerprints from the Army vehicles and farmhouse contents. But it was a hurried plan and hastily executed. The now poorly painted yellow Army truck just drew attention, and the bonfire of army uniforms, balaclavas, empty mailbags and other items created too much smoke.

Bruce Reynolds and Roy James were amongst others who left the farm to arrange transport for the remainder. It had been planned that others would visit the farm and clean and/or burn it down, but with such heat, it would be foolhardy for anyone to venture there without very good reason. It was all going seriously wrong.

While the plan to rob the train had been detailed and perfectly timed, the getaway had been largely ignored. That didn't matter to Hill or the Krays, they had had kept the job at arms' length and ensured that their cut had been whisked to safety very quickly. But for the majority on the ground, the absence of escape planning would cost them dear.

Within 24 hours Roger Cordrey, because of his naivety, and without the guidance of his fellow Raiders, was arrested in possession of his full cut of £141,000. He had travelled to Bournemouth and attempted to rent with stolen cash, premises from a policeman's widow.

Aldridge continued his part by ensuring the statements of key railway staff fitted the version of events that suited him. The key signalman had his police statement shaped by Aldridge and told lies to the British Rail hearing on the subject.

A great deal of forensic evidence might have been available on the locomotive 'footplate' where the driver and his colleague had been overpowered and on which the robbers had travelled to Bridego bridge.

And the two TPO coaches would potentially provide an even greater source of forensic evidence. The signals and telephone lines on which the robbers had worked were other places that forensic science might help. But Aldridge ensured that both the locomotive and the two stricken coaches were moved up country before any forensic work could be done.

Soon, the Metropolitan Police Flying Squad took over the investigation and coordinated the joint efforts of Buckinghamshire Constabulary, Bedfordshire Constabulary, British Transport Police and the Post Office investigation branch.

The senior Met detectives soon realised there must have been collusion in the robbery by one or more British Rail and/or Post Office employees. Official records bear witness to the fact that British Transport Police HQ CID and Post Office investigators were given the job of discovering who insiders might be. Yet despite years of work and interviewing many hundreds of rail and postal staff, they were unable to identify any firm suspect.

The following year, Aldridge's remarkable dedication to duty over a protracted period, led his doctor to conclude retirement was necessary on health grounds. Aldridge retired on full pension and moved away, apparently to somewhere quiet where he would never be reminded of the past.

Although the Metropolitan Police brought Danny Pembroke in for questioning, he had left no clues at the farm and was not a known robber. They had no evidence with which to charge him and he was released. A few weeks later, Danny disappeared from view. Over 20 years later he returned to South London and bought a rather nice house for his family. He had been living under the radar in the USA. Financially secure, still unknown to the police, he became a black cab driver in London, just for appearances sake. He wasn't named as one of the robbers until after his death when Tom Wisbey shared his name with me.

Once Freddie Sansom became aware of Roger's arrest he, like Danny, realised that it would only be a matter of time before the police came knocking. But unlike Danny, Freddie was a well-known robber from a family of robbers. So Freddie decided the best thing he could do was to continue his life of crime on the basis that no one who had just pocketed £141,000 would be risking their neck trying to steal a few thousand. As a result, perhaps to his relief, or even perhaps, as planned, he was arrested six months later for theft and sentenced to a period of imprisonment. He must have smiled as the door was locked behind him. But not everything goes to plan, shortly after being imprisoned, Freddie became ill and died. Where did his assets end up? Who knows?

As for the others, Gordon Goody was on the run for just seven weeks. At his subsequent trial the judge made it plain that Goody was the leader on the ground (though the judge was sure he was not the boss behind it all). He sentenced Goody to 30 years.

Roy James, who it seems was on the brink of a successful career as a racing car driver, remained at large until early December that year. He was subsequently sentenced to 30 years.

Bruce Reynolds evaded capture for three months and later sentenced to 25 years. After his release he portrayed himself as the leader of the gang. There is no reason to believe it true, and very good reason to believe it false.

Jimmy White, remained free until April 1966. He was subsequently sentenced to 18 years.

Buster Edwards was on the run for three years. He got 15 years.

John 'Paddy' Daly was acquitted (wrongly).

Biggs was sentenced to 30 years before escaping and fleeing to Brazil.

Charlie Wilson was arrested within two weeks of the crime. He was sentenced to 30 years and for no apparent reason, was the last of the robbers to be released (1978).

Tom Wisbey was arrested four weeks after the robbery and got 30 years. After release he got mixed up in the theft of mails again, and that's when I met him.

Bob Welch evaded arrest for just over two months, and was then sentenced to 30 years. After I had completed the first draft of this book I shared parts of it with Bob Welch. He became very aggressive and warned me against publication.

Roger Cordrey was sentenced to 20 years, reduced to 14 on appeal.

Jim Hussey was arrested on September 7, 1963 and subsequently sentenced to 30 years.

Others were caught within a few months, but for some reason, the police never questioned Billy Hill or the Krays,

Remarkably, perhaps uniquely for such a big gang and such a massive crime, and with all the pressure and underhand tactics to which the police would have resorted, none of the robbers ever informed on any other. Why? Billy Hill and the Krays.

No one was ever charged with the Irish Mail job.

During the Great Train Robbery trial, Judge Edmund Davies specifically mentioned that certain robbers had escaped arrest and the mastermind had gone undetected. So too had the person or persons who supplied the inside information. The mastermind's close associations with Tangier (Hill's second home), was also mentioned by the trial judge. Edmund Davies, an experienced judge, had heard every word of evidence, yet his conclusions about Goody being the leader on the ground, and the identity of the mastermind have been studiously ignored in the interests of maintaining a modern 'Robin Hood' myth.

The instructions for the robbers to take all the proceeds to Leatherslade Farm had been a contentious one. Their preference was an immediate return to London. And, had it not been for their use of the farmhouse, the robbers might have escaped arrest.

During their many years in prison and afterwards, each of them must have reflected long and hard on the instructions from Hill to take all the proceeds to Leatherslade Farm. Why would he have insisted on that? Well, perhaps Hill thought the police and their masters would be content as long as some of the robbers were caught. After all, there was little chance of them 'talking' when he had a grip on their families. And of course, if all the proceeds had gone straight back to central London, there would have been no chance for Hill and the Krays to fly their share out before the balloon went up.

As for Alfredo, he was of course safely ensconced in Italy within 24 hours of the crime. Within weeks he was joined by Shirley and Tony, and a few months later, his mother and father too. Alfredo and his family bought a café near the town where his extended family lived. According to Tom Wisbey, Alfredo ran a successful café that became a successful restaurant. He and Shirley had so many children that Tom lost count. They were happy it seems, and if Alfredo and Shirley are still alive, they will be in their early 80's now.

The End.

# Main Characters and other notes

**Billy Hill**

Real character – though the true criminal structure behind the Great Train Robbery has never been proven, from the earliest days after the robbery, his name featured as the most likely. Billy Hill was the most feared London gangster of the late 50s and early 60s.

Hill was the most successful armed robber of his time and was an experienced railway mailbag thief (Brighton line). In 1952, he organised the Eastcastle Street Post Office mail van robbery. Over a quarter of a million pounds had been unloaded from a train at Paddington and was being carried across London. Hill had inside knowledge and knew the route the Post Office van would take. In addition, he had managed to ensure the postal van's alarm had been deactivated. The robbery was efficiently carried out, no one was caught and the money was never recovered.

Apart from masterminding the occasional 'spectacular', Hill ran various rackets in the West End and beyond. His main income now came from protection rackets, illegal gambling, gambling swindles and witness intimidation. A few years before, he had dabbled in kidnapping. In his early days he had been a mail thief, burglar, 'smash and grab' expert, handler of stolen property and hired thug. He spent the Second World War making a fortune on the black market.

Hill had expensive homes in London, Brighton and Tangiers. After the Great Train Robbery, he moved his base to Tangiers where he lived out the rest of his life in luxury enjoying the odd visit from the Krays and their like.

Hill was known for his careful planning, his charm and when necessary, the use of extreme violence. It is generally accepted that the Krays regarded him as their mentor. Hill built strong connections at Westminster and at very senior level at New Scotland Yard. Despite Scotland Yard suspecting him of being the brains behind the Great Train Robbery, he was never arrested or questioned about his involvement.

**The Krays**

Real characters – well known East End gangsters from the early 60s. I have used the Krays to fill the role of two brothers who Tom Wisbey refused to name, though at one point, without any real conviction, he suggested the Harris brothers. They were real characters that Tom had 'worked with.' In truth, the Krays were not regarded with particular respect by Tom, or many others who saw them as 'ponces' (living off the earnings of 'decent thieves'). But there can be no doubting their capacity as enforcers, or their desire to be close to, and emulate, Billy Hill. But I have only the smallest amount of circumstantial evidence to suggest they were involved in the Great Train robbery, and absolutely no direct evidence.

## Danny Pembroke

Real character – Danny was a lifelong friend of Tom Wisbey's and one of the Great Train Robbers who was never caught. Tom stayed friends with Danny right up to the time of Danny's death. Remarkably, Tom told me Danny had expressed more than once, that he wished he had been caught back in 1963, just like most of the gang. One can only speculate as to why that might have been. Danny was the leader of The South Coast Raiders. Recent claims that Roger Cordrey was the boss are miles wide of the mark.

## Freddie Sansom

Real character – Tom Wisbey revealed to me the identity of this Great Train robber. My book, 'Great Train Robbery Confidential' revealed this for the first time.

Freddie was born in Brixton, South London a couple of years after Tom Wisbey. He was a robber by trade and made a good living from robbing banks, sub post offices and stealing mailbags. He had properties in London and Brighton. Tom was well known to the Sansom family, indeed their families were close. Freddie's two brothers were named as suspects, but perhaps because of Freddie's car accident he was never questioned

## Other Train Robbers

All robbers named are real characters but for Alfredo.

## Alfredo

A fictional character – a handsome, young, proud, professional boxer and husband of Shirley, mother of his baby son, Tony. Shirley and child are also fictional.

## Frankie Fraser

Real character – Frankie Fraser was born in the Waterloo area of London in 1923 and died in 2014. Much has been written about him and I have no idea whether he ever helped the Raiders. He was certainly well-known to Tom Wisbey and to Billy Hill, with whom he was associated for many years. He was undoubtedly a violent and fearless criminal who spent a huge proportion of his life in prison. His relationship with the Wisbey family was a strong one, and Tom's daughter Marilyn, and Frankie, became partners and lived together for some years prior to his death.

## D/I Dennis Aldridge

A fictional character – the identity of the person who supplied all the necessary inside information to enable the Great Train Robbery remains unknown. Whoever it was, he must have had access to highly confidential Post Office security information and unquestioned access to all parts of the railways. It has long been suspected it might have been a senior official in the Post Office. My professional experience leads me to the more logical conclusion that it is more likely to have been a Transport Police detective. I do suspect a particular individual but don't have enough proof to name him in any publication. Instead, I have created the fictional 'Aldridge.' I should add that it might well be that a postman working the TPO on the night of the attack was also involved.

## Roy 'Brummie' Walcott

A fictitious character – Roy is an honest, though lacklustre Transport police detective who is transferred from Birmingham to London to help out on Aldridge's over-stretched mailbag squad.

## The Irish Mail Train Robbery

A true event. Little has ever before been said about this robbery. The details in this book are based on the actual accounts of the restaurant car staff, the guard and the ticket inspector who were swept up in events that night. They match the accounts as reported to the police and detailed in 'The Forgotten Train Robbery: The Guard's Story' (By Arwel Owen 2013 Kindle Books). In addition, Tom Wisbey confessed to me his participation in this crime. None of the men responsible, named by me for the first time, was ever questioned or charged with the crime. The account given to me by Tom Wisbey is, I later discovered, substantially corroborated in the book by

Guard Howell's son. The only real variance is that Tom Wisbey was certain that it wasn't just one soldier who came to the rescue of the train staff, he insisted that there were at least six. All the names of the train crew mentioned in this account, and details of their participation, are accurate to the best of my knowledge and belief. However, I have given particular train robbers particular roles within the Irish Mail Robbery which I cannot prove. It would after all, be impossible to know now the exact action and words spoken by each of the participants.

I hope you enjoyed the read. If so, please don't forget that review!

www.ingramcontent.com/pod-product-compliance
Lightning Source LLC
Chambersburg PA
CBHW030123180626
46812CB00002B/540